I've travelled the world twice over,
Met the famous: saints and sinners,
Poets and artists, kings and queens,
Old stars and hopeful beginners,
I've been where no-one's been before,
Learned secrets from writers and cooks
All with one library ticket
To the wonderful world of books.

© Janice James.


The wisdom of the ages
Is there for you and me,
The wisdom of the ages,
In your local library.

There's large print books
And talking books,
For those who cannot see,
The wisdom of the ages,
It's fantastic, and it's free.

Written by Sam Wood, aged 92

# THE BRASS DOLPHIN

Lila Cunningham was almost twenty-one when she learned with a shock that her artist father faced financial disaster. With the loss of their home imminent, they had no option but to accept an offer of a house in Malta. But war was looming, and Malta became the focus of Hitler's attention just as Lila became the focus of attention for three very different young men. As bombing devastated the island and Lila, along with the other inhabitants, learned to live with privation and fear, she also came to realize the value of true love in all its forms, and the difference between hope and illusion.

*Books by Caroline Harvey*
*Published by The House of Ulverscroft:*

**LEGACY OF LOVE**
**A SECOND LEGACY**

JOANNA TROLLOPE

WRITING AS

CAROLINE HARVEY

# THE BRASS DOLPHIN

*Complete and Unabridged*

# CHARNWOOD
*Leicester*

First published in Great Britain in 1997 by
Doubleday, London

First Charnwood Edition
published 1998
by arrangement with
Doubleday
a division of
Transworld Publishers Limited, London

British Library CIP Data

Harvey, Caroline
The brass dolphin.—Large print ed.—
Charnwood library series
1. World War, *1939 – 1945*—Social
aspects—Malta—Fiction
2. Love stories 3. Large type books
I. Title II. Trollope, Joanna
823.9′14 [F]

ISBN 0–7089–8987–X

Published by
F. A. Thorpe (Publishing) Ltd.
Anstey, Leicestershire
Set by Words & Graphics Ltd.
Anstey, Leicestershire
Printed and bound in Great Britain by
T. J. International Ltd., Padstow, Cornwall

This book is printed on acid-free paper

For Ian

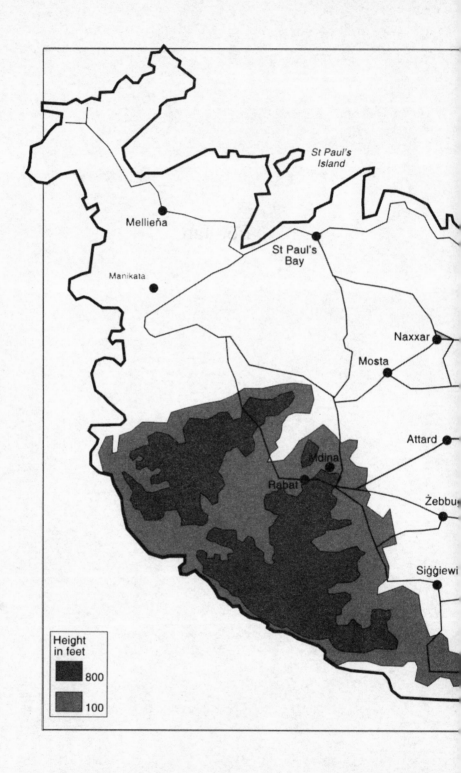

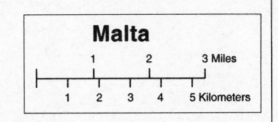

# Malta

1     2     3 Miles

1   2   3   4   5 Kilometers

N

Sliema

VALLETTA

Birkirkara

*THREE CITIES*

Hamrun

Qormi

Zabbar

Paola

Tarxien

Luqa

Zejtun

Gudja

Gñaxaq

Mqabba

Żurrieq

Birżebbuġa

Kajafrana

# Part One

*1938*

# 1

'THE last day of March,' Lila wrote in her diary, '1938. Rain all day and the sea is throwing shingle off the beach at the sea wall. Got sent home early because I had a headache. I didn't *say* I had a headache, but I must have looked it, and Mrs Perriam noticed. Have just counted my Running Away Fund. Twenty-seven pounds, three shillings and fourpence. Not bad, but not enough to run away with yet. At least, not to London.'

She paused and put her pencil down. London. When she was eighteen, she had promised herself that by the time she was twenty-one, she'd be in London. There were now three months until she was twenty-one and the prospect of London seemed even further away than it had when she had been eighteen.

"Why London?" Mrs Perriam had once asked, after Lila had, on impulse, confided in her.

"Because it's where things happen," Lila had said, and then after a pause, more truthfully, "because it's all I can think of."

She picked up her pencil again and put it between her lips, as if it were a cigarette. Mrs Perriam hadn't said anything further about London, but had merely looked as if she hoped Lila was really thinking about it. They were like grandparents to her, those old Perriams, employing her as assistant in their meticulous

3

and scholarly research into children's games and songs, for which they had an international reputation, but treating her less as an employee and more as if she were some stray young female relation they'd found huddled on the doorstep one night in a storm. They were the right age to be grandparents, after all, and it wasn't as if she had any real ones. She hadn't any real anything when she came to think of it, no mother, no aunts and uncles, no brothers and sisters, no cousins. There was just her. Her and Pa, living in this tall thin house, one room balanced on top of another, like a tower of children's building blocks, with the little town at its back and the North Sea, as cloudy as ginger beer, crashing away in front.

She got up, pulling the edges of her cardigan tightly across her body for warmth, and went to the window. Her room was the very topmost one in the house, and except when you stood right in the window, you could see nothing but sky. Pa had given her this room. He'd said that if he had the room above hers, he'd keep her awake by thumping about with his wooden leg. He'd had his left leg amputated in a field hospital after the Battle of Verdun and he wore a peg leg a local fisherman had made in exchange for a painting of his boat, and another of his tar-paper-covered hut from which he sold the day's catch. At night, Pa kept the peg leg beside his bed, to wallop potential intruders with.

Lila gazed down at the narrow roadway that separated their house and all the others in the seafront terrace from the beach. It was empty, except for a gull or two riding the gusts of wet wind, and the road and the sea wall and the shingly beach and the sky and the sea itself were all uniformly grey, blurred by the rain and the gathering dusk. Lila shivered. Pa would be home soon, stumping and whistling through the puddles, and the house, now so narrow and still and dark, would feel as if the human contents of a jovial pub had suddenly been emptied into it.

Lila took a paraffin lamp off the mantelpiece, turned up the wick, and carefully lit it. The house had gas, but half the mantles in the lights were broken, and Pa was no kind of a fixer of things. Pa liked company and talk and noise and distraction — even while he was painting he sang and whistled — but he didn't like fixing things. When things got broken, he adjusted to their brokenness at once, as if they had never been whole. That's how he had been about his lost leg, and everyone admired him for it. "Wonderful fellow, Claude," they'd say. "One leg gone and never a grumble." But had he been like that too, Lila sometimes wondered, when her mother had died? Lila had been hardly two, not much more than a baby, when her mother had died of pneumonia. What had Pa been like then? Blithely going forward as if he'd never had a wife in the first place? Or different, changed and sorrowful in a way she couldn't see because she'd been too young? There'd been some kind of family quarrel, at least that much she knew. Her grandmother, Lilian, after whom she'd been named, tried to take her, to bring her up, but

Pa had resisted. He'd resisted, as was his way, with a great amount of sound and fury, and had deliberately brought Lila to the other side of England from her grandmother's house, to this tall thin house in Aldeburgh where the sea was never still and seldom silent.

Lila went out onto the landing outside her bedroom, and began to descend the steep stairs all the way down to the kitchen. The lamp threw glancing, darting shadows over the varnished banisters and the green linoleum treads and the pictures that hung on the walls, packed so closely together that there was hardly space between them. Some were framed, and some were just held behind their glass with strips of black passe-partout. They were all Pa's, every one, row upon row of ships of every size and kind from the grandest three-masters to the lowliest dinghy, from destroyer to tug. They were painted at sea and in harbour, in storm and calm weather, at dawn and at dusk, ship after relentless ship, always sailing from left to right, and always without one single sign of human life on board.

Lila seldom looked at them. Not only were they as familiar to her as Pa's face or the backs of her own hands, but she privately didn't think them much good. The ships were all right, she supposed; it was their surroundings that weren't. Pa's seas were quite static and his skies were dead flat with flat clouds slapped onto them like icing on a cake. There was no movement in Pa's paintings and no light. Lila couldn't, somehow, believe in them.

But Pa believed in them all right. Pa thought they were wonderful. He would drag unsuspecting guests off around the laden walls saying, "I've got just the thing for you, old boy! Just the thing! Right up your street! You'll love it! Promise you, you will!"

Sometimes, out of sheer embarrassment, the guest would buy a painting, and Pa would chortle over his two guineas with shameless satisfaction while Lila quietly expired of mortification in the background.

"You don't have to, you know," she had whispered once to a summer visitor Pa had dragged in from the beach. The man, tall, stooped and scholarly looking, had glanced from the painting to Pa and back again and had said quietly and tensely, "I do, you know."

Pa said that selling paintings made the difference between bread, and bread and butter with jam on Sundays. Lila doubted it. Small scatterings of guineas at infrequent intervals seemed to make no difference at all to how they lived except to convince Pa that he was a professional marine artist of considerable quality. Which, Lila thought now, stepping down into the kitchen and praying that every last black beetle would have had the grace to go home before she entered, was no help at all. If they didn't have the money that the Perriams paid Lila, there probably wouldn't even be bread most days, let alone butter or jam.

She put the lamp down on the scrubbed wooden table. A single beetle, caught by its light a foot from a table leg, froze in terror.

"Get out!" Lila shrieked. She pulled off her shoe and flung it randomly. "Get out! Get out!"

The beetle fled. Hopping round the table to retrieve her shoe, Lila thought without enthusiasm of the haddock there was for supper. The Perriams' cook had taught her to cook white fish in milk, with a little seasoning, and a bay leaf. She had given her a store of bay leaves, from the trees that grew in the pots in the kitchen garden, in an old brown envelope which said 'Mrs Perriam. Culver House' on it. Mrs Perriam never used anything once that could be used twice.

The small, cold larder smelled earthily of potatoes and, faintly, of fish. The haddock lay on a slate shelf between two plates. Beside it was a winter cabbage, also from the Perriams' garden, and a few carrots which their gardener stored in boxes of sand in a dark shed. Looking at it all, Lila couldn't think exactly what it was that she would like to eat, but she knew with great certainty that it wasn't haddock or cabbage or carrots.

She scooped up the cabbage and the carrots and took them over to the heavy white sink. She had cooked for Pa and herself since she was twelve, when the last daily housekeeper had departed in a black cloud of offence, pursued by bellowed accusations that she had helped herself to the supplies in the larder, to the little piles of small change that Pa left all around the house like clues in a paper chase, and to Pa's monthly bottle of dark Navy rum. During the lunch hours from school in Saxmundham, Lila had subsequently and haphazardly shopped for food, bringing home on the bus to Aldeburgh a string bag bulging with things that had caught her fancy but which neither she nor Pa had had the first idea how to cook. A swede had quite defeated her, she remembered — she couldn't even get a knife into it, as had a spiny length of oxtail and a tallow-coloured lump of suet the butcher assured her would make a wonderful piecrust. Pa, luckily, didn't care what he ate. She could dump plates in front of him, saying 'bubble and squeak', or 'steak and kidney', and he'd rub his hands together and say, "Capital, capital," and then pay the food no further attention whatever except to shovel it into his mouth. He, at least, wouldn't feel discouraged about the haddock.

Lila ran water into the sink and rummaged in the drawer beside it for the broken knife she used to scrape carrots. Sometimes she almost wished Pa would get discouraged by something. He was so blithe, so determined to ignore difficulties or potential problems, so cheerfully, resolutely thick-skinned about other people's sensitivities if they interfered with his sunny view of things, that Lila couldn't help thinking that it was often more like living with a large, jolly dog than with a parent. She didn't want to depress him, but she did sometimes feel that the burden of managing their domestic lives and money, and often in opposition to Pa's carefree wishes, was one that somehow took away quite significantly from the expected pleasure of being twenty and having, as Mrs Perriam often said to her, "all her life before her". She didn't feel a drudge exactly, but she did sometimes feel careworn, and by nasty, mean little cares, cares about the price of mutton chops or the ceaselessly dripping tap in the bath which had now made a large hideous green and orange stain in the bottom, like a livid bruise. It was such cares which, two years ago, had led her to resolve to find herself in London by the time she was twenty-one. London had to be better, had to offer more horizons, more freedom, more people, more *life*. Didn't it?

Sometimes, cycling to work — in from the sea through the alleys to the High Street, out of the town past the church, right up the Leiston road towards South Warren, and Culver House where the Perriams had lived all their long, quiet, self-sufficient married life — she made herself swear, out loud, that this time next year she wouldn't be on a bicycle going to Culver House. "Promise!" she'd shout into the wind if there was no-one coming, "promise! promise!" Some days she even believed herself. Other days, she took stock of what she was and what she had and could believe nothing at all. Twenty years old, adequately educated but without distinction, possessed of an unremarkable domestic competence and an irrelevant store of knowledge about children's games and rhymes down the ages, it seemed to her, on those darker days, the sum total of nothing, of the hopelessly nondescript, of the reverse of potential.

She dropped the carrot she was scraping

into the sink and went to peer in the tiny looking glass that one of the long procession of past housekeepers had insisted that Pa put up in order that she could make sure her hat was on straight before she went home. The light in the kitchen wasn't good on account of the paraffin lamp, and by its wavering glow, Lila thought her face looked thinner than usual and her eyes larger and darker and her hair, which she had scraped back with grips while she wrote her diary, depressingly lank. Pa was sturdy and ruddy-complexioned, with thick tufts of pepper-and-salt hair, and Lila's mother had been quietly pretty and brown. It was from her grandmother, Lilian, that she had inherited these thin dark looks, these long arms and legs that had made her look, as a child, like some kind of fragile, jumping insect.

From beyond the closed kitchen door that led to the alley behind the house came the sound of whistling, snatched at intermittently by the wind. Lila made a face at herself in the glass and went back to the sink.

"Yo ho ho!" shouted Pa, and flung the kitchen door open. "Hail to thee! Desperately dark in here, isn't it?"

Lila said, without turning, "You could always mend the gas mantle."

"Could," Pa said heartily. "Oh yes. Could. But haven't."

He limped across the kitchen and aimed a kiss at Lila's cheek.

"Good day?"

"Not particularly. I came home early. I had a headache."

Pa clicked his tongue. "Poor girl. Better now?"

"Well — "

"That's it! That's the spirit! Mind over matter."

"Been at the club?" Lila said, finishing the last carrot and lifting the double handful, dripping, out of the sink. Pa loved the seamen's club. He could pretend there that he'd really been a seaman, and the real seamen, the retired sailors and fishermen, were very tolerant of him on account of his peg leg and his cheerfulness.

"Mm," Pa said. His voice was very loud. Too loud.

Lila turned round, holding the carrots. Pa had hitched his stump, as was his wont, onto the corner of the table and was staring down into the glass funnel of the lamp which threw a weird light up into his face and made it grotesquely craggy with shadows.

"Pa?"

He didn't look at her. She noticed, for the first time, that he wasn't just wet, but really wet, soaked through, as if he'd been walking for hours, stumping unevenly through the pouring rain for miles.

"Pa? Pa, where've you been?"

"Out on the marshes," he said. His voice was suddenly much quieter. "By the sea. Better by the sea."

She leaned forward and put the carrots on the table.

"What's happened?"

He sighed. A little line of raindrops suddenly collected in the edge of his tufty hair above his left eyebrow and ran down his face, like tears.

"Took a chance," he said, "years ago. Never thought I could lose. Never thought it would come to this."

"To what?" Lila said. Her voice sounded sharp.

He gave her a quick glance. His little blue eyes, usually so bright with expectation, were clouded with something very like apprehension.

"Not really a punt," he said. "Not really. Perfectly above board, with the bank and all. Everybody does it."

"Does what?"

"Borrows," Pa said. "Money."

Lila held onto the edge of the table.

"Pa, you've been borrowing money from the bank?"

He looked at her again.

"Not much. Just a bit. Here and there. There was always the house, you see. Worth a thousand pounds, this house. Well, eight or nine hundred at least. Bank didn't mind. Bank liked it."

"So what," Lila said, struggling to understand him, "has happened?"

There was a pause. Pa gave a huge sigh, a huge, deep, heartfelt sigh. Then he opened his arms and made a sort of hopeless, shrugging gesture, as if whatever had happened had been no fault of his, had not, in some way, even had a connection with him.

"Bank's got the house."

Lila stared at him.

"What? *What?*"

"Borrowing here, borrowing there, never counted, never thought to count. Now, would you believe it, it's all gone. No more left to borrow."

Lila said slowly, "Do you mean that you've borrowed and borrowed from the bank against the value of the house until there's nothing left and this house belongs to the bank?"

He nodded. He shot her another of his quick, fearful glances. "They say we can rent. Rent it back. Rent from the bank." He tried a small, anxious smile. "All's not lost?"

Lila looked at him. She looked at him for a long, long time, at his wet face and hair and clothes and at the pleading in his eyes, and then she leaned forward and picked up the paraffin lamp and went slowly and deliberately out of the room with it, leaving him in the dark.

# 2

THE drive to Culver House wound through a grove of birches, planted by the Perriams thirty years before. They gave the place a clean, northern, almost Scandinavian feel with their gleaming white trunks and soft, whispering leaves and the way the earth stayed almost bare beneath them, brown and soft and crumbled looking, only blurring into sheets of blue here and there, when the bluebells were in flower in May. Lila liked the birches; they seemed to her graceful feminine trees, giving her open glimpses, as the drive curved among them, of Culver House, so red and foursquare and Edwardian and welcoming. They were like a kind of pretty chorus, dancing lightly across the front of the stage before the star made her entrance.

There was always a sense of homecoming about arriving at Culver House. Every weekday morning Lila left her bicycle in an outhouse propped against an old copper boiler — still used for the weekly laundering of sheets — and went into the house through the kitchen. It was a big kitchen, warm and comfortable, the table pale from its daily scrubbing with salt, the great deal dresser hung with cups and jugs and measures. Mrs Tuttle presided here, a small, square, straightforward woman, whose husband worked in the garden. Together they inhabited

15

a red brick cottage the Perriams had built for them beyond the glasshouses and the shed where Tuttle, a keen rabbiter, kept his ferrets.

Mrs Tuttle never said good morning to Lila. Instead, she said things like, "Get that wet coat off," or, "Doesn't look to me like you had your breakfast this morning." She'd had two sons, both of whom cycled to work each day for a builder in Leiston, and she was used to speaking to the young in purely practical terms. Their feelings were their business, just as hers were hers. Lila, she was aware, was more governed by her feelings than either of the Tuttle boys had ever been, but she still considered that they were Lila's affair. Besides, dwelling on feelings wasn't good for you; it made you nervy.

She looked up this morning from the shortcrust pastry she was making for lunchtime's rabbit pie, and regarded Lila. She looked, Mrs Tuttle thought, poorly, as if she hadn't slept, and she was drooping somehow, like a cyclamen needing water.

"There's porridge still," Mrs Tuttle said, "in the bottom oven. They never finished it."

Lila unwound her scarf from her neck. "I'm not sure I — "

"And cream," Mrs Tuttle said, as if she were instructing someone, "with some of that West Indian sugar. The dark kind."

Lila said apologetically, "I'm not really hungry."

Mrs Tuttle, rolling her pastry, nodded her head towards the great black range which Tuttle fed all day with hods of coke.

16

"Tea just brewed, then. You ought to have some tea."

"Thank you," Lila said. She pulled her coat off and hung it, with her scarf, on the hook behind the outer door. "I didn't sleep very well."

"It was windy," Mrs Tuttle said. She held up a teaspoon. "Sugar?"

"No, I —"

"Better. It's better, if you're tired, to have sugar."

She held a cup out to Lila, a big cup, patterned, as all the Perriams' everyday china was, with stylized peacocks and azaleas, pink and green and black, on a cream ground.

"You get that down you."

Lila said, taking the cup gratefully, "Are they in the library yet?"

"Indeed they are. Early start today. Porridge for both of them, stewed fruit for Madam and a kipper for Sir. They didn't touch their toast. I shall have to give it to the chickens." She glanced at the clock. "You'd better go in. It's gone nine."

Lila nodded. "Thank you for the tea."

Mrs Tuttle grunted. She picked up her rolling pin again and resumed her smooth practised movements across the pastry.

"Rabbit pie," she said, "with apples and prunes. And some juniper berries, if I can find them."

Lila, holding her cup carefully in one hand, pushed open the heavy kitchen door with its outer, muffling overcoat of brass-studded baize,

17

and found herself, as she did every working morning, in another world. The architect of Culver House had had baronial tastes, and the hall was pillared and galleried and panelled, with a great staircase marching impressively up to the first floor, wide enough for four people to climb abreast. On the floor, the Perriams had laid silk Chinese carpets, and instead of the antlered heads the architect had planned, they had filled the hall with tall Chinese vases and long scroll-like paintings, as delicate and elegant as the birch trees outside, from Japan. In the centre of the hall stood a drum table, laden with books and papers and, in the middle, an enormous pale green orchid, like a flight of immense butterflies, stood in a porcelain pot as big as a bucket, wreathed in blue dragons.

Lila went down the hall towards the front door, and knocked on one of the pair of double doors that flanked it. There was a pause. There was always a pause. Then Mr Perriam's voice, calm but faintly abstracted, said, "Come!"

"Good morning," Lila said, "I'm afraid I'm a little late."

They looked up from either side of the huge partners' desk at which they worked. They both smiled.

"Are you?"

"Yes. Three minutes. Mrs Tuttle pointed it out."

"Mrs Tuttle," Mr Perriam said, "was put out by our wanting breakfast ten minutes before the usual time." He half rose from his seat and gave her a little bow. "Good morning, Lila."

18

"Good morning," Mrs Perriam said. Her tiny frame was draped, as it was all year round, winter and summer alike, in several fine wool Liberty shawls of oriental pattern, and her hair was screwed up into its usual tight little grey bun, skewered with a great prong of tortoiseshell. She gave Lila a clear glance through her round-framed spectacles. "You look tired, dear."

The cup in Lila's hand shook very slightly.

"Oh, the wind — "

"There's wind most nights," Mrs Perriam said.

Lila licked her lips. She looked round the room for a moment or two, at the distinguished, scholarly clutter of books and papers, of chairs and reading lamps, of prints and pictures propped haphazardly against anything handy that was upright, and then she said, "I'm so very sorry to interrupt you, but I wonder if — I wonder . . . "

There was a small exchange of glances between the Perriams, and an even smaller sigh of polite disappointment. Mrs Perriam put a slip of paper into the open book in front of her, to mark her place, and Mr Perriam took off his gold-rimmed spectacles, folded them carefully, and laid them down across the monograph he had been studying, by a German disciple of Wittgenstein, on the significance of the colour black in the world of children's play. Then they both, kindly and patiently, folded their hands and looked at her.

Lila swallowed. She put the teacup down on a pile of educational pamphlets — *Clay Toys*

19

*from the Iraqui Marshlands* the top one said — and put her hands behind her back.

"Won't you sit?" Mr Perriam said.

"No. No, thank you. No, I — " she stopped.

"I do hope," Mrs Perriam said gently, "that you aren't going to tell us that you plan to leave us?"

Lila burst into tears.

"My dear — "

"Lila. Dear Lila — "

"Sorry," Lila said, gasping and scrabbling for a handkerchief. "I'm so sorry."

Mr Perriam rose, removed a pile of books and a primitive puppet from a nearby upright chair and carried it over to where Lila stood.

"Please sit down. Sit down and tell us what is the matter."

Lila subsided gratefully onto the chair and blew her nose.

"Now," Mrs Perriam said, "tell us."

Lila said, in a rush, "I don't think Pa meant to. I mean he didn't think far enough ahead, he isn't very good at thinking of the consequences of what he does, his mind just doesn't work that way."

"No," Mr Perriam said patiently. To someone like Mr Perriam, Claude Cunningham was as alien a creature as if he'd alighted from another planet. Mr Perriam could see no connection whatever between Lila and her father, no connection of appearance or temperament or aptitude. So whenever Claude Cunningham did anything arbitrary, the last thing Mr Perriam felt was surprise.

20

"It's so awkward, talking about money," Lila said, "and I don't want you to think I want more, because I don't, I think you are very generous to me but — "

"But?"

"I — I, well, I didn't realize that we were spending more than we had. I mean, we don't spend much, but we were still spending too much for — for what was coming in. So there was a gap, you see, between what was coming in and what was going out and my father — well, my father borrowed some from the bank. Over the years. Over lots of years. Using our house as security." She paused and then said simply, "You see."

"And now," Mr Perriam said, putting his fingertips together, "there is no more left to borrow?"

"No."

"And the bank will take possession of the house."

"Yes."

He looked gravely at her.

"And you have spent the night worrying that you no longer have a roof over your heads."

"Yes," Lila said. "The bank would allow us to rent the house back but — but we can't afford that." She left her mouth open to say, "We can't afford anything, actually," but decided against it, for fear of sounding self-pitying, and closed her mouth again.

"Poor child," Mrs Perriam said. "Poor Lila."

"My father says we should go and live in France. In Dieppe or Le Havre or somewhere.

21

He says it's very cheap to live there and — and that it would be a good place to paint his pictures. And," she added faintly, "to sell them."

"And you?" Mr Perriam said. "What would you do, in Dieppe?"

"I thought perhaps I could teach English."

"Perhaps."

"Or work in a school. Or a shop. I don't mind, I don't — "

"You should mind," Mr Perriam said. "It is your life too, and you have ability. Teaching English to the daughters of French ironmongers is not enough for your ability."

"I don't feel I have ability," Lila said. "To be honest, I only feel at the moment that I have fear and dread."

There was a pause, during which Mr and Mrs Perriam looked at each other in the silently communicating way that Lila had always found so beguiling — so different, too, from Pa's boom and bluster.

"Lila," Mrs Perriam said, not turning, "Lila, I wonder if you would take a little walk in the garden."

Lila sprang up.

"Of course."

"Fifteen minutes," Mr Perriam said. "Just a quarter of an hour."

"Thank you," Lila said. She bent and retrieved her teacup. "I'll go and find Tuttle."

"Mulching the rosebeds," Mrs Perriam said, "I hope."

"I didn't mean to burden you," Lila said

suddenly. "I don't mean you to think of a solution. I just had to tell someone, I had to ask advice and — well — " she paused and looked down into her teacup. The tea was cold and had turned the colour of the winter sea. There had been no-one else to tell actually, only the Perriams. Simple as that.

"A quarter of an hour," Mr Perriam said.

★ ★ ★

Out in the rose walk, Tuttle was forking chunks of compost, as dark and dense as Christmas cake, around the unyielding thorny stems of the ramblers. It was a task that should have been done in January, to catch the winter frosts, but Tuttle with steady, silent obstinacy, had omitted to do it until Mrs Perriam had openly confronted him. Tuttle didn't like roses. Ugly things, he said to Mrs Tuttle, ugly, bare things except when the blooms were on them. But Mrs Perriam loved roses, loved all the old ones with untidy flowers and strong scents, and seemed impervious to the work they involved for him, all that pruning and feeding and dead heading and tying up, with your hands cut to ribbons in the process. In the privacy of his mind all those solitary gardening hours, Tuttle had made a bargain with Mrs Perriam. He would tend her roses, and in return he would, in defiance of her instructions, grow the monster cabbages and marrows and leeks in which his heart rejoiced. Vegetables, now that was real gardening.

23

"How do," Tuttle said to Lila, not looking up from his forking.

Lila looked down at the compost.

"That looks nourishing."

"'Tis," he said. "Two years old. You could do with a bit of something like it."

"Tuttle," Lila said, pulling her coat round her and holding it hard across her, as if she had a pain, "Tuttle, were you born here?"

"Nope," he said.

"But near?"

"Nope," he said. "In Devon." He gave her a brief grin. "Can't you tell? I don't sound like a Suffolk man."

"Do you miss Devon?" Lila said.

He whacked a lump of compost to break it up.

"No," he said. "Well settled here. More'n thirty years now."

"Does it," Lila said carefully, "take thirty years to get used to something new? Even if you didn't very much like what you had in the first place?"

Tuttle paused for a second.

"What you getting at?"

"Change," Lila said, "choices. I always thought the one thing I wanted was to get away, and now I may have to, because of circumstances and not because of choice, and I — well, I suppose I'm frightened."

Tuttle straightened up and threw her a quick glance.

"It's no good talking in riddles to me."

"No. No, I'm sorry. I should not have come

24

out and interrupted you — "

"But I'll tell you one thing," Tuttle said, cutting across her as if she had never uttered, "and that's this. If you don't take your chances young, you don't take them. Chances don't suit us later. Later, we like to be settled." He shook a forkful of compost evenly through the tines. "But you don't want to get settled yet. You don't want to get fixed. There's times you don't know where you're going but you know you've got to go somewhere. Those times," Tuttle said, and he was grinning again, "you just got to hold your nose and jump."

★ ★ ★

In the library, Mr and Mrs Perriam had moved from the partners' desk and were sitting composedly either side of the fireplace in high-backed wing chairs upholstered in pale grey damask. They motioned Lila to sit between them, on a padded stool. Down there, she felt more granddaughterly than ever, small and submissive on a stool between their thrones.

"It is always unpleasant in life," Mr Perriam said, "to find oneself without the means to sustain oneself, to go forward. But you were right to subdue your pride and come to us. You were right to ask us for help."

"I only meant advice," Lila said. "I only meant that you should tell me what to do, advise me. I didn't mean to ask for help, I never meant — "

"But we would like to help," Mrs Perriam said.

"You're so kind — "

"What you may not like," Mr Perriam said, "is the help we have in mind."

He leaned forward and, from the low table that stood between the two fireside chairs, lifted a huge quarto volume, bound in dark blue cloth. He laid it on his knees and opened it and Lila could see maps across the pages, maps of land masses in green and brown, and maps of oceans in pale blue.

"Now," said Mr Perriam, "we agree about the proximity of sea for your future life. We see the necessity for a marine ambience for your father. But not the English Channel. Not Dieppe."

Lila waited. Mr Perriam turned the great book slowly, and lowered it to the floor in front of Lila's stool. Across the double-page spread ran the broad blue sweep of the Mediterranean, an exotic idea to Lila with as much reality to it as the moon.

"There," said Mr Perriam He picked up an ebony ruler like a wand and brought the tip down on the open pages of the atlas. "The southern shores of Spain and France. The tip of Italy. The island of Sicily. And below, the north coast of Africa, Tunisia, Tripoli. And between, between Sicily and Tunisia, what do you see?"

Lila held her knees and peered over them at the atlas. The ebony ruler had come to rest on a small oval of green with a jagged north edge.

"An island — "

"An archipelago," Mr Perriam said. "An

26

archipelago of three little islands of which the chief is — " The ebony ruler beat lightly on the green oval. "What is the name of this chief island?"

Lila bent closer. Her knowledge of geography was shamefully inadequate, she knew it. In a questioning voice, she read out a single word: "Malta?"

"Exactly," Mr Perriam said. "Malta it is."

# 3

"**D**ON'T understand it," Pa said. He sat propped on one corner of the kitchen table, fiddling with the old battery wireless whose battery was dead. He put his ear to the silent mesh panel that hid the loudspeaker. "They could declare war tomorrow and we'd never know. Would we? Dead as a dodo."

"Not," Lila said, "if you bought a new battery."

"Don't understand it," Pa said. "Why Malta? What's going on?"

Lila sighed. She was sitting on a high wooden stool with her elbows propped behind her on the edge of the sink. In the sink lay four beetroot Tuttle had left in her bicycle basket. She didn't want to think about them.

"It's perfectly simple. I told you. The Perriams have a house in Malta. They never use it. They say we can use it. They say they have a friend there who might give me a job."

Pa banged the wireless twice with the flat of his hand.

"Heard a capital song today. 'Jeepers, Creepers'. First rate. 'Jeepers, creepers, where d'you get those peepers?' Topping. But why Malta?"

Lila closed her eyes.

"Because Mr Perriam's father was an archaeologist and Malta is full of prehistory.

28

He went there so often, he bought a house. Mr and Mrs Perriam had their honeymoon in that house. But no-one lives there now. It's empty. It's been empty for years."

"There," Mr Perriam had said that morning, putting a sepia photograph, faded almost to buff, in her hand. "My father's house. Villa Zonda. In my father's day, it had a small vineyard. That has now gone, but you can see the courtyard garden, and the well. The wellhead is Roman. Late, I must admit, but Roman."

The house in the photograph was difficult to make out, but Lila thought she could see a balustraded roof and long windows and a balcony. It looked huge.

"You're so kind, you're unbelievably kind, but we couldn't take a house like this, such a house — "

"Then take a room or two," Mr Perriam said, "take what you need. Doubtless you will find it overrun with Maltese in any case, the caretaker's children and grandchildren. And goats, I shouldn't wonder, in the salone."

He'd taken down several books after that, big, dark volumes full of big, dark photographs protected by sheets of crackling translucent paper. 'A. E. O. Perriam' they said on the spines: 'Tarxien: 1907'. 'Mnajdra: 1908'. 'Hagar Qim: 1910'.

"My father's excavations of Maltese stone age temples," Mr Perriam said. "His methods were entirely scientific. He was a devoted follower of Sir Themistocles Zammit."

"Yes," Lila said. She had looked at the names

29

on the spines. "Hagar Qim?"

"A curious language," Mr Perriam had said, "Semitic in structure, and probably descended from the speech of Hannibal. It's been overlaid by Arabic of course and Italian, and Spanish and English, but the Semitic roots remain. My father spoke it fluently. This caused him to be regarded with great suspicion by the 'high people' as the Maltese upper classes call themselves. The high people speak English and Italian and do not like to be seen to understand Maltese."

Lila said, hesitatingly, "I can't imagine this, I can't imagine what you're offering us — "

"A roof," said Mrs Perriam. "A roof on a Mediterranean island. It will be even cheaper to live in Malta than in Dieppe."

Lila had put her hands over her eyes.

"Half an hour ago," she said, "I'd hardly heard of Malta."

"There was a siege there," Pa said now. "In Malta. Long time ago. Turks and galleys and the Knights of St John and what have you."

"Yes," Lila said, "but this is now!"

"What's the deal?" Pa said. He smacked the wireless again. "I mean, what's the bargain? This house for what?"

"Nothing."

"Nothing?"

"They own it but never use it. They don't like leaving home. They said they'd like to think of us there." She paused and then she said, carelessly, "There's a long naval tradition in Malta of course. Lots of boats. Boats everywhere."

Pa pretended not to notice what she'd said.

He picked a corner of the mesh away from behind its wooden fretwork and blew into the loudspeaker.

"And I could work for a historian there. He was a young pupil, long ago, of Mr Perriam's father. He lives somewhere called the Silent City."

"Ha!" Pa said. "Silent! Why silent?"

"Almost no traffic, I suppose," Lila said.

Pa gave the wireless a last thump and got off the table. He limped over to the window and looked out into the alley behind the house where the sun never came except in high summer. Across the alley was the storeroom for one of the town's greengrocers, and the double doors to this were wide open showing a jumble of boxes and crates, and a carpet of trodden cabbage leaves.

"Boats," Pa said softly.

Lila waited. Then she said, without particular enthusiasm, "And gulls. And rocks and sea and harbours. And villages with yellow stone churches. And sun. Hot sun. For months and months every year. Blue sea and hot sun."

There was silence. Lila leaned back against the sink and Pa stood crookedly by the window, staring at the cabbage leaves.

"Sorry," Pa said suddenly. "Sorry. Didn't want to be a burden. Didn't mean to turn us topsy-turvy . . . "

"No."

"But boats — "

"Yes."

"And sea. Sea all round."

"Yes."

31

He looked at her, one of his quick almost furtive glances.

"You choose," Pa said.

"What?"

"Don't want the responsibility," Pa said. "Might make another muddle. You choose."

Lila took her elbows off the sink and sat up straight.

"Pa — "

"Yes," he said and then, under his breath, humming to comfort himself, "Jeepers, creepers, where d'you get — "

"Pa," Lila said, and her voice was harsh, "Pa, d'you really think we've got a choice? D'you really think we've got such a luxury as choice *left*?"

★ ★ ★

Lila lay in her cold bedroom and waited, without much hope, for sleep. She was cold, as well as her bedroom, despite wearing a cardigan over her pyjamas and some of Pa's thick white wool fishermen's socks. Pa always had spare socks. After all, he only ever needed one sock at a time. Lila washed them in the sink in the kitchen and then hung them to dry on the wooden pulley suspended from the ceiling where, in winter, they dripped despondently for hours. At least in Malta there'd be sun to dry Pa's socks.

She turned on her side and stared towards the window. The curtains, though drawn across, were very thin, made of unlined checked cotton, and through them she could see the ghostly

gleam of the moon, coming and going fitfully
behind chasing clouds. Over lunch at Culver
House, Mr Perriam had also said some sobering
things about the situation in Europe, about the
unsettled nature of things now that Germany
was mobilizing her armies.

"You may well be safer in Malta," Mr Perriam
had said, cutting neatly into the rabbit pie,
"more out of the way of things. Now that Hitler
has appointed himself War Minister, I think we
can no longer delude ourselves that Germany's
intentions are other than aggressive." He laid
a triangle of Mrs Tuttle's excellent pastry on
the topmost plate of the little pile before him.
"I have no faith, I am afraid, in the hopes of
Mr Chamberlain. I have no faith that Europe's
problems can be settled amicably."

Lila said uncertainly, "Pa thinks Winston
Churchill is right . . . "

"Ah," said Mr Perriam. He sounded mildly
surprised. "Then your father and I are in
agreement. Perhaps, in that case, we might also
agree on Malta as a solution to your present
difficulties for other reasons than — than — "
he paused, holding a spoonful of gravy, halted
by his own delicacy.

"Money," Lila said.

He gave her a little twinkling glance.

"Quite," he said and then, after a pause, and
almost to himself, "a face saver."

But Pa's face didn't need saving, Lila thought.
Pa didn't think he'd done anything wrong. What
dismayed Pa was that he'd been stumped, for
a little while, for an answer, and then because

33

it came from another source than himself. Pa liked the illusion he could manage life, he liked people to say, when in difficulties, "Oh, ask old Claude. Claude'll know what to do. Claude'll see you right." What Pa would have liked was to have thought of Malta himself, and not to have to be beholden to the Perriams. But as to getting himself and Lila into a situation where they had to be beholden to somebody in order to survive, that he was perfectly comfortable about. Losing the house was the way of the world. It had nothing to do with him.

Lila had said over supper — a dismal affair of beetroot in white sauce and potted meat spread on cream crackers — that Mr Perriam had advised her that they should go all the way to Malta by sea, from Southampton.

"A year ago," he said, "I should have advised taking the train down through France, and then taking a ship from Marseilles. But France is calling up its reservists and although France is undoubtedly our ally, I should prefer to think of you both in British hands, all the way. I should be more than happy to assist in arranging your passage."

"No!" Pa had shouted over the beetroot when this was reported to him. "No! Perfectly capable! Won't be pushed around! I'll see to our passage! I'll do it!"

He had become very animated then, and had thumped up to his room and returned with a heap of maps and charts which he then spread on the kitchen table and covered with cracker crumbs.

"There!" he said triumphantly, stabbing with a smeary knife. "There! Malta!"

"I know," Lila said.

"And Gozo. And Comino. It is," Pa declared importantly, "an archipelago!"

Lila shut her eyes briefly. "I know."

"Ship from Southampton. Steamship. Port side out, port cabins. All the way to Valetta. Grand Harbour, in Valetta. Grand defences. Best in the Mediterranean." He glared at Lila. "Don't tell *me* how to get there."

Now, lying in her chilly bed watching the moon wavering in and out among the clouds, Lila couldn't help feeling that the getting there was nothing — nothing, that is, compared with the arriving there, the being there. Of course it would be chaotic, everything that concerned Pa always was, and their luggage would be immense and unwieldy and peculiar, burdened with Pa's painting stuff, and his telescope and all the household things that she, Lila, would be timidly, unadventurously afraid to leave behind in case they weren't obtainable in Malta. But while they were travelling, that was all they could do — travel. They were human parcels, with no decisions to make, no initiatives to take. It was when they got there that the difficulties would begin; when they got to this hot, bare place with stone churches and fishing boats, to this neglected house full of goats and caretaker's grandchildren, to this unknown historian living so disconcertingly in a silent city who might very well not want an assistant who knew about nothing but seventeenth-century children's street games. Or who — even worse — wouldn't want her, but would take her on only in deference to Mr Perriam's wishes, and they would both become trapped in hopeless courtesies. And if she didn't get the job, what would they do? Even in Malta, Pa's pension was too small to live on.

"Bugger all!" Pa used to say cheerfully of his pension in the seamen's club where he felt salty language to be appropriate. "That's what they think I'm worth! Bugger all!"

Lila sat up, slowly. Plainly the idea of sleep was useless. She felt restless, as well as cold. She leaned over the side of the bed and groped on the floor for her overcoat, which also had to serve as her dressing gown, and struggled into it, still sitting up in bed. Then she swung her feet out from under the covers and padded, in Pa's socks, to the window.

She slid the curtains back. Being threaded only on wires, and not on rings, they slid silently. She peered out. The sea was black and, where the moon caught it, glittering and almost oily-looking. Between the sea and her window, the darkness was unvaried, giving no hint of beach or wall or road, except for a faint glow, just below her, from Pa's window. He had a lamp lit. He, too, for all his bluster, couldn't sleep. She pictured him down there in his striped flannel pyjamas and the thick dark blue jersey he wore over them in winter, poring over maps of the Mediterranean with little emphatic grunts and exclamations. By morning, she knew, he'd have adjusted himself completely. He'd know all about Malta. He'd doubtless then tell her — and anyone else who would listen — all about Malta. By the time she got back from Culver House after work the next day, he'd have been to the seamen's club and Malta would have become his pet project, his very own idea.

"Malta?" he'd be saying, "Malta? Planned to go there for years. Years! Wonderful climate. Excellent material for a painter. So we're seizing the chance. Selling up and going before old Adolf puts the slammers on us. Seize the chance, I say! Always have!"

Lila sighed. Beside her, to catch the light from the window in the daytime, stood the wobbly little table, streakily varnished the colour of black treacle, at which she wrote her diary. As her eyes accustomed to the faint light of the moon, she could even see her diary, the fat exercise book with purplish marbled covers which she had bought in the stationers in Saxmundham on her last day at school. She had kept it pretty faithfully for almost three years, which was, she reflected, a seventh of her whole life, this life which had been lived so far almost entirely in this narrow house by the sea. And now . . .

She opened the front cover. It had figures listed inside, under a heading which seemed to her suddenly childish now, unrealistic: 'Fund for London. For Running Away'. And then below it, the laborious slow chart of her savings, shilling by shilling with a five pound note at Christmas, from the Perriams. She had started with ninepence halfpenny. Three years later, she had twenty-seven pounds, three shillings and fourpence.

She went back to her bed and knelt down, pushing her arm in deep between the mattress and the creaking iron-mesh base. She drew out a bag, a stout green calico bag which one of the long ago housekeepers had made her, to hold her indoor shoes on the way to school. Now the bag was worn and knotted halfway up, above the hard knobbliness of the coins packed down into the bottom.

Lila carried the bag over to the window and picked the knot undone with her fingernails. Then she emptied the contents across the open first page of her diary, a clatter of silver and copper and a thin roll of big white five-pound notes, carefully tied with a broken bootlace. She poked the pile of coins with her finger, stirring it about, trying — hard though it was — not to feel too possessive about it. It was plain, painfully plain, that every farthing of it would have to go towards those sea passages to Malta which Pa, down there below her, was at this very moment so excitedly planning.

She made a sudden movement, and swept the coins off the diary. Then she sat down at the table and, fumbling in the dimness, found her pencil and turned the pages to the entry of the day before. It was difficult to see, but not impossible. She drew a thick unsteady line across the page and then she wrote underneath the line in big, rough capital letters, 'April Fool's Day'. She added several exclamation marks and hoped they looked as heavily ironic as she intended them to. Then, with a deep breath, she wrote rapidly:

This is the end of the diary. This is the end of this part of my life. I meant the next part to start of my choosing, but that isn't happening. The next part is starting because it has to, and I have to, too. In one sense, I've got my wish. I'm running away. But something's happening that I never thought of. I'm running away all right, to Malta, which is an island in the Mediterranean between Tripoli and Sicily and which, before ten o'clock this morning, I had scarcely heard of. But the thing is — Pa is running with me.

She paused for a second and then, in the same capitals as she had written April Fool's Day, she wrote 'End' and then, not caring if Pa heard her or not, she slammed the diary shut and hurled it to the floor.

# 4

THE sunlight was merciless. Lila had never seen anything like it. When she opened her eyes to more than mere slits, it bounced at her, brilliant and harsh and bullying. When she had said to Pa, all those weeks ago, "Hot sun, blue sea," in an attempt to reconcile him to the fact that going to Malta was an imperative and not a choice, she had imagined the sunlight as golden and benevolent, an enriching, glowing thing and not in any way this fierce, white glare which hit one like a headache.

She had a headache, anyway. In fact, there was scarcely an inch of her that didn't ache after those appalling, tossing days at sea. Pa had said, lurching robustly about the heaving decks, that seasickness was merely a state of mind and of a pretty feeble mind at that. He himself ate three square meals a day and spent the time in between meals getting in the way of the crew, who treated him with extraordinary forbearance. Several times a day, scarlet in the face, with streaming hair and oilskins, he would fling open the door of Lila's cabin and shout, "Yo ho ho! And how does my hearty do?"

Lila, shivering and unutterably wretched, wracked by ceaseless nausea, had never hated anyone as she hated Pa at those moments. If she had had the energy to murder him, she

40

knew she would have had no qualms in doing so. She had no idea she could feel so utterly, purely terrible, nor that such terribleness could go on so remorselessly, day after night after day after night until the end of the world seemed to be the only thing worth hoping for. Her own death didn't seem to her enough — this kind of suffering called for a grander gesture, no less than the death of everything.

And then the ship passed through the Straits of Gibraltar and the winds dropped, as suddenly and completely as if they had never had an idea of blowing in the first place. Two sailors, with grins Lila did not at all care for, came down to her cabin, escorted by Pa, and carried her up on deck in a canvas chair and left her there in the clear May light and gentle breezes. She lay in her chair, as limp as a rag doll, with her eyes closed, and tried to ignore Pa who circled round her, full of triumph and well-being, suggesting a turn on the quarterdeck and bacon and eggs. He brought other passengers to visit her, as if she were some kind of exhibit, and those who knew Malta already told her what a splendid little place it was, a really snug berth and of course, properly British in attitude.

"Don't worry about the language," one woman said to her, "English is the lingua franca. Quite rightly in my view. If you get lost in a village, find a girl to speak to, a schoolgirl. They teach English better to the schoolchildren than the adults and better to the girls than the boys. So find yourself a bright-looking girl. I always do."

Lila nodded. She found herself nodding at most of her visitors, at the cups of broth she was brought (dreadful stuff, tasting of bones), at the information she was given about how much coal there was in the hold of the ship ("Great coaling station, Valetta. Did you not know?"), about the suspension of the Maltese constitution ("Simply got to keep our eye on Mussolini, you see, Miss Cunningham"), and how she must never wear shorts or ignore the water rationing regulations in summer. ("They're frightfully proud of their water. And they've got this Spanish modesty thing about women, veils and whatnot. Best to oblige, don't you know.")

"Jolly coves, what?" Pa said, after each instructive visit.

"No," Lila said.

"What?"

"I said no. I thought they were awful."

"Jeepers, creepers," Pa said cheerfully. "You'll get used to them."

And then this morning came. Slackening speed, the ship steamed slowly out of the great blue spaces of the Mediterranean and into the harbour at Valetta, the Grand Harbour of the island of Malta. And the sunlight changed. The sunlight of the open sea, kind for all its brilliance, was replaced by this other sort, bouncing and glaring off yellow walls, cliff-like yellow walls and ramparts and bastions, bigger walls than any Lila had ever seen or imagined. She stood on deck as the ship steamed in, her eyes narrowed as far as they could go without entirely closing, and felt the light and the hard

42

yellowness hit her in the face like a smack with a shovel. Around her, the English voices of her fellow passengers brayed and bellowed, and through it all she could still hear Pa, loud and clear. He was singing. On the journey out, the sailors had taught him a new song, and he loved it. He loved it even more than 'Jeepers, Creepers' and he was singing it now, out of sheer exhilaration at finding himself in this awful flaring yellow hell. The song was called, 'Flat Foot Floogie with a Floy Floy' and with it, at the top of his voice, Pa was singing them both into their new life in Malta.

★ ★ ★

"Spiru will be at the harbour to meet you," Mr Perriam had said. "I have written to him with express instructions to bring a cart down for your luggage. You will find him very useful. He must be almost seventy now, but my father taught him to read and write English as a child and he is much attached to the family. I have sent a physical description of you both, so that no mistakes will be made. I have also instructed him to prepare rooms for you."

There were no carts on the waterfront. There were crowds and shouting and piles of goods and boys with handcarts full of coal and fish and oranges, but no empty cart attended by a faithful servant waiting for their luggage. Lila sat down on a salt-stiffened pile of fishing nets and tried to ignore the steady stares of a group of barefoot children nearby, while Pa went stomping up and down the waterfront shouting, "Spiru, Spiru, Villa Zonda, Villa Zonda!" like a railway conductor announcing the name of the next station. Lila wished she had a hat, or a scarf, or even a newspaper she could hide behind. The children seemed to find staring second nature to them, their dark eyes steady on her face and her thin arms and legs where they protruded from her cotton dress. One of them seemed to be fixated by her feet. Under his unwavering gaze, Lila felt her feet grow bigger and bigger until she hardly dared look at them herself for fear of what she might see.

"May I help?" someone said in accented English.

Lila said, without looking up, "I really don't know — "

"Have you just come in the ship?" the voice said. "In the SS *Meridian*?"

"Yes."

"And you would like a dghaisa to take you across the harbour to your hotel?"

Lila shot a glance sideways. A young man was standing six feet away, dressed in a blue shirt and trousers and holding a straw hat in one hand.

"A what?"

"A dghaisa. A boat to take you across the water."

"Your boat, I suppose," Lila said, disagreeably.

"No," he said, apparently not at all put out by her tone. "Not my boat. I am a schoolmaster."

Lila risked another glance. In her experience

44

schoolmasters were middle-aged or elderly with an invariably desiccated air. This young man wasn't thirty and had vivid dark looks.

"I am only presuming to speak," the young man said, "because you looked so lost."

Lila said stiffly, "My father is with me. He has gone to find our — " she paused, wondering how to refer to Spiru, and then said, feeling absurd, " — our manservant. I am merely — merely tired, thank you."

The young man gave a little bow. "Then I am sorry to have troubled you."

She said nothing. There was a moment's pause, and then the young man moved past her and said something sharp and incomprehensible to the group of barefoot children. They scattered at once, their feet slapping lightly on the stones of the waterfront.

"They don't beg," the young man said, "but they like to look."

At that precise moment, Lila felt keenly that she would have preferred to have been begged from than stared at. She hadn't looked in a mirror for days, since one disgusted glance she had taken soon after she had stopped being seasick, for fear of still looking, as Pa so encouragingly put it, "as limp as a halibut fillet." She put up a hand now and tucked a long strand of hair behind her ear, as if to indicate some small remaining measure of composure.

The young man was still standing where he had been to reprimand the children, and was gazing along the waterfront.

"Please," he said, "is this your father?"

Lila looked up. Pa was stumping energetically along towards her, nodding and beaming at people as he passed, his face shining with exertion. Lila rose from her pile of fishing nets and was conscious of the young man's eyes on her, as the children's had been, all down her thin, unhappy, weary length.

"No sign!" Pa shouted merrily from several yards away. "Not a dicky bird! Been right along. No Spiru, no cart. What's to do?"

Lila smoothed her crumpled dress down her sides.

"Perhaps he never got Mr Perriam's letter."

"No!" Pa cried. "That'll be it!"

He sounded entirely undismayed, as if finding oneself in a foreign harbour with all one's worldly possessions in an ungainly pile, and no means to transport them to a very uncertain destination, was simply a matter of course.

"Jolly crowds, though," Pa added. "Topping harbour. Top hole boats."

Still standing respectfully at a little distance, the young man cleared his throat. Pa turned, beaming. "What ho!"

The young man said, more deferentially than he had spoken to Lila, "My name is Angelo Saliba, sir."

"Ha!" Pa said, still beaming.

"I am a schoolmaster. Today, being the feast of Our Lady of the Rosary, my school is closed. Are you and your daughter — are you strangers in Malta?"

"I'll say," Pa said. He winked at Lila.

She said quickly, "We have a house to go to,

46

the house of English friends — "

"Zonda," Pa said, interrupting very loudly and clearly as if speaking to a halfwit. "Villa Zonda. Know it?"

The young man nodded his head.

"We have Mr Perriam's instructions," Lila hissed at Pa. "Near some aqueduct, he said, on the way towards this — this Silent City. We don't need — "

"The Wignacourt Aqueduct," the young man said gravely. "The road to Mdina, to Rabat." He hesitated and then he said, directly to Pa, "May I help you? May I help you find transport?"

Pa stumped forward and clapped his hand on the young man's shoulder. "Capital!" he said. "Lead on, my hearty!"

Lila said, "Pa, we can't, I mean, we can't just ask, we can't — "

Angelo Saliba looked at her gravely.

"I am a Roman Catholic, miss," he said. He sounded severe, almost as if he was reproving her for harbouring suspicions about his honourableness.

She could feel herself growing red, in awkward blotches up her neck and cheeks.

"I didn't mean — anything, Mr Saliba. I just meant we couldn't impose, being total strangers — "

"That's why we need help!" Pa cried. He limped back towards Lila and shook a finger at her. "What else are we to do? Kind young man, answer to prayer. Don't be a nincompoop." He turned back to Angelo Saliba. "Very civil of you. Very civil indeed. Something to take my

47

daughter in and something for all our traps. Just the ticket."

"Perhaps," the young man said, to Lila, "you will come and sit down at my mother's house. While I make arrangements. It is only a few steps this way. My mother does not speak English but she will be — " he paused, glanced at Lila's face and said stiffly, "very happy."

For some sudden reason she could not fathom, Lila was seized by the feeling that she was, inexorably, going to cry. She sank down again onto the pile of fishing nets and, pulling up her knees, attempted to hide her face in her hands behind them.

"My mother's house," she heard Angelo Saliba say offendedly above her head, "is very clean — "

"Dear boy!" Pa cried. "Dear boy! 'Course it is! Undeniably spotless!" He lowered himself awkwardly onto the knee of his good leg beside Lila and hissed at her, "What are you thinking of? Eh? What manners. What a display of manners. Kind young man, only trying to help — "

Lila raised her face from her hands and glared furiously at Pa. "Go away!" she screeched. "Go away the whole lot of you, and leave me alone!"

And then Pa's face seemed to loom at her, huge and weirdly quivering like the reflection of a face seen in moving water, and she fell abruptly away from him, across the fishing nets, in a dead faint.

She came to sitting on a wooden kitchen chair

with her head between her knees, staring at the cobbles of the waterfront. Some hands were on her shoulders, not unkind but very decided, holding her down. When she moved her eyes slightly sideways, she could see a dark stuff skirt and black stockinged legs and a pair of black canvas shoes with rope soles. Presumably the feet in the black canvas shoes and the hands on her shoulders belonged to the same person.

"I'm fine," Lila said uncertainly.

The person above her appeared to take no notice. Lila pushed her shoulders up with such strength as she could muster, and the hands relaxed. Lila raised her head slowly and looked across the waterfront to the harbour which seemed to shimmer in the brilliant light like something seen through flames.

A glass of water was thrust under her nose and a woman's voice said something she did not understand.

"Thank you," she said, taking the glass and drinking gratefully. "Thank you. Did I faint?"

"Iva," the woman's voice said.

Lila twisted her head round.

"I've never fainted in my life before."

She looked up. A middle-aged woman with an earthenware jug in one hand was standing beside her. She had her head bound up in a black scarf, and there was a gold cross round her neck, on a cord. She lifted the jug, to pour more water into Lila's glass.

"Where is my father?" Lila said. "Where did he go? Are you Mrs — " She paused. What had the young man in a blue shirt said his name was?

"Are you the schoolmaster's mother? Where is my father?"

The woman bent down towards Lila and spoke rapidly. She was not, at close quarters, as old as her clothes made her seem, and she had good teeth, white against her dark skin. She set the jug down on the stones and took Lila's free hand and patted it. Her hands were hard, unadorned with anything except a wedding ring.

"It's so awkward," Lila said, "not being able to understand you."

"Villa Zonda," the woman said, and then, more slowly, "Villa Zonda. Angelo Saliba."

"Ah," Lila said, nodding. "You are Angelo's mother."

"Iva."

"And this — " turning a little in the wooden chair, "is your house."

"Iva."

Lila took her hand out of the woman's grasp and laid it on the wall behind her. The wall was warm, and made of pale stone, yellowish pale stone, and up it grew a plant Lila couldn't identify with flowers that seemed to be exactly the same as the leaves except that they were a brilliant pink, and as papery and fragile as tissue.

"Pretty," Lila said politely. She touched a flower.

"Sabih."

"Sabih? Pretty?"

"Iva," the woman said again, and smiled down at Lila. She had a gold tooth, brassy,

Lila now saw, among the white ones. They regarded each other for a second or two, and then Lila looked away and down at the glass of water she still held. She observed that the hand that held it was shaking very slightly, and, at the same moment, that a vision had risen in her mind, a vision so powerfully attractive that she almost cried out with the sudden longing for it. It wasn't a vision of that tall thin house with its damp, salt-smelling rooms that she had left behind, but rather one of the Perriams' library on the first morning of April, with the fire burning and herself crouched on a stool before it, with the map of the Mediterranean spread at her feet, and the idea of Malta only a sunlit kind of dream, a possibility, a chance made unalarming by the security and civilization of the surroundings in which she had been offered it. There, in the Perriams' library, among the books and pictures and contented scholarly quiet, the idea of Malta had seemed a little disconcerting, but no threat; it had seemed something she could manage as easily as she managed being part of the Perriams' gentle, ordered lives. And now here it was, the reality of it, hot and yellow and incomprehensible, and there was no single thing about it that did not dismay her to her very depths.

She stood up unsteadily and held the water glass out to Angelo Saliba's mother.

"Thank you," she said, "you have been very kind. No doubt your son is still being kind and that my father is somewhere about with him. I hardly care. I'm sorry you can't understand what

I'm saying, but perhaps it's just as well because I have to tell you — at least I have to tell *somebody* — that I have never been anywhere in my life that I wanted less to be than here, and that all I want to do, absolutely *all* I want to do, is to go home."

# 5

"VILLA ZONDA," Angelo said, turning round.

He was sitting beside the driver on the box of the curious old-fashioned phaeton he had found to carry Lila and Pa. Pa had been vastly amused by it, by the enormous wheels with gilded spokes, by the black oilcloth seats with tufts of horsehair springing through the splits, by the elderly driver who looked, Pa remarked several times, like nothing so much as a pickled walnut. Behind them, at some distance, a low cart on bone-shaking ironbound wheels was carrying all their luggage.

"These gates," Angelo said, "this is the entrance."

The dusty roadway had been bordered for some time by a stone wall, over which nothing much could be glimpsed but unfamiliar trees, some unnaturally dark, some twisted and silvery. But now there was a break in the wall, and two immense iron gates, painted black long ago and now peeling in dry, greyish flakes, stood ajar, just open wide enough to allow a person, but not a vehicle, through. The gates were hung on stone pillars, each one surmounted by a stone finial. The left hand finial had its top broken off and below the right hand one was a darker stone, set into the face of the pillar with the words 'Villa Zonda' carved into it, in capital letters.

53

"Well!" said Pa, patting Lila's knee. "Home sweet home!"

Lila said nothing. She watched in silence as Angelo jumped down off the box and pushed the gates open wide enough to allow the phaeton through. They turned off the road and into a driveway darkened by tall trees, seeming suddenly very silent after the sunlight outside the wall.

"I hope — " Lila said, and stopped. Her voice did not sound trustworthy.

Pa looked at her. "It'll be first rate," he said. "You'll see." He patted her again. "First *rate.*"

The phaeton moved softly forward over the drive, which was carpeted with pine needles. Angelo did not get back on the box, but ran easily beside them and the sight of him escorting them in this simple, courteous way only added to Lila's resentful feeling that she was in a place of quite impenetrable foreignness. She said, despising herself, "If it's hopeless — " and stopped.

"Hopeless?" Pa said. "Why should it be hopeless? What's hopeless, I'd like to know?"

Lila shook her head. She said desperately, "If we can't belong, if we find we can't manage, if — "

"We've been here three hours," Pa said. "Three hours! Three hours and you want to give up?"

"There!" Angelo called from beside them. "Look ahead! There is the Villa Zonda."

Ahead of them the trees of the driveway

ended, and the sunlight blazed down on a big bare yellow house with rust-coloured shutters, all closed. A balustrade, broken in places, ran around the roofline, and under a group of crooked palm trees planted in front of the main doors, a donkey was tethered to a stone. Apart from the donkey and a few dusty hens scratching in the dry earth without much enthusiasm, there was not a sight or a sound of life.

The driver brought the phaeton round the neglected sweep by the palm trees and stopped in front of the shallow flight of steps leading up to the main door. The donkey raised its head from its reverie, regarded them all dully for a second or two, and looked away again.

"Will I knock for you?" Angelo said.

"Capital!" Pa cried, struggling with the latch on the phaeton's door. "Good man! Capital place!"

Lila stayed where she was and gazed up at the house's façade. Little wiry clumps of weed had seeded themselves here and there in holes and crevices, giving the house the look of needing a thoroughly good shave, and the little balcony below the centre pair of first-floor windows was whitely streaked with bird droppings. There were urns punctuating the balustrade at the corners of the roof, and one of these was broken and another sprouted a single leggy stem, knobbly and bent, like some grotesque antenna. It all looked forlorn, neglected, like the houses so beloved of all the Perriams' fairy tales, which revealed themselves as containing something of great good and beauty or, more often, something of great evil and spite. Those houses, Mrs Perriam had said, those shuttered mansions and castles of the ancient story world, were images for life, the Pandora's Box of life. They had to be entered with great caution, Mrs Perriam said, being full of traps for the unwary. Lila would have given anything in the world at that moment to have had Mrs Perriam beside her, small, bespectacled and shawled, and incapable of being disconcerted by anything.

She watched Angelo run up the steps and hammer on the tall flaking main doors with his fist. Pa had got out of the phaeton — admiringly watched by the driver for his nimbleness — and was standing, in his familiar crooked stance, at the foot of the steps, waiting for the doors to open and his new Maltese dwelling to welcome him in. He wouldn't have noticed, Lila knew, the weeds or the broken urn or the blistered paint or the despondency of the donkey. He only saw a new door opening, literally and metaphorically, and a new prospect revealing itself, bright and beckoning.

Angelo turned on the top step. He called down, "I think no-one can hear me."

The horse between the shafts of the phaeton sighed as if to suggest that it had been hopeless to suppose, in such a place, that anyone would.

"I will go round to the courtyard," Angelo said. "I will find somebody in the courtyard."

Pa limped forward.

"I'll come with you, old chum. Introduce myself, what?" He glanced at Lila. "You stay there. No more fainting fits."

56

She watched the two of them move together along the façade of the house and disappear out of sight round the corner. Then she watched the luggage cart creak painfully into the drive and come to a rattling halt behind the phaeton, and the two drivers gesture and grunt at one another. Then she watched the donkey for a while, and the tattered hens, and then she closed her eyes and thought of the clean, cold North Sea and the birch trees, dancing so gracefully across the façade of Culver House and the pale green orchid in the hall there, in flight from its translucent porcelain pot wreathed in blue dragons. Clean things, cool things, things of green and grey and blue and silver, with a clean wind whipping up clean salty air . . .

"Now there's a thing," Pa said loudly.

Lila opened her eyes.

"What a to-do," Pa said. He was holding onto the side of the phaeton and his eyes were bright with drama. "Never seen anything like it. Weeping and wailing and gnashing of teeth. Everyone in black, 'cept the baby. Bet they'd put the baby in black, for two pins. Angelo said we just missed the body. They'd had the body there on the kitchen table for two days, all in its Sunday suit."

Out of the corner of her eye, Lila saw Angelo, hesitating at the corner of the house. She looked hard at Pa.

"Whose body?"

"Whose d'you think?" Pa said. "Spiru's. Who else? Heart attack, Angelo said. The son-in-law told him. He was out there thinning his carrots

57

and wham, bang, heart attack. Head of the family. Everyone in hysterics. Gone to pieces."

Lila licked her lips.

"So — what happens?"

Pa beamed.

"In we go! Settle in!"

"But — but if the whole family is in mourning — "

"Cheer 'em up!" Pa said. "We'll cheer 'em up!"

"But if Spiru's dead, and no-one else speaks English — "

"There's a child who does," Pa said, "funny little object. Little girl. A few words anyway." He rattled the latch of the door. "Lila," he said, and his voice was different, less blithe. "Got to get out, old girl. Got to go in. Got to face it. You said it to me, now I've got to say it to you. No choice."

Lila stood up in the phaeton. She glanced along the house to where Angelo still stood, waiting to see what they would do next.

"Pa — "

"Yes?"

"I think — maybe we should thank Mr Saliba and ask him to go now?"

Pa shrugged. "If you want."

"I — I sort of feel he's seen enough."

"Up to you, old girl. As you wish."

"But I don't quite know how we thank him."

Pa beamed again. "Easy."

"Is it? I mean, can we give him money?"

"Money? Certainly not. For one thing, we

58

haven't got any. For another, I've the perfect notion."

"What?"

"Simple," Pa said triumphantly, "simple. I'll paint him a picture."

\* \* \*

"Here," the child said.

She wore a black shawl tied round a much-washed blue cotton frock and her pigtails were finished with black rags. She stood in the tall doorway of a first-floor room and gestured for Lila to look inside.

"Here," she said again, and then, as an afterthought, "big."

Lila peered in. The room was wholly shuttered so that the sunlight fell only in narrow lines through the crevices, as if ruled across what appeared to be a very dusty tiled floor. There seemed to be an iron bed in the room, and a big cupboard and a table with a jug on it and a couple of upright chairs. Lila couldn't see any curtains, or anything on the floor but dust. Above the bed a single picture hung, dark and difficult to make out but looking, even from the distance of the doorway, suspiciously holy.

"Good?" the child asked.

"I don't know. But, as you say, big."

"Another big," the child said. She took Lila's hand and drew her along the tiled floor of the upper landing to another tall doorway. "There."

This room had three beds in it and a

59

washstand and a revolving bookcase shrouded in a piece of flyblown muslin. There were rolled up mattresses on the beds, covered with black and white ticking and tied with rope. A single shutter was open in this room, allowing a square of sunlight to fall on the floor, and in this square, stretched out luxuriously, lay an immensely pregnant yellow cat. Was it here, in these gaunt and dusty rooms thirty years before, that Mr and Mrs Perriam had had their honeymoon?

"And salone," the child said. Her voice was awed. She ran ahead of Lila, her bare feet light on the tiles, and pushed open a pair of double doors at the far end of the landing. A smell of mould surged out at once; a smell of neglected fabric and leather and paper, of quiet decay.

"Oh Lord," Lila said.

The salone was huge, running the whole depth of the house with three walls of windows. It too was shuttered, but two shutters had splintered holes in them, letting in enough light to see that the room was as crammed with furniture as the bedrooms had been empty of it. The floor was covered with an immense Turkey carpet, red and blue and green, over which other rugs had been laid, and on this layered base stood a flotilla of chairs and sofas and tables and padded stools, lamps and cabinets and bookcases inlaid with brass. Every lamp bore a fringed shade, every chair and sofa a tasselled cushion, every table a shawl-like cloth. And everything, every bronze cupid statuette, every plaster cast of a classical head, every landscape on the walls framed in

60

black and gold, bore a thick layer of pale dust, as even and opaque as velvet.

"This room," Lila said, "hasn't been touched for thirty years. Has it? Simply not been *touched*."

The child leaned forward and laid a respectful finger on the arm of a nearby chair. It was a vaguely oriental lacquered chair, and when she took her finger away, there was a round black spot, neat and shining, where it had briefly been. She blew the dust off her finger.

"My name," she said, "is Carmela."

"And was Spiru your grandfather?"

Her head drooped at once and she crossed herself devoutly.

"Sorry," Lila said.

Carmela closed her eyes.

"He is with the saints."

"Yes. Yes, of course. But did he ever come in this room?"

Carmela's eyes flew wide open with shock. "No!"

Lila walked past her to one of the windows which had a hole in its shutter. The windows were high narrow casements, fastened by vertical sliding metal rods and knobs ornamented with acanthus leaves. From the doorway, Carmela watched as Lila wrenched the windows open, and then the outer shutters, releasing a scatter of dead flies and a shower of dust and paint flakes. Then she came carefully over the carpets between the pieces of furniture and stood beside Lila at the window.

Below them, in the courtyard, only the men of

61

the family were grouped around the wellhead. Pa was with them. Pa was talking and gesticulating and the men were watching him, polite but uncomprehending. They looked rather as Angelo Saliba had looked when Pa had, wreathed in cheerful smiles, told him to run along now and he'd be rewarded, in due course, with a painting of the harbour.

Angelo had said, "I have offended you?"

"No, no," Pa said, hearty with exaggerated reassurance. "No, no, nothing of the kind. But we'll have to forage about for ourselves now, don't you see? Bite the bullet."

Angelo had looked puzzled and then angry, and then, with a swift glance at Lila which most speakingly — and accurately, she knew — laid the blame for this dismissal at her door, turned on his heel and went rapidly down the drive beneath the umbrella pines. She had been filled with shame at treating him so badly and with a simultaneous unreasonable anger that his courtesy and kindness should have shown up so baldly a reciprocal ungraciousness in herself.

"I'm tired," she told herself, averting her gaze from that swiftly disappearing blue back, "I've been ill." But neither, she knew, was a real excuse for a needy stranger to treat an hospitable native so badly. She had behaved exactly like those English people on the ship whom she had told Pa she thought were so awful. She had been awful to Angelo Saliba, cold and superior and rude. She had punished him for behaving better than her and — come on, she told herself, *truth* please — for being better-looking than her too.

62

And, with both those advantages, for being the son of a fisherman.

She took her gaze away from the group by the wellhead and looked down at Carmela. Nobody could call Carmela good-looking. She was small and skinny, with a disproportionately large head and a froggy little face, wide mouthed and popping eyed. Perhaps she was nine or ten, perhaps less; it was difficult to tell and Carmela didn't seem sure. All she could tell Lila was that she had been making lace for three years, with her mother and her aunts, and that if the lacemaking orders were heavy, she didn't go to school. On those days, they all sat in the courtyard on kitchen chairs, backs to the sun, with the lacemaking cushions propped up against the wall in front of them, and the glass bobbins flew about and clicked together in the disciplined webs of white threads. Carmela hadn't learned her English at school, she said, she'd learned it from her grandfather, who could read it, too. At the mention of his name, Carmela crossed herself again and bowed her head.

Her mother and grandmother and aunts had been unable to speak to Lila. She had seen them, through an open doorway, in a big room she took to be the kitchen, a huddle of black clad women from whom rose a curious wailing sound, half a sob, half a lament, almost rhythmic. There was a wicker basket on two stools by the doorway, and in it Lila could see a black-haired baby bundled up in shawls like a little chrysalis. It was when she had stooped to look at the baby that Carmela had detached

63

herself from the group of women and come forward, standing in front of Lila with her hands composedly folded across her limp blue cotton skirts.

Lila said now, her voice not as certain as she would have liked it to be, "We are going to live here. In these rooms. My father and me."

"Yes," Carmela said.

"Where do you live?"

Carmela leaned out of the window, and pointed downwards, across the wall of the house to the shuttered ground-floor windows.

"There is my living."

"And your mother and father?"

"And my sisters and brothers."

"And your aunts and uncles and grandmother? And the baby? How many?"

Her lips moving in Maltese, Carmela began to count off her relations on her fingers. She got right across both hands once, and then stopped to start on her toes.

"Seventeen," Lila said. "Maybe — "

"Seventeen people down there?"

Carmela nodded. There seemed to her to be an enormous amount of space downstairs. For the last year, she had only, after all, had to share a bed with one cousin, not two. They had brought the extra bed down from the first floor as they had, over the years, brought down cupboards and chairs and sheets and tables as they needed them. Her father Salvu, in fact, had been planning to bring down the three mattresses quite soon, and had already tied them up prior to throwing them out of the window, to save carrying. It was perfectly acceptable, she knew, to take things as the downstairs family grew, as long as you only took things from the bedrooms. Her grandfather had made that very plain. It was the salone that must never be touched. The salone was sacred. The salone belonged to the English master who had found Spiru working in a cellar as a coppersmith, in the slums of the Manderaggio below Fort St Elmo, and had brought him to live at the Villa Zonda. For Spiru and for all his family, the salone was a shrine. To be standing in it beside the English lady gave her an excited, guilty feeling, like being in church without her head covered.

"We must sleep here tonight," Lila said.

Carmela nodded again.

"And," Lila said uncertainly, "buy food."

"Bread," Carmela said, spreading her fingers out again, "timpana, lampuki."

"Lampuki?"

Carmela screwed up her face. "Fishes," she said and then gestured wildly, as if to indicate that it was something more than fishes, but exactly what was beyond her powers of explanation. "Fishes," she said again.

"Carmela," Lila said. "Carmela, will you help me?"

"Help?"

"Will you help me to sweep the rooms and make the beds and buy fishes?"

Carmela looked doubtful. Her days were already, it seemed to her, crammed with sweeping and bedmaking and errands. And the baby — though she knew his arrival had been the will of God — had only added to all these obligations.

"I'll teach you more English," Lila said. "I'll teach you English so that when you're older, you can get a job in Valetta, in a — in — "

"A shop?" Carmela asked, brightening.

"Yes, yes, I'm sure, if that's what you want."

"A shop," Carmela said firmly. She looked down at her bare feet and added decidedly, "With shoes."

"Yes, I — "

Carmela held up her hand, commanding silence.

"At once," she said. "At once I fetch brushes," and then she raced from the room, leaving Lila alone among its mouldering Edwardian glories.

# 6

SALVU found Lila a bicycle. He gave it to Pa to give to her because, like all the men of the house, he preferred to speak to Pa and to pretend that Lila wasn't there. When he spoke to Pa, he spoke respectfully, as a younger man to an older one, and as one with blessedly whole limbs to one who had been damaged in the glory of service to his country. Salvu was a passionate patriot. For his taste, there were far too many English living in Malta, living *off* Malta, as he suspected the English girl was. Her father, painting pictures of Maltese boats on Maltese seas under a Maltese sky, he could see some small use to; but not the girl. The girl looked pale and strained and kept to herself on the first floor of the house. What's more, she and her father were sleeping on two of the mattresses Salvu had earmarked for his own children, now that they were growing. For all that, when Pa, through Carmela, asked Salvu to find Lila a bicycle, he didn't refuse. He didn't smile about the task, but he didn't refuse. He also accepted a painting of a dghaisa crossing the Grand Harbour in payment, and hung it in a place of honour, beside a picture a nun in the little convent at Zurrieq had painted of Saint Venera, who was his wife's nameday saint.

"There!" Pa said.

He stood beside Lila at the open window

of the salone, and regarded the bicycle with triumph. It leaned against the wellhead in the courtyard below, heavy, black, extremely upright and decidedly old-fashioned. It had only one mudguard, a broken basket in front and, at the back, a wooden box tied with rope to a sort of flat metal carrier.

"Thank you," Lila said faintly.

"Just the job, eh?"

"Oh yes."

Pa spun round. The salone behind him, to the horror of Spiru's family downstairs, had been emptied of half its furniture, and the carpets had been brushed. Lila had done it herself, and washed the windows, never mind dragging great chests and sofas about with no one to help her but that funny little frog child. She'd seemed determined, Lila; determined to wear herself out getting things shipshape, imposing some order. It was time she got outside, time she got some air and sunlight; time — even Pa hesitated over this — time she went off in pursuit of this employment Mr Perriam had suggested and brought home, to put it crudely, a bit of bacon. Pa jingled the coins in his pocket. When those were gone there was precious little to replace them with and Lila, so practical about money in England, seemed different in Malta, less prepared to accept responsibility, even quietly, persistently angry, as if coming here in the first place hadn't been her idea, her doing. Pa had the distinct feeling that Lila bore a grudge against him, and wasn't going to let that grudge go until she was good and ready. She didn't seem prepared to appreciate the efforts he was making, bartering paintings for things they needed (how else, he'd like to know, would she have had her bicycle?), forgoing his daily tot of rum, enduring those endless plates of fish she produced, bristling with bones. "Fish is the cheapest," she'd say meaningfully, "so we eat fish."

Pa turned back to the window and waved a hand down towards the bicycle.

"Fancy a spin?"

"I might," Lila said. She knew exactly what Pa was getting at and was in no hurry to oblige.

"Out — mm — out Mdina way?"

"Maybe," Lila said.

"Do you good, cooped up in here — "

"I'm used to here."

Pa sighed. He looked down at the bicycle and then he looked at Lila. She was wearing a yellow cotton dress with white spots and a narrow white belt round the waist. It didn't suit her. She didn't have enough colour to wear yellow. He sighed again.

"I'll be off then," Pa said. "I'll leave you to think about it."

Lila said, "Where are you going?"

For a moment, Pa hesitated again. He had found a wonderful street in Valetta, a street of bars and clubs and easy virtue which drew the sailors like a honeypot. Its proper name was Straight Street but the sailors called it the Gut, and Pa loved it. It knocked the seamen's club in Aldeburgh into a cocked hat. But somehow, Pa held back from mentioning the Gut to Lila. It would be difficult to describe its particular charms to Lila in a way she would understand.

Pa said airily, "Oh, down to the harbour, as usual — "

"Did you," Lila said awkwardly, "see Angelo Saliba again?"

"No," Pa said cheerfully, "never did. But if I do, I'll tell him I haven't forgotten his painting. He can have a merchant ship. Why not? There's a new one just come in."

When Pa had gone, Lila went slowly out of the salone and into the room she had made her bedroom. It had an armchair in it now, as well as the iron bed and the cupboard, and a looking glass she had taken from the salone, in a green and gilded frame with two doves at the top looking affectionately at one another. Lila had hung this on one of her bedroom walls, as well as a watercolour of a garden which looked comfortingly English, with blue spires of delphiniums against a brick wall, and a beehive and a rabbit hutch. The picture that had looked suspiciously holy had turned out indeed to be an engraving of the martyrdom of St Sebastian, all arrows and agony. Lila had wrapped it in a piece of cloth when Carmela wasn't looking, and hidden it in the bottom of the cupboard.

She went across the room to the dove mirror, and looked at herself in it. It amazed her that, even though she never saw anything different when she looked in the mirror, she always hoped — even expected — that she would. She released her hair from the ribbon she had tied it back with

70

that morning, brushed it vigorously, and put the ribbon back again as an Alice band. It made her look younger, which was a pity, but less tired and severe, which was an improvement. She looked down at her frock. It was perfectly clean, but really she had no way of knowing if yellow cotton was suitable for calling upon the high people of Malta or not. If you had to do it on a bicycle, there wasn't, in any case, much option. Perhaps she ought to add stockings, and take some gloves and maybe change her canvas shoes for leather ones. She'd had a string of pearls once, little graduated pearls that had belonged to her mother, but Pa had borrowed them, to buy paints with he said, and they'd never come home again.

Carmela came out of the kitchen when Lila emerged into the courtyard, and inspected her appearance with interest. She should have been at school that day, but the baby had kept her mother awake all night, so she had stayed at home to mind him while her mother slept. The baby was sleeping too, worn out by the activity of the night, and Carmela was bored.

"Look," she said, pointing at Lila's stockinged legs.

"I am going visiting," Lila said, "to Mdina. To the Silent City."

Carmela touched one of Lila's cotton gloves. "And look."

"It's to be polite," Lila said.

"I am coming?"

"No," Lila said, "I am going on my new bicycle."

They both regarded it. Lila said, "Is it far? To Mdina?"

Carmela, who had only ever been there twice in her life, nodded vigorously. It was miles away, *miles*. You had to go to Attard, almost, and past the hospital for the mad people — God preserve them — and up a hill. It was a huge hill. Lila would have to get off her bicycle at Rabat, where all the best lacemakers lived, and push it up the hill. She, Carmela, could come too and help push. She could ride on the metal carrier at the back.

"No," Lila said, "I am going to meet complete strangers, people I don't know at all." She patted her pocket, in which Mr Perriam's letter of introduction lay, inscribed, alarmingly, to Count Tabia Is-Sultan. "I have to go alone. And you have to mind the baby."

"Bring the baby," Carmela said. "Baby in basket."

"It wouldn't be safe. I couldn't hold us all steady. The baby might fall out."

Carmela's eyes filled with tears. She said unsteadily, "I scream — "

Lila put her gloved hands on the cracked rubber grips of the handlebars of her new bicycle.

"Carmela, I am going to see a count."

Carmela gulped.

"And his sister is a baroness. In her own right. I don't think I can take the baby."

Carmela scuffed her toes in the dust. "Next time?"

"Maybe," Lila said. She wheeled the bicycle

72

away from the wellhead. "But maybe there won't be a next time. Maybe the high people will turn out to be too high for me."

★ ★ ★

Out in the dusty roadway, Lila paused, squinting in the sun. Ahead of her, across the road, and quite familiar now, were the marching stone arches of the aqueduct, which in the early seventeenth century had run for almost ten miles to bring water into Valetta. Now it was disused, and broken in places, and the only creatures to use it were small flocks of goats who sought shade underneath it. When Carmela — and sometimes her older cousin, Maria — took Lila to the market in Santa Venera, they turned left out of the gate and followed the aqueduct along past the big house with the stone lions on the roof where, Maria said, Sir Harry Luke lived. Her grandfather, Spiru, had been an admirer of Sir Harry Luke, Lieutenant Governor of Malta for eight years and, like his old English master, a rescuer and admirer of Maltese buildings. "There are *some* good English," Spiru had said. "The good ones are the friends of Malta." Maria recounted this every time they passed Sir Harry Luke's house and stopped to look at the four stone lions, and Lila was very tired of it.

Now, however, she was to turn the other way and travel a road that was completely strange to her. Mr Perriam had given her a map — "Out of date, I fear, but still, I am

73

sure, serviceable" — on which, in Indian ink, he had traced her route to Mdina. It looked at least straightforward. From the point where she now stood, one foot on the ground to steady her bicycle, the road seemed to run south-west across the island uninterrupted by corners or turnings. The only village she would pass was Attard, where the Governor General lived in a country palace which Mr Perriam much admired — "Such fine gardens, and a most impressive stable courtyard, both of them testimony to the fact that the original builder, Grand Master de Paule, was an unregenerate hedonist to the end."

She gave herself an energetic push and set the bicycle off towards the sun. Her gloves felt hot and prickly, despite being made of cotton, and the straw hat which Carmela's mother, Doris, had sent out with strict instructions that it must be worn, oppressive. There was a warm wind, puffing up the dust in plumes and swirls, but the air felt clear still, clear with the new warmth of early summer, and Lila, despite her misgivings, despite her apprehensions, despite the weight of the bicycle and the constrictions of hat and gloves and stockings, felt a sense of exhilaration and freedom at being out on the open road and began, very cautiously, to enjoy herself.

The road, being flat, was relatively easy to ride on despite the stones and the potholes, and the weight of the bicycle gave it momentum. There wasn't much traffic, only donkey carts and a lorry or two and a few fellow cyclists, some of them English servicemen in khaki shorts, who yelled cheerfully at Lila as they bumped by. And the countryside amazed her. It was so stony and so inhospitable-looking, yet, in a curiously mysterious and Maltese way, so extraordinarily cultivated. There seemed to be very few trees, except for here and there the lumpy outline of a prickly pear, or the strange dark trees that grew in the garden of the Villa Zonda, but instead there were walls. Lila had never seen so many walls; walls dividing up tiny fields, walls round farms, walls round villages, walls round houses so that they looked enclosed and secret, declining to let the outside world look in. Some of the field walls were made of rubble and stones, but the village ones were smooth and pale gold, and the houses were flat-topped and made Lila think of pictures she had seen of houses in North Africa, where you spread your mattress on the roof under the stars, for coolness at night. There were figures in a lot of the fields too, the women in black, and donkeys with panniers strapped either side of them, and little stooping children, apparently picking up stones. It was fascinating and somehow impressive, pedalling through this landscape where people were behaving as they had behaved down through the ages, just going about the simple, relentless, necessary business of staying alive.

"You will find," Mr Perriam had said gently, "that the Maltese are very different. They believe their islands to be the hub of the universe and, in consequence, to have a special relationship to God. Their history has given them a siege

75

mentality and, I may say, a passionate puritanism rare among Mediterranean peoples. You must go carefully, Lila. You must take trouble not to offend." He had paused and then he said, "The Maltese are, I do believe, even more Catholic than the Irish. Particularly out in the countryside."

Lila glanced sideways as she rode. Those people out there, in their tiny fields of green-gold wheat and potatoes and red clover, were just the people Mr Perriam had spoken of, proud and independent and pious, bending over their stony earth and living privately behind their windowless walls. It was sobering suddenly. The sight of them made her feel, for the first time, not alarmed and dismayed by the foreignness of Malta, and its initial inhospitable impression of ugliness, but respectful, as if the Maltese knew as well as she did what it was like to struggle, but didn't kick against life all the time and shriek at fate and glare at themselves irritably in mirrors. There was, she discovered, screwing up her eyes against the brightness of the light, a curious comfort in the thought. Heaven knew why, but there was.

And suddenly, so absorbed had she been in the surprising relief of her feelings, there was something else too. The road, having jolted its way through a succession of fields and walls, suddenly seemed to pull itself together and become more formal. The surface became smoother, and the sides were edged with a leggy double line of umbrella pines, and fields of red clover, undivided by walls, stretched away on either side in a rich carpet of colour. And ahead lay something wonderful, the hill which Carmela had spoken of; but she had never said what it was crowned with, never mentioned that a magical small city sat up there behind ancient golden walls, with domes and towers and cupolas outlined against the blue summer sky.

Lila got off her bicycle and propped it against an umbrella pine. Then she stepped down into the thick soft mass of the nearest clover field, and shielded her eyes to look. Running up the lower left-hand slope of the hill ahead of her was the sprawl of a modern town, no doubt the place Carmela had spoken of so respectfully as being renowned for its lacemaking, but it didn't touch the little citadel at the summit. There was something timeless about the look of that small city up there, as there had been about the people working in the fields, something serene and untouchable, protected as it was by the great guarding walls and ravelons rearing out of the surrounding seas of clover.

"Silent it is," Mr Perriam had said, "as you will see. But also something else. It was called Notabile, as a compliment by Alfonso V, King of Aragon. It is, indeed a notable city."

Lila climbed out of the clover field, adjusted her hat, straightened her stockings, mounted her ancient bicycle and, with a high heart, rode on.

# 7

THE room was very quiet. Lila didn't think she'd ever been in such a quiet room. Nor in one that was so beautiful. It was on the first floor, long and lofty, and the ceiling was coffered in dark wood with faint gleams of ancient gilding. The walls were panelled too, and hung with tapestries of flowery gardens and hawking scenes in leafy spring woodland. In the centre of one wall a great fireplace rose halfway to the ceiling, surmounted by two blithe carved stone dolphins, and all down the length of the opposite wall, windows opened onto a courtyard full of orange trees. Then there were the globes and astrolobes and the bronzes of nymphs and dancers, and the candlesticks as big as those in a cathedral, and the long tables, covered in Persian rugs, on which prints and maps and open books were spread. And everywhere, on the floor, on the tables, in the window embrasures, were flowers; huge tubs and troughs of lilies and amaryllis, white and blue and as glowingly orange as a sunset.

A manservant had left Lila here. He had led her up a stone staircase from a stone hall hung with elaborate fans of swords and pikes, and bowed her into the wonderful room, and left her. He had not seemed, when finally she could make anyone hear her from outside the great house's silent, shuttered walls, at all surprised to see her. The door had swung open — enormously tall, and bearing an immense brass dolphin knocker set too high for anyone but a giant to reach — and revealed him, formal and courteous, in a black suit over a white shirt, with his hand already held out for her visiting card. Lila had no card. She had put Mr Perriam's card into his hand, and waited.

He motioned her in.

"Good afternoon," he said, and inclined his head.

Lila found herself stammering. "G-good afternoon." She had stammered too at the great entrance gate to the city, when confronted by a priest who had looked severely at her legs and asked her, in thickly accented English, what she wanted. "The T-tabia Palace," she had said. "The C-count of Is-is-" She stopped. There was no point trying to say it all. Instead she said, as firmly as she could, "I have an introduction."

The priest had surveyed her again, with disapproval. Then he turned and indicated across the tiny square behind him.

"St Peter Street. Five turnings on the left."

"Thank you," Lila said. He was a small man in a scruffy soutane, but he was oddly intimidating. So, in its way, was this quiet, quiet place, muffled by the afternoon sun. It seemed sacrilegious to mount her bicycle again, so she had pushed it and walked beside it as softly as she could. It was like being in a dream, in a fairy tale, moving silently down the little sleeping curving streets between high walls and shuttered windows and bolted doorways, beneath balconies and porticos too noble for pigeons or pots of geraniums or washing.

This room was noble, too. It was not just impressive and lovely, but exalted, as if the people who occupied it only did high-minded, cultivated things in it, not ordinary everyday things like squabbling or reading newspapers or sewing on buttons. Even the air in the room was special, and smelled of beeswax and flowers; no cooking smells, Lila decided, could ever be permitted anywhere near.

She crossed diffidently to one of the open windows and looked down into the courtyard. It was, if anything, even lovelier than the room. It was filled with orange trees and pomegranates, planted in as precise an order as pieces on a chessboard, and there were rosebeds, and huge terracotta pots full of jasmine and plumbago, blue as the sky, and, in the centre, yet more dolphins frolicking in a fountain. There was nobody in the garden that Lila could see, but somebody had lately been there. On a stone seat, supported on little crouching lions, by the fountain, someone had left a book and a pair of spectacles and a hat wreathed in a white chiffon scarf.

"Miss Cunningham?"

Lila spun round.

A small man stood just inside the doorway, a dapper, old-fashioned looking man in a white waistcoat with hair as smooth as if it had been painted. He was smiling. He gave Lila a little bow.

80

"Julius Tabia, Miss Cunningham."

"Oh — " Lila said. How did one address counts? What did one call them? She clutched her straw hat tightly.

"Any friend of my dear friend Arthur Perriam is a friend of mine."

"It — it's his son I worked for — "

"Who I also know. And his charming wife. They came here for their honeymoon, and I recall a wonderful breakfast picnic at the temple of Hagar Qim. It was spring and the flowers were unforgettable. Have you visited Hagar Qim?"

"I'm afraid," Lila said, turning her hat round and round, "that I haven't been anywhere."

Count Julius came further into the room and took Lila's hat gently out of her hands.

"You mustn't be nervous. Call me Count Julius. It is the simplest, you see. Maltese surnames are too exotic for the English to get their tongues round."

Lila managed a small smile.

"I feel — well, I feel a bit impudent, coming to you like this — "

Count Julius laid Lila's hat courteously upon the nearest table.

"Our friend, Mr Perriam, has told me that you were an admirable assistant, conscientious and intelligent. I am writing a naval history of Malta, so you may imagine how useful a native English speaker might be to me with Britain and Malta's long maritime connection."

"Oh!" Lila cried, "oh, but you mustn't feel — "

"I never do anything I don't want to," Count

81

Julius said, "as you will discover. I have a heart of flint. And I never have anything in my house which, as your admirable William Morris once said, is neither useful nor beautiful. My sister will confirm that. I hope you will stay and meet my sister."

"I'm afraid," Lila said, horribly conscious of an uneven blush flooding up her neck and cheeks, "that I came on impulse, that I'm dreadfully unprepared. My father found me a bicycle this morning so — so, well, I got on it, and I came."

Count Julius was laughing.

"I loved it," Lila said. She put her gloved hands up to her hot face. "I loved the ride, the countryside, those walled villages."

"Our casals," Count Julius said. "The famous casals of Malta. Almost every one with its own church, magnificent churches. We are a godly island." He glanced at Lila. "And your father, I believe, is a painter?"

"Yes."

"And you are living at the Villa Zonda?"

"Yes," Lila said. "The Perriams have been so kind, a sort of lifeline."

"In Arthur Perriam's day," Count Julius said, "the garden at the Villa Zonda was everything a Mediterranean garden ought to be, a paradise of walks and cypress trees and groves of oranges and tangerines, and in spring, acres of jonquils. I was a young man then, and more romantic than I seem capable of being now, and I remember being quite transported in springtime by the scent of the jonquils at the Villa Zonda."

"I'm afraid it is all overgrown now. Or given over to growing vegetables. Spiru's family, you see — "

"Ah, the excellent Spiru."

"He died. He died just before we arrived. The family are all so shocked."

Count Julius sketched a quick crossing movement above his breast.

"May he rest in peace. Good heavens, then who is to look after you?"

Lila said, shyly, "I do it."

"My dear!"

"I'm — I'm quite used to it, you see. In England I looked after us anyway. I have, since I was twelve. In — in England, it's nothing extraordinary."

"I shall send someone back with you," Count Julius declared. "We can spare someone, I am sure. My sister — "

"No," Lila said earnestly, "no really. It's so kind of you, but I am quite used to it. I — I prefer it. I like the independence."

There was a pause. Count Julius surveyed Lila with a keenness of eye which took in, she knew, the quality of the cotton of her dress and her gloves, the inevitable dustiness of her shoes, the home-cut, home-washed amateurishness of her hair.

He said gently, "But you must earn money."

She nodded.

"There will be little difficulty in that."

"But not as a favour," she said anxiously. "Not as a kindness."

He smiled at her again.

"I told you, did I not, that I don't know the meaning of kindness? I think only of myself. If you turn out to be of no use to me, I will tell you so. Now!" He clapped his small, well-manicured hands together. "You have come all this way on your bicycle and I have not offered you so much as a mouthful of water. My sister will scold me. Come with me, please, my dear Miss Cunningham, and meet my sister." He paused and twinkled at Lila. "My sister is a baroness. Her title is even more obscure than mine. My sister is the Baroness of Ferroferrata, of St George, of Manikata and of Ibn Dalam."

★ ★ ★

The hat swathed in white chiffon on the stone seat belonged to the Baroness. By the time Count Julius had escorted Lila down to the courtyard, the hat was on the Baroness's head and she was deadheading the rosebushes with a pair of gilded scissors shaped like fish. Besides the hat, she was wearing a soft grey afternoon dress of perfect cut, grey suede shoes and several strings of immaculately matched pearls.

"Caterina," Count Julius said, "I have brought a new English friend to meet you."

The Baroness stopped snipping and turned round. She was somewhere, Lila supposed, between fifty and sixty, small like her brother, and as perfectly finished. She did not smile.

"She comes on the warm recommendation of Edward Perriam."

"Ah yes," the Baroness said. She glanced

swiftly and tellingly at Lila's feet.

"You remember, Caterina," Count Julius said, "my telling you of the letter I had had from Edward Perriam? He is glad to have the Villa Zonda occupied. He thinks very highly of Miss Cunningham."

The Baroness laid her fish scissors down in the basket she carried full of decapitated rose heads. She regarded Lila.

"Do you speak Italian?"

"No, I'm afraid I — "

"Or French?"

"Only a little. There was never much chance to practise it, in Saxmundham."

"Where?" said the Baroness.

"Saxmundham. On the east coast of England."

"I do not," said the Baroness quellingly, "know the east coast."

For a fleeting second, Lila was tempted to say rudely, "Well it's there, all the same," and fought it back. Instead, she said, "I've never seen anywhere like this."

"This?" said the Baroness. "What do you mean?"

"This house," Lila said. "This garden. This city."

The Baroness looked at Lila's cotton gloves, now grubby.

"That is because there *is* nowhere like it."

"Caterina," Count Julius said, "you must allow Miss Cunningham her enthusiasm. And we must also provide her with refreshment." He gave Lila a smile. "I shall ring the bell."

He moved away from them and picked up a

85

small brass bell from the rim of the fountain and shook it vigorously. Almost immediately, the manservant who had opened the door to Lila appeared at the edge of the courtyard.

"Tea," the Baroness called. "Tea. Unless," she said, turning to Lila and somehow managing to convey the subtlest contempt, "you would prefer lemonade."

Lila shook her head. She was desperately thirsty and the idea of lemonade was ambrosial. She said, "No thank you. Tea please."

"Tea, you see, like the English," Count Julius said. "You will discover that we Maltese have profited from the endless invasions of our islands to take the best from every nation — pride from the Spanish, grace and the visual arts from the Italians, gardens and courtyards from the Moors. And tea from the English."

"The Union Club in Valetta," the Baroness said, "has seven thousand members at present. Almost all of them British servicemen."

Lila waited politely.

"The social life of the British in Malta since the last war has been perfectly phenomenal. But I imagine I need not inform you of that, Miss Cunningham. I imagine you are entirely familiar with dances and picnics and film shows given on the quarterdeck by your — *hospitable* navy."

"No," Lila said, "no, I'm afraid not. We've only been here a month, and I've met nobody, we've — well, we've been very private."

"Why?" demanded the Baroness.

"Caterina — "

"Because we have no money," Lila said,

suddenly and too loudly. "Because we came here when — when we were ruined in England. We are here because of Mr Perriam's kindness and for no other reason. For the last month, I've been trying to clean our rooms, and to learn to cook on an oil stove and to adjust to — well, to a very different way of life. And it doesn't," Lila said, now not caring if she sounded rude, "include parties on the quarterdeck."

She heard Count Julius take a breath in, lightly but sharply. The Baroness laid her basket down on the stone seat, and turned to face Lila.

"You are a very outspoken young woman."

Lila said nothing.

"You are a perfect stranger to me," the Baroness said. "Why should I not assume that you are like other English girls of my acquaintance?"

Lila was trembling, very slightly. Count Julius said soothingly, "Caterina, cannot you see that Miss Cunningham is considerably more enterprising than any of the other young Englishwomen we know? She has bicycled all the way here from Villa Zonda and has found us out, all on her own initiative."

The Baroness considered a moment and then she said, "Perhaps."

"You mustn't, my dear sister, allow your views of young Englishwomen to be coloured by reports of behaviour at these naval parties Miss Cunningham has the misfortune not to attend." He glanced at Lila. His eyes were twinkling again. "There is a young officer's

87

wife, I'm told, who in view of the brilliance of her chevelure and the exuberance of her spirits, is known in Valetta as the Southsea Bubble."

Lila said gratefully, "I don't really want to go to parties."

"But you would like to work."

"Yes. If — "

Count Julius held up his hand.

"We will deal with the ifs later. In the meantime, you must enjoy my sister's roses and tell her how much you admired the lilies in the tapestry room. My sister is an expert at lilies. She understands what gluttons they are."

"Ah!" the Baroness said suddenly.

Lila turned quickly towards her, so changed was her voice from the cold reserve with which she had previously spoken. Her 'ah!' was full of warmth and happy surprise, an 'ah!' of delight and love. She was looking past Lila to where the manservant was emerging from the house bearing an enormous silver tray laden with tea things.

"Tea," Count Julius said. But the Baroness was not looking at tea, she was looking beyond the servant, past him at something, someone behind him.

She opened her arms.

"My sons," the Baroness said, and her voice was rich with satisfaction.

# 8

'I AM sorry,' Lila wrote rapidly in her clear, upright handwriting, 'that I haven't written to you before now. After all your kindness to us, I'm aware that it's been very wrong of me to stay so silent, but the truth is' — she paused and looked up from the paper at all the tiny brass-handled drawers on the bureau at which A. E. O. Perriam had presumably also written letters and made careful archaeological notes — 'that I found it very strange here, much stranger than I had imagined. I hope you don't think I am ungrateful in saying this. The fault lies with me. I had always thought that, given an opportunity, I would prove very adaptable, but I'm afraid I disappointed myself. But things are so much better now, things have really changed. Since three days ago.'

Lila put her pen down and held her writing wrist with her other hand. In front of her, blue fronds of plumbago from the Tabia Palace gardens stood in a wineglass of water. Anton had picked them for her, Anton Ferroferrata, using his mother's little fish scissors. Both he and his older brother, Max, were much taller than their tiny mother and uncle, taller and darker and broader. They had had, Lila gathered, a northern Italian father who had, perhaps, proved unequal to the united competition of Ferroferrata, St George, Manikata and Ibn

Dalam, and had faded from the scene, leaving it undefended from his wife, and leaving too these boys, these young men, these specimens of a kind of young manhood that Lila had scarcely dreamed of, let alone encountered.

Max was the older. He was also bigger, quieter and kinder in manner. Anton was fascinating. He had sparkle and energy; he looked a little dangerous. When he had picked the plumbago, he had attempted most deftly to insert a spray under her hair ribbon, and when sharply prevented by his mother, had, without smiling, put it behind his own ear instead and refused to remove it. It was among the other sprays now, in the wineglass in front of Lila. She had held them, all the journey home, sitting in the front seat of an open Ford which the Baroness had imported from America, with Anton driving and Max sitting behind them and Lila's bicycle — looking suddenly more absurd than ever — strapped to the back.

When they reached the Villa Zonda, the brothers had insisted on escorting her inside, and all Spiru's family had seeped out of the house to stand, in awe and wonder as at a golden calf, around the Ford. The brothers had spoken to them in English, friendly but lofty.

"I don't think they speak English," Lila said hesitantly. "At least, only Carmela does."

"And we," said Anton, "don't speak Maltese."

Lila stared at him. He smiled back, wholly unabashed.

"It's a peasant language. Absolutely impossible! It wasn't even written down until this century."

"But — "

"At home," Anton said superbly, "we speak Italian." He paused and looked at Lila, and then added lightly, "Everybody does."

"But English — "

"Oh, *English*," Anton said and his eyes were bright with mockery, "English is so *useful*."

"Enough," Max said. He looked up at the house. "My uncle is anxious you are not comfortable here."

Lila thought it was as well that neither of these magnificent young men had seen the narrow house in Aldeburgh. She said, with some asperity, "Well, not by the standards of the Tabia Palace, but very much so by ours."

Anton bowed, smiling. "Touché."

They had insisted on coming upstairs and seeing the rooms, standing about in them looking like two marvellous museum pieces in a bric-à-brac shop. But Anton stopped teasing. He found water for the plumbago and admired Lila's arrangement of the salone. When they left, both brothers kissed her hand and asked to be allowed to call again. And Max had said, quite soberly, "You would be of real use to my uncle, you know. He needs a fresh eye, a new intelligence. And you would like to work in the palace?"

"Oh, I would love it."

"And we should of course find you a car, for the daily journey."

"But I can't drive."

"Then," Max said gravely, "we will teach you."

When the Ford had driven away beneath the umbrella pines, Carmela had come skipping upstairs.

"Those gentlemen — "

"Well?"

Carmela wriggled.

"Were they kings?"

"Not quite."

"So — " Carmela said with energy, "so — so *sabih*."

"Beautiful. Yes."

"Here," Carmela said, indicating her head, "and here," all down her body, "and *here*," reverently touching her feet.

"Yes," Lila said, "very beautiful. All the way down. Two beautiful young barons in beautiful clothes and beautiful boots. In my house. It's like a dream or a fairy tale."

"Fairy?"

"Something magic," Lila said. "Something you might dream of but never expect to see because dreams usually melt when they touch real life."

Carmela had stopped listening. Her eyes were back on her feet, whose bareness offended her so.

"Kings," Carmela said firmly, "have shoes."

'Most of all, I think,' Lila went on, in her letter to the Perriams, 'I must thank you for the introduction to Count Julius Tabia. My father found me a bicycle and I rather forwardly went to Mdina and presented myself. I was quite overwhelmed by the place, by the palace and by his kindness. He is, as I'm sure you know,

92

writing a naval history of Malta and has at present just reached the period of the Great Siege of 1565. I am to help him three days a week. He is pleased that I can type. I also met his sister and his nephews — ' Lila paused and looked again at the blue flowers, 'who are', she wrote quickly, 'very charming. They are to teach me to drive. The Baroness grows wonderful lilies.'

She stopped again and put her pen down once more. Writing to the Perriams was indeed like writing to grandparents, carrying as it did an obligation to give as much information and as little as possible away at the same time. She picked up her pen again.

'There is some bad news, though, I fear. Spiru died, very suddenly, of a heart attack while working in his vegetable garden. His family were in great disarray when we arrived, but they are being very kind and I find presents of vegetables left on the stairs, and sometimes an egg or a piece of honeycomb. I have sort of adopted one of them, a little girl called Carmela who is probably about nine. She is one of Doris's children, who you will remember is Spiru's daughter. She is very quick and speaks some English. The sole ambition of her life is to own some shoes, which I hope to be able to realize soon.

'My father' — Lila shut her eyes for moment, took a breath and plunged on; 'My father's well. And busy. I hardly see him all day.' At least that was true. 'The open air life around the harbour suits him. I know he would wish to join me in

93

thanking you, over and over again, for giving us this chance.

'Please give my best wishes to Mr and Mrs Tuttle. As you know, the favourite meat of the Maltese is rabbit and every time I see it, I think of Mrs Tuttle.

'With love from your affectionate

'Lila.'

She opened one of the bureau's little brass-knobbed drawers, and took out an envelope. It was made of thick cream paper, perhaps twenty-five years old, and stamped on the back, aslant up the opening, were the embossed words, 'J. Azzopardi, stationer, Old Mint Street, Valetta.' Bought, no doubt, by A. E. O. Perriam, as had been the writing paper, equally thick and smooth. She folded the letter, inserted it into the envelope, licked the rim of the flap — it tasted pleasingly of peppermint, even after all the years — and sealed it firmly. Then she turned it over, and wrote on the perfect cream surface, 'Mr and Mrs Edward Perriam, Culver House, Aldeburgh, Suffolk, England,' and was astonished to discover for the first time since her arrival, that she felt no pang thinking of England, of the grey North Sea and the silver birches and the firelight dancing in a book-lined room.

A small commotion arose in the courtyard below the open windows of the salone. There was often a commotion in the courtyard. The yellow cat would be discovered sleeping suffocatingly upon the baby, a hen would lay an egg and all the other hens would wish to join clamorously in the occasion, mice would be found living contentedly and plumply in the flour sack. But this commotion was slightly different, since Lila could hear, above the human voices and the bark of the gaunt black dog which spent most of its life chained to a barrel, the distinct roar of a motor engine.

She was on her feet in an instant, and fleeing to the dove mirror to peer at herself. No time to do anything about her hair, except shake it loose, no time to change the shorts she wore indoors for the more decorous dress the Maltese expected for even the least public appearance; no time, in fact, to do anything but lick her finger and rub vigorously at the smear of ink on her cheek. Perhaps the young barons, being modern young men, would for all their elegance and the rarefied air of their world, forgive the shorts.

She ran downstairs to the courtyard, meeting an excited Carmela halfway down.

"Come, oh quickly, quickly come!"

In the courtyard there was indeed a motor car. But it was not the young Ferroferratas' open Ford, long and dashing, but instead a tiny car, a kind of sports car, and it contained not two young men, but a very large elderly woman. She wore a man's white felt hat, a voluminous white driving coat against the dust of the road and, when she turned a square pink face towards Lila, a monocle.

"Aha!" she cried.

Lila went forward. Carmela, either to comfort or be comforted, took her hand.

"Miss Cunningham?"

"Yes."

"Wizard!" the woman cried, whipping off her hat and revealing a huge Edwardian cottage loaf of grey hair and pearl earrings as big as gooseberries. "Miss Cunningham! Excellent! I am Trixie de Vere!"

"Oh," Lila said, smiling. "How — how nice — "

Miss de Vere opened the door of the tiny car and began with much strenuous heaving to extricate herself from the driver's seat. Lila hovered, uncertain as to whether it was more mannerly to help or to watch, and Spiru's family, as was their habit, began to emerge from doorways around the courtyard, curious as young cows.

"There!" Miss de Vere cried triumphantly. "Out! Out always harder than in!" She surveyed Lila and then put a large pink hand on each shoulder. "How are you, my dear? Settling in? Angelo Saliba sent me."

"Angelo — "

"He's an excellent young man. One of my protégés. The first member of his family to read and write. He told me he brought you up here on your first day."

Lila was scarlet.

"Yes. Yes, he did."

Miss de Vere waved a hand at the house.

"This has got in a shocking state, of course. The Maltese always mean to look after things, but they never do. Except for churches and by heaven do they look after *them*." She glanced at Lila. "May I come in?"

"Of course," Lila said. She indicated her shorts. "I'm afraid nothing's very ready for visitors — "

"Well, what do visitors expect, if they come unannounced? My dear, you're too thin."

"I just am thinnish."

"In the face," Miss de Vere said, "thin in the face. And I'm too fat. I've always been fat. I remember in the nursery hearing my mother say to Nurse, 'Nurse, Miss Beatrix is stout beyond the call of health.' I always have been."

"Would you like tea?" Lila asked.

Miss de Vere fanned herself with her hat.

"No, my dear. I should like a large chair in the cool, and a glass of water. I never drink tea. I drink coffee and water and whisky in the winter. It would make my poor mother spin in her grave to know I even thought of whisky, let alone drank it. She founded a temperance society here in Valetta. It had seventeen members: sixteen ladies and an elderly gentleman who was stone deaf and slept through every meeting."

Lila said, laughing, "In Valetta?"

"Oh yes. I was born here, and so was my father. We de Veres are Malta through and through. The de Traffords, the de Veres and the Stricklands, we're Malta. Have you met Mabel?"

"Mabel?"

"Mabel Strickland. Runs the *Times of Malta*. Admirable, formidable and impossible."

Lila said shyly, ushering her visitor up the stairs, "I'm afraid I haven't seen a newspaper since we got here. And the wireless broke and my father — well, my father hasn't had time to mend it."

Miss de Vere began to climb, breathing heavily.

"Then when war breaks out, my dear, it will be a great surprise to you."

Lila's voice was high.

"War?"

"Undoubtedly. And a good thing too, if you ask me. We have to send this beastly fellow Hitler packing and we have to make it plain to that bully Mussolini that he can't make eyes at Malta."

Lila reached the top of the stairs and held a hand down to Miss de Vere.

"But I thought — I mean, the people I used to work for in England, very scholarly people, thought — I mean, they gave me to understand that if war broke out, we'd be out of it, if you know what I'm saying, sort of not involved, here in Malta."

Miss de Vere reached the top and stood, heaving for breath for a moment, still clutching Lila's hand.

"My dear child. Don't be so perfectly idiotic. If you'd had even the briefest look at Valetta, you'd have seen that it's all dockyards, that the harbour is heaving with ships and none of them are pleasure boats. No, my dear, no. For us, for us British, Malta is the watchdog of the Mediterranean. If we go to war, Malta goes with us."

Lila stared. Miss de Vere reached out her free hand and patted her shoulder.

"Don't fret about it. Fret about finding me a chair and sending that child for some water."

"Carmela," Lila said.

Miss de Vere looked down the staircase. Carmela was fidgeting eight steps below, scuffing her feet and twisting her hands up in her skirts. Miss de Vere said something to her in fluent Maltese.

"Oh!" Lila said.

"Why 'oh!'?"

"I thought — well, I was told the other day that, well, nobody spoke Maltese."

Miss de Vere winked at her, very lightly, and patted her cheek.

"That's what happens if you mix with the Tabia Palace people."

"Heavens, how did you — "

"I know everything. There's almost nothing in this place I don't know. Now then," she said to Carmela in English, "water, water, water, quick, quick, quick," and to Lila, dropping her hand and taking her arm companionably instead, "we shall go now into Arthur's salone and start to make friends. That is why I've come, as well as to satisfy my curiosity. You will find, my dear girl — do you have a Christian name, I wonder? — that I will prove a very useful friend indeed."

# 9

"NO," Anton said. "No." He leaned slightly towards Lila and put one hand on her knee. "Depress this pedal, the clutch, with the left foot. Then with this hand — " he moved his hand to hers — "move the gear lever to the left a little bit and then up."

"And with my right hand?"

"That will do the steering."

"And my right foot?"

"As you bring your left foot up from the clutch, you press this pedal down with your right one. This one is the accelerator."

Lila took both hands and feet away from the controls and folded her hands in her lap.

"Impossible."

"What is this impossible?"

"It is absolutely impossible to do four different things simultaneously."

"Look at me," Anton said.

She did, willingly. His face was perfectly serious, except for his eyes.

"Some things, Miss Cunningham, are difficult. Almost nothing is impossible. Driving is very possible. Apes and very stupid people can drive with no trouble."

Lila said, gazing at him, "I'm neither an ape nor very stupid. *That*'s the trouble. I have a brain which says that to ask both feet and both hands to do four separate things all at once flies in the face of nature."

Anton said, "Put your hands back on the wheel."

She didn't move.

"Do it."

"No," Lila said, "I'll just go on riding a bicycle."

Anton leaned sideways again, picked up both Lila's hands and laid them carefully on the steering wheel. Then he leaned a little further — she could feel the weight of him — and turned the ignition key. The engine leaped to life. Lila squealed.

"Left foot on the clutch!" Anton shouted. "Left hand on the gear stick! Right foot on the accelerator! Left foot *down!*"

She felt her left hand being firmly taken, the gear moving smoothly sideways, heard the brake released, let her right foot go down and the car sprang forward, wildly, apparently entirely of its own accord, and buried itself in a spiny bush on the opposite side of the dusty road.

"Bravo," Anton said.

Lila sat rigid.

"Excellent first try."

"It was *terrible.*"

"Well, I agree it wasn't a miracle of co-ordination, but it wasn't terrible."

"It was very frightening."

"Miss Cunningham," Anton said, "do you frighten very easily?"

"I'm called Lila, and I expect I do. By male standards anyway. Men and women are

101

frightened by different things."

"How interesting. Now you must let me into the driving seat so that I can extract the car from the bush and we can try again."

"Oh no."

"Lila," Anton said, and his voice was quiet, "oh yes, Lila. Yes, yes until we can do it."

Lila got thankfully out of the car and wandered to the edge of the road. They were on the southern edge of the island, on a high remote headland above the sea, quite close, the brothers said, to some of those prehistoric temples which were, Lila increasingly felt, fundamentally responsible for getting her here. It was extraordinary up here, on this bleak, empty, lonely height, with the sea, wrinkled and glittering far below, and no sign of life anywhere except, far away now, the tiny figure of Max, who had abandoned them to the driving lesson, and taken his new camera — a Kodak, also American — to find, among the boulders and shadows that they cast on this bright day, a suitable subject. There was almost no wind, just enough to whisper among the dry grasses and hollow stalks of weeds, bleached blond already by Malta's summer sun, and there was an overwhelming impression of light and air and space. And, apart from the sound of the Ford being skilfully reversed, of peace. It was very peaceful, in the way Lila felt that only ancient places are peaceful, full of endless time and infinite knowledge. She squinted up at the sky. It was very difficult to imagine those serene blue spaces torn up by the planes of war which Miss de Vere seemed to think were so inevitable.

"Come back!" Anton shouted.

She turned. He was standing by the Ford, holding the driver's door open. He wore cream flannel trousers and a white linen shirt with the sleeves rolled up and his skin was the colour of perfectly browned toast.

"I really don't want to."

"That has nothing to do with it."

She crossed the road reluctantly and climbed in.

"I don't like doing things I don't know how to do."

"But you are *learning* how. Now then, put your feet on the pedals again, and feel them, up and down. The centre pedal is the brake. Very useful. Miss Cunningham — Lila — this car is only a machine, it has no initiative. It is you who have that." He moved round to the passenger side of the car and vaulted lightly in. "Now," he said, "left foot down. Good. Left hand move gear into first gear. Good. Release brake. Good. Press accelerator down gently while releasing clutch. Good! There, you see? Not so difficult."

Lila looked about her in puzzlement.

"But nothing's happened."

"Hasn't it?"

"No. I mean, we aren't moving."

"No," Anton said, "nor we are. I wonder why that could be?"

She stared at him. He shrugged.

"Only a little detail. Only the smallest trifle

103

of omission." He grinned at her. "You forgot to turn the engine on."

★ ★ ★

Later, they drove her into Valetta. "A gentleman's city," Max said. He was at the wheel, and he sounded as if he was quoting. "Built by gentlemen, for gentlemen." Gentlemen or no gentlemen, Lila was enchanted. It was a golden city of elegance, with narrow streets running the length and breadth of a little peninsula, some of them so steep they dissolved into steps, and some of them giving glimpses of the harbours on either side, glinting with water and busy with shipping. The houses were shuttered and balconied, and some of them had urns on their rooflines and statues and stone medallions set into their façades. There were little squares with trees and fountains, and a great cathedral with marble steps, and convents and shops and terraced gardens hanging over the Grand Harbour, and a great quiet yellow building which the brothers said had been the hospital of the Knights of St John in the sixteenth century, renowned throughout Europe, whose main ward was also one of Europe's longest rooms. The patients, Max said, who had included the insane and the destitute, slept in linen sheets and ate off silver plate. "It is now," he added, and his voice was heavy with sarcasm, "the headquarters of the Malta police."

"And that," Anton said, pointing, leaning over the back seat of the car between Lila

104

and his brother, "that is Fort St Elmo, and the St Lazarus Bastion. But of course, you know about the Great Siege. You know Malta's history."

Lila let a tiny pause fall. "Of course."

Max glanced sideways, to check that Anton had not offended her.

"Perhaps you should examine my brother on English history?"

Lila smiled at him. "Perhaps."

Anton said, "We defeated the Turks, you know. It was one of the most decisive actions of the Western world. Suleiman the Magnificent sent the largest fleet of ships the world had ever seen, a hundred and eighty-one of them, and we defeated him."

"The Knights of St John did," Max said in a friendly voice, turning the car in the cobbled space outside the Fort gates, and heading back towards the harbour. "And the Turks were not exactly defeated. They withdrew."

"We sent the Turks packing," Anton said, taking no notice. "We saved Europe from Islam. And we'll send the Italians packing now, if we have to. And the damned Germans. Look across there."

Lila looked. Below them, the harbour stretched raggedly away to the east, a mass of creeks and bays and buildings. And shipping. Not pretty shipping, not graceful masted boats with sails and rigging, but brutal, martial shipping, ironclad shipping, destroyers and fortified merchant ships and battleships spiky with radar equipment.

"Look at that," Anton said. "There isn't much question, is there?"

Lila looked away from the harbour, along the side of the little tree-lined street they were on which hung above it on a narrow terrace of rock.

"If there's war — what will you do?"

"Enlist," Max said.

"Of course," Anton said.

"I'm sorry to seem stupid — but for whom?"

"For the British," Anton said. "You may be using us as a garrison, but we are all on the side of civilization, after all."

Max let the clutch in smoothly and the car glided forward.

"Actually," he said over his shoulder to his brother, "*actually*, we've been a British possession since 1814. Just, as you would say, a little detail."

"That doesn't make me British!"

"In war it does. In any case, most Maltese identify with the British now. We've worked in the British dockyards now for too long to think otherwise."

"I would fight for the British on my own terms!"

"I am sure," Max said drily, turning the car easily down a street so narrow that Lila could have touched the walls on either side, "they are most appreciative of that." He glanced at Lila. "My brother is a noble patriot, you see."

"So is Salvu," Lila said.

"Salvu?"

"He's one of the family at the Villa Zonda.

He hates British domination. He's polite to my father and me but you can see he is smouldering underneath."

There was a pause, then Anton leaned back in the seat behind and said distantly, "I think you are a little confused. What I mean by patriotism and what a — a peasant means, are very different matters."

"In England," Lila said, looking straight ahead, "we never speak of peasants."

"What do you call them then?"

"People," Lila said.

"But — "

"Society is arranged very differently in England," Max said smoothly. The car emerged into a space before the City Gate. He waved a hand to the right. "There," he said. "The Church of St John's Cavalier."

Lila looked obediently.

"I think," Anton said, "that we should take her to the Phoenicia."

"The Phoenicia?"

"The Phoenicia Hotel. It's just outside the City Gate. I want to buy you a gin fizz and lecture you about society. Heaven knows what notions this Aldeburgh place has filled you with."

★ ★ ★

When they dropped her, in the dusk, back at the Villa Zonda, Max said he would be back in the morning to pick her up for a day's work with his uncle.

107

"No, no. I shall cycle."

"Out of the question. None of us will hear of it. I shall be here at nine-thirty."

Lila, happy and exhilarated, and a little unsteady with gin, sketched a wobbly curtsey.

"Thank you, kind sir."

They smiled at her from the open car, their teeth in the fading blue light as white as their shirts.

"And thank you for today, for this afternoon."

"We enjoyed it. We were so bored before you came along, you can't imagine."

"Oh," she said, and shook her head, laughing.

They kissed their hands to her then, and Max took the car down the drive beneath the pines at tremendous speed, waving until they turned out of the gateway onto the Mdina road. Even then she could still hear them as the car raced away, carefree and confident, the car that she had been in all afternoon, that would be there in the morning to collect her.

In the courtyard, Carmela was waiting. She wore a cotton skirt and a spotted blouse too big for her, and her pigtails had been pinned up in loops either side of her head, like bat's ears.

"Oh dear," Carmela said.

Lila stopped.

"What do you mean?"

Carmela shook her head. She looked very grave.

"Oh dear," she said again.

"What do you mean, 'oh dear'? That I have been out all afternoon? I've been having a driving lesson."

Carmela shook her head.

"Not you. Not you."

"Who then?"

Carmela, as was her custom when she wanted to show Lila something, took her hand.

"Where are we going?"

"Up," Carmela said.

She led Lila into the house and up the staircase to the first floor. There were things lying about on the staircase, a cabbage which perhaps Doris had left, and a newspaper, and a shoe. Lila peered at the shoe. It was an old misshapen brown brogue, heavy soled, with knotted laces. It was Pa's. She tore her hand out of Carmela's and raced ahead of her.

A lamp was lit in Pa's bedroom, the paraffin lamp which was absolutely the only domestic feature that was common both to the Villa Zonda and to the house in Aldeburgh. It stood on a chest against the wall, and threw enough half-hearted light across the room to reveal that Pa was on the bed, fully dressed, and that his peg leg was still strapped to his stump. Pa never lay down with his peg leg on, he said that was the only time it hurt him — not the peg, but the leg that wasn't there any more.

Lila snatched up the lamp and hurried to Pa's bedside.

"Pa? Pa! Pa, what is it? Are you ill?"

She peered at him. He looked flushed, feverish, and he was sprawled on the bed, his face squashed into the pillows, as if he were unconscious and couldn't help himself. Lila put a hand on his shoulder and shook him slightly.

"Pa, Pa, what's the *matter*?"

Pa stirred, gave an enormous, stentorian grunt and rolled over. He opened his eyes.

"Buggered," he said indistinctly. "Jiggered. Jiggery pokery. Pokered. Pooped." He burped, loudly. "Sorry," he said, and giggled.

Lila straightened.

"You're drunk."

"Well done," Pa said approvingly.

"You're horribly, disgustingly drunk and you stink of rum like a — like a — "

"Shewer rat?" suggested Pa helpfully.

"Where have you been? How did you get like that?"

"Here and there. Up and down. Mostly down. *Lot* of down, falling down. Y'know. Glass here, glass there. Bottle just gone. Here one minute then — *gone*."

Lila said, "How did you get back here?"

Pa thought a bit.

"Flew?" he suggested, and then as an afterthought, "swam?"

"You're not funny," Lila said, "you're disgusting and I'm ashamed of you."

Pa rolled over onto his face again.

"How awful," Lila said furiously, "to do this in a foreign country, in front of the Maltese. In front of people who are being so kind to us."

Pa seemed to be trying to say something. Lila bent closer.

"What?"

"Floogie," Pa said waveringly. He was trying, she realized, to sing. "Flat floot floogie. Tra la — " He paused, feeling her angry and

110

disapproving presence very close. "La," he said lamely, and closed his eyes.

"You can stay there," Lila said. "I'm going to leave you there and don't think you're going to get any supper, because you aren't. You aren't getting anything. And I hope you have a horrible night and wake with a blinding headache. Good *night*."

"What ho," Pa said faintly from his pillow, and then there was silence.

Lila marched out onto the landing and banged the door behind her. Carmela was waiting, hopping from foot to foot.

"Fetch doctor?"

"No."

"Fetch water?"

"Yes, but I'll do it. In a minute. Carmela — "

"Please?"

"Who brought my father home?"

Carmela spread her hands.

"Nobody."

"I think someone must have. Perhaps you didn't see?"

"No," Carmela said decidedly. "I was in the courtyard all afternoon and nobody came." She stamped her foot for emphasis. "*Nobody*. Father came home — " She looked about her for inspiration and then said, suddenly remembering, "Fairy! Father came home by fairy!"

# 10

"THE traditional oared galley," Count Julius said to Lila, "was the typical Mediterranean warship of the sixteenth century. There were commonly twenty-five oars each side, with five men to an oar. These men, the galley slaves, were of course chained." He paused and ran a hand across the print he had laid out before them both. "It was regarded, somewhat naturally, as the most hellish life on earth."

Lila, slightly dazed by the rapidly accumulated knowledge of the morning, nodded in silence.

"My task now," Count Julius said, "or rather yours, is to discover exactly who built the galleys used by the Knights of St John during the Great Siege of Malta."

"Yes."

"Where the timber came from — because of course Malta has almost none of her own — and the money to pay for them. There is a model of a Maltese galley in the National Maritime Museum in London which I greatly covet. I would be so very grateful to discover a model maker who could furnish me with a model of my own. Entirely precise to scale, of course. I am a fanatic for precision."

"Yes," Lila said again. Her head was reeling, spinning with a kaleidoscope of facts and figures, of images of howling Turkish Janissaries storming gallantly defended forts and brave little parties of small ships boarding Turkish frigates and seizing their standards. Indeed there had been moments during the morning in this quiet, studious room where the air had seemed rent apart with the boom and crash of artillery and the screams of the wounded. Count Julius had talked and talked, opening books, unrolling maps, sliding prints out of drawers; he had shown her his card index system housed in a black japanned cabinet, his copious notes filed in small portfolios between marbled board covers and, with a proud little flourish that even his urbanity could not disguise, the first chapter, in a perfect old-fashioned hand, of his great work, *A Maritime History of Malta.*

"Which must, of course, be typed."

"Of course," Lila said, thankful to see something she knew she could do.

"With a duplicate copy."

"Naturally."

Count Julius' library was a very different apartment from the tapestry room. It was as large, but the walls were entirely lined with mahogany bookshelves, each bay surmounted with a pediment and a Roman numeral painted in gold. There were tables in the room, and tall desks at which one stood to read, and map cases, all of them illuminated by brass lamps with green glass shades. The room was very dim, which was, Count Julius explained, to protect the books. The blinds must be drawn down at all times, and air was only introduced into the room through a series of filtered grilles — a method

113

of his own invention. He did not seem to find working in this shuttered, viewless seclusion in the least oppressive, nor to consider that anyone else might find it claustrophobic. When Lila left the room, he explained, if she was the last person in it, she must close the shutters and extinguish every lamp. "Light, Miss Cunningham," Count Julius said, "is the enemy of old ink."

He bent again over the print.

"One mast was common, you see, and a triangular lateen sail. Five guns were mounted in the bows, the centre one a heavy bombarde capable of firing a fifty-pound cannon ball. Can you, Miss Cunningham, conceive of a cannon ball of fifty pounds?"

Lila, her jaw aching with the effort of suppressing a yawn, said no she couldn't.

"There might be an additional eight guns on board. The Turks, of course, had smaller galleys and fewer guns, and favoured the regrettable practice of using poisoned arrows. In the sixteenth century, war was still extraordinarily savage." He glanced up. "Miss Cunningham, I do believe you are sated with war for one morning."

"Perhaps."

"Just one more introduction," Count Julius said. "Just one more, and then you shall be rewarded with luncheon. Please permit me to introduce you to Grand Master La Valette."

Lila turned round. Count Julius, dapper in his white waistcoat and faultless suit — 'Irish linen, Miss Cunningham, English tailoring' — was standing beside an almost black bronze bust

114

on a column of green marble five foot high. It was the bust of a bearded man, wavy-haired and handsome, with a curious indented star upon his armoured breast.

"The hero of the Great Siege," Count Julius said, "the Grand Master of the Knights of St John, and something of a fanatic. His life was the Order, and a world without the Order was unthinkable to him. Valetta, is of course, named after him."

Lila regarded him respectfully.

"A hero to his men," Count Julius said, "and to me also."

There was a moment's silence. Lila felt the atmosphere in the room to be suddenly not just airless, but imprisoning, as if she was quite literally trapped with the terrible glories of the past while air and light beckoned to her from beyond the blinded windows. She put a hand out behind her and felt for the nearest table edge, for support.

"I find it," Count Julius said dreamily, his eyes upon La Valette, "so hard to tear myself away from this room; so hard. It often seems that there is more reality to the past for me, than there is to the present. This attitude exasperates my sister. And so," he added, suddenly brisk, "would our being late for luncheon."

★ ★ ★

Luncheon was set out at one end of a gleaming table that would have seated twenty. Four places had been laid, with linen napkins. Between the

115

four places was a large silver bowl full of white roses and in a shadowy corner two servants stood silently, their hands folded under cloths.

The Baroness was already seated, and beside her was Max. There was no sign of Anton. There had been no sign of him all morning. The Baroness, who had been speaking to her son, gave a small nod in Lila's direction.

"Miss Cunningham."

Max rose and came round the table to hold a chair for Lila. It occurred to her, for a mad and fleeting moment, to say that if they would all please forgive her, she would be so very much happier eating bread and cheese alone in the courtyard. She glanced at Max.

"I — "

He smiled at her, encouragingly. "Please sit. You'll be exhausted. My uncle shows no mercy where history is concerned."

Lila sank into her chair. She had found a dark blue cotton dress with a white collar to wear which had seemed to her, earlier that morning, to be entirely appropriate to the day ahead. Now, under the Baroness's eye, it felt cheap and crumpled. The Baroness was wearing softly pleated mushroom-coloured silk. And pearls.

"Well," the Baroness said, "and how was this morning?"

She did not look at Lila. One of the servants detached himself from the shadows and slid in front of each of them a shallow white bowl of cold soup, palest green flecked with darker green.

"We have swum the Grand Harbour under

116

cover of darkness," Count Julius said, "and scuttled several Turkish warships. My sister, Miss Cunningham, remains unmoved by history."

"Not in itself," the Baroness said, "but only by its quantity and the obtrusiveness of its presence in this house." She picked up her soup spoon. "And how, Miss Cunningham, is your father?"

Lila hesitated. It was difficult, sitting in this dining room beneath the painted gaze of past Tabias in their ruffs and silks, at a table formally laid with linen and silver and fine glass, to adjust to the recollection of Pa. It wasn't an edifying recollection in any case. Pa had been crumpled and groaning and unwashed that morning, limping up and down the landing bellowing and holding his head and then going soggy with remorse at the sight of Lila, and wanting to apologize. She had refused to let him. She had left a jug of water in his room for him to wash with and the means for making coffee on the tin-topped table in their primitive kitchen, but she wouldn't speak to him.

"Didn't mean to," Pa said. "Never meant to. Met a chap. Nice chap. Very friendly. Whole thing friendly. Can't you see? Never meant to upset you. Never did. Silly old Pa. Made a mistake, that's all. A mistake."

Lila said now, without conviction, "My father is very well, thank you."

She could feel Max's eyes upon her. Max had seen how they lived at the Villa Zonda, in those three dusty rooms full of the kind of furniture that wouldn't be countenanced within a thousand miles of the Tabia Palace. Max had

117

seen how makeshift everything was, how worn. Max probably knew that if anything got cleaned, it was Lila who did the cleaning. She dared not look at him.

"We should be so pleased to meet your father," Count Julius said. "It would be so interesting, for me especially, to meet a marine painter."

Lila froze. Was there the smallest teasing edge to his voice, or was she imagining it?

"I don't think," Max said, "that Mr Cunningham has time, or even perhaps the inclination for social life."

Lila stared intently at her soup.

"Why not?" the Baroness demanded.

"He's a painter," Max said, as if that explained everything.

"Nobody," the Baroness said, "can paint twenty-four hours a day."

"No," Max said, his voice still pleasant and reasonable, "but creativity is very tiring, and perhaps Mr Cunningham chooses to relax in — other ways."

There was a small silence. Lila took an unsteady spoonful of soup. Under the table, for a fleeting second, something touched her foot.

"Nobody in this house," Max said, "knows the meaning of work."

The Baroness gave him a sharp look.

"In the sense of labour, my dear Max, I should hope not." She turned to Lila. "Miss Cunningham, I hope you are making acquaintances in Malta?"

Lila put her spoon down. The soup was

delicious, but in the circumstances of this panic-inducing prospect of Pa and the Baroness ever setting eyes upon one another, quite impossible to eat. She took a deep breath and raised her gaze to look straight at the Baroness whose eyes, she now saw, were the startling blue of cornflowers.

"This afternoon," Lila said, "I am to have tea with Miss Beatrix de Vere. In her house on Kalkara Creek."

The Baroness also laid down her soup spoon, with some surprise.

"Well," she said faintly, "I commend your enterprise."

★ ★ ★

Max insisted on driving her.

"No, really, I — "

"You can't possibly bicycle. Or walk. It's far too far. Right round the far side of the Grand Harbour, even past Senglea and Vittoriosa."

"I could get a taxi."

"You cannot afford a taxi," Max said, firmly but not unkindly. "I am free to take you and willing to take you, and I will cost you nothing."

Lila, thinking how luxurious it must be never to be beholden to other people, submitted and climbed into the car.

"Thank you. And — thank you for — for what you said at lunchtime."

"That was nothing. We needn't speak of it."

Miss de Vere's house stood almost on the

119

water's edge. It had no garden, being backed by the road, and no space either side, being sandwiched between other buildings. Its glory lay in its views. On the waterfront side of the house, the façade was hung with balconies at every level and of every size outside almost every window, and from these one could see right across the creek to the tip of Vittoriosa, and Fort St Angelo, and beyond that to the great spaces of Grand Harbour and the skyline of Valetta, golden in the mornings, said Miss de Vere, and mysteriously, softly dark later on, against the setting sun.

She took Lila into a room which resembled nothing so much as Lila's idea of the old sheep's shop in *Alice in Wonderland*. It was jumbled with stuffs; shawls and cushions and cloths and lengths of damask and taffeta had been layered and twisted and flung across and wound round things until the room gave the impression of having no corners or hard planes at all, these being entirely obliterated by a soft and colourful riot.

"I love colour," Miss de Vere said unnecessarily, "love it. Not on myself, mind you, being as pink as a York ham, but on everything I look at. White for me, rainbows for everything else. Sit there, dear child. Yes there, on the yellow brocade. You'll find there's a perfectly serviceable chair underneath."

Lila sat, startled.

"Oh!"

"There. What did I tell you? Now, tea and McFarlane Lang's ginger cake."

"May I help you?"

"No, thank you. Rosanna will bring it. Rosanna keeps me in order in the house, and Zanzu on all my projects."

"Projects?"

"My little schools, my hospital, my natural childbirth scheme, my literacy campaign — "

"Heavens," Lila said.

"What else was I to do?" Miss de Vere said. "The only surviving child — my brother died on the Somme — of prosperous parents, and the only man I ever wanted to marry first marrying someone else and then dying of dysentery in Cairo — well, I didn't think I had an option. Fling yourself into life, Trixie, I said to myself, just *fling*. If you can't have a family, make one. What was the alternative? Sitting about learning Italian or taking trips to Switzerland for health cures? No, indeed. I made a list of all the things that are the matter with Malta, and off I went. Tornado Trixie, my father used to call me. Nice man, my father."

The door opened and a slender young woman came in with a tray, stepping nimbly over the swathed and brilliant floor.

"Lila, dear, this is Rosanna."

They looked at one another. Lila smiled; Rosanna nodded gravely.

"Rosanna considers this house impossible. And its owner close to impossible too. But we are her mission. It is her mission in life to stop us sliding into unutterable chaos. Is that not so?"

Rosanna nodded again, and stooped to set the tea tray down.

121

"Thank you," Lila said. Rosanna glanced at her again, almost assessingly. Then she turned to Miss de Vere. "That is all?"

"Yes, Rosanna, for now that is all. Thank you."

When the door had closed behind her, Miss de Vere picked up the teapot — silver, Lila noticed, and crested, and extremely battered as if it had spent a good deal of its life being regularly dropped on a stone floor — and said, "Of course, you know her brother."

"I do?"

"Young Mr Saliba, who rescued you your first day."

"Oh," Lila said. She looked down at her lap. "He — he is rather on my conscience. I wasn't very polite to him, I'm afraid. He was very kind and helpful, and I was tired and sick and hating everything and he could see it. I didn't want him to see I couldn't manage our arrival — that — well, that all I wanted was to go home."

Miss de Vere passed Lila a cup painted with poppies.

"And now?"

"Now?"

"Do you want to go home now?"

A vivid picture of the driving lesson on those high, exhilarating clifftops shot through Lila's mind.

"No. Well, not so much anyway."

Miss de Vere, busying herself with the ginger cake and a cake knife shaped like a scimitar, said, almost unconcernedly, "And what has changed your mind?"

"I've got used to things, I suppose," Lila said. "To the Villa Zonda. And the family there."

"And now," said Miss de Vere, "there is the Tabia Palace. I noticed that one of those young princes drove you here."

Lila said firmly, "Count Julius is giving me some work. As a sort of secretary and research assistant."

"I see."

"I need the money, Miss de Vere. We have my father's tiny pension, but it isn't enough to live on, not even with the Perriams' kindness."

"No."

"So I need to work."

"Of course. But there are all kinds of work, are there not? Work doesn't have to be researching the naval strategy of sixteenth-century Turkish admirals, does it? What about hospitals, schools, clinics, libraries? What about work for other people? Useful work?"

Lila put her teacup down. She said in a tight voice, "I'm only doing what I've been trained to do. Besides, my father — " she stopped.

Miss de Vere said, in a kinder voice, "Ah yes. Your father."

Lila felt a sudden flash of anger. She said furiously, "Miss de Vere, I don't know why you think you have the right to criticize me. You don't know me, you don't know what my life is like, what it's always been like, what a haven of peace and civilization working for the Perriams was, and how I think I can see the same calm and refinement working for Count Julius. You're too quick to make judgements and tell me what

123

to do. You don't know anything about me."

She stood up hastily, almost knocking over the poppy-painted teacup. Beatrix de Vere regarded her calmly.

"Good."

"What d'you mean, good?"

"It's good to see you roused. Good to see you can feel things with some strength. And you misunderstand me."

"Do I?" Lila almost shouted.

"Calm down. Yes, you do. I can see more than you think I can and I am under no illusion as to what your life is like. With your father."

"Don't mention my father!"

"I have to, dear, don't I? We can't leave your father out of it, can we?" She paused, and then added a little mockingly, "But nor, perhaps you think, can we introduce your father to the Tabia Palace?"

Lila stared at her.

"Especially not after last night."

Lila subsided onto the arm of the yellow brocade smothered chair.

"What do you mean?"

"Your father was in the Gut all yesterday afternoon. He is there most afternoons. I don't expect you know about that and I don't expect you know about the Gut either. I wouldn't expect you to. But your father was found there yesterday in no condition to look after himself, and was taken home."

There was a pause. Lila fixed her eyes on Miss de Vere's big pink hands, which still held the scimitar cake knife.

124

"Who," Lila said at last, "took my father home?"

Miss de Vere smiled. She leaned forward and put the cake knife down and briskly dusted crumbs off her hands.

"Who do you think?" she said. "Angelo Saliba, of course."

# 11

THE great door of the Tabia Palace swung open. Teseo, the manservant who was, Lila supposed, a kind of butler, stood as he always did, just inside, one hand on the door, head bent in a small, token bow.

Lila indicated the dolphin knocker.

"Are those traditional?"

Teseo looked up.

"In Mdina, yes. In Valetta, not so much."

Lila stepped inside.

"What do they mean?"

He shrugged, as if to say he neither knew nor cared.

"They are not a fish. They are an animal. Like a — a — " He spread his arms and blew.

"A whale?"

"Yes. A whale."

"I like them," Lila said. "I like these dolphin knockers."

"The family is not here."

She looked at him.

"Not here?"

"No. They are in Gozo. They have gone to Gozo for three days. They will put the Ford on the ferry."

"Oh."

"But Count Julius has left instructions. For you. With the typewriter."

"I see."

"In his library."

"Teseo — "

"Yes?"

"As the typewriter is quite small — "

"Yes?"

"Could we carry it into another room, with windows?"

Teseo considered. His employers were people of such exactness in their taste and habits that Lila's suggestion seemed little short of revolutionary.

"Out of the library?"

"Yes. For more light. For — for my eyes. And then put it back again, exactly where it was, at the end of the morning. Then we needn't put any lamps on in the library, at all. Count Julius would like that."

Teseo said doubtfully, "It is not usual."

"No. But no harm will be done. And harm *might* be done, to me, if I have to type for hours in the half dark."

Teseo looked at her. He looked at her with something of the same reservation she sometimes saw in the fleeting glances Salvu threw her.

"Very well."

"Good," Lila said. "Thank you. You need take no responsibility. It will all be mine."

He gave another little bow of the head, and trotted up the stone stairs of the house towards the first floor. Lila followed him.

"The tapestry room, perhaps."

"The tapestry room?"

"It would be so very comfortable, putting the typewriter on one of those carpeted tables. If

127

I have to move even one book, I will put it precisely back again. And I won't eat anything or drink anything."

"No!" Teseo said, much shocked. "I am to bring you luncheon, in the courtyard, at one-thirty. Count Julius has ordered your wine, and Baron Anton your flowers."

"Flowers?" Lila said, "Baron Anton?"

"Yes."

"You are sure?"

"Yes."

"Oh," Lila said, the prospect of three hours' typing suddenly becoming irradiated in a remarkable way, "*Oh*. Thank you."

Teseo carried Count Julius' black and gold Remington from the library — where it lived in a cupboard in order not to defile, by its utilitarian presence, the aesthetics of the room — and set it respectfully on a table by a window in the tapestry room. He then brought a chair, its seat covered with a minutely stitched petit point of a garland of olive leaves, and a carafe of water on a tray lacquered with golden peonies. Then he hovered.

"Teseo?"

"Miss."

"Please don't worry. I won't spill the water, and I won't type for so long that the typewriter makes marks in the carpet."

He twisted his hands.

"It was not the instructions, miss."

"No. I've changed them. The cats have gone to Gozo, so the mouse is going to work in a place better suited to her."

"Please?"

"Go away," Lila said kindly. "Go away, and don't worry. Nothing will come to any harm."

Reluctantly, he left the room and closed the door carefully behind him. She waited until his footsteps had retreated along the stone-floored passage outside and then she sat down, with some pleasure, on the olive leaves, and smoothed her skirt. It was her yellow cotton dress again, and without the Baroness there to induce feelings of immediate sartorial inadequacy, she felt perfectly at ease with it. She also felt entirely at ease sitting on a seventeenth-century chair and leaning her elbows comfortably on a table covered with a sixteenth-century silk carpet. To her left and right, on the table, she could see the leather-covered portfolios — red and ochre and crimson, like old wines — in which the Baroness kept her collection of botanical prints and drawings, and ahead of her, between two huge ornamented lead tubs planted with lilies as pure and stiff and clean as if they were made of the best parchment, the double window, open to the blue air and the soft-leaved trees of the courtyard. There was no sound beyond the smallest murmur from the trees in the breeze, and the gently falling water in the dolphin fountain and the odd bird, as controlled and contented-sounding as most things seemed to be in this lovely and perfectly ordered place. Even the prospect of three hours of Count Julius' manuscript — he was as portentous a writer as he was a light and amusing speaker — couldn't dim the fact that Lila knew herself to be, sitting there in this place, at this moment, entirely happy.

She picked up two sheets of typing paper, the second one thinner than the first to make the copy, and inserted between them a frail, faintly waxy piece of blue duplicating paper. Was this happiness wrong? Was this kind of contentment and security in lovely surroundings what Miss de Vere had suggested so forcibly to her to be the wrong kind of work; an easy option? Miss de Vere had money after all, private money which meant she didn't have to go out, like Lila, and earn it. Yet she plainly didn't spend the money on herself, she used it for the things she believed in, and she had been very firm about those things, about the necessity to use the privilege of one's own taken-for-granted education for the benefit of people not so privileged. She had also been very plain, even if by inference, about the people at the Tabia Palace. Grand, she said, indubitably and genuinely grand as the old Mdina aristocracy all were, but also proud, and with a kind of pride not well suited to a world changed after a great war, and threatened by another. Don't, she had seemed to say, let them corrupt you. Don't let them turn your head.

Lila inserted her neat sandwich of papers into the typewriter and rolled them carefully round. Having your head turned implied being made a fool of, of that she was very well aware. But there were things Miss de Vere was not aware of about her, about Lila Cunningham, whose childhood and growing up had been so oddly confined and solitary, and who had always known herself to be plain. Nobody had ever tried to tell her otherwise. Housekeepers had congratulated her sometimes on looking neat; the Perriams had worried if she looked tired and clucked relievedly when she didn't; Pa, as far as she could recall, had never once commented on her appearance either way. She had learned to accept, early on, that her thin dark looks were ordinary at best, and almost ugly at worst. At least, she thought she had. But when she met the young barons from the Tabia Palace, and they, so beautiful in themselves and presumably with the pick of European female beauty to choose from, behaved towards her with an interested gallantry, she realized that her acceptance of her looks was only skin deep. She might have spent her life telling herself she was reconciled to her appearance, but she had been fooling herself. She did care, she cared very much, which was why it was so seductive, so astonishing to dare to believe, with the attentions of the young Ferroferratas to prove it, that there was a possibility that she might be just a little more than plain and neat. She bent her head over the keys and a smile spread helplessly, happily over her face. To order flowers, special flowers, to be placed on a luncheon table was the sort of thing men did for — well, for pretty girls. Lila took a deep breath, put her hands on the keys, glanced sideways at Count Julius' opening page, written exquisitely and without correction, and began to type like the wind.

★ ★ ★

131

"I don't want you to go," Lila said.

Pa stood leaning against the kitchen doorframe, his weight on his good leg.

"No harm — "

"There is harm. It's where the sailors go. You disgraced me the other day."

"Just a mistake. Got caught out. Won't do it again."

"We can't afford it," Lila said. She was standing by the chipped enamel bowl on a stand they used for a sink, holding a glass of water. She was hot and dusty from the ride back from Mdina, and had arrived home just before Pa had planned to set out on his afternoon jaunt to the Gut. Between them, on the table, lay one of Anton's white roses. Lila had not dared to bring the whole vase.

"Rum," Pa said with certainty, "is cheap. Very cheap."

"That's not the point. If you're carousing in bars, you aren't painting. I thought you were going to paint to — to help us out."

Pa said nothing. He had no intention of getting drunk again — that had been a pure, if merry, accident — but Lila couldn't seem to see the difference between a convivial drink or two, with a lot of what the Irish called the crack, and getting drunk. There was a lot Lila didn't see, couldn't or wouldn't see. She'd never see about the girls, in the Gut. She'd never see how easy they were with him, with his wooden leg, how accepting, nor how infinitely comforting it was to be treated by a woman as if you were a proper man, a whole man and not some tiresome, troublesome child. He squinted at Lila.

"No freedom then?"

She sighed.

"Don't treat me like this," she said impatiently. "Don't *make* me nag you."

Pa watched her for a moment. She'd never been pretty, poor scrap, not like her mother who'd been as pretty as a picture. Lila was like that angular old beanpole, her grandmother, his mother-in-law, all long limbs and big eyes, no softness and grace. But she looked better today, there was a kind of glow to her, and she'd gone a nice colour, cycling in the sun, and her hair had a bit of life to it. If only her attitude did. If only she could be like twenty-year-olds were supposed to be, carefree and careless, taking the odd risk. It was to be wondered, Pa reflected, if Lila even knew how to take a risk, if she knew how to stop being careful and confined in everything she did. It was making her crabbed, this carefulness, and Pa was truly sad to see it. He shifted his weight a little and put his hands in his pockets.

"Lila."

She took a swallow of water.

"Yes?"

"I may be a burden to you. I may be an old nuisance. But I'm not as much of a burden as you make me."

She waited.

"You torment yourself," Pa said. "You dwell on things."

She bent her head, and her hair swung forward.

133

"It's how I'm made. Or, how I've become."

"*All* because of me?" Pa said.

She shot him a quick glance.

"Maybe not."

"It's not good for girls to lose their mothers," Pa said. "It's not good for chaps to lose their wives. Takes away their anchors. Leaves them floundering. But — " he stopped, and looked awkward.

"But what?"

"Difficult to say," Pa said. "Difficult to spell out."

"Try."

"Well," Pa said. He rubbed a hand over his hair. "We've still got each other. I may not be what you'd like as a pa, but I give you, faults and all — " he paused, screwed his eyes up and continued — "somewhere to come from. A starting point. I've known you all your life. No one else has."

Lila finished her glass of water and put the tumbler down, with a clink, on the tin-topped table.

"*Do* you know me?" Lila said.

"Yes," Pa said unexpectedly, "I do. And I don't think you are now how you're going to be."

"What d'you mean?"

"When you've let go a bit, you'll be different. When you stop worrying about the dust and the pennies."

Lila closed her eyes. A picture of that morning rose up and printed itself clearly behind her lids, the security of the Tabia Palace, its calm

134

assumptions both of lovely surroundings and also of ample funds to pay for them, the white linen cloth on her luncheon table, the green glass, the silver knife and fork, the vase of white roses . . .

"I'd open up," she said, "if I wasn't worrying. Of course I would. But if you won't worry, I've got to. There isn't a choice."

Pa limped forward and leaned on the table. He seemed about to say something else serious, but then to change his mind.

"Well," he said, and his voice was jaunty again, "and how's the job?"

"Lovely," Lila said.

"And the people?"

"Amazing," Lila said. "Grand, very grand. Wonderful clothes. But kind to me. At least — my employer is, and his nephews. They are teaching me to drive." She leaned forward and gave the white rose an elaborately careless nudge. "One of them gave me that."

Pa looked at the white rose, almost sadly. He said, after a pause, "Talking of young men — "

"Yes?"

Pa shifted a little, his eyes still on the rose.

"You — you know who brought me back the other night?"

"Yes."

"Miss de Vere tell you?"

"Yes."

"Good sort, Miss de Vere. And that Saliba boy. First rate. Very respectful." He gave Lila a quick glance. "He asked after you. Often does."

135

"Oh."

"Asks me if you're settling down. Asks me if you like Malta."

Lila said, with the same carelessness with which she had touched the rose, "Do you often see him?"

"Most days," Pa said. "He comes to find me. After his school closes."

"In — this Gut place?"

"It's a street. Yes, he comes to find me. Reminds me of the time."

Lila turned away.

"You go," she said.

"What?"

"You go. Into Valetta, if that's what you want. I don't mean to nag, it's just that our life seems so — so fragile, and sometimes that scares me."

Pa looked at her back, at her narrow waist encircled by the cheap white belt, and the hair on her shoulders, so dark it was almost black. He stood upright and steadied himself into his habitual, crooked stance.

"Lila — "

"Yes?"

"Don't want to lecture. Haven't any business to lecture. But must say this. What you need to learn is what to be really afraid of. You need to learn what matters. What you're doing now is shying at shadows."

Lila didn't turn. Pa waited a moment and then he said, in his ordinary voice, "Toodle-pip, my hearty," and she heard him stump out, familiar and uneven, along the tiled landing and then, even more raggedly, down the stone stairs to the courtyard. When he emerged, Salvu might also appear, his expression its usual mixture of courtesy and resentment, and offer Pa a lift, on his motorbike.

Lila sighed. She turned round slowly and surveyed the kitchen, the peeling plaster on the walls, the cracked tiled floor that was so difficult to clean, the various unmatching jugs and cups that had come from Aldeburgh now hanging on wooden pegs, not metal hooks, but still dispiritingly themselves. Pa might be right in saying that she was afraid of the wrong things, of little things, mere details, because she wasn't experienced enough to have a better sense of proportion. But he wasn't right in supposing she didn't know that, wasn't keenly aware of the narrowness of her preoccupations so that when she encountered a richer world, a freer world where people took control of their lives instead of just responding, day in, day out, to imposed limitations and restrictions, she turned towards that world both greedily and naturally, like a flower seeking the sun. A flower. Lila bent forward and picked up the white rose, and carried it along to the salone to find one of Arthur Perriam's Edwardian silver vases to put it in.

# 12

"AFTER the war," Anton Ferroferrata said, "Max is going to be a lawyer. And I shall be a financier. I shall go to America and enter one of the big houses on Wall Street. Or the City of London maybe. We have family connections in both places."

"Oh," Lila said with dreamy irony. "How useful."

They were lying on their backs in the small space of shade afforded by the car, after another driving lesson.

"Of course it's useful. I don't think you understand the influence of the Maltese nobility. When my grandmother went to England in 1880, and attended one of Queen Victoria's Drawing Rooms, the queen permitted my grandmother to kiss her cheek, like an English peeress, instead of kissing only her hand."

"Oh good," Lila said.

There was silence. Anton raised himself on one elbow and contemplated Lila. She was shredding a full seedhead of grass, scattering the tiny seeds across herself and into the small breeze.

"Do you know one of the things I like about you?" Anton said.

"No," Lila said, almost holding her breath.

"You're so impudent. Cheeky. You have no respect for me. For my name. It used to drive me wild, but now I am fascinated by it."

"I can't respect a *name*," Lila said, "not for its own sake. I can only respect people. And the way they live."

Anton reached over and took the seedhead out of her hands.

"What about my family then? What about the way we live?"

"Wonderful," Lila said. "Enviable."

"Because we are rich?"

"Only partly. Because you are civilized. And free."

"Max doesn't think so. Max thinks we are artificial."

Lila turned to look at him. His face was startlingly close.

"Why does he stay then?"

"Because we don't come into our money until we are twenty-five. He must wait one more year. For me, it's two."

"And then you will be rich and really free?"

"Yes," Anton said, as if it were the most natural thing in the world. "Max will go to Zurich or Geneva. I will go to New York."

"Except for this war."

"Except for that."

Lila said, "You are staring at me. Please don't."

He said, easily, "I am trying to decide why I want to look at you so much when you are really not pretty."

She turned her head away.

"Don't look at me then."

"I told you. I want to. Did you like my flowers?"

Still staring away from him, Lila nodded.

"I knew you did, actually," Anton said.

Her head whipped back.

"How?"

"Because you took one."

He was grinning, delighted with himself. She stared at him, willing herself not to blush.

"You counted — "

"Twelve. Twelve roses. And eleven when I got home."

Lila said, "You are disgustingly sure of yourself."

"Am I? If I was really sure, I wouldn't play games with roses. But I want to *be* sure, you see."

She tried desperately hard not to say, "Of what?" but failed, and said it.

"Of you," he said. "Whether you — like me."

Lila rolled rapidly and suddenly away from him and sat up.

"You can't talk like this," she said primly. "I am your uncle's secretary and, as you never cease to remind me, vastly your social inferior. I'm not in your rarefied orbit."

"I know," he said. He was smiling. He put out an elegant brown hand and took her wrist, very lightly. "That's why I am so fascinated. You are not pretty, you are not well-born, you are not worldly. But I think about you all the time. If I stay away from you, it's to see if you will miss me."

140

Lila's hands were shaking. She pressed them together and pushed them down, hard, into her lap.

"That doesn't show a very nice nature."

"I haven't got a nice nature," Anton said. "Of course I haven't. I should be ashamed to have anything so boring. Is that what you really want, anyway, a nice nature?"

"My father says," Lila said unwisely, "that I ought to let go a bit."

"And do you think," Anton said sliding towards her to put his free arm round her waist, "that your father is right?"

"I don't know."

"I do."

She looked down at his hand on her wrist and felt an inward sliding sensation, as of the moment before a leap, a spring, a surrender to freefall . . .

"What would your mother say?"

"She will not be given the opportunity to say anything. This is between you and me."

"What is?"

"This," said Anton, and took his hand away from her wrist so that he could turn her face towards his, and kiss her, with great confidence, on the mouth.

A little later he said, his mouth still almost on hers, "I think you haven't been much kissed."

"Not *much*."

"How much? Once?"

Lila, her immediate horizon filled both literally and metaphorically by his face, remembered an inexpert and tentative episode in the cinema in

Saxmundham, and a more practised but rough encounter in a bus shelter with a sixth former from the local boys' school who, when she rejected him with some force, said he'd only tried to kiss her for a dare anyway, and she had believed him, and suffered several subsequent days of deep humiliation.

"More than once," Lila said, and then, enjoying herself, "but never in Malta."

"I should think not. I shall lock you up if you even think of it."

"Do you have a dungeon in the palace?"

"Of course. All the best palaces have dungeons."

He took his hand away from her cheek and laid it on her shoulder, pressing her gently down onto his encircling arm until she was lying down once more in the cool shadow cast by the car.

"You kiss nicely," Anton said, "but too sweetly."

"Sweetly?"

"Like a child. Like a girl."

She lay there, waiting. His dark head and shoulders hung above her, and beyond him was nothing but blue air, blue air and sunshine and space.

"In a minute," Anton said, and his voice was very low, as if the thing he was about to say was truly private, even on these empty cliffs, something meant only for her, "I shall teach you some more driving. But before that — before that, I am going to teach you something else."

★ ★ ★

In the courtyard of the Villa Zonda, Carmela sat on a kitchen chair in a patch of shade cast by the house wall. She was supposed to be doing arithmetic. She was also supposed to be minding the baby. She had an exercise book open on her knee, and a stump of pencil in her hand, and at her feet the baby lay in a cradle improvised from a drawer from the kitchen dresser, his previous basket now being required for the harvesting of summer vegetables. He seemed, Carmela thought, perfectly contented in the drawer, lying on his back in his unvarying cocoon of shawls, and gazing at her with his round dark eyes, as if he were trying to fix her face, once and for all, in his memory.

Carmela did not want to do her arithmetic. She had been set ten simple sums, five addition and five subtraction, in an attempt to compensate for all the days she had spent away from school recently. Her schoolmistress, a zealous young woman from the little fishing village of Marsaxlokk, had been to the Villa Zonda to find Doris, to explain most vehemently that Carmela's education must take precedence over lacemaking and baby minding and carrot pulling. Doris had stared at Miss Bezzina with a blank, bovine expression. If she had been a priest, she would have listened to her intently, but as she was merely a schoolteacher and a woman — a childless, unmarried woman — she saw no need to pay her any attention. Miss Bezzina told Doris that Carmela was quick and clever, and that her talents must not be wasted, and when she departed, her voice by then shrill with exasperation, she left schoolwork for Carmela to do, arithmetic and English spelling exercises and a book of stories for reading practice. Carmela read the stories all night, by the light of a candle, whizzing over the words she did not know in eager pursuit of the narrative, and left the sums and the spelling to gather dust in a corner of the kitchen. It was Lila who had made her pick them up again, and blow the dust off the exercise book covers.

"I don't *like*," Carmela said.

"I know. But if you can't write English and you can't do sums, you won't be able to work in a shop."

"Today," Carmela said, giving all her attention to standing on one foot with her hands linked on top of her head, "I am not interested in shop."

"Nor shoes?"

Carmela considered.

"Maybe . . ."

"When you're grown up," Lila said, "do you want to be like Doris, all babies and kitchens?"

Carmela lowered her foot to the floor very slowly.

"He is a good baby," she said loyally, "he is the gift of God."

"So are you."

"I am not boy."

"That has nothing to do with it. God likes girls quite as well as boys. What He doesn't like is clever girls who won't work. Who won't work with their brains. A priest would tell you

God gave you your brains."

Carmela slid her hands down to hold the sides of her skull, as if feeling for her brains.

"You could do those sums in ten minutes," Lila said, "and the spelling in half an hour. If you weren't so lazy."

Carmela hopped up and down, fizzing with indignation.

"I'm not lazy!"

"Oh?" Lila said, as if she had suddenly lost interest in the whole business. "Aren't you?"

No, Carmela thought now, fidgeting on the kitchen chair, and flicking the pages of the exercise book, I am not lazy. I could climb the carob tree or run all the way to the market or beat seven carpets hung on the line or pick four baskets of cabbages or sing lullabies to the baby for three hours or sweep Miss Lila's stairs or scrub five buckets of potatoes or skip ten skipping games without stopping or . . .

"Hello," someone said, in Maltese.

Carmela sprang up, and the exercise book flew off her lap and landed in the drawer on the baby.

"Oh!"

"I remember you," the young man said. "I remember you very well. I've been here twice before." He smiled, and then he said in English, "You speak English."

Carmela regarded him. It was the young man who had first brought Miss Lila and Mr Claude to the house, and who had then brought Mr Claude back the day he couldn't stand up, and had told Carmela that she was to forget she had seen him. He had a roughly wrapped paper parcel in one hand and he was wearing dark trousers and a short-sleeved shirt and a tie. And shoes. Carmela climbed onto the kitchen chair, and squatted down like a hen, pulling her skirts over her bare feet, to hide them.

"Have you been to school today?" Angelo Saliba said.

Carmela jerked her head towards the drawer, where her exercise book lay upside down over the baby's body like a little cardboard roof.

"I do schoolwork here. I had to mind the baby."

Angelo Saliba picked up the exercise book with his free hand and looked at the first page.

"You haven't got very far."

"The *baby*," Carmela said, with emphasis.

Angelo looked at the baby. The baby looked back at him, without surprise.

"That baby doesn't look like much trouble to me."

Carmela looked piously heavenwards.

"He is an angel sent straight from God."

Angelo Saliba said, in a voice that suddenly had a certain tenseness to it, "Is Miss Lila in?"

Carmela nodded. It was Miss Lila who had told her not to stir from the kitchen chair until the sums were done, and who had said she was not to be disturbed until the shadow from the wellhead reached the foot of the carob tree.

"But not to be spoken to."

"Where is she?"

Carmela took one hand away from pinning

146

down her skirts and indicated the first-floor windows of the salone.

"There. But private."

Angelo Saliba glanced at the parcel in his hand.

"I will only be quick — "

"No!" Carmela said. She jumped off the chair and jigged agitatedly about in front of him. "No! No!"

"Is she asleep?"

"Yes. No. Perhaps."

"If she is asleep, I will go away again. Will you go and see if she is asleep?"

Carmela considered. She looked at Angelo and his clumsy parcel. She looked at the baby, gazing intently up from his drawer. She looked at the exercise book.

"All right," she said, "but do not take your eye off the baby for one *second*," and then she skipped away across the courtyard and vanished into the house.

Angelo sat down on the chair and put his parcel on his knees. Then he leaned forward and loosened the baby's shawls enough to extract a tiny curled hand. The hand opened and shut a few times, experimentally, but the baby's gaze didn't waver from Angelo's face.

"That better?" Angelo said. "Good to move something other than just your eyes?"

The baby blinked. Angelo bent again and moved the little hand into the baby's line of vision.

"There. That's yours."

The baby looked amazed.

"And you have a second one."

He drew out the baby's left hand, smoothed it out and then let it curl round his forefinger. The baby looked from hand to hand, dumbfounded. Then he gave an eager little jerk of his swaddled body and his toothless mouth opened in the beginnings of a smile.

There was a sudden slamming sound from the direction of the house. Angelo glanced up. The shutters at one of the windows of the salone had been flung back, and with them the windows themselves, squeaking on their metal rods. A moment later, Carmela came darting back across the courtyard, her pigtails bouncing on her shoulders.

"She wasn't asleep."

Angelo said quickly, "What did she say?"

"Oh!" Carmela exclaimed in outrage, noticing Angelo's forefinger tight in the baby's grasp. "Oh, this is dreadful, this is quite wrong, he will catch his death of cold!"

She swooped down on the drawer, and swiftly tucked both tiny hands back inside the shawls, pulling the folds up tightly and imprisoningly. The baby, deprived of his first minute taste of freedom, opened his mouth, screwed his eyes up, and began to howl.

"Please," Angelo said, "please. What did Miss Lila say?"

Carmela, full of busy indignation, scooped the roaring baby out of the drawer and began to walk rapidly up and down, holding him against her shoulder.

"She said — there, there, baby, don't cry,

148

don't cry, what a fright you've had."

"What did she *say*?"

"Oh," Carmela said impatiently, as if she had far more important things to deal with right now, "she said you could go up. For *five minutes*."

Lila was sitting in an upright upholstered chair by the open window of the salone apparently reading. Angelo stood just inside the door, and waited. He hadn't knocked but he knew she knew he was there. He adjusted the parcel from one hand to the other, and the paper it was loosely wrapped in crackled faintly.

Lila closed her book and looked round.

"Mr Saliba."

He came forward, into the square of sunlight where she was sitting.

"Thank you for seeing me."

She indicated a chair opposite. He sat down in it clumsily, cradling his parcel. It was the kind of chair to make one feel too big, too ungainly, to make one conscious of one's dusty shoes. He gave her a quick glance. She wasn't, to his surprise, looking superior, but more disconcerted, as if, albeit for different reasons, she felt their meeting to be as awkward as he did. She was wearing a dark blue cotton dress, he observed, and she looked immeasurably better than she had the first time he had seen her, crouched on the pile of fishing nets on the harbour front, quite dazed with fatigue and strangeness. She had put on a little weight and her hair was longer and thicker. She had scooped it off her face with two red combs.

"I suppose," she said, looking down at her

149

book, "Miss de Vere sent you."

He looked startled.

"No! No. Why should she?"

Lila hesitated. Then she said, in a rush, "So that I could apologize. For behaving badly to you. And — and thank you. For — well, for looking after my father. Miss de Vere thinks I owe you an explanation."

She wasn't, he noticed, looking at him. She was keeping her eyes fixed on the book she still held in her lap. No doubt she found his appearance as distasteful as she had previously, his clothes and haircut and manner all wrong. Or wrong, at least, by her standards.

He said, "I have not spoken to Miss de Vere about you. I am not interested in what Miss de Vere thinks."

"Oh."

"I am glad," Angelo said, unhappily conscious of how stiff he sounded, "to help your father. If he permits me."

Lila said, almost angrily, "It's so embarrassing — " and then stopped.

"That he should sometimes need help?" Angelo said. "That I should be the one to help him?"

Lila gave a little exclamation and stood up abruptly, throwing her book onto a nearby sofa. She said furiously, "He shouldn't put us in this position!"

Angelo rose too.

"Of obliging you to feel you should thank me? I don't want thanks. I don't help him to be thanked. I did not come here to be thanked."

150

She looked at him properly for the first time since he had come into the room. He was a broad young man, but hardly taller than she was, and for a moment they regarded one another, absolutely on a level. Then she said, less abruptly than she had spoken before, "Why did you come then?"

He indicated the parcel.

"To give you this."

"To give — "

"Your father told me you liked them. I have an uncle with a small foundry, who makes them. I thought, now that you are a little settled in Malta, that you might accept one."

He held out the parcel with one hand, and folded back the rough whitish paper of the wrapping with the other. Inside lay a brass dolphin knocker, perhaps eight inches long, complete with its benevolently moulded eyes and mouth, and elegantly triple-forked tail.

"Oh."

"I hope you like it."

"Yes, yes I do. It's — it's charming. It's very kind of you."

"It's for good luck, in a way. You can put it on your door and feel that maybe Malta can be a home for you, after all."

Lila looked at the dolphin. It was lovely, but somehow she couldn't touch it.

"You — you shouldn't give me things."

"Why not?"

She made a confused gesture with both hands.

"We don't know each other, we — we,

well, we have nothing in common except your kindness to my father, we have — we have no relationship — "

There was a pause. They both looked at the dolphin. Then Angelo said, in a voice without much expression, "And you don't want us to be friends?"

"It isn't that. It isn't — anything so — final. So unkind. It's just that I feel you can't make relationships where — well, where it isn't natural, isn't easy — "

"I see."

"I *am* grateful to you. I *do* value your kindness. But I can't pretend. I can't do anything that — that might be artificial. It wouldn't be right. It wouldn't be fair. To — to you."

He raised his eyes from the dolphin and looked at her directly. She seemed genuinely distressed, as if she was struggling not to say what was really in her mind, what was the true obstacle to her accepting the dolphin. He folded the paper back over the knocker and moved to lay it gently on the nearest sidetable, beside a little bronze statue of Mercury, complete with winged cap and heels.

"I shall leave the dolphin," he said, "all the same. It was made for you, so you will see that I cannot return it."

"You shouldn't do this!" Lila cried. "You shouldn't put me in a position like this! You shouldn't force me to accept something I don't want in order to put me under an obligation to you!"

152

He hesitated. He looked at the parcel and then, fleetingly, at her. Then he seemed to give himself a little shake, as if he were coming back to his senses.

"No," he said, "no. That would be the last thing I would want," and then, with a sudden decisiveness of movement, he leaned forward, picked up the knocker and its wrappings, and went swiftly past her and out of the door before she had even recovered sufficient presence of mind to say goodbye to him.

# 13

"**D**RAGUT," said Count Julius musingly, "now, there's a name that fascinates me."

He sat at his desk in the shrouded library, leaning back in an armorial chair, his fingertips touching. Lila, six feet away and checking her typescript for errors, said nothing. In part, it was because she was attempting to concentrate, and in part — the greater part — because she could think about little except that she had found that morning, in the drawer of her typing table where she kept pencils and erasers and new black typing ribbons on metal spools, a single white rose. It lay tranquilly among her pencils on a strip of pink blotting paper, silently, thrillingly eloquent. Anton must have borrowed a key from Teseo, and come in secretly in the early morning having cut the rose, thinking of her and . . .

"The great sea wolf of the Mediterranean," Count Julius said, "known as Turgut Reis to the Turks. In 1551, he raided Malta and sacked the citadel of Gozo. He was killed in the Great Siege by a splinter of stone shattered by a cannon ball from Castle St Angelo. I expect you know the spot. Dragut Point."

"Mm," Lila said. She longed to look at the rose again. She longed, even more, for lunchtime, when Anton would appear and they would have this delicious secret, each knowing about the rose in the drawer, and neither saying.

"I think," Count Julius said, with a slight note of teasing in his voice, "that you are not much interested in Dragut."

"Only because I am trying to concentrate on your semicolons."

"Ah," Count Julius said. "The semicolon! A punctuation mark of great subtlety. To be used to indicate a division in a sentence which is greater than a comma yet does not require the balancing weight of a full colon."

"Yes."

Count Julius leaned forward. Out of the corner of her eye, Lila could see his linen-clad arms and his white shirt cuffs and the oval gold cufflinks that bore the Tabia crest.

"Lila."

"Yes, Count Julius."

"Lila, I believe my nephews are teaching you to drive."

She did not look up.

"Yes. Yes, they are."

"This is excellent. With a war coming, we shall all need to learn how to drive. I hope you are proving an apt pupil."

Lila, recalling the kissing lesson on the clifftop, bent her head lower over her typescript.

"And I hope my nephews do not have to leave before your instruction is complete."

There was a pause. Under Lila's gaze, a sentence which began, "The continuing battles against the infidel . . . " seemed to writhe slightly on the page.

155

"Leave?"

"Oh yes," Count Julius said. "My sister has decided that she can wait for Herr Hitler no longer. She is to go to America. We have family connections in America and she has decided to take the precaution of using them as a lifeline for supplies, should Malta in any way become cut off."

"Cut off?" said a voice in Lila's head. "Lifeline? Leaving?" She put down her blue correction pencil, swallowed, and said in as normal a voice as she could manage, "Is — is the Baroness a pacifist?"

"Certainly not. Why should you suppose such a thing? But she is a pragmatist. And she wishes to provide a haven for her sons, should they need it."

"Are — are they going to America too?"

"No indeed. They are going to Cranwell."

"Cranwell?"

"Yes. Surely you have heard of it? The Royal Air Force flying school. My nephews have elected to be pilots and thus must be trained."

Lila turned slowly to face Count Julius, hoping her face betrayed nothing.

"Was — was this a sudden decision?"

He shrugged.

"We have been talking of it since March, since Hitler invaded Austria. But the papers from Cranwell only arrived two days ago."

Two days. The day after that last driving lesson . . .

"They will leave next month. I, of course,"

156

Count Julius said, linking his hands comfortably on the orderly pile of papers before him, "will remain. I am too old to fight but I am not too old to resist. I would resist to the death any German attempting to drink my Waterloo Madeira. In any case, the palace might be of use, to British officers."

Lila rose from her chair and went over to the bronze bust of Grand Master La Valette. She put a hand out and lightly touched the sharply indented star on his breast.

"I had no idea — "

"That things were so imminent? Well, we cannot be sure but I fear we must plan for the worst. And it is so easy here, in this enchanted place, to believe that we are somehow removed, untouchable." He paused, and then he said looking straight at Lila, "Don't you think?"

Lila turned to look at him.

"Why — have you suddenly told me this?"

"Because you needed to know," Count Julius said; and then, more gently, "because it will affect you too."

"My — my working here?"

"We might not find it possible, my dear, to fiddle while Rome burns. But I was not thinking so much of work."

Lila waited. She took her hand away from La Valette's cool bronze breast and put it behind her back, with her other one.

"I would not insult you," Count Julius said, "by assuming you do not know what I mean."

Lila did not move. Nor did she look at him. She looked, instead, straight ahead, and while

157

she looked, she counted. She counted slowly and steadily, holding her hands rigidly behind her back, and when she had reached fifty, she unlocked her hands and went back to her desk and the typescript and the blue correction pencil. Count Julius watched her for a while, sitting composedly behind his own desk and then, with a little smile she did not observe, returned to his papers.

* * *

Luncheon had been laid in the courtyard, under the trees. Her sons, the Baroness said, had insisted upon it. Despite the dappled leafy shade, a huge white canvas umbrella had been erected above the Baroness's chair which gave it the look of a throne belonging to an Eastern potentate. The Baroness was wearing cream silk, spotted and edged with black, and impenetrably dark sunglasses. Anton had sunglasses too, and a peach-coloured silk shirt. There were white roses on the table, in a huge silver bowl, and to Lila, after the news of the morning, they looked like nothing so much as a gigantic tease.

The Baroness, already seated beneath her white umbrella, gave Lila her usual small, formal bow. And, also as usual, Max held her chair for her. They might be eating in the open air, but no visible concession had been made to informality and the table was laid with all the ceremony and precision with which it was laid in the dining room. Lila looked at the array of silver and glass, at her glossy white napkin, and felt that she was in the middle of some subtle and complicated game, a game that wouldn't have been out of place in one of the Perriams' fairy tales, a game that she was bound to lose because she didn't, unlike everyone else round the table, know the rules. She was aware of Max watching her. Whether Anton was or not, she dared not look to see.

"And this morning?" the Baroness said to her brother, as was her custom. "What exploits have you exhausted Miss Cunningham with this morning?"

"Piracy," Count Julius said, unfolding the huge stiff square of his napkin, "and — " with a glance at his nephews " — piloting."

Max said quickly, "You spoke of Cranwell?"

"Indeed I did."

"Uncle Julius," Anton said, and his voice was tense, "Cranwell is our business. It is for us to tell Miss Cunningham."

Count Julius looked quite unperturbed. He raised his water glass and looked at Lila over it, as if he were toasting her, then he said easily, "Miss Cunningham and I have no secrets."

Max said to Lila, "We were going to tell you ourselves. This afternoon."

She felt Anton's face turn towards her, his eyes hidden behind his sunglasses.

"That's very kind," Lila said stiffly, "but really, there is no obligation to inform me of family matters."

The Baroness looked at her sharply.

"Precisely."

Anton said, "I disagree."

159

His mother smiled at him.

"Dearest, disagreeing is second nature to you."

Two servants emerged from the house bearing trays laden with silver domes.

"I am not a child," Anton said. "This decision is mine and information about it is mine also."

The Baroness, with a swift sideways movement of her eyes, indicated the servants.

"Dearest, please — "

"I'm afraid I had no idea," Lila said quickly, too loudly, "that you all believe a war to be more — probable than possible. I think I felt that, living here, because it's so unlike England, we were all somehow out of the way of the rest of Europe."

She stopped. They were all watching her, Anton inscrutably from behind his sunglasses, Max with some sympathy, Count Julius with amused detachment.

The Baroness said coldly, "You are quite mistaken."

"It is easy," Max said, "to be so mistaken."

"Perhaps," the Baroness said, picking up her fork as a signal that the rest of the table might begin to eat, "perhaps, Miss Cunningham, you would prefer it if your father would take you home to England?"

"My father — "

"Indeed."

Lila said hastily, "I don't think — I mean I can't quite see — " and then stopped abruptly. There was a small commotion happening at the side of the courtyard, inside the doorway that led

160

to the house, a confusion of voices and unsteady footsteps.

"Excuse me, sir," Teseo could be heard saying, "excuse me. The family are at luncheon — "

He emerged backwards into the courtyard, his arms straight out in front of him as if he were trying to restrain someone else in the passage behind.

"Teseo!" Count Julius called sharply.

He turned his head briefly, and they all caught an expression of extreme agitation on his face and then there was a sudden flurry of movement from within the doorway, and Teseo seemed to be brushed aside.

"Bunkum," a voice said cheerfully. "Bunkum and bosh."

Lila froze. From the pedimented doorway of the Tabia Palace, an unmistakable figure crookedly and confidently emerged. He wore a none-too-clean blue workman's shirt, a red bandanna round his throat, and his tufted hair stood blithely on end. He stood unsteadily for a moment, blinking in the sunshine and beaming upon the group at the table, who gazed back, quite paralysed by his appearance.

"Well," Pa said, his smile broadening into a huge grin. "*Well*. What ho?"

★ ★ ★

"Of course I shan't apologize," Trixie de Vere said. "Why should I? He is your father and he is perfectly entitled to see where you work and to meet the family you work for."

161

Lila lay face down on one of the hard Edwardian sofas in the salone. The bolster under her cheek smelled of mice and dust. Rage and mortification swelled in hard, undigestible lumps in her chest and made it impossible to speak.

"He merely said to me that he should like to see where you worked. What could be more natural than that I should offer to drive him? We may have made an error in forgetting that life in the Tabia Palace ossified about a hundred years ago and that luncheon is still a sacred rite there, but beyond that I cannot see what objection you might have. *Except*," said Miss de Vere with emphasis, "ones that you should be ashamed of."

Lila moved her position a little so that she could put her fingers in her ears. She would have liked to have closed her eyes too, but dared not, since she had discovered that when she did, images immediately printed themselves behind her closed lids which she never wanted to recall again: images of Count Julius' expression as he turned his gaze from Pa to Lila and back again after her stumbled introduction; of the glances Max and Anton had exchanged; of the Baroness rising from the table and sweeping past Pa into the house, only pausing to give him a small bow, a bow which conveyed a thousand things, none of them pleasant. It was at that moment that Lila, already distressed by the news of the morning, and now in a perfect turmoil of confused shame, loyalty, longing and apprehension, had burst into tears, howling like

162

a baby into the starched folds of her table napkin. And it had only seemed to her a few more moments after that, that she, consumed only by the need to get Pa out of the place as quickly as possible, had hustled him out of the Tabia Palace, and into the narrow street where the brilliant early afternoon light cast shadows on the golden stone walls as black and dense as ink.

"Why couldn't we stop?" Pa had demanded. "What's the hurry? Nice fellow offered me wine — "

"You shouldn't have come. You shouldn't have surprised me."

Pa had been very quiet on the journey home. Crammed beside him in Miss de Vere's tiny car, Lila had stared resolutely ahead at the yellow walls and fields and villages which, only a few weeks before, she had ridden so exultantly among. She had declined to speak. Miss de Vere hadn't spoken either, but Lila knew she was going to, she could feel Miss de Vere's decided opinions seething round her like a cloud of wasps.

"It's time," Miss de Vere said now, to Lila's obstinate back, "it's time that you grew up. It's time you stopped yearning for what might be, and faced what is. Nothing's as bad as you think it's going to be when you face it."

There was a series of creaking sounds. Miss de Vere was plainly extracting herself from the chair she had chosen as a suitable vantage point from which to lecture Lila. Lila did not turn. Would not.

"Tomorrow, I shall collect you to come with me and visit my clinic. I shall be here at ten o'clock."

Lila didn't stir.

"Count yourself lucky," Miss de Vere said, "count yourself very lucky, to be rescued in the nick of time."

When she had gone, Lila lay on the sofa for a further ten minutes or so, and then she rose and went over to the window and looked down into the courtyard. There was only Salvu to be seen, testing a bicycle tyre for punctures in a bucket of water and, by the kitchen door from which the murmurings of women's voices came, the baby in his drawer propped on two stools, and shrouded in an old piece of fishing net against the maraudings of the yellow cat. The afternoon light lay soft and golden on the wellhead and the pots of marigolds and the shaggy dark branches of the carob tree, but to Lila it looked harsh, a harsh light on a forlorn and shabby place, a place in the end like any other place, sunshine or no sunshine, a place where the same cares had followed her so doggedly.

She turned from the window and went across the layered rugs of the salone, and down the tiled landing to her bedroom. The shutters were open, but the light in the room was shadowy away from the sun. She lay down on her narrow iron bed and put her face into the rough cotton of her pillow. Perhaps, silent in his own room next door, Pa was doing the same thing, his peg leg sticking out of the jug on his washstand where he had taken to leaving it when lying down. She pulled her pillow round her head as if it could muffle her thoughts. She didn't want to think about Pa. She didn't want to think about him, or Miss de Vere, or any of the consequences or implications of this awful day. Nor did she want to think about the future. If there was one. If she couldn't have her dreams, if she couldn't have at least the chance of a dream, then she wasn't sure a future had any meaning, and that, she remembered with a sinking heart, was what she used to fear, all the time, in England.

* * *

Carmela pressed her ear to Lila's door. There was no sound. It was almost dark, but still too early to be asleep for the night unless, like her grandfather, God rest his soul, you rose with the sun and went to bed with it also. But Lila was not like that. Lila lived her life by her wristwatch. After shoes, Carmela most coveted a wristwatch.

She gave the door a tiny tap. There was no reply. Holding her apron bunched up in one hand to secure what was inside, Carmela turned the stiff brass knob with difficulty and opened the door just wide enough to peer in. Lila was indeed on the bed, her shape just visible in the dusk and her hair very dark on the pillow.

Carmela opened the door a little wider.
"Please?" she said.
Lila stirred. She turned her head a little.
"Hello?"

165

"Me," Carmela said. She pattered to Lila's bedside.

"Heavens," Lila said, raising herself on one elbow. "What time is it?"

"The baby is in bed," Carmela said, "and the man came."

Lila pushed her hair back from her face. She sat up properly and peered at Carmela in the dim light.

"What man?"

"He said not to disturb you. I said yes, yes. He said no, no." She leaned forward until her bunched apron was resting on the sheet. "He gave this."

Lila looked down at the apron.

"What?"

Carefully Carmela opened the folds of her apron.

"The flower," she said. "The high man with the car."

On the rough cream calico, a white rose lay.

"And this," Carmela said. She slid her hand under the rose and drew out a piece of paper. "Look."

Lila, in a sudden tumult of feelings, took the paper. It was very small, not as big as a postcard. She held it up close to her eyes in the gloom. There was one word on it, black on the white paper.

'Wait' it said.

# Part Two

*War, 1941*

# 14

LILA woke slowly, postponing consciousness as she had learned to do in the last six months, clinging to sleep. Sleep was brief oblivion. Consciousness was — well, it was such a mixture of things these days and required so much courage and resourcefulness, that one only wanted a very little of it at a time. But of course, one wasn't allowed that. Being awake meant being immediately active, alert and watchful. Lila shut her eyes tightly against acknowledging that she really was awake, and burrowed down under the bedclothes.

Even down there, it wasn't really warm. There were too few blankets to go round the household now, they'd given so many away, and the ones that were left were worn and thin. And in any case, she could hear that it was raining. It had rained for days, it seemed, cold, steady, northern-feeling rain that had turned Malta from a yellow island into a grey one, a grey island scarred now with swathes of destruction left by the raids of the Italian bombers. The first raid had been on June 11th, the day before Lila's twenty-fourth birthday, and she had been woken on her birthday morning by a curious wailing, shuffling sound, like the sound of a herd of distressed cattle coming nearer and nearer. When, with Carmela, she reached the gate in her nightgown to see what it was, she saw that

169

it was indeed a herd, a sobbing, limping crowd of refugees fleeing from the harbour area where the bombers had struck. She had stood there for half an hour, dazed and helpless, watching the endless stream of people, clutching bundles and babies and kettles and canaries in cages, making unsteadily for the countryside where they believed sanctuary might be found. Later that day, a special constable brought twenty gas-masks to the Villa Zonda, in cardboard boxes, and announced that they should be carried everywhere, at all times, without fail. There was even one for the baby, except that he was a baby no longer but a sturdy three-year-old, named Spiru, for his dead grandfather. Little Spiru was the only one of the household who showed any enthusiasm for his gas-mask.

Lila's was under her bed right now. She had never taken it out of its box, but she carried the box everywhere, as they all had to. She had taken it to church the day before, to the afternoon mass held in the cathedral in Valetta, a mass for Christmas Eve.

"You have to come, my dear," Miss de Vere had said, "for the Maltese. Forget God by all means, but never forget the Maltese. They need our solidarity."

The cathedral had been packed, there'd hardly been standing room. Lila and Beatrix de Vere and Rosanna Saliba had been crushed together and pressed out of the nave into a little side chapel dedicated to St James so that they could see nothing except the dim, smoky spaces above the crowd, and angles of ornately gilded pillars and the frescoed ceiling, vaulting far above them, glimpses of limbs and wings and drapery, blue and red and amber. The crowd had smelled of damp wool, its united voice rising and falling to the timeless, rhythmic phrases of the Latin mass. Some of the older women wore the faldetta, the ancient sweeping black silk headdress of Malta, its edge stiffened with cardboard, framing the face like a great wing. But most of the other women were shawled, and the men all wore hats or caps. Many of them, men and women, were weeping.

Five more minutes, Lila thought, and I'll get up. I'll get up and light the stove and make Pa a cup of what passes for tea these days and take it in to him and say 'Happy Christmas!' because that's what you say on Christmas Day, happy or not. Pa hadn't come to church on Christmas Eve. He had offered to stay at home and look after Spiru, as he often did these days, so that the women of the family could go to mass. The men would go too if they could, but Salvu and his brothers were now trainee gunners in an anti-aircraft battery down in Senglea and seemed never to be off duty. There had been fifteen air raids in December alone, already. And over two hundred since the bombing began. Pa counted them, and timed them. Tiny as Spiru was, Pa was teaching him his numbers that way. And when Malta's three ancient Gladiator planes — nicknamed Faith, Hope and Charity — took off to brave the incoming enemy, Pa would take Spiru out into the courtyard and they would cheer and wave and yell encouragement.

It was one of the few occasions these days when Pa looked really happy, something like his old self. It wasn't any good, Lila reflected, thinking Pa was just the same, because he wasn't. He was quieter, more withdrawn, and his breezy assumption that everything would turn out for the best had lost its assurance. Just as he had. There was no stumping jovially about on the harbour front now, no jolly visits to the Gut, no boastful talk of painting — indeed, no painting itself. Instead, Pa spent most days with the family downstairs, sitting on a kitchen chair, whittling away at something that never turned into anything, with a penknife, and singing funny little songs for Spiru. The women of the family treated him easily, as if he were as much a fixture in their kitchen as the chopping board or the mangle. Lila was pleased to let him stay down there. After all, it was where he seemed happiest, most at home.

Lila took a deep breath and threw back the blankets. The room was raw and chill and black. Even when dawn broke, the light would still be dim because of the newspapers, the sheets and sheets of old copies of the *Times of Malta* that Pa had pasted across the windows to minimize the effect of splintered glass, should a bomb fall nearby. Pa had wanted them to go and sleep downstairs with the family, but Lila had resisted. Safety or no safety, her last privacy and independence lay up here in these dusty, underfurnished rooms. There was nothing much to recommend them but they had become, in a weird way, home. Or at least, all the home there

172

was to be had just now.

She swung her legs over the edge of the bed, feeling on the floor for the pair of Pa's old socks which she used as slippers, and as she moved, something smooth and warm slipped around her throat on its retaining piece of ribbon and came to rest against her skin. She put her hand up to hold it, as she always did; to hold it like a talisman. Anton's ring.

★ ★ ★

Pa was lying humped under his blankets with only his tufty hair visible. Lila, holding the oil lamp carefully in one hand — every drop of kerosene was becoming more precious by the day — set a mug of tea down on the battered old chest that now served Pa as a bedside table.

"Happy Christmas, Pa."

Pa rolled over. He looked up at her with his little blue eyes.

"Happy Christmas, shipmate."

She sat down on the edge of the bed, feeling his warm bulk through the blankets.

"I'm afraid a mug of tea's all I've got for you."

"Aha," Pa said. He twisted himself slightly and felt under his pillow. "I've done better than that!" He pulled a flat red and gold tin out from underneath and slapped it into Lila's hand. "How's that, eh?"

She peered in the lamplight.

"Chocolate?"

"No less!"

"Pa!" she said, beaming. "Pa! Where did you get it?"

He struggled into a sitting position. "I didn't get it. I got someone to get it for me. You won't want to know who." He tapped the tin in Lila's hand and said triumphantly, "Cadbury's!"

Lila leaned across and kissed his stubbly cheek.

"*Thank* you."

Pa looked at her sideways.

"Any — any more presents?"

Lila's hand went instinctively to the ring hanging under the old coat she still wore as a dressing gown.

"No."

"None?"

She said quickly, "I wasn't expecting anything. When you're flying — " she stopped.

"Where's he flying?"

She swallowed.

"I don't know. It's secret. You know that. Everything's secret."

"Ho hum," Pa said. He reached out and picked up his mug and took a noisy swallow of tea. "Ho hum."

"I'm working today," Lila said. "Down at the hospital. So I'm afraid I won't be here, to be Christmassy."

"Christmas!" Pa said, and gulped his tea again. "Never could get on with Christmas. Your mother — " He paused.

"What about her?"

"She liked it. Christmas. Holly and ivy and whatnot. Carols." He put a hand out and patted

Lila's briefly. "Sorry," he said. "Sorry. You've never had one of those."

Lila stood up.

"I don't suppose I'd recognize one if I met it in my porridge."

The bedroom door opened silently against the darkness of the landing outside.

"Oh hallo," a voice said, in accented English.

Pa's face lit up. He leaned forward in the bed.

"Hallo, my hearty!"

Spiru came forward into the room. He wore a woman's shawl tied tightly round his little body over his pyjamas, and clumsy green baize boots Pa had made him from the lining cut out of a bureau drawer in the salone. He too was holding a red and gold tin.

"Happy," Spiru said.

"And to you, old son."

Spiru came unsteadily to the edge of the bed, impeded by his shawl, and held up his arms. Pa put his tea mug down and bent to lift him.

"Happy," Spiru said again and then, with even more emphasis, "hallo!"

Pa settled him on his knee, loosening the shawl so that he could move his limbs more easily. He gave Lila a little wink, and then bent his head over Spiru's.

"Quite," he said.

★ ★ ★

It was raw outside, and barely light. Lila, dressed in an old shirt of Pa's, two jerseys,

175

khaki trousers from forces supplies, men's boots and her dressing gown coat, wheeled her bicycle out from the shed in the yard where the family kept their rabbit hutches. When she had first come to the Villa Zonda she had been innocently surprised to see that a family with so many mouths to feed should amuse themselves by keeping half a dozen cages of pet rabbits stacked neatly in a shed and fed regularly with all the vegetable peelings. It didn't take her long to realize that feeding all those mouths was exactly what the rabbits were for. Mrs Tuttle, so many miles and now years away in Aldeburgh, would have been shocked. Eat a tame rabbit? Never. If you wanted a rabbit, you sent Tuttle off with the twelve-bore. There had to be sport in it, in Mrs Tuttle's view — that was only fair.

But the Maltese, Lila reflected, averting her gaze from the soft quiet shapes in the hutches, didn't see it that way. There was a lot they didn't see the same way, a lot that had to be learned if you were going to live with them and work with them. They were the product of so much resistance, so many invaders, and their roots were tough and ancient and secret. Even their curious language seemed a kind of secret. Lila pulled the purple woollen mittens that Carmela's mother had knitted her out of her coat pockets and put them on. No time to reflect upon the riddle of the Maltese now. Miss de Vere — she had said to Lila, "You may call me Trixie," but Lila somehow couldn't — had said she wanted Lila down at the hospital at eight-thirty sharp, and Lila knew that she herself would be there at

176

eighty-twenty-nine, ostensibly already busy, but still sharply looking out.

It wasn't really a hospital, though Miss de Vere liked to call it one; more a first-aid centre. After the fall of France in June 1940 and the sudden subsequent increase of attacks on Malta, first-aid centres had sprung up everywhere, mostly in the schools, and Miss de Vere had immediately offered to staff one in Kalkara with nursing auxiliaries whom she persuaded the military hospital in Valetta to give a month's training to. Protesting that she still had her own life to live — "*Do* you?" Miss de Vere had asked brusquely in what had become her refrain over the last two years as she sought to involve Lila ever more deeply in Maltese activities. "So a sixteenth-century war is to take precedence over one that is actually happening all around you, is it?" — Lila found herself a daily companion to a patient Maltese nurse whose job it was to show her the sluices and instruct her in bedmaking, simple wound dressing and bed baths. Lila had been sick twice the first day, once in front of a patient. He was a kindly middle-aged naval mechanic, who handed her his own glass of water and remarked that if he had to do what she had to do, he'd probably bring his own breakfast up even faster. By the end of a week, she found she wasn't even flinching.

"There," Miss de Vere said, sounding not triumphant but merely matter-of-fact. "There. What did I tell you?"

Lila bumped out of the drive of the Villa Zonda and out onto the road. In the east, pale

177

streaks of light lay low on the horizon as if anxious about disturbing the blackout. The rain had stopped and the air smelt washed and cold, almost like English air except for the undertone of singeing, of burning, which hung over Valetta like a pall now, a raw menacing legacy from all those bombs. Putting her head down against the early morning wind, Lila began to pedal at a steady speed towards the city.

★ ★ ★

Miss de Vere was in her makeshift office in a corner of what had once been the school's secondary classroom. She was dressed in her usual winter uniform of a thick white flannel skirt and a huge white cable-stitched cricketing jersey which had belonged to her brother. Over them, she had pinned an apron made of flour sacks with 'Msida Mills' stencilled across them at regular intervals.

"Happy Christmas, dear."

"And to you," Lila said.

"We lost that child in the night," Miss de Vere said, "little Getju Debono. He'd been too badly crushed. I should have sent him up to the hospital. I didn't realize it was his lungs. I want you to go and see his mother."

Lila hesitated.

"He was her eldest," Miss de Vere said, regarding Lila levelly, "her eldest boy. You know what that means to the Maltese."

Lila said, "Shouldn't Rosanna go? She's Maltese after all."

"Seems to me," Miss de Vere said, "that putting yourself in the place of someone in a state of grief has nothing to do with nationality. Or shouldn't have. Don't you think?"

Lila stuffed her purple gloves into her coat pockets and took the coat off. She turned away from Miss de Vere to hang it on a nail driven into the wall.

"Why do you keep asking me to do extra things, difficult things?"

"Because I know you can do them."

"It's as if," Lila said, "you were continually setting me some kind of test."

"Perhaps I am. Perhaps I have a better idea of what you can do than you do."

"Or perhaps," Lila said, "you still disapprove of what I want."

"That hasn't changed?"

Lila's hand went automatically to the spot beneath her jersey where the ring lay. It had come four days after her twenty-third birthday, a circle of little pearls in a jeweller's box from Bond Street in London, and accompanying it a pressed white rosebud wrapped in tissue paper. There had been no letter. Lila hadn't needed a letter. Not then, at any rate.

"No," Lila said.

"And have you," Miss de Vere said, "had Christmas salutations from the Tabia Palace?"

Lila's chin lifted a little. It had been eighteen months now since her last session in Count Julius' library, and six since she had heard anything from him.

"No."

179

"Nor from the Baroness in America?"

"No."

"And no word from the gallant Max?"

"No."

"Then," said Miss de Vere, rising stiffly and smoothing down the flour sacks, "we must abandon dreams for today and proceed with reality. Don't you think?"

She looked at Lila, at the hand touching something under her jersey by her breastbone. Then she came out from behind the table that served as a desk and put a large pink hand on Lila's arm.

"Mrs Debono," she said gently, "in the main ward, sitting on a chair by the bed we put Getju in. She speaks a little English."

# 15

"**B**AD news," Pa said.

He leaned in the kitchen doorway, holding a copy of the *Times of Malta*. Mabel Strickland's father had had a huge cave dug to house the printing machines, and the paper was coming out steadily every day, bombs or no bombs.

Lila was peeling potatoes in an enamel bowl. They were nearly at the bottom of the sack of potatoes Salvu had given them in September and Lila couldn't quite think what they would do when the sack was finished. Not having enough food had hardly occurred to her when war broke out because she had been too preoccupied with — to her — much more important things. But now she peeled the remaining small, softening potatoes as thinly as possible, and kept every scrap of peel for the rabbits.

"Hitler's woken up," Pa said. "Taking a nasty interest."

"In us?"

"He's going to bomb all the supply ships to Malta. He's stationing the Luftwaffe in Sicily for the purpose."

Lila dropped her knife into the earthy water. "What'll happen?"

Pa pointed at the enamel bowl.

"Fewer of those. No kerosene. No medicines. That aircraft carrier the other day was just the

181

first. Dive bombers got her, didn't they?"

"The *Illustrious*," Lila said.

She put her hand into the water and felt about for the knife. It had been awful. The ship had come limping in to Grand Harbour, and ambulances had gone racing down to pick up the wounded. There'd been dozens of them, dozens and dozens, some so badly burned it was just a question of helping them to die peacefully. Almost everyone at the first-aid centre had been sent up to Imtarfa Hospital to help, and Lila had been left in charge, with two Maltese orderlies, in Miss de Vere's absence. To her surprise she had quite liked it; there had been a kind of freedom to the day, especially as she could send two patients home at the end of it as being sufficiently recovered to cope without help. The only awkward moment had been when Angelo Saliba had come in, gaunt in the face and hollow-eyed after nights of firewatching, to ask, in his courteous stiff English, if she was well.

"Of course," she said, going on rolling bandages, "in so far as anyone can be just now."

He was silent for a moment. Out of the corner of her eye she observed that he was looking at her intently, almost scrutinizing her, as if he could learn more from how she looked than what she said. Then, almost hesitantly, he said, "Have you enough to eat?"

"As much as anyone has," Lila said shortly. "And I expect more than a lot of people."

"I could bring you some eggs."

Lila picked up her pile of rolled bandages and

stacked them in an old shoebox.

"If you've got spare eggs, you should give them to your schoolchildren."

"I do."

"Angelo," Lila said, turning to face him, "did you come today because you knew Miss de Vere was up at the hospital?"

His face was quite open.

"Yes."

"Your sister told you?"

"Yes."

Lila sighed. She and Rosanna Saliba worked together because they had to, but it was no good pretending that they were in any way natural companions. Lila often wondered if Rosanna was jealous of the interest Miss de Vere took in Lila, and also resentful of Lila's treatment of her brother. Whatever the reason, relations between them required an effort, on Lila's part at least, to seem cordial. She made such an effort, now, not to sound impatient.

"Don't come," Lila said. "Don't waste your time."

"Or yours?"

"I didn't say that."

"No," Angelo said. "There are many things you don't say from which I learn a great deal."

And then he was gone, as quickly and silently as if he had dissolved where he stood, leaving her feeling as he always left her feeling, that somehow he had behaved much better than she had, and also that he knew her better than she wanted him to. They had hardly ever met, and never talked at length, but he unnerved her, by his perceptiveness. Only Pa, for all the confusion of her feelings about him, was permitted to see her as keenly as that.

"Thing is," Pa said now, brandishing the paper, "time has now come. To abandon ship."

Lila, having found the knife and the last walnut-sized potato, said warily, "What ship?"

"This," Pa said. "Up here. Time to go and sleep down there. With the family. In the cellar."

"No."

"Raids coming," Pa said. "Raids all the time. Worse raids. Germans more accurate than Italians."

"No."

"Nothing heroic about being killed for being stuck up," Pa said.

"I'm not stuck up!"

"You are," Pa said calmly. "Stuck right up about some things."

Lila opened her mouth to shout her defiance, but got no further. From less than a mile away, the first growing wail of a siren was beginning. She flung the knife and the potato back into the water.

"Damn! Damn, damn, damn, damn!"

"Come on," Pa said. "Quick march."

He dropped the paper on the floor and seized Lila's wrist.

"It's two o'clock in the afternoon!"

"So what? Any better to be flattened at midnight?"

He dragged Lila from the kitchen and along

the tiled landing. Carmela, her pigtails bouncing on her shoulders, was hopping about on the stairs to the courtyard, her skinny figure silhouetted against the sharp winter sunlight outside.

"Oh come quick, come quick. It's a big one, it's a such big one! They said on the wireless it was coming, they said the Germans were coming! You must bring the gas masks, you must. Spiru has put his on and he's calling for you!"

Stumbling down the stairs after Pa, Lila felt Carmela seize her hand.

"Come on, come on, we've had raids before, hundreds — "

"Not like this! Not so big! The Germans want to ruin the Grand Harbour!"

The family kitchen was empty, and the yellow cat, taking advantage of everyone's absence, was helping himself to the scrawny chicken carcase that lay, suddenly abandoned, part-dismembered on the table, ready for the stockpot.

"Geroff!" Pa bellowed.

The yellow cat knew when to take no notice and merely turned her back. The cellar door, a narrow plank door giving onto a precipitous staircase into blackness, stood slightly ajar. From it came the rhythmic sound of voices, low and murmuring, voices joined together in prayer.

"I'll stay here," Lila said. "I'll stay in the kitchen — "

"No!" Pa roared. "No! No!"

He seized her waist with his free arm, propelling her across the room with extraordinary force, and almost hurled her through the cellar door and down the staircase. Her hands went out instinctively, clutching vainly for support and scraping down the rough walls, and then she fell, bumping and tumbling into the blackness.

At the bottom of the stairs, Doris's voice said, "Miss Lila?"

"Ow!"

A candle was held near her.

"Broken?" Doris said, in Maltese. "Broken bones?"

"I don't think so."

"Better," Doris said. "Better a broken bone down here than to be up there in that madness."

Lila felt herself gingerly, and then the cellar space around her.

"Where's Carmela?"

"Here."

"And Pa?"

"Here," Pa said. She felt his hand on her leg. "Stumps don't care for stairs. Well now. Got the whole crew?"

Lila looked round. It was Doris who was holding the candle, and its faint yellow light fell on all the women of the family, huddled in dark lumps against the cellar's darker walls, and on Spiru, solemn and grotesque inside his gas-mask.

"Our men," Doris said brokenly. "Our men up there. My Salvu — "

From above came the last scream of the siren and then a noise, so enormous, so deafening, so complete, that the cellar door slammed shut and the draught of it blew out the candle.

"God preserve us," Pa said in a shocked

186

voice in the darkness. "God in His mercy preserve us."

* * *

It wasn't until almost sunset that the all clear, the pealing of church bells all over Malta, sounded. The noise that had first so stunned them had gone on and on, for more than a couple of hours, interspersed with the muffled scream and whine of the diving planes and their bombs. It went on for so long that Spiru, still in his gas-mask, went to sleep in Pa's arms, and Lila, frightened in a way she had never known before, and simultaneously obscurely ashamed of that fear, had envied his oblivion deeply. Doris and her mother and sisters had prayed steadily, their voices rising and falling, their rosaries clicking persistently in the thick, damp darkness.

"I'm going into the city," Lila said, at last out in the freedom of the courtyard.

Pa looked at her.

"Ah."

"I want to see. I want to go to Kalkara and find Miss de Vere. I want to see where the bombs have fallen."

"You shouldn't go alone."

"There's no-one else to come. I don't want to risk Carmela. Doris has enough to worry about."

Pa looked at her again, more thoughtfully.

"It's going to be bad."

"I've seen bomb craters before."

"Not like this," Pa said. He stopped and then said, "Wish I could come. Wish I could come with you."

"They need you here."

He glanced down, at his wooden leg.

"Don't seem to be able to manage him like I could. Don't seem so nimble."

"I have to go," Lila said gently, "I have to see."

He nodded. He limped past her to the rabbit hutch shed and opened the door. Everyone had forgotten the rabbits, who were now pressed into the far corners of their cages, as deep into their meagre bedding as they could dig themselves. Pa wheeled Lila's bicycle out into the courtyard.

"Poor little beggars."

Lila put her hands on the handlebars.

"If I don't come back, it's because I'm needed. I'll get a message to you somehow. But I'll be all right."

"We never know that," Pa said. "We never do. But we hope it."

She glanced at him. He looked suddenly much older to her, and fragile, standing there crookedly with his hair on end and his face smudged from the cellar.

"Pa," she said, "you go back to Spiru. Thanks for getting my bike."

He nodded. She took the bicycle at a run out of the courtyard, to get up enough speed for the bumpy driveway, and then she turned and headed for the city, not knowing what she would find.

'I have to write to you,' Lila wrote to the Perriams two days later, 'because I have to tell someone what we are going through. I don't expect England is having much of a time either, especially London, but somehow I need to think of you and Culver House and that clean, cold sea. I need to think something, somewhere is changeless.' She paused, and moved the candle she had stuck in an old beer bottle so that its wavering flame fell rather more on the paper than on her hands. The paper was the old writing paper she had found in A. E. O. Perriam's desk, thick, old, small-sized paper with Villa Zonda, Santa Venera, Malta embossed in one corner in black. She had it balanced on her knee, on an old atlas for support, and she herself was sitting on the floor of the family kitchen, close to the cellar door. In the cellar itself were all the family and Pa and the gas-masks and a pile of bedding. She had promised faithfully that at the first squeak of a siren, she'd be down those stairs to join them all, like lightning.

I don't quite know where to start. It is like some kind of hell in the Three Cities. The streets are full of rubble, everything is burned and broken, there is the stench of TNT. When I went down to Kalkara after the first raid, I was so shocked I could hardly breathe. There wasn't anything that wasn't violently damaged and there were people everywhere in tears

189

because they are now beggars. And if they aren't beggars, they're dead or wounded, and the refugees are pitiful, struggling out of the city with their children and their sad bundles. You wouldn't recognize the Three Cities. I wonder if you'd recognize Malta.

And there are more raids to come, we're promised another big one tomorrow. Sometimes it's so frightening you feel you'll go mad. But you can't, because people need help, all the time, so you have to fight down everything you're feeling and do what you can. Miss de Vere is amazing. The hospital was hit, but not destroyed, and she found several bottles of whisky in her own house and brought them over and the patients poured in all night and she wouldn't let us turn anyone away, not even the poor mother who brought in a dead child who'd drowned in a blown-up sewer. I'm sorry to write these things, but I have to. And about the human head I saw, blown off its body, with a towel over it. And the starving dogs the policeman shot because they were trying to eat corpses. But we're lucky here, with the cellar. We spend the nights down there now but I don't sleep much because I can't, I can't make my mind stop seeing pictures. I try and make it see you, and your library and the Chinese rugs and the birch trees, but sometimes I'm too tired to stop it seeing all the horrible things it seems intent on seeing. Miss de Vere says I am useful and I can only hope she's right. Everything one does is so tiny and what people need is so huge. I wish I was back with you. I wish I was in the kitchen with Mrs Tuttle drinking tea, or making notes in the library. I'm so sorry to write like this but it's all rather overwhelming. Pa is well, I suppose, but not the same, not so sure that the sun will always come out again. I feel I must look after him too, but differently. Please write to me. Write to me and tell me ordinary things, familiar things. This letter is childish. I know it and I'm ashamed of it. But I have to write it all the same.

The candle gave a little sigh, and the flame sank down into the pool of wax. Lila watched it for a moment and then, very gently, blew it out. She sat there for a moment in the quiet kitchen and listened to the silence, a silence that was always eerie now because it was like some monstrous thing holding its breath before it sprang. Then she slipped her letter inside the cover of the atlas, laid the atlas on the cold kitchen floor and, huddling herself up into the folds of her coat, twisted round until her cheek was pillowed on the atlas. Then she closed her eyes.

★ ★ ★

"I am so sorry," a precise voice said, "to disturb you."

Lila opened her eyes. Her gaze, focussing slowly, took in a pair of elegant polished boots, and the hems of some smooth dark trousers, sharply creased.

"I should not have walked in like this," the voice said. "And of course, without the present emergency, would not have dreamed of doing so. But I tried the upper apartments, and finding them empty, assumed that you and your father must be spending the nights down here. I was evacuated at dawn, you see, from the Tabia Palace. Another major raid is feared today."

Lila whipped upright like a sapling.

"Count Julius!"

"Miss Cunningham. Do forgive me. Hardly a welcome guest. But I felt you would not refuse to shelter me."

She scrambled to her feet; pushing her hair off her face. Count Julius wore an immaculate dark overcoat and a homburg hat. He smelled, very faintly, of some citrus-based cologne and he was holding fawn kid gloves. Standing there in the family kitchen, in the shabby, homely clutter lit only by the new daylight from the courtyard coming in through the door he had opened, he looked like a creature from another planet. She stared at him.

"I think it will only be for a night or two. I have no intention of allowing Herr Hitler to make it more. I would have gone to Gozo, but the travelling is so difficult and here you were, but a few miles away." He paused. "Miss Cunningham? Is — is it not possible for you to receive me?"

Lila swallowed. Then she gave Count Julius a slow, radiant smile.

"Oh yes! You can see — " she gestured about her, " — you can see how we live. But of course you're welcome. I'm very — very flattered."

"I have brought provisions, of course. Teseo motored me here, with the Ford. I expect — "

Behind Lila, the cellar door creaked open. From it, Carmela emerged, crumpled with uncomfortable sleep, streaked with soot and wrapped in a tattered brown blanket over her everyday clothes of a too-big tartan dress and worn black canvas plimsolls. The plimsolls were her first ever shoes, and she regarded them as if they had been crocodile pumps. She drew a long, astonished breath.

"Oh!"

Count Julius bowed. "Good morning."

Carmela stared. Count Julius looked from her to Lila, in her dishevelled overcoat, and back again. He said in a gentler voice, "You must tell me your name."

Holding on to the cellar doorpost with one hand, and her gas-mask with the other, Carmela made a deep unsteady curtsey.

"Carmela, sir."

"Charming," Count Julius said. He turned back to Lila. "Apart from provisions, I have brought something else that will please you. News of my nephew."

Lila held her breath. Count Julius smiled.

"My nephew Max."

# 16

COUNT JULIUS stayed three nights. On the day of his arrival, there was indeed, as threatened, a German raid as savage as the first one and which removed yet more of Miss de Vere's little hospital in Kalkara. Lila was actually at work when the raid began, and although the German aim was yet again to sink the aircraft carrier *Illustrious*, now moored in the Grand Harbour, high explosives were dropped all over the Three Cities, and a pall of black smoke, stifling and sickening, hung over the shattered streets. For almost six hours, Miss de Vere, Lila, Rosanna Saliba and all the Maltese nursing staff crouched with their patients in a makeshift shelter that had been hastily dug out of the sloping land towards Vittoriosa. It was far, far worse than being in the cellar at the Villa Zonda. With every scream and crash came the sickening certainty that the rock stratum above their heads simply couldn't hold, but must inevitably break in the end and bury them all under boulders as big as small houses. Miss de Vere did not want Lila to go home after the all clear.

"I must. Because of Pa."

"We will get a message to him somehow and I can't see how you are going to make the journey in any case."

"I know. But I must try. After that raid, particularly."

Miss de Vere considered her for a moment.

"I need every hand I can get."

"I know. I'll be back at eight. Earlier if you like. I just have to get back for a few hours."

"Lila — "

"Yes!"

"Is your father the only reason?"

Lila looked at her in the dusky light, attempting to make her look completely direct and open.

"Oh, of course."

There was a tiny pause.

"I see," Miss de Vere said. "Just remember, I want you back at first light."

It proved hopeless to try and reach the Villa Zonda. Lila's bicycle had vanished, no doubt by now a tangled heap under some masonry debris, and probably also now virtually useless in streets choked with rubble. For the same reason, no other vehicle, even moving cautiously in the blackout, could get through. The only hope would have been to get out into the countryside to the east and then try to work her way round, hitching lifts where she could, behind Tarxien and Qormi, but it soon became plain that that idea was hopeless. After an hour's fruitless and exhausting struggle, having stumbled round in circles and cut herself twice on shards of splintered glass, Lila gave up. Everything had gone — streets, houses, even the possibility of moving around at the simplest level. She stood for a moment leaning against one of the few remaining walls of the great Dominican church in Vittoriosa and watched the dim shapes of the rescue teams still digging persistently on in the ruins of the priory for survivors, and knew herself to be beyond tears. In fact beyond, at that moment, almost anything. "It's enough to be alive," Miss de Vere had said, at one point in that fearful day, to a desperately weeping woman. "That's enough for any of us." But was it, Lila wondered now, gazing up at the night sky, unbelievably innocent-looking after all the day had witnessed. Was it enough just to breathe and be? Or did that *have* to be enough; did she have to simply set her teeth and make it so?

She wrapped her coat tightly round her and sank down against the wall to the ground. No-one would find her here, no bossy warden would come and tell her to find shelter, because they were all too occupied just now. If she had to go back to the hospital — which she did — she would compensate herself with just ten minutes alone in this broken, holy place, with the night horizon still hideously glowing with the fires the bombs had left behind. She wouldn't look at them. She wouldn't look at anything. She pulled her coat up over her head and put her head down on her knees and wrapped her arms around them.

"Please," Lila said, inside the tent of her coat. "Oh please. *Please*."

* * *

"Can't offer you much," Pa said. He grinned. "It's rum or rum. Take your pick."

Count Julius was seated on a shabby brocade

chair with claw feet, in the salone. The blackout was up, and the salone was lit by a single kerosene lamp which threw out a weird harsh ring of light on their hands and faces, and the dusty table which held a squat black bottle and two imperfectly washed tumblers.

"Rum, I think," Count Julius said.

Pa pulled the stopper out of the bottle with a jerk.

"Nothing fancy. Get it from Belin Sultana."

"Ah," Count Julius said.

He wore the suit in which he had arrived, with the addition of a plaid travelling rug round his shoulders as a shawl. He looked perfectly shaved and brushed and not in the least as if he had spent the previous night in a Maltese peasant kitchen on a bed made from an old door balanced on a bench and two stools. There had been delicate moments in deciding where Count Julius should sleep. The salone or Pa's own bedroom were clearly the most fitting, but also the most exposed, and it was felt acutely by everybody that, war or no war, the least exposed place — the cellar — was entirely out of the question. The kitchen, where Count Julius had found Lila, asleep between a wooden milk pail and a backless chair with a candle in a bottle on it, was plainly, being close to the cellar but not actually in it, the best compromise. Teseo had devised his master a bed out of an old door found in an outhouse, padded it as best he could with the Count's own possessions, and retired to sleep in the Ford, from which he would not be parted. Count Julius said he had slept excellently on the door. It reminded him of the hard beds of his childhood, constructed in order to encourage a military bearing. When he got back to the Tabia Palace, he remarked, he would immediately take steps to find another door to sleep on.

He raised his glass to Pa.

"To our shared relief that Miss Cunningham is safe."

Pa closed his eyes briefly. His face, unwashed for several days, was now also thickly stubbled, and smudged with fatigue.

"Didn't sleep. Couldn't. Not a wink. Couldn't believe she stood a chance. Didn't believe it until the Saliba boy came."

"Miss de Vere is no risk taker. If Miss Cunningham had to be in any hands in these terrible times, let us be thankful they were the hands of Beatrix de Vere."

Pa took a swallow of rum.

"Good girl, my Lila."

"Very good."

"But never — " Pa paused, and laid his finger to the side of his nose. "Never quite — content with things. Mind you, things have been pretty bad, *are* pretty bad. All the same . . . "

He looked at Count Julius, and then he patted his chest.

"She wears his ring, you know. Round her neck here. Day and night."

Count Julius took the smallest sip from his glass, wincing faintly.

"Ah."

"Tell me," Pa said, "what's he doing, your

nephew Anton? What's he up to? Never writes. Something hush-hush?"

Count Julius put his glass down.

"Very."

"Thought so," Pa said. "Told her so, too. Told her — " he paused.

"What did you tell her, Mr Cunningham?"

Pa squirmed a little.

"Difficult . . . "

"I know. But do tell me. It's a matter that concerns me so much too."

Pa hesitated a moment and then he said, "Won't wash, you know. Won't do. Dreams and stuff — "

Count Julius leaned forward.

"My nephew Anton is, and I make no bones about it, the apple of his mother's eye. He may not be the elder, but he is everything to his mother. And my sister, Mr Cunningham, is a most forceful and strong-minded woman."

Pa winked.

Count Julius smiled at him. "As you remember."

"Lila thinks that boy is everything too," Pa said. "Everything. Sun, moon and stars."

"I know."

"And him? What about him? Playing games?"

"Not playing games, Mr Cunningham, but not facing reality either."

"What's reality, eh?"

Count Julius looked round the salone, at the neglected, overstuffed Edwardian furniture, at the stained walls, the dusty curtains hanging across the blacked-out windows.

199

"You will spare my having to spell it out, Mr Cunningham."

"Not good enough," Pa said quietly. "Not enough blood. Not enough money. Not good enough."

"We can wish things otherwise most earnestly but we can't make them so by wishing."

Pa threw the last of his glass of rum down his throat.

"And your other boy? The other nephew?"

"Max? Ah now, Max is much loved by his mother, but not so ardently cherished."

"*She* don't love him, though," Pa said.

Count Julius leaned back in a brocade chair.

"Max is to be made a pilot officer in the Royal Air Force. He is making every effort to be posted back to Malta, on anti-aircraft duty, and we have hopes that these recent raids will assist those efforts. I should hope that we in Malta are going to be very much on Mr Churchill's mind."

"I know a boy," Pa said abruptly, "good sort of boy. Boy that brought the message from Lila. Gone from schoolmastering to being a firewarden to manning a Bofors gun. Down at Senglea Point."

Count Julius watched him.

"Now there's a boy," Pa said. "Brave boy. Maltese. Good sort."

"But not perhaps," Count Julius said, slowly, "the sort of boy that dreams are made of."

Pa sighed. He looked across at Count Julius.

"Her mother was a dreamer. Dreamed of a settled life with four children and a motor car and the vicar to tea. I used to say to her, 'If that's what you wanted, why did you marry me?'"

Count Julius smiled.

"And why did she, do you think?"

Pa winked again. "To get away from her mother." He looked down at his empty glass, his expression suddenly forlorn, almost crushed. "I hope," he said, and there was abruptly nothing jaunty in his voice, "I hope Lila doesn't dream these dreams just to get away from *me*."

Just after Mdina and the Tabia Palace were deemed safe for Count Julius' return, and the Ford was being respectfully packed for his journey, Lila, dirty and grey with fatigue, pedalled slowly into the courtyard of the Villa Zonda on a borrowed bicycle. The family were enchanted, all the women surging out of the kitchen with little cries of thankfulness and welcome and Carmela in ecstasies. Spiru put on his gas-mask in her honour.

"I'm all right," Lila said, grateful and touched, "really I am. I'm filthy and I could sleep for a week, but I'm all right."

"You must eat," Doris said. "You *shall* eat. The Count brought such delicacies you can't imagine! We don't know what half of them are!"

"The labels on the jars are in French sometimes," Carmela said. "The English ones I can read *easily*. There is a whole duck squashed into a tin."

"Where's Pa?"

"Sleeping. In his own bed. He was up half the night with Count Julius."

Lila stared. "Was he?"

Doris shrugged. "A bottle of rum."

"Oh no!"

"Don't worry. The Count was very quiet this morning too."

Carmela said, "He wore silk pyjamas. In our *kitchen*."

Doris bridled slightly. "He said he slept excellently in our kitchen!"

Lila leaned against the wellhead. "Heavens."

"All is well," Doris said, "This is an emergency! It makes us all children of God together."

"I think," Lila said, "I'll go and sleep."

"You must *eat*."

"Afterwards."

"And wash," Carmela said sternly.

"Afterwards."

"Miss Cunningham!"

Lila turned a little. Advancing from the house in his homburg hat and carrying his fawn kid gloves, was Count Julius.

"My dear. We are so thankful for your safety. You have had an unspeakable time."

Lila smiled at him tiredly.

"Extraordinary perhaps, and certainly frightening and sad. But not unspeakable."

"I rejoice at your return. These good people here have looked after me so well."

"I'm so glad."

"And now I am permitted to return home. I have a foreboding I shall have to transfer the contents of my library to the cellars in the coming days. What a choice. All those precious books to be either burned by bombs or drowned by damp."

"Will — " Lila said and then paused. She took a breath and brushed a strand of hair away from her grimy face. "Will I see you again soon?"

There was a tiny pause.

"My dear! Naturally. How can we live four miles apart on a war-torn island and not meet? I am so grateful for the shelter of the Villa Zonda." He turned and smiled at the group of women behind him. "I am so grateful to you *all*. Perhaps," he glanced at Carmela, "you would convey how grateful I am, in your own language?"

There was another little pause, no less awkward than the first, and then Count Julius bowed to Lila, and walked away with measured step towards the waiting Ford.

"He never took his hat off," Carmela said, her voice full of reproof.

★ ★ ★

"I am sorry," Angelo Saliba said.

He leaned against the wellhead in the courtyard where Lila had leant two hours earlier, and turned a dirty cap in his hands.

"What for?" Pa said.

"For coming again without announcement."

"Don't need announcement," Pa said. "Not here. Not with me."

"I — I knew you were all alive after all," Angelo said, bowing his thanks. "I knew that.

203

I just needed — to see."

Pa glanced at him.

"She's asleep, old son."

"I — I am glad to hear it."

Pa leaned on the stick he had taken to using. It had belonged to old Spiru, and the knob at the top was shiny from handling.

"I think . . ."

Angelo waited.

"I think, like you, she's seen things she'd rather never have seen. I saw too many myself. In the last to-do — 'fourteen to 'eighteen. So she won't talk about them. So we can't ask her how she is. So we have to wait. Be patient."

Angelo turned his cap slowly, fingering the torn place where the peak was parting company from the top.

"I miss my school."

"Of course you do."

"I don't really know what teaching they are having now. Of course everyone is doing their best but it is all so difficult. They are in the shelters all day and night just now, the poor children." He bit his lip. "I should like to be with them."

Pa said, "You're doing a grand job where you are. *Grand*. Proud of you."

"Thank you, sir."

"Don't 'sir' me," Pa said. "Don't 'sir' anyone. Not with what you're doing for us all."

There was a silence. Angelo glanced up at the clear winter sky and the fading light, and sighed. Then he rolled up his cap and put it in his pocket and stood upright.

"I must return. Will you . . . "

Pa waited.

"Will you say I — I am glad for her safety? When she wakes."

Pa nodded.

"Thank you," Angelo said.

When he had gone, Pa limped over to the kitchen door and looked in. The table was half covered with the extraordinary provisions Count Julius had brought from the Tabia Palace, and the women were standing round and gazing, as if transfixed.

"Blackout, girls," Pa said. "Time for blackout."

He went on to the courtyard staircase, where Carmela sat with a candle, wrapped in a blanket and apparently earnestly reading.

"School's done," Pa said. "Blow that out."

Carmela read doggedly on.

"Blackout is *orders*," Pa said. He stooped, leaning on his stick, and blew out the candle.

"Need to save those. Candles. For the nights."

"Was that Angelo Saliba by the well?"

"It was," Pa said, "*if* it's any business of yours."

"When I marry," Carmela said, "it will be a prince with gloves and a car from America."

"Not you too," Pa said.

He stumped slowly on up past her to the landing. It was very quiet, with that unnatural quietness there was these anxious days, between raids. He had to wake Lila, however tired she was, and get her down to the cellar before the light went, taking with them, he supposed, those fancy jars of stuffed quail, and the apricots in

205

brandy. Nice chap, the Count, nice chap in many ways. Shouldn't take against a chap just because he wore silk socks and had a taste for the kind of food that went out with the Arabian Nights.

He went into the salone, to put up the blackout. The empty rum bottle still stood there, and the two tumblers on the dusty table. Clear those away tomorrow, in the morning, in the daylight. Do it first thing, before Lila saw them. Lila. Pa paused, shaking his head, remembering the night before. Poor little Lila.

# 17

THE rain was falling, as it had at Christmas, steady cold rain turning the powdered masonry in the ruined streets to a sticky yellow mud. By day, the German raids continued, though none quite as fierce as those in which they had attempted to sink the *Illustrious*, and between them, and at night, an eerie silence fell as if all human life had indeed been obliterated. Miss de Vere moved her little hospital permanently into the shelters despite the fact that the only water supply was two standpipes, one at either entrance, from which everything had to be carried in buckets.

Lila now worked three-day shifts, sleeping in the shelter during snatched hours, with twelve hours off to go home if she could be spared. The shelter itself was a long series of roughly hewn little rooms cut out of the rock, crudely propped with timbers, each room opening into another to minimize the effect of bomb blast. It was dark inside, and airless, and increasingly full of inevitable smells, but the patients, those local people not considered acute enough cases to warrant transfers to the big hospitals, seemed to mind none of those things, but only the confinement.

"I must return," they'd say to Lila, "to St Lawrence Street, or St Scholastica Street — you know it? — and see what's left of my house. I know there won't be much, but I must see it. I was born there, you know, and so was my father. They say the Germans have bombed the old auberges of the Knights of St John. Well that's sad, to be sure, but it's my house I worry about, it's my house I want to see."

Every day, whatever happened, a newsboy came panting round with a canvas satchel of copies of the *Times of Malta*, and at midday a group of orderlies were despatched to the nearest victory kitchen, set up by the government to provide one hot meal a day, to collect the hospital's ration of bread and goat stew, cooked sometimes on wood from bombed-out buildings, but invariably tasting strongly of paraffin.

At the Villa Zonda, things were less subterranean, but little different. Relations of the family, bombed out of the Three Cities, had joined the days in the kitchen and courtyard, and the nights in the cellar, adding to the burden on the ever-dwindling food and fuel supply. Pa brought all the smaller, worthless pieces of furniture down from the upper rooms to the courtyard and chopped them up resolutely for firewood. When Lila was on duty, he added a pile of his pictures to the stack, much to Spiru's horror at seeing the boats and ships and spaces of sky and sea splinter under his axe.

"More use this way," Pa said. "Never were much use as they were. You ask Lila."

Lila came back and forth, tired and grimy and hungry. The grinding anxiety of the days and weeks prevented most conversation being about anything but the most practical things, and Lila would huddle immediately under the blankets with her clothes on, and sleep as if felled by a blow, until it was time to go back on duty, or the siren sounded. The family saved her an egg if they could, or a rabbit joint from a stew, or a slice of precious bread smeared with a little of last year's honey — and it was the last year, because the bees had fled and the hive stood dusty and empty in a corner of the near-exhausted vegetable patch.

Carmela made her own efforts. "I'm doing the reading."

"Oh good."

"Every day I do it. Not at school, but I do it. And the number book, every day."

"That's wonderful."

"I will do it every day until the Germans go away. My father said they are bloody fascists and my mother crossed herself. What is a fascist?"

"Someone who is against socialism and wants to win by force, and sometimes violence."

"And bloody," Carmela said reverently, savouring the word, "is blasphemy."

Very occasionally, Lila would wake before Pa came to shake her gently. It was disturbing when this happened, because it gave her time to think, and thinking was the least desirable activity just now. There was so little she knew, even less she could be certain of, and still less she could hope for. You could work yourself to the bone for other people but, unless you were what Doris would call a blessed sainted martyr, there was always some little voice inside asking for some small thing for oneself. And all she asked, all she ever asked, was that this ring she wore so faithfully, day in, day out, signified that there was at least a glimmer ahead, the merest glimmer of a promise even if there couldn't be the promise itself. The thought that that tiny glimmer might not even be there made Lila feel quite desperate.

Pa found her one sunset, lying awake and staring at the ceiling.

"Chop chop. Blackout time."

"I know."

"You on duty tonight?"

"Yes."

She turned her head to look at him.

"Tonight and the next night and the next."

He came closer to the bed and looked down at her. He said, in a much quieter tone than usual, "You bearing up?"

"I think so. Just like anyone else."

He came closer still, and sat down crookedly on the side of the bed.

"Hard. Isn't it?"

"Yes, very. Especially as we don't know how long it will go on."

"Just wondered — " he stopped.

"What did you wonder, Pa?"

"Whether — " he eyed her, "whether we should try and get you home."

Lila sat up, pushing her tangled hair off her face.

"Why? Why do you ask?"

"Wasn't prying," Pa said firmly, "just found it."

"What? What did you find?"

"Doing a geography lesson with Carmela. Showing her where England was. Where we lived. Opened the atlas — and out it fell."

There was a silence. Lila pleated up the top blanket between her fingers.

"My letter to the Perriams."

"Yes."

"That was nearly six weeks ago."

"Might mean it still. Mightn't you? Only asking."

"How would I get home?"

"Not sure. Plane maybe? Ask Count Julius to pull strings. It's a risk, but then, everything's a risk just now."

Lila turned away from him and began to struggle out of bed on the far side.

"Pa?"

"Yes."

"Thank you."

"Don't thank me. Should have seen. Should have noticed." He stood up, unsteadily, feeling for his stick. "Only so much anyone can stand."

Lila put her hand up to her breastbone.

"Do you think — "

"What?"

"Do you think — he's still in England?"

"If it's hush-hush, more than likely."

She said suddenly, on a kind of cry, "Why doesn't he write?"

Pa said slowly, "Some don't. Some men. Can't do it. And war. Well, war means nothing's normal."

"Sometimes," Lila said, "I think I'm forgetting

what he's like. Sometimes I think I'm just remembering what I imagined, not what happened." She paused. "And not much did happen, really. Did it?"

"Don't know," Pa said. "Doesn't need much, sometimes. If it's right."

"It *was* right," she said. "It was lovely. It was perfect."

He grunted. "You think about it," he said. "You think about going home. The Perriams'll have you, they'll give you a home. England may be almost as bad as this, but there'll always be a home for you, at the Perriams."

Lila stood up.

"Pa?"

He looked at her.

"Wouldn't you be coming too? If I decide to go home, won't you come with me?"

He looked down, at his wooden leg, at his stick, at the floor where the dust now lay as thick as grit in places.

"No," he said gently, "I wouldn't do that. Not now," and then he turned away from her and limped out onto the landing.

* * *

There was a dawn raid the next morning. The rain had cleared and as the early February sun rose slowly into a pale sky, the Stukas came screaming out from Sicily, and the harbour front exploded again in flames and smoke and choking clouds of debris. The raid lasted almost two hours, and when it was over, Lila and Rosanna

Saliba, working steadily through the patients in the shelter to count them, discovered that a man they had all admired for his steady cheerfulness, and whose leg wound was sufficiently recovered for him to have soon joined his family out in the countryside, had had a heart attack, and was sitting against the stone wall, quite dead, his rosary between his fingers. It was, oddly in the middle of such universal distress, deeply distressing. They carried his body outside the shelter, and laid it in the shade of a scrubby thorn bush, crossing his hands on his chest, and closing his lids over his sightless eyes. Then they covered him with a grey blanket. It was all they could do, until the orderlies were back on duty.

Two hours later, Lila found herself in sudden tears. It wasn't just the quiet weeping of a private grief, but something altogether more convulsing, so much so that she had to put down the slop buckets she was sluicing and hurry out into the open air, in order to find something to lean against, to support her. It was deeply embarrassing, but she seemed to have no control over these wrenching, heaving sobs, nor to have a handkerchief either. All she could do was to lean against the rough yellow rock wall of the shelter and wait for this tumult to subside.

"Are you ill?" someone said.

She shook her head violently, throwing her arm up over her face. She felt a hand on her shoulder.

"Come on," Rosanna Saliba said. "Come on,

sit down. You're tired. You're hungry."

"So are you!" Lila wailed.

"We break at different moments."

"I'm not breaking!"

"Sit," Rosanna said. The hand on Lila's shoulder pressed harder. "Sit. Tell me what it is."

Lila subsided slowly and shudderingly to the ground. The stones and weeds outside the shelter were still wet from the rain, but the damp felt clean and reviving.

Lila said unsteadily, "There's nothing to tell. Anyway you wouldn't want to hear."

"Why wouldn't I?"

"Because — "

Rosanna waited.

"Because you only work with me because you have to."

Rosanna seated herself on a small boulder opposite Lila. Even in a dirty flour-sack apron she looked neat. She folded her hands in her lap.

"We could be friends," Rosanna said, "if we tried. But I have always thought that you didn't want to try."

Lila picked up the cleanest corner of her own apron and blew her nose on it.

"Last night my father asked me if I wanted to go home."

"Home!"

"Yes. Home to England. To the house of the people I used to work for."

"Is England safe?"

"Not very."

"Safer than here?"

"Perhaps a little. In places."

Rosanna said, "Are you exhausted by being frightened? Do you want to go where you won't be frightened so much?"

Lila sighed.

"I don't know. I mean, I know I long, like everyone, for it all to be over, but I don't know if that's why I want to go home."

There was a silence. Rosanna, hands folded, feet together, regarded Lila steadily for some moments. Then she said carefully, "Perhaps I shouldn't mention my brother . . . " Lila waited.

"But I must tell you that that was why he wanted to give you the brass dolphin. Maybe it was a little bit romantic, but he hoped you might be starting to feel that Malta was beginning to be home." She leaned forward. "Did you love your home in England?"

Lila gave a shaky smile.

"Not very much."

"And here? The Villa Zonda?"

"I — I'm sort of used to it, I suppose. I've grown very fond of the family, of Carmela."

"Could you leave them?" Rosanna said. "Could you leave them now, in this war, and go back to England?"

"I don't know."

"And your father?"

Lila looked at Rosanna directly for the first time.

"He wants to stay here. He wouldn't come with me."

"And you could leave him?" She stood up. "There must be something very strong in England to make you think of going back. Without him."

Lila took a breath and lifted her chin a little. "There is. Or at least, there might be."

"Only you," Rosanna said, and her voice hardened, "can decide. Only you can know which is the right thing to choose."

Lila stood too.

"The *right* thing. You sound like Miss de Vere."

Rosanna came up suddenly very close to Lila, and pushed her face into Lila's, her dark eyes blazing.

"Yes," she said, "yes! There is duty, Miss English Lila, there is duty for all of us, men *and* women, as well as heart's desire!"

★ ★ ★

Their usual newsboy was late that day with the *Times of Malta*. He came scrambling down the slope to the shelter, caked in mud, explaining that the last raid had blocked his usual route in several crucial places so that his round had taken three times as long. He was a wiry boy, perhaps thirteen or fourteen, with the usual dark Maltese skin and hair, and uneven teeth of startling whiteness.

Lila took the paper from him.

"We did wonders today!" the boy said proudly. "We got so many of them! Five out of every wing of German planes!"

"That's amazing."

"Carrying thousand-kilo bombs they were! Fifty to a wing. And they've lost some prize officers — in the newsroom they could hear German radio asking for news of them!"

Lila smiled at him. "That's wonderful."

"We're going to win!" the boy said. "We are! We've got ninety-two anti-aircraft batteries out there, and we'll win!"

Lila put her hand in her pocket. In it lay the hard bread roll that had come as part of her midday meal ration from the victory kitchen. She held it out to the boy.

"Here."

"Hey!"

"You take it," Lila said. "You need it."

"Hey," he said again, "thanks!" and seizing the roll, was off again up the steep slope above the shelter, his canvas bag banging on his back.

Lila shook the paper open. 'Parachute mines dropped — most intercepted', ran one headline and below it, 'All young men aged 21 to be called for military service on March 3rd'. Then, below that, in smaller type, 'Significant buildings to be requisitioned for the military. Four palaces in Mdina to become army headquarters as Malta's defences are significantly strengthened.' Lila's gaze narrowed. 'Count Julius Tabia-is-Sultan has offered the Tabia Palace as an officers' mess.'

Lila swallowed. An officers' mess! In the Tabia Palace. The Tabia Palace full of English officers who just might know of, even have met,

217

or heard of — she shut her eyes briefly, and folded up the paper. The chances were tiny, but they were there, and being there was all she'd ever asked of chance. She turned and hurried back into the shelter, thrusting the paper at Rosanna as she passed her.

"It's wonderful," Lila said, "we've done brilliantly. We shot down five out of fifty Stukas this morning."

Rosanna paused in checking the fever chart. "*We?*"

Lila laughed. She gave Rosanna a quick glance and hurried on.

"Oh yes," she said.

# 18

"AEROPLANES," Pa said. "English aeroplanes. There are now over two hundred English aeroplanes in Malta to fight the Hun."

Spiru nodded. He was sitting cross-legged in the dust under the carob tree in the courtyard, close to Pa's stool. The June sun was bright beyond the tree's dense shade, and the last two hens of the family's flock were scratching listlessly round the base of the old wellhead. They looked thin and scruffy now, and one of them had lost most of her neck feathers.

"Planes," Spiru said. He had given up wearing his gas-mask now, but still carried it about with him, like a good luck charm.

"Hurricanes," Pa said. "Planes called Hurricanes."

Spiru nodded again. He spoke in a mixture of Maltese and Pa's staccato brand of English. "Planes," he repeated, "planes. Bang. Bomb." And then, after a pause, "Hun."

"That's it," Pa said. "That's about the picture."

He turned the piece of wood he was holding over in his hand, tapping it with his penknife. He'd been going to make it into a boat for Spiru, but now it seemed to him that it would make a better plane than a boat. It would make a Hurricane. He could make a Hurricane for Spiru

219

with English markings. It would give him, Pa, something to do. Even with all the help he gave Doris, and his newfound capacities as vegetable grower and shoe mender and coat patcher, there wasn't enough to do, and during the last six months, when the raids had been so heavy, it was peculiarly difficult not to have enough to do.

"I do worry," Pa said to Spiru. "I worry about Lila. Shouldn't. Pointless. Quite pointless. But can't stand seeing her waiting. Waiting for something that doesn't happen."

Spiru began to pick up small pebbles that lay around him in the dust, and to drop them down the air tube of his gas-mask.

"Bang," he said quietly, as each one fell.

"She's been there," Pa said. "She's been up to the palace, to the officers' mess. Found some young chaps to take her. *Pleased* to take her. 'Course they were. But no-one knew anything. She didn't say, but I could tell. If I make you this plane, old lad, I'll have to make you a Stuka too. To shoot down."

Spiru looked up.

"Stuka."

"That's it. Stuka. Hun plane."

Spiru looked away again. He was a placid child, used to the slow exploration of his confined world. His gaze travelled over the wellhead and the scratching hens and the peeling, neglected façade of the Villa Zonda to the gateway from the courtyard to the drive beyond.

"Man," he said calmly.

220

"What," Pa said, "in your plane? Want a chap in your plane?"

Spiru put down his gas-mask and got, without hurry, to his feet.

"Man," he said again.

Pa looked up from his whittling. A tall dark man in RAF uniform stood uncertainly in the gateway, his cap in his hands.

"Jeepers creepers," Pa said. "Man indeed!"

He stooped for his stick, waving wildly with his free hand.

"Halloa, halloa! Come in!"

The man came a little way into the courtyard. Spiru, towing his gas-mask in its box like a dog on wheels, advanced hospitably towards him.

"Mr Cunningham? Mr Cunningham — it's Max. Max Ferroferrata."

"By George! By George and Jove, so it is!"

Pa stumped forward, holding out his hand.

"Well! Well, I'm blowed. Blowed and dashed. Never thought — never hoped — *well*. How are you?"

Max took the proffered hand and bowed a little.

"Very well, sir." He indicated his uniform. "As you see."

"Wings! Pilot Officer Ferroferrata!"

Max smiled. "The other boys just call me Ferret."

Spiru said, "Bang!" with great energy.

Max looked down.

"Spiru," Pa said, "the baby of the house. My little shadow. We come out here and count the planes."

221

Max smiled down at Spiru.

"I hope you'll now have a lot more English planes to count." He held his cap out. "Want to try that on?"

Spiru's eyes shone. He glanced at Pa.

"Go ahead, old son. If the gentleman says you may, you may."

Spiru took the cap with awe. He inspected it very slowly, and then, equally slowly, lifted it and put it on his head. It engulfed him. He stood there inside it, quite upright, blinded by its size, and rapturous.

"When did you land?" Pa said.

"Two days ago, sir. At Hal Far. It's quite quiet down there. We're billeted in Hal Far House which feels odd because I remember going to parties there. We're four to a room." He smiled a little. "Waiting for some action."

Pa squinted at him.

"What are you sir-ing me for?"

"Habit," Max said and then, with a shy glance, "it should have been a habit before." He looked round him. "How have you all been?"

"All still here," Pa said. "But it's been rough. Six months of raids now. Food not so plentiful. All the boys from the family down with the AA guns. So it's me, and the girls and — " he gestured towards Spiru, still motionless under Max's cap, "and him."

"And Lila?" Max said.

"Working for Miss de Vere. In her first-aid set up."

"Is she all right?"

"No," Pa said.

There was a pause. Spiru put his hands either side of Max's cap and lifted it by inches off his head. His face was scarlet.

"I don't understand you," Max said.

"She wears his ring," Pa said. "She waits for letters. She waits for news. No news. No letters. Waiting isn't good for you. Stops you living."

Spiru sat down in the dust at Max's feet, and laid the cap across his knees, cradling it like a baby.

"Sorry," Max said. "Sorry, I just don't get — "

"Your brother," Pa said. "Your brother sent her a ring. And a flower. It gave her hope. She keeps hoping."

Max looked down at Spiru.

"I didn't know this."

"Didn't you?"

"No, I — "

"Haven't you seen him? Your brother? You've been in England together for two years and you haven't seen him?"

"I've been at Cranwell — "

Pa grunted.

"I'm sorry," Max said. "It's useless to say so, but I'm sorry. I'd no idea . . . "

Pa sighed. He banged his stick against his wooden leg.

"Well," he said, "there's a thing."

"I'm afraid," Max said, "I have no message. Nothing."

Pa stopped banging his wooden leg, and looked up at Max.

"Well," he said again. "Well, Mr Pilot Officer

223

Ferret. You'd better get yourself down to Kalkara and tell her so, in person."

★ ★ ★

Rosanna Saliba was spreading washed dressing cloths and bandages on the rocks outside the shelter to dry. Miss de Vere disapproved of this practice — she disapproved of anything that might even begin to diminish the effectiveness of Malta's war effort, and that included the visibility of white bandages on yellow rocks — but as she was not at the hospital just now, Rosanna felt she could safely be ignored. Anyway, hot rocks were easily the fastest drying method and she badly needed a moment alone in the open air. It was so stuffy in the shelter, and so crowded, and the rising summer heat made the afternoons hard on everyone's tempers. Lila had fainted the day before, just keeled over without warning, with her arms full of bedding. Miss de Vere had said it was hunger, but Rosanna remembered her mother telling her about reviving Lila the very first day she landed in Malta, and had fainted on a pile of fishing nets. She had been being pestered by some children. Angelo had come to her rescue, and then she had fainted.

"The mind couldn't manage," Rosanna's mother had said then, recounting the incident. "It was hot, to be sure, and she had been sick on the ship coming. But in the end, it was the mind. You could see it, in her face."

You could see it yesterday, Rosanna thought.

You could see some shadow in her, in those moments before her consciousness came back and she started apologizing to everyone. There was a great deal in Lila that Rosanna disliked heartily, but there was also something that intrigued her, and roused her pity. She was like someone on a journey who didn't know where they were going, they were just travelling on hope, and hope was wearing thin. Rosanna had a pretty good idea where Lila's hopes lay, and an equally low opinion of those hopes, but that didn't prevent her from feeling both curiosity and even compassion. Whatever pain Lila might be in, and whatever Rosanna's opinion of that pain, Lila was bearing it in silence.

Someone shouted from the rough path that ran along the slope above the shelter. Rosanna straightened up and shaded her eyes against the sun.

"Is this the Kalkara First Aid Centre?"

It was a man. An English-sounding voice.

"Yes," Rosanna called back.

"I'm looking for Lila Cunningham."

"She's here," Rosanna said. She allowed her voice no inflection. "She works here."

"Thanks!" the man shouted. "I've got a gharry waiting. I'll come down."

Rosanna stood and watched him. He was tall and in uniform. He came down the rough path fast and with agility, leaping the last few feet to land beside her. He was, she couldn't help noticing at once, handsome as well as tall. Tall, dark and handsome. The Hollywood dream.

"I'm Max," he said, "Max Ferroferrata. I

225

knew Lila before the war."

Rosanna didn't smile.

"She's on duty," she said. "She's on duty all day. But I'll fetch her."

"I'd be grateful," Max said. He paused, and then he said, "I'd be grateful to know your name too."

She hesitated, then she said, without grace, "Rosanna Saliba."

"Ah. From Valleta?"

She took a step away. She felt full of resentment but couldn't decide at whom.

"I was born in Grand Harbour."

"A true Maltese."

She shrugged.

He said, "I was born in Geneva, but my mother is Maltese. We come from Mdina."

Rosanna shrugged again.

"I'm proud to be Maltese," Max said. "This war has made me proud."

"I'll get Lila," Rosanna said.

She went past Max into the dark stuffiness of the shelter. Lila was sitting by the straw-stuffed mattress of a woman whose right arm had been hit by a shower of splintered glass. Every day, and twice if there was time, her dressings had to be removed, and yet more tiny shards of glass that had worked themselves to the surface had to be picked out with tweezers. The woman submitted to these painful probings in absolute silence. Her husband and son had been buried alive when their house had been hit by a bomb, and for her, the point of life was over. An armful of glass was simply irrelevant.

Rosanna crouched down beside Lila.

"You have a visitor."

Lila didn't look up. The cloth spread on her knees was covered with tiny bloodstained chips of glass.

"I don't know anyone."

"He says you do. He says you knew each other before the war. He's in RAF uniform. He says he's called Max."

Lila's hand holding the tweezers froze inches from the woman's arm.

"Max."

"Yes. You know who he is. You do."

Slowly, Lila's other hand fell from the woman's arm.

"Sorry," she whispered.

Rosanna put a hand out for the tweezers.

"I'll do it. I'll take over."

"Just for five minutes."

"Yes."

"Sorry," Lila said again.

"Don't be sorry," Rosanna said. "Just be quick."

Lila picked up the cloth of glass pieces and stood up.

"Thank you."

"Just hurry," Rosanna said, "will you? I'll cover for you, but hurry." She took the cloth and then she said, with an edge that was almost spiteful, "You don't want to keep the young Baron waiting, do you?"

★ ★ ★

227

"Lila!" Max said. He held his arms out. She stood back, dazzled by the sunlight and by the unexpectedness of him. "Lila!"

She stepped forward and he put his arms round her, right round her and held her firmly, flour-sack apron and all.

"It's wonderful to see you!"

She said, "I didn't know you were coming, I didn't know — "

"Nobody did. We're being flown in from various carriers, in batches. Force H is escorting us. I came in two nights ago. I've been to see Uncle Julius and your father and now you."

"You've been to see Pa!"

"Of course. Why not?" Max dropped his arms. "It's been two years."

"I know."

He put his hands on her shoulders and scrutinized her.

"You look worn out."

"Thanks a million."

"You've been a heroine, though."

"No, I haven't. I've just done what everyone else has done. Or tried to."

Max said seriously, "I'm really pleased to see you."

She looked at him properly for the first time. He looked wonderful. There was no other word for it. Just wonderful. His face had settled and matured, and his uniform — so new, so clean — gave him a kind of authority, as well as taking away the slight air of the dilettante that had always hung around him in civilian clothes. She said, laughing ruefully, "We all look so awful."

"No. You don't. You do look tired but you look admirable. You are admirable. Everybody thinks so. Churchill does. So does the King."

"Oh, the King!"

"Yes, the King. We're going to try and get some supply ships in from the east now. Get some more food in." He took his hands from her shoulders and picked up one of hers instead. "Lila."

"Yes?"

"I know what you want from me, but I haven't got it. I haven't got anything."

Lila swallowed. She looked away for a moment at the ragged rows of dressing cloths drying in the sun.

"Have — have you seen him?"

"No."

"Do you know where he is?"

There was a little pause and then Max said, "No. Not exactly."

"Is it secret?"

"Yes. Yes, I suppose so."

"Is what he is doing secret?"

"Lila," Max said, folding her hand between both his, "don't ask me any more questions because I don't know or I can't tell you."

"He told me to wait," Lila said. "I know it was ages ago, but he never said stop waiting. So I haven't. I don't want to. I'll wait for ever, if I have to."

Max swung her hand a little.

"I've come to distract you."

"What?"

He jerked his head upward.

"I've got a gharry up there. I was going to take you to bathe."

"Bathe!" Lila said. Her face was illuminated. "Bathe! Oh Max, oh Max, I'd *love* to. But I can't."

"I know. I see that. But I'll come back for you. I'll come back and take you bathing and to have a drink and to see Uncle Julius and maybe we'll go riding. Or dancing. What about that? What about dancing with me, Lila?"

# 19

"WELL," Count Julius said, "and what do you think my sister would say?" They were standing by the open windows of the tapestry room in the Tabia Palace, looking down into the courtyard. The flowering shrubs were still there, the roses and the jasmine and plumbago, and the dolphins still played in their fountain, but the graceful benches had gone, and the weathered urns of lilies, and in their place were regimented groups of khaki canvas chairs, set round card tables with huge white china ashtrays in the middle. Behind them, the tapestry room no longer had its tapestries. The long tables had lost their carpets too and were covered with lengths of heavy green cloth, resembling blanket. The gilded leather portfolios of prints and drawings had been replaced by newspapers, packs of cards and more enormous ashtrays, and every other available square foot of space was taken up with clumps of chairs, canvas chairs like those in the courtyard, and a strange assembly of armchairs and sofas of all shapes and sizes.

"We had to take the tapestries down," Count Julius said, "after the first mess dinner party. The nymphs, which you will remember, proved an irresistible target. Why do the English find it so hard to enjoy themselves without throwing food?"

"The Australians like it, too," Max said gently. He was watching Lila. She was wearing a dark blue dress with a white collar he remembered her wearing before the war, when she was still working for his uncle. It had hung rather awkwardly on her then, given her a diffident, schoolgirlish air, but now it rather became her, even fitted her better, as if the body underneath it, for all its deprivations, had more assurance. Lila must have had that dress five years. He thought of his mother. The only garments his mother kept for five years were her sables.

"Where do you live?" Lila said to Count Julius. "I mean how can you live, with the house like this?"

"Teseo and I have withdrawn to the kitchen quarters. I sleep in the room that used to belong to my sister's housekeeper. I find I rather like it. My own bedroom, you see, now has three officers in it, and my library, four. We have moved the books to the cellar." He glanced at Max. "So far, I have managed to keep your mother's bedroom sacrosanct. I have declared that no-one under the rank of colonel shall have it, but that I know your mother would definitely prefer a brigadier or, better still, a general."

Max smiled. Lila said diffidently, "Have you heard — ?"

"From America? Oh, indeed. My sister is spending the winters in Washington and the summers in California. She is of course already fund-raising for the rebuilding of Malta, after the war." He glanced again at Max and to Lila there seemed something significant in his glance, as if some private signal was passing between them. "A formidable fund-raiser, your mother."

Max moved away from the window. He was in civilian clothes, shorts and a dark blue shirt, the kind of clothes that most of the young soldiers and airmen on the island wore off duty.

He said, "I'm going to take Lila down to bathe. And then we'll try and find dinner somewhere. She's done nothing but work for months. May I borrow the Ford?"

Count Julius smiled at Lila.

"No."

"Uncle — "

"I have, like everyone else, almost no petrol. And I am extremely selfish about what I do have. You'll have to take a gharry."

Max looked at Lila and shrugged. "Sorry."

"I don't mind. I don't mind at all. I haven't even been in a car for two years."

Count Julius leaned forward and patted her arm.

"You are an example to us all, my dear. You put us all to shame."

Max put a hand under Lila's elbow, and held it.

"Don't patronize her, Uncle."

Count Julius smiled at Lila. His face, she noticed, had got thinner, and his teeth, by contrast, looked sharper and somehow less civilized. He gave a little bow. "I wouldn't dare."

★ ★ ★

233

"You can't imagine," Lila said, "how wonderful this is. How delicious and lovely and wonderful."

They were sitting side by side drying off on a towel on the beach, with two bottles of beer half buried in the sand by their feet to keep them upright. They had swum for half an hour in the clear, cool sea watching the afternoon light change on the great cliffs running away to the west and — in Lila's case at least — feeling that the sea was gently peeling layers and layers of fatigue and anxiety and grime away, dissolving months and months of tension.

She lifted her tangled, salt-damp hair off her shoulders and pushed it behind her neck, to feel the last sea drops in it slide down her skin.

"You've let your hair grow," Max said.

"I sort of forgot it. I suppose I could cut it myself, or get Carmela to, but it doesn't seem to matter. And it's easier, longer. You can tie it up out of the way for work."

"It suits you," Max said. He picked up his shirt from the sand and took a packet of cigarettes from the breast pocket. He offered one to Lila. She shook her head.

"I smoked like a chimney at Cranwell. Got so bored at times. It'll be the same here, if we don't get some action soon. Would you like to see my machine?"

"I'd love to."

"We all look after our own. I run it up most days, and test the magnetos. It's all right while it's dry like this, but I dread to think what'll happen when it rains; we'll all be bogged down in the mud. I can't imagine why we didn't think of building underground hangars, before the war."

Lila put her arms round her knees.

"Do you love flying?"

"Yes."

"More than anything?"

Max looked at her.

"More than a lot of things. I haven't — well, I haven't done much in my life before, that you could say was useful. Neither of us — did."

Lila laid her cheek sideways on her knees and looked at him.

"Do we talk about Anton?"

He blew out a cloud of smoke.

"If you want to."

"I did," she said, and then she stopped. She looked at Max's hand, holding his cigarette. "I did most terribly but now I find I don't — at least not so much."

He said slowly, "Maybe that's just as well since there's so little I can tell you."

She straightened up.

"I don't quite understand all this mystery about him."

"War," Max said shortly.

"That's what everyone says."

"Then you must believe them." He turned his gaze from the distant blue horizon where the sea met the sky and looked directly at her.

"You aren't wearing his ring."

Lila's hand went up automatically to her breastbone.

"I took it off. Before we swam."

"And will you leave it off?"

She stared at him.

"Heavens. Why do you ask that?"

He shrugged.

"Independence, maybe."

"Independence?"

"Just showing yourself you can live without him."

"Oh," Lila said quietly, "you too. You and your uncle and my father."

Max stubbed his cigarette out in the sand.

"I'm on your side, Lila."

"Are you?"

He took her hand.

"Absolutely."

She said, rather uncertainly, "That's nice to hear."

Max leaned forward and put his free hand under her chin, and then kissed her lightly on the mouth.

"I mean it. Absolutely. And now we're going back into the sea, and after that, I'm going to find something other than goat stew to feed you on, even if it kills me."

★ ★ ★

Moonlight lay on the courtyard at the Villa Zonda in silvery pools, making even its workaday, battered appearance almost romantic. Lila came softly round the corner from the drive, holding her still damp bathing suit rolled in a towel, and found Pa sitting on his stool in the kitchen doorway.

"Cellar's terrible," he said. "Smells like a

236

monkey's armpit. Couldn't breathe. Sometimes you wonder — "

"What, Pa?"

"What you're saving your life *for*."

Lila sat down on the step of the kitchen doorway.

"I've been dancing."

"Holy smoke," Pa said.

"In another cellar. In the cellar of the Phoenicia Hotel. We had corned beef and warm Spanish champagne, and then we danced."

"You and Pilot Officer Ferret?"

"Yes."

"Good," Pa said.

Lila leaned her cheek against the stone doorpost. It was still faintly warm from the day's sun. Max had kissed her twice more, once on the dance floor and again, in a more considered way, when he left her at the gate of the Villa Zonda.

"I know you're on duty now for three days," he said, "but I know where to find you, and I'll be down to interrupt you, believe me."

"I feel — so *different*," Lila said to Pa. "I can't remember when I felt like this before."

"Needed it," Pa said, "didn't you? Needed a break. Needed to go dancing. Your mother liked dancing. Now — why would she do that?"

"What, like dancing?"

"No. Marry a chap with a wooden leg if she liked dancing?"

They both looked out into the moonlit courtyard, at the shaggy black shadows cast by the carob tree, and the wellhead, which had seen

237

all those long, long centuries before inventions such as aeroplanes were even thought of.

"Do you think of her much, Pa?"

"Seem to. Just lately. Didn't do very well by her. Meant to, but didn't."

"Am I like her?" Lila said.

"No," Pa said. "Except for the dreaming."

Lila stood up slowly, and stretched. "I don't need to dream tonight."

Pa grunted.

"And I'm going to sleep in my own bed."

He looked up at her. He was grinning.

"Don't blame you."

She stooped and kissed him.

"'Night, Pa."

* * *

"I gather," Miss de Vere said, "that the eldest Ferroferrata is back."

"Yes."

"And much improved."

"He was always nice."

"Those bits of him," Miss de Vere remarked, "that his mother hadn't managed to ruin."

Even Miss de Vere, Lila thought, had lost weight. She sat behind her improvised desk in the shelter and Lila could see that her customary white summer suit — now inevitably dingy — hung on her in considerable folds. She had her account book open, one of the long, maroon-covered books in which she recorded every expenditure, from the wages she paid her helpers and orderlies to the last box of matches

238

or roll of gauze bandage.

"I always do it, every day," she had told Lila. "My father did it, and so do I. 'Trixie,' he said to me, 'Trixie, it doesn't matter if you've bought a house or a halibut, it's all money and it all adds up.'" She glanced up now at Lila. "You look better."

"I feel it. I had an amazing day. I almost stepped out of the war, just for a day. We went swimming, actually swimming, in the sea."

"Good Lord," Miss de Vere said. "How did you manage to find an inch of beach that wasn't bristling with barbed wire?"

"Max knew somewhere. Down beyond Zurrieq. It was lovely."

"How's your father?"

"Quiet," Lila said.

Miss de Vere looked down at her columns of items and figures.

"Look at that. Two shillings and sixpence for an egg. An egg! I ask you. I often think, you know, that stoicism takes more out of you than active bravery. It's bearing things that takes the toll. I don't suppose we'll ever know what goes on in your father's mind. Now then. We're an orderly short until noon, so no more time for chat."

By the afternoon, the atmosphere in the shelter was so stifling that all the patients who could be moved were brought out into the sunlight, and propped against boulders. It was an unspeakable relief to everyone, except to Lila who was instructed, with two orderlies, to spray the corners of the shelter with a strong solution of Jeyes Fluid against cockroaches, now thriving and swarming in the heat and dirt. It was a disgusting job. She tied her hair up in a scarf and her nose and mouth in a second one, and manhandled the clumsy metal spraycan around the rough and insanitary corners of the shelter, while one orderly held an oil lamp and the other chased the cockroaches out of their comfortable lairs with a broom. When at last she came out into the sunlight again, filthy and reeking of tar, she found Max in uniform, perched on a boulder, in conversation with Miss de Vere.

"Your friend has found me four boxes of bouillon cubes," Miss de Vere called, "and three tins of processed cheese from Holland!"

"Oh good," Lila said. She untied her scarves, and dropped them on the ground. They'd have to be burned. She should have used rags.

Max stood up.

"I'm sorry I can't take you to bathe again. You look as if you need it."

"I do," Lila said shortly.

Rosanna came up to her, holding a chipped teacup of water. She looked, as she always seemed to, neat and controlled. And pretty. However cross one might be about the cockroaches, you could not deny that Rosanna Saliba was very pretty indeed.

"Thank you."

Rosanna said in a low voice, "I'm sorry you had to do it. I should have done it too. I should have offered."

Lila looked up.

"Thank you again."

"I will sweep up the dead ones."

"Rosanna," Lila said, "we can do that together."

She glanced up. Max was talking to Miss de Vere again, but he was watching them. She drank her water. It was extraordinary what a difference he made, just sitting there, what a lift he gave to this undeniably shabby, even sordid scene. And how good his manner was, how easy. She saw him bend away from Miss de Vere to say something to an old man, his leg swathed in none-too-clean bandages, who was propped up close by, and saw the old man smile and then laugh and then clap Max on the shoulder. She became aware that Rosanna, standing silently beside her, was watching Max too.

Lila said, "I — I knew him, before the war."

"I know," Rosanna said, "I remember."

"He's come back for anti-aircraft duties."

"Yes."

"He's — he's changed."

"Perhaps," Rosanna said, "he is happier in wartime. He has something to do. It must be terrible to have nothing to do."

Max waved across at them.

"Come over here!"

They made their way carefully among the patients, Lila still holding her teacup.

"I can't come very close. I smell terrible."

"An honourable smell," Miss de Vere said.

Max was smiling.

"I've had a small triumph."

241

"Have you?"

"Uncle Julius will lend me the Ford. For one day only and on condition I don't drive more than fifty miles."

Lila's face lit up.

"So, on your next day off, I'm going to take you out. We'll go to Buskett. Take a picnic."

"How lovely!"

"Good," Max said, his eyes full on her, "good. I'm glad you're pleased." He stood up. He turned to Rosanna and gave her a little bow. "It would give us great pleasure, Miss Saliba, if you would come too."

"I don't think so," Rosanna said, colouring, "I think I must be here."

"No," Miss de Vere said, "certainly not. One day off after all these months? I won't hear of you refusing."

Lila felt a swell of pride in Max's generosity, and a small cold edge of something else she was nothing like so gratified by. She said, with some little effort, "Do come."

"Yes," Max said. He was smiling directly at Rosanna now. "Yes, do come."

She looked up at him, and straightened her shoulders.

"Thank you," she said.

# 20

FOUR days later, there was another dawn raid over the Grand Harbour. It was, by comparison with the raids of the previous six months, relatively minor, and the all clear sounded after only forty minutes, releasing the family from the airless confinement of the cellar of the Villa Zonda. Lila had been dressing for work when the warning siren had sounded, and emerged into the kitchen from the cellar wearing her underclothes, a cotton blouse and a blanket, from which, although all her limbs were perfectly decently covered, the women of the family piously averted their gaze. They wore their black dresses day and night, raids or no raids. Doris was even attempting to get Carmela into a black dress as befitted, in Doris's eyes, her approaching adolescence. So far, however, Lila was delighted to notice, Carmela was resisting this, and had merely exchanged her winter tartan frock for a summer one of green spotted cotton, in an equal state of disrepair.

"I'd better go," Lila said to Pa, "I'm sure that's it for today."

He peered at her.

"You look all in."

"I didn't sleep much."

He gave one of his little grunts. She'd come in late last night from this expedition to Buskett Gardens, and he'd waited up, partly to have something to do, and partly in case she wanted to talk. But she didn't seem to. She said the day had been lovely and she'd gone to sleep under the trees and Rosanna had shown them how to eat prickly pears.

"Max let me drive a bit."

"Did he now. Could you remember?"

"Oh yes," she said.

And then she'd gone to bed. She never slept in the cellar now, and with the raids easing off he wasn't going to nag her. He'd tried once and she had told him that Miss de Vere had slept in her house in Kalkara every single night since the war began, and Kalkara was in the thick of the bombing. Pa couldn't help feeling that, however foolhardy this was, it showed the right attitude. He wouldn't go down to the cellar himself any more, if it wasn't for young Spiru. Spiru wouldn't sleep if he wasn't there. Doris was inclined to get sentimental about this and talk of the spirit of her sainted departed father and the holy presence of the blessed dead and similar claptrap. Pa couldn't bear such talk. But nor could he bear to let Spiru down. So, night after night, he and Spiru and Spiru's gas-mask box and the little wooden aeroplane slept uncomfortably together in the stifling darkness on a heap of potato sacks. It was the least, Pa felt, that he could do.

He said to Lila, "Better eat something."

"No."

"I've saved some bread. Bread and oil and tomato paste is about all it'll be any minute. Remember those bloaters? Aldeburgh bloaters . . ."

244

"Pa," Lila said, "the food we ate in Aldeburgh was pretty nearly as awful as the food we're eating now."

She bent down to put on her sandals. Pa watched her absently, waiting, almost idly, to see Anton's ring swing forward, as it always did, on its ribbon, out of the neck of her blouse. It didn't. He peered. It wasn't there. He cleared his throat.

"Well, now."

She buckled the second sandal and straightened up.

"What?"

He patted his chest.

"Gone."

"What's gone?"

Pa winked.

"Ring."

Lila looked self-conscious.

"I've decided not to wear it. For working, that is."

"Ah."

"In case it gets lost."

Pa winked again.

"Good thinking."

"Stop it," Lila said. "It's not important, it's not — *significant*."

"If you say so," Pa said.

She leaned forward, as she had now taken to doing whenever she came and went, and kissed him.

"Bye, Pa. See you on Sunday."

He patted her shoulder.

"Toodle pip."

In the courtyard, Carmela waited with Lila's bicycle. It was, by now, about the fourth bicycle, since bicycles seemed to go missing with astonishing regularity. This one was a man's bicycle, and Doris had told Carmela it was immodest for a lady to ride it.

"I must come with you," Carmela said, fixing her eyes urgently on Lila's face.

"To Kalkara? I'm afraid you can't."

"Here," Carmela said, "it is nothing. Nothing, nothing, *nothing*. Every day, nothing."

Lila looked at her. Her froggy little face was lengthening as she grew older, and she had taken to pinning her pigtails on top of her head in a sober and matronly way.

"After the war," Lila said, "whatever I do, you can come with me."

Carmela thrust her face upwards.

"You promise?"

"I promise."

"Today," Carmela said, "I read *The Children of the New Forest*. I found it in the salone."

"Good."

"If I read," Carmela said, "I can go *anywhere*. Can't I?"

★ ★ ★

Two Maltese orderlies met Lila at the mouth of the shelter.

"Have you seen her?"

Lila propped her bicycle behind a small thornbush.

"Who?"

246

"Miss de Vere."

"Isn't she here?"

"No. That's why we ask you. You are late and she is not here."

"There was a raid," Lila said, tiredly, "that's why I'm late. The siren went just as I was setting off."

"But Miss de Vere isn't here at *all*."

She looked at them. They were gawky boys of fifteen, too old for school under current circumstances, and too young for the active war duties they longed for. No-one except Miss de Vere could have persuaded them that most of the tasks they did each day were not, in fact, women's work.

The taller one, whose huge hands and feet indicated he was going to get taller still, said, "She's never late."

"No," Lila said, "no, you're right. She never is." She looked at her bicycle. "I'll go there. I'll go down to the creek and see. Is Rosanna here?"

"Yes. She is worried."

"Tell her I've gone," Lila said. "Tell her I've gone to find Miss de Vere. I'll be as quick as I can."

\* \* \*

The road behind the waterfront on Kalkara Creek was choked with rubble, too deeply piled to get even a bicycle through. On the mounds of fallen masonry the usual patient teams of men with wooden handcarts were sorting out

247

the blocks of stone and moving them slowly, steadily, to the side of the street. The Germans had been aiming, one of the men said to Lila, for the great Naval Hospital on the headland.

"Missed," he said, and grinned.

Lila left her bicycle hidden, she hoped, in a narrow alley between two buildings which were still, albeit drunkenly, standing, and began to scramble over the rubble piles towards Miss de Vere's house. It appeared that the buildings that had taken the greater force of the bomb had been those at the back of the street, away from the water, buildings which had been evacuated months before, when the German bombings began in earnest. Only Miss de Vere, with her dauntless, eccentric courage, had continued to live in the eye of the target.

"I have to do it," she'd said. "It won't harm the war effort, but it'll harm me to stay away. I've slept in that house for thirty years and it's like a ship to me. If it goes down, I'll go down with it."

The façade that faced the street looked, as far as Lila could see, almost intact, except that several windows were blown out, and through them could be seen spaces of sky where the roof should have been. The street door, with its dolphin knocker, stood slightly ajar, and as she approached it a man came out, a Maltese in working clothes, carrying a bucket.

"Fire's out," he said to Lila. "Only a small one."

"But Miss de Vere," Lila said. "Miss de Vere! Is she all right?"

"Who?"

"The lady who lived here — "

He swung his bucket. "She fell through the floor. The blast took the floor away. She's a bit bruised — "

Lila pushed past him into the passage that ran the width of the house, parallel to the creek. She shouted, "Miss de Vere? Oh, Miss de Vere!"

Zanzu appeared in an inner doorway, holding a towel. He was covered in dust, and had been darkly bruised down one side of his face.

"Oh, Miss Lila — "

Lila ran forward.

"Where is she? Is she all right? Was she badly hurt? Are you all right?"

Zanzu felt his face.

"The wall fell on me. Knocked me out for a while."

"And Miss de Vere?"

"Come," Zanzu said.

He folded the towel trimly over his arm as if he were a waiter with a napkin, and ushered Lila through the door into the kitchen of the house. It was a narrow room, and rather dark, despite windows looking out towards the creek, and the far end of it was almost entirely taken up by a huge wicker chaise longue which Lila recognized from its usual place in the riotously colourful sitting room upstairs. On it, Miss de Vere lay with her head tied up in a turban of pink silk, and the rest of her swathed in an immense pale grey wrapper patterned with peonies.

"Oh, Miss de Vere — "

The pink turban moved slightly.

"My dear."

Lila ran forward.

"Oh, are you all right? Are you?"

"Yes," Miss de Vere said firmly. "Certainly."

Lila knelt by the chaise longue. If anything, Miss de Vere's face was more bruised than Zanzu's, and uncharacteristically pale, so that the bruises stood out like wine stains.

"Just knocked about a bit," Miss de Vere said, "as you see. The ceiling fell on me. Luckily it wasn't a very substantial ceiling, but all the same, there was a lot of it. And then it and I proceeded to fall through the floor. We ended up on the ground floor and to my amazement, I was still in bed."

"But with all that on top of you."

Miss de Vere moved uncomfortably.

"I *am* a little stiff."

"I should think you are. It must have been terrifying."

"More enraging," Miss de Vere said. "I had a perfectly good house last night and now look at it."

Lila put her hand gently on Miss de Vere's arm.

"What can I do for you?"

"Just do without me for a few days. Till the worst subsides. Zanzu is marvellous and we have plenty of arnica for the bruises." She looked slightly behind Lila. "Did Rosanna come?"

"No."

"Ah."

"I — I just came the minute I heard. Rosanna's at the hospital."

250

"I should like to see her."

"Of course."

"When you get back," Miss de Vere said, "perhaps you could take over for a while?"

"Oh, yes."

Miss de Vere closed her eyes for a moment and Lila saw, with a pang, how tired she looked, how abruptly old, how vulnerable.

"Rosanna has looked after me for seven years. Since she was sixteen. I've known her since she was a child."

Lila rose to her feet.

"I'll go now. I'll go and send her down."

"Thank you," Miss de Vere said. She turned her head away so that Lila could see almost nothing but pink turban. "Thank you."

* * *

Rosanna was waiting. She was ostensibly occupied with the daily round of temperatures and pulses, but Lila could tell, from the tenseness in her body, that she was waiting.

"She's all right," Lila said. "Badly bruised, but very much alive."

She crouched on the floor of the shelter beside Rosanna, breathing hard. She had ridden back from the creek like the wind.

"Oh good," Rosanna said. Her voice was hard and small.

"Hey," Lila said, "what's the matter? Aren't you pleased? I thought you'd be sick with worry, like me — "

Rosanna laid the thermometer she was holding

251

in a chipped enamel kidney dish.

"Excuse me," she said to the patient she was attending. She turned to Lila. "Could we speak outside for a moment?"

Lila got to her feet.

"Of course, if that's what you want."

"I do."

Lila followed her out into the sunshine. The moment they were out of the immediate earshot of anyone in the shelter, Rosanna said, with open fury, "How dare you!"

Lila stared at her.

"How dare I what?"

"How dare you take it on yourself to be the one to go and see if Miss de Vere was all right?"

"But I — "

"I was waiting," Rosanna shouted. "All through that raid, while I was alone on duty here, I was waiting! I was waiting for you to come so I could go down to the creek! Don't you see? I could see the raid from here, I could see where the bombs were falling, I knew there was a chance she might be hit! And what do you do? You come down here after a good night's rest and you don't even *think* to come and find me! Do you? Oh no. It has to be you to go and see Miss de Vere, doesn't it? It has to be you!"

Lila put her hands to her face.

"I'm so sorry, I didn't think — "

"No. You don't think. You just *do*. It's me who has looked after Miss de Vere all these years. Isn't it? You may think you are her special friend because you are English and you

252

are educated, but you are wrong. Do you hear me? *Wrong*."

Lila took her hands away. She straightened. "She is asking for you."

"Is she?"

"Yes. She asked me to ask you to go down to her. Now."

There was a small silence. Then Rosanna said, "What has happened to her?"

"A ceiling fell on her, and then she fell through the floor. She's badly bruised, as I said, but I don't think anything's broken."

"She will be shaken," Rosanna said, "and shocked." She looked at Lila, and for a moment Lila wondered if she was going to say she was sorry for losing her temper. But she didn't. She simply said, "I will go now then."

"Take my bicycle."

"Thank you."

When she had gone, Lila sat down on a boulder. She found she was shaking a little. In a minute, she told herself, she would go back into the shelter and resume those daily duties which every day became harder to do without the adrenalin of emergency; but for a few minutes, she would sit here and attempt, at least, to collect herself. There had been moments yesterday, during the picnic in Buskett Gardens, of knowing that Rosanna had stiffened somehow, withdrawn — moments of real awkwardness. Lila had marvelled at Max's patience with her, and courtesy. And she herself had strained every sinew not to emphasize, even *indicate*, the familiarity between herself and Max. She had imagined she had succeeded, indeed had told herself that the effort of succeeding had probably been the reason why the day had lacked something carefree. And of course Rosanna was devoted to Miss de Vere. Of course she was. But did it really matter, in wartime, who went to see if anyone was safe, as long as someone did? Or did wartime just sharpen up everyone's sensitivities? Doris was fond of saying that at least war reminded all humankind that they were, without social distinction, all God's children, but maybe this was more wishful thinking than realistic. It certainly didn't seem, right now, that Rosanna Saliba had any desire whatsoever to be Lila's sister in God.

There was a shout from the top of the slope. Lila looked up. Max stood up there, in uniform, waving. She rose, waving enthusiastically back.

"I've got five minutes!" he called. "Come to see you both!"

He came leaping down the stony path from the road above.

"I can't hug you on duty, can I?"

"No," she said, delightedly, "you most certainly can't."

He gave her a swift kiss on the cheek.

Lila said, "That was such a lovely day. Thank you."

He smiled.

"Where's Rosanna?"

"Gone to see Miss de Vere. Her house was hit last night. She's all right, just pretty battered. Actually — "

"Actually what?"

254

"I've just been ticked off good and proper by Rosanna. That's why I was out here. Cooling off."

Max's attention seemed to focus suddenly.

"Ticked you off? Why?"

"For going to see Miss de Vere without telling her. For presuming to be the first to go."

"I see."

"Do you?"

"She's a proud girl," Max said, "like her brother."

Lila was startled.

"What d'you mean, her brother? What — "

"I went to find him," Max said. "After the way she spoke about him yesterday, I thought I'd like to meet him. I've just been in Senglea."

Lila looked away.

"He's a great fellow," Max said. "Brave. Like her. Makes me ashamed."

"Ashamed? Why should you be ashamed?"

"Of — how I was. How we were brought up to be. Thinking of the Maltese as peasants, who only spoke a kitchen language. *I'm* Maltese, for God's sake."

Lila moved away a little. "I'd better get on."

He smiled at her, suddenly relaxed again.

"Me too. When will I see you?"

"Sunday?"

"Sunday it is," he said, "Germans permitting."

# 21

SOME days, during the long and hungry afternoons, Carmela would read to Pa. She would join him and Spiru in the shade of the carob tree and read long passages of English prose and poetry in a steady sing-song voice that took no account whatsoever of either punctuation or verse rhythms. She had just discovered A. E. O. Perriam's copy of Tennyson's poems, bound in a curious purple cloth faintly resembling leather. The poems were printed on thin, crackling paper with gleaming gold edges, which Carmela much admired. She had told her mother — to Doris's outrage — that she thought the book as beautiful as a Bible. She also thought the poems were beautiful, especially 'The Lady of Shalott' and poor Mariana sighing in her moated grange. In her present state of confinement there was solace to be had for Carmela in these portraits of romantic imprisonment.

"She only said the night is dreary He cometh not she said," read Carmela, "She said I am aweary aweary I wish that I were dead."

Spiru gazed at her respectfully.

"I do," Carmela said. "I do wish that I were dead."

Pa was patching some trousers of Salvu's. Salvu hardly came home now, but when he did he was silent and blazing-eyed, and his trousers were worn through at the seat from blistering, grinding contact with the seat of an anti-aircraft gun. Pa was not delicate with his needle, but he was effective. He was sewing, with big, even stitches in heavy-duty black buttonhole thread, a large plaid patch cut from an old shirt, onto Salvu's khaki drill trousers.

"Not sure," Pa said, "that we don't all wish it sometimes."

Carmela patted the book.

"Did she get rescued? The Mariana lady? Did he come?"

"Doubt it," Pa said.

"But Baron Max has come back for Lila."

Pa glanced at Carmela.

"Looks like it."

At the mention of Max's name, Spiru's face had gently lit up. There was the memory of the wonderful airforce cap.

"Bang," Spiru said reverently. "Plane."

"That's the one," Pa said.

He knotted off the thread and shook out Salvu's trousers.

"Reckon those'll last three raids."

The black dog, who had been idly scratching himself in the shade of his barrel, suddenly rattled his chain and stood up and barked.

"Oh goodness," Carmela said, getting up and holding the Tennyson to her green cotton chest, "look who's come."

Angelo Saliba, in a drill shirt and worn dark trousers, was standing in the entrance to the courtyard with a bundle in his arms. Pa was delighted.

257

"What ho!"

Spiru stood up too, holding his aeroplane.

"Come on over!" Pa called. "Come and join us! We're reading poetry."

Angelo crossed the courtyard, smiling. Even his sturdy frame seemed diminished now. He looked down at Carmela's book.

"What poetry?"

She pouted, swinging herself from side to side and refusing to answer.

"Tennyson," Pa said. "Lovely ladies. Lovely ladies in lonely places."

Angelo grinned at Carmela.

"Of course."

"Shut up," she said rudely.

"Now, now," Pa said, "no need for that. Must learn to take a little teasing."

Angelo said to Pa, "I'm glad to see you, sir."

"Look at me," Pa said, "look at me. Stitching away like an old crone."

"Or a sailor."

Angelo settled himself easily in the dust, cross-legged. He put his bundle, tied up in an old checked tablecloth, on the ground in front of him. Spiru watched him for a moment, then came and settled down next to him, cross-legged too.

"Hallo," Angelo said.

Spiru looked up at him. He held his aeroplane in both hands.

"I remember you. They'd trussed you up like a chicken."

"It was *necessary*," Carmela said fiercely.

"Nice to see you have all your arms and legs," Angelo said to Spiru.

Silently, Spiru offered Angelo his aeroplane.

"Very fine," Angelo said. "Where did you get that?"

"Pa," Spiru said.

"Is that what he calls you, sir?"

"Yes," Pa said, "they all do."

"I've come to ask a favour, please."

"Any time," Pa said. "If I can do it." He folded Salvu's trousers up and picked up Lila's all-purpose winter coat. He had offered to mend the torn lining and sew on the buttons more strongly.

"I've had to move my parents," Angelo said. "They've stood all these raids because my father couldn't bear to be away from the Grand Harbour, but the last raid got the houses either side of them and they've been ordered to move because their house isn't safe any more. I'm taking them out to Mqabba, to my mother's sister's house. It — it isn't ideal because my mother and her sister quarrel, but at least it's away from the worst of the bombing. I just wondered — " he paused and touched the bundle in front of him. "My mother thinks that if she takes some of her most precious things to her sister's house, her sister will take them from her. So I wondered if I could leave them here?"

"Why not?" Pa said. "Why not?"

Angelo leaned forward and untied the bundle.

"They are things, you understand, of value to my mother."

259

"Of course."

Angelo folded back the tablecloth. Spiru got onto his knees to have a better look and Carmela, despite herself, put down the Tennyson and craned forward. There, tenderly wrapped in clean rags, lay several brightly coloured plaster statues of saints, two pictures of the Virgin Mary, one holding the Christ child, and one a lily, two amber glass candlesticks, a small looking glass edged with shells, a paper Spanish fan, a small engraving of King George V and Queen Mary, and a wooden crucifix on a stand. There was also a parcel, wrapped in whitish paper. Pa pointed to it.

"What's that?"

"It's a brass dolphin," Angelo said, "a door knocker." He paused and then he said, "It was meant to be a present, once. For your daughter, sir."

"Ah," Pa said. He seemed to concentrate suddenly on a long rip in the lining of Lila's coat. "Wouldn't take it?"

"No."

"I'll take it," Pa said. "I'll keep it. Insurance policy."

"I don't understand you, sir."

"No," Pa said, "people seldom do." He winked. "But I know what I mean."

Angelo looked down at his mother's treasures. Carmela was brooding over them, over the pretty pink-faced Virgin in her blue robe holding the lily before her as if it were a candle.

"This is beautiful," she said.

For three days Miss de Vere stayed on the wicker chaise longue in the kitchen of the damaged house on Kalkara Creek. Short of lifting her bodily, nobody could persuade her to move, and as she was both of independent mind and independent means, they finally left her there. Zanzu looked after her by day, while she did her account books, read the *Times of Malta*, and dozed, and at night he went up to the hospital to keep Lila company, while Rosanna took his place with Miss de Vere. Lila did not accompany her. There was nothing in Rosanna's manner to encourage this, and, as far as Lila knew, Miss de Vere had not asked for her.

The three days of duty seemed somehow even more interminable than usual. There were no more raids, it was very hot and Lila spent many angry hours wondering why they couldn't, since the intensity of the German onslaught seemed to be over for the moment, move the hospital back into some kind of building, where at least there would be light and air. It seemed to her, just now, that whatever Miss de Vere was thinking or planning, she, Lila would be the last to know.

On Sunday morning, pale still, but in excellent spirits, Miss de Vere reappeared. Her face was still smudged with bruises, but she had removed the pink turban and replaced it with a white drill solar topee, lined in dark green. The patients revived visibly at the sight of her familiar white suit and the atmosphere of resolute optimism she brought with her.

"Off you go," she said to Lila.

"But can you manage?"

"Perfectly well. How do you think I managed before?"

"But the others, Rosanna — "

"Left her at home to sleep. It's all she needs. She can sleep all day, if she wants to."

"Thank you," Lila said. There had been moments during the last few days when she had wondered if she would have to forego her precious Sunday.

It was a hot day, already, the sky the pale whitish blue it seemed to be in Malta in summer, lacking those northerly breezes that keep other parts of the Mediterranean sky so deeply blue. All Malta looked bleached out by the heat: the broken streets and the rubbly heaps that were once houses; the roads; the dusty countryside where farmers and off-duty soldiers struggled to grow at least something for the coming winter. It was, Lila thought, pedalling on while the sweat ran down her in rivers, as if Malta had been sucked dry and left out to bleach to a husk in the sunlight. The lion sun, the Maltese called it, as if it was some fierce and greedy beast, sucking the marrow out of the island, and leaving only the dry bones behind.

Max was already in the courtyard of the Villa Zonda. He and Pa were sitting on kitchen chairs in the shade that the house itself cast in the mornings.

"I'm not fit to be considered," Lila said, stopping the bicycle six feet from them. "Don't even look at me until I've washed."

"Honest toil," Max said, standing up and bowing to her. "What's the shame in that?"

She laughed, and wheeled the bicycle past him and into the rabbit shed. There was only one pair left now, and even they seemed reluctant to breed, crouched at opposite ends of their cage as if the mere thought of contact was too much for them.

"I'm taking you to Mdina!" Max called.

"Oh! To the palace?"

"No," Max said. "Better than that. My uncle's been lent a house by a friend of his, a friend who's spending the war in Switzerland. Uncle goes to read there. He says it has hardly any furniture but it's cool and the views are wonderful. It's in the walls, the south walls."

"Splendid," Lila said. "And what do we do there?"

Max indicated a basket by his feet.

"Picnic," he said. "Sardines, bread and beer. What more do you want?"

★ ★ ★

"This," Lila said, "is one of the most lovely houses I've ever seen."

She stood on a dusty tiled floor in a long, high room whose windows, set in embrasures six feet deep, looked south over the clover meadows that ran up to the very walls of Mdina, and gave it, in spring, the impression of rising out of a rose-red sea. The ceiling was coffered, the windows were shaded with delicate screens of latticed wood, and around the tops of

263

the walls, washed pale saffron, ran a frescoed frieze of birds and flowers and peacocks, docilely drinking from fountains in graceful pairs. There was, as Max had promised, almost no furniture, beyond a huge round table, its top inlaid with pietra dura, two great carved chests and several chairs like thrones, with high backs culminating in pediments.

"It's like being in a castle and a ship, all at once."

Max was setting out their picnic on the marble table; the tin of sardines, the loaf of hard-crusted Maltese bread, the two beer bottles.

"The man who owns it, Uncle says, almost never comes here." His tone was faintly contemptuous. "He thinks Malta is primitive."

"This house isn't," Lila said. She touched the catch on one of the window lattices and swung it wide, letting a slab of sunlight fall in, glowing on the tiles. "This house is perfect, just a tower of rooms in the walls, all looking out over this lovely view. I lived in a house like a tower once, but it wasn't remotely like this, it didn't have any romance or poetry and the sea it looked at was almost always grey. I could imagine living in this house. I could imagine being really happy in this house. It has the right atmosphere to be happy in. Don't you think?"

Max flipped the cap off one of the beer bottles and held it out to her.

"I don't think lovely houses necessarily make for happiness. I've lived in beautiful houses all my life and I can tell you they don't. It's

264

people that do that. It's people who make for happiness."

Lila took the beer bottle. It was warm from the journey in her bicycle basket in the sun.

"Perhaps," she said, "I'm only just learning that."

Max took a swallow of his own beer, and pulled a face.

"It's as hot as tea." He looked at her. She was wearing shorts, and a sleeveless open-necked blouse she had cut down from the old yellow cotton dress after the skirt had been torn by her bicycle chain.

Max said, "You're not wearing the ring."

"No."

He put his beer bottle down on the table.

"Why not?"

She looked directly at him.

"I don't need to."

He smiled.

"Good."

She licked her lips. She went past him and put her own bottle down on the table next to his.

"I don't need to, you see, because you've come home."

He said nothing. He was watching her intently, as if what she next said or did was of supreme importance.

"You've made such a difference to me," Lila said. "You may have changed, but so have I. I think I never saw you properly, before. I was so dazzled by Anton. I think I never realized that it was you, really, all the time. You."

She smiled at him. He was still looking at

her with that concentrated gaze. She moved forward, still smiling and reached up to put her arms around his neck, and felt his arms come round her, tentatively, as if the moment had a significance that must be respected.

"Max," Lila said softly, and kissed him on the mouth.

Gently, he turned his head away.

"Max — "

"Sorry," he said. He moved one arm to hold her head against him, almost protectively. "Sorry."

She pulled away a little.

"Max? Max, what's the matter? I thought — "

"I'm so fond of you," he said, his face still averted, his arms still loosely holding her. "I'm so fond of you. I always have been. And I owe you so much."

Lila took his hands in hers and detached them from her sides, as if she were handing something back to him.

"I — I don't think I want to be owed anything."

"But I do," Max said. He turned his head to look at her. "You were the first person to show us how wrong we were, the way we lived, the way we thought and treated people. I wouldn't be where I am now without you."

"Thank you," Lila said. Her voice was hard. She moved away from him and stood by the table pushing the beer bottles about. She said loudly, "I must be very stupid. Mustn't I? Very stupid indeed."

"Why," he said. "Why so?"

"Oh!" she said, fighting tears. "Oh, for assuming things. For assuming that if a man constantly seeks your company and takes you swimming and dancing, and kisses you and is generally sweet to you, that he may actually feel something for you! How amazingly, densely stupid to assume any such thing!"

"I do feel something," Max said. "I do. I have from the beginning."

"But you were flirting with me! You were!"

"I wanted to cheer you up, I wanted to do something for you. You are my dear, dear friend — "

"Don't say it!" Lila shouted. "Don't say it! *Don't*." She rounded on him. "Why, just now, did you say 'good' when you noticed I wasn't wearing Anton's ring? Why was that good, if it wasn't that I wasn't carrying a torch for him any more?"

"Just that," Max said. "He's my brother, but he's no good for you."

"I see," she said. She was shaking. She leaned on the marble table to steady herself, gripping the edge. "I see. He's no good for me, but you don't want me."

"I do," Max said. He came round the table, and tried to take her hand. "I do. But not as a lover. As a beloved friend, but not as a lover."

"Have you any idea," she said, "how humiliating this is?"

"Yes," he said. "I never meant it to happen. I — I didn't read the signals right."

She stood up abruptly, snatching her hand

back and putting both in the pockets of her shorts.

"No, you most certainly didn't."

She looked at him. There was something in his expression that suddenly made her feel that she didn't know it all, that awful as this present scene was, it had to become more awful before it was over.

"Max?"

He looked at her. His eyes were wary.

"Yes."

"You did think you were in love with me, didn't you? Just for a little? Just at the beginning?"

He took a breath, and nodded.

"Yes."

"When you first came back?"

"Yes."

Lila took her hands out of her pockets, and folded her arms.

"Right. So, then what happened?"

There was a long pause. Max looked down at the floor where their feet had swirled the dust into long, feathery patterns. Then he looked back at Lila and she read both apology and exultation in his eyes.

"I met Rosanna," he said quietly. "That's what happened. I met Rosanna."

# 22

THE summer and autumn ground away in days so slow it seemed that some of them would never end. The Germans, deflected by Hitler's Russian campaign, ceased to bombard Malta for the time being, and the nervous vibrancy induced by having to be on the alert day and night subsided into boredom and gloom. There was time — unwelcome time — in which to realize just how hungry and tired and miserably uncomfortable everyone was. News of the war in other areas — the desert, the fall of Crete — was hardly encouraging, nor was the fact that although the island was briefly outwardly tranquil, life on it was ever more restricted. Every beach which could possibly be called a beach was out of bounds, as indeed was most of the coastline, however rocky, so that nobody, except a few soldiers and gunners manning remote concrete pillboxes, had any access to water for swimming. The sun, high in the white sky, was pitiless.

By August, even Miss de Vere was convinced her hospital could be safely moved out of the shelter, and the by now dwindling number of patients were shifted into the ground floor of a warehouse that had once held the goods of a ships' chandler, and which still smelled faintly of tar and twine. The windows were mostly broken, it was plagued by rats and mice, but it had, as

Lila had longed for, both light and air. As there were so few patients left, Lila was sent as an auxiliary teacher to the dockyard school, whose staff was by now seriously depleted because of the need to prepare stronger anti-aircraft defence. Her job was to teach English to a group of children whose ages ranged from eight to fourteen, in a classroom only usable in good weather since one complete wall had been neatly blown away, leaving an uninterrupted view of the devastated spaces beyond, where patient clearance work went on, day in, day out. She became perfectly used to teaching against a continuous noise of shovelling and shouting.

Most days, she took Carmela with her, balancing her perilously on the crossbar of her bicycle. Carmela was passionately eager to come, and enormously proud of her speaking and reading skills in English. Her Maltese was also invaluable. It took over an hour to get there, with both of them dismounting for the hills, arriving at the end of each journey as dusty and sweat-soaked as the dockyard workers whose children they were teaching. It was, for Lila, infinitely preferable to nursing. She liked the children; she liked their spirit and curiosity and the way they accepted the war as a restriction upon their activities, but not an impossible one and certainly no catastrophe. They were also wonderfully distracting.

Lila needed distraction. She had done her best — or, as she told herself, the best that *she* could do — to make herself into the valued platonic companion that Max had said he wanted that hot and unhappy Sunday in Mdina. She had gone to visit his plane with him, and the house where he was billeted at Hal Far, and had even endured a singularly unsuccessful expedition with Rosanna as well, to the Inquisitor's Summer Palace, sitting like a little English manor house above its pretty valley. But it had all been no good. She could feel nothing but the humiliation of her position, jealousy of their happiness and a good deal of sheer misery. She had made, she told herself, a clumsy, dreadful mistake and could not bear to watch it paraded about constantly in front of her. So even though Max came up frequently to the Villa Zonda, having, like all his fellow pilots, far too much free time just now, Lila avoided him.

"Don't tell me," Pa had said. "I can guess."

"Can you?"

"I can guess enough."

"I feel," Lila said, "such a fool."

"Shouldn't feel that," Pa said. "I read the signals same as you."

She glanced at him.

"Did you?"

He nodded.

"Then we were both wrong."

"Never a door shuts," Pa said, "but another opens."

She looked at him. Her own expression was very doubtful.

"Does it?"

Pa had grown almost a sack of potatoes for the household from seed potatoes as small as withered marbles. He had also achieved two strings of onions, a box of carrots carefully stored in sand just as Mr Tuttle used to do, a bag of dried figs, laid out in the sun and increasingly resembling, Lila thought, large squashed beetles. Doris was delighted. Pa had become her pet, her substitute father. He was the only person she trusted with Spiru, her last gift — she crossed herself as she said this — from God. Pa was given a special chair, with a hard cushion made from cotton wadding and a pair of blue felt slippers, embroidered in cross stitch, which had belonged to old Spiru. He was entrusted with killing the last two rabbits as well as being awarded the privilege of presiding at the head of the table when the resulting stew was produced. Looking at him sometimes Lila saw that despite the fact that he was, like everyone, thinner and tireder and increasingly shabby, he was happy. He was useful and active, deeply appreciated and, most important of all, respected. "You must ask Pa," Lila would hear Doris say to her sisters, or her children. "You must seek advice from Pa."

"Mad," Pa said, "mad as a hatter. Might as well ask advice from a donkey as ask me." But he was beaming.

As the autumn wore on, more and more young English pilots appeared, accompanying their Wellingtons and Blenheims and Swordfish. Some of them were as young as nineteen, racing about the island in search of horses to ride or enough other people for an impromptu game of cricket. Count Julius befriended several of them, giving them oranges from the Tabia Palace courtyard and wine from its cellars. Once or twice, he asked Lila to meet them and she spent an hour or so in the tapestry room listening to them laugh and shout and complain about how little action there was.

"Honestly, might as well be a civilian for all the action I've seen."

"I'm fed up, do you hear me, fed up with being here doing nothing."

"What I can't stand is the thought that we might miss everything."

One of them, a tall thin boy whom she had difficulty imagining folding himself up into the confined space of a cockpit, asked her to a cinema show at another mess in the city.

"*The Big Store*, Marx Brothers. Brilliant," he said. He was grinning.

She smiled back at him. She couldn't tell him that everything about his appearance, manner and attitude made her feel a hundred. Instead she said she had to be at home at nights because of her father, and the Maltese family they lived with. The young pilot looked amazed.

"Maltese? You live with them? I say. Good show."

Bicycling home, Lila told herself she had been priggish. Priggish and pompous and untruthful. But there was something about these young men, for all their decency and courage, that made her feel she had grown beyond them, and also beyond their particular kind of English boyishness.

"They think," she said later to Pa, "that death

273

is just somehow a hazard of the chase."

Pa looked at her. He looked at her for a long time, far longer than was customary for him, and then he took her hand for a moment, and gave it a little shake.

"Perhaps they're right," Pa said.

* * *

Just before Christmas, the Germans returned. There were alerts every day, and raids on most days, even Christmas Day. No church bells rang on Christmas Day, and there were no customary candles in any windows. Pa made Spiru a primitive crib out of corks and cardboard with pipe-cleaner figures dressed in scraps of patching fabric with the foil out of cigarette packets for halos.

"I thought," Lila said, "you thought all this was tommyrot. I never had a crib."

Pa winked. "Never asked for one."

On New Year's Day, there was an official broadcast announcing that the year ahead held the distinct threat of invasion.

"Stay in your village or town and take cover. Church bells will no longer be rung as the all clear signal and if you hear them, you will know they mean danger of general attack. Take your gas-mask, water, food and candles to your shelter. The blockade of Malta is tightening."

The rain began, heavy, steady rain which turned the airfields into quagmires and the shelters into mouldy catacombs. One convoy of supply ships got through, the next two

274

were sunk. Kerosene was severely rationed, then bread. Miss de Vere opened her hospital again.

"I think," she said to Lila, "I won't ask you to come back."

"No."

Max Ferroferrata was now down at the hospital working alongside Rosanna every hour he could spare. He had been in two dogfights, but the organization of the Malta Station was so haphazard that he was often left champing impatiently on the ground without orders, while German and Italian planes screamed through the veiling clouds above. Miss de Vere could hardly be under any illusion as to the reason for Rosanna's glowing face, nor for Lila's thin one. She patted Lila's shoulder.

"Work is the great healer."

"Is it?"

"I should know," Miss de Vere said.

Work might heal pain, Lila thought, but did it heal pride? She looked at her ill-assorted class: at the two little sisters who came every day, war or no war, in starched white pinafores; at the vast ragged majority who sported a Dickensian assortment of hand-me-down clothes and cast-off shoes; at the boy who took almost two hours every day to get to school, but who still came, as regular as clockwork, and she thought that what enabled her to try and live up to their cheerful courage was that they didn't know about her pride. To them she was just Miss Cunningham, a fixture in their lives now like the school or the sound and position of the anti-aircraft guns

275

about which they were so knowledgeable, and with the infinite advantage of having been born English so that she didn't have to learn her own impossible language. For them, the enemy was nothing yet inside themselves, but something outward and much simpler — the Germans.

"Jerry won't win," they said to her and to each other. "We'll never give in, will we?"

★ ★ ★

In April it was announced that King George VI was giving the George Cross medal to the whole island of Malta, for courage.

"Does that mean us?" Lila said.

Pa grunted. He was staring at the headlines in the *Times of Malta*.

"Must do. We're living here. Done our bit." He glanced at Lila and grinned. "Rather have a leg of lamb, though."

Lila didn't like leaving the Villa Zonda these days. The raids were so frequent and so heavy that nowhere seemed safe. March had been a month of terror and death.

"We go on," Pa said. "We have to, don't we? We do our bit where we have to do it. What good would it do for you to stay here?"

"None," Lila said. "It's only superstition."

All the same, whenever she reached the last stretch of the long road beside the aqueduct that led to the Villa Zonda, and saw that the tree lines were still the same and the battered roof was still there, nestling among them, she felt, however consumingly tired and hungry, a surge

276

of relief. Some things in her life had to *be* there, to *stay* there — things that could be counted upon. And who would ever have thought, she sometimes reflected, that this neglected yellow house, the first sight of which had so appalled her, and her exasperating parent, could have come to represent those changeless things?

For three solid days, there were raids around the school area every morning. First the sirens' warning wail, then the scramble of everyone down into the shelters, then that fearful, helpless waiting while the sinister whistling of falling bombs was followed by the crash and roar of explosions. After the last raid on the third morning, everyone was sent home. Several of the children, their eardrums pierced by the endless blasts, needed medical attention; others, for all their brightness of spirits, were too distracted by tension to concentrate on anything. Lila, in a similar state, was only too thankful to collect Carmela and set off on the long journey home in the middle of the day.

It was a clear day, with the irresistible optimism of atmosphere of a spring morning. Trudging up hills pushing the bicycle, Lila couldn't help noticing that among the blackened ruins of so many buildings, a number of spring flowers were resolutely pushing through broken masonry and rubble. She and Carmela didn't speak much; they needed their breath for walking. In any case, Lila was preoccupied by a new anxiety about Carmela. On the backs of her hands and wrists, as she pushed the bicycle, Lila could see the rough red patches which she knew to be the first symptom of scabies. Not enough calories. But nobody had enough calories, from labouring men to newborn babies. She moved forward to take the bicycle from Carmela, to relieve those reddened hands and wrists. When they got back to the Villa Zonda, she would bath Carmela and scrub her with soft soap. Maybe Miss de Vere would have some benzyl benzoate and she could rub that into Carmela, every inch, from her chin to her toes, to stop the hideous little parasite burrowing on, all down her half-starved small body . . .

"Look," Carmela said. Her voice was quite flat.

"What?"

"That house. It's gone."

They paused.

"They've never bombed this far out before."

"I expect it was a mistake. What's the point of bombing civilian suburbs?"

"A lady lived in that house," Carmela said. "Didn't she? She had two children. We used to see her hanging out their washing."

Lila indicated the bicycle.

"Hop on. It's the last flat mile, thank heavens."

Carmela perched herself sideways on the bicycle crossbar, as was her custom.

"She had a dog too. A little black curly dog. Do you think the dog is dead?"

"I can't talk," Lila said, "and pedal."

She bent her head against Carmela's half-turned green cotton back. Poor lady, poor children, poor dog. Poor Carmela, with her infested hands. It was hard work, pedalling like this, hard work with two on the bicycle, even a thin two, and nothing inside you since yesterday but half a slice of bread and a mug of something called coffee which tasted of nothing but dust and bitterness; hard work to summon up sympathy for the dead lady and her departed washing when all your energies had to go on going on, on and on . . .

Carmela screamed. She took her hands away from the centre of the handlebars and put them to her face, and then, still screaming, she threw herself off the bicycle into the road. Lila braked violently and skidded to a clumsy halt.

"What — ?"

"No," Carmela shouted. "No, no, no!"

Lila looked up. Ahead of them, the familiar road stretched between the wall and the aqueduct, and behind the wall rose the equally familiar trees, shaggy and dark, with the occasional silvery gleam of olive or eucalyptus, that partly concealed the roofline of the Villa Zonda. Except that the roofline wasn't there now; there wasn't anything there except steady black plumes of smoke rising against the clear blue April sky. Lila flung the bicycle aside, stepped into the road to pull Carmela to her feet, and ran as she had never run before.

★ ★ ★

The house was roofless, but bravely still half standing. There was no sign of a bomb crater, only the extraordinary sight of the salone, ripped apart and spilling sofas and chairs and desks down into the smashed-up chaos of the family rooms below. The other end of the house, the kitchen end above the cellar, *seemed* to be more or less intact up to the first floor. As far as their bedrooms. Lila and Pa's bedrooms. The fires had been in the outbuildings, the sheds and barns and huts that had surrounded the courtyard to the east, where the potatoes were stored, and bicycles, and timber for repairing things, where the rabbits had lived. Against the wall of the rabbit shed, the black dog lay slumped, his chain snapped from the barrel by his last desperate leap for freedom, away from the fire. But the fires were no more than smouldering now. Someone had been there. Someone had doused the fires, doused them so thoroughly that nothing was left except the choking columns of smoke rising upward into the blue sky, as calmly as if they were from cooking fires.

Carmela, her wrist tight in Lila's grasp, began to scream again.

"We don't know," Lila said. "Oh please God, we don't know — "

A figure, summoned by the sound of Carmela's screams, appeared at the far side of the courtyard, at the gap in the wall, now raggedly, brutally enlarged, that led to the vegetable garden. At the sight of them, the figure began to run, stumbling and weeping.

"Oh Lila, Miss Lila! And my little one, my child, my little one — "

Carmela tore herself free from Lila's grasp

and flung herself against her mother. Doris's face was smudged with black and there was a gash in her cheek.

"Oh may Heaven preserve us, you are safe!"

Lila stared at her. She seemed suddenly far away, like a figure reduced to miniature by being seen through the wrong end of the telescope.

She said, in a voice that sounded as faraway to her as her perception of Doris, "Where's Pa?"

Doris had wrapped her arms around Carmela, and was covering her with sooty kisses.

"We were saved, by the mercy of Our Lady. We were in the cellar. We were saved! And now you are saved!"

"Were you all in the cellar?"

Doris paused in her kissing. Carmela's face was streaked with soot and blood. There were other people now in the entrance to the vegetable garden; Doris's sisters, little Spiru, a neighbour or two, an aunt who had fled from the bombed Manderaggio. A sudden silence seemed to fall, a silence punctuated only by the sighing of the smouldering timbers and Carmela's little whimperings.

"Where's Pa?" Lila said again.

Doris looked up at her. Her eyes, Lila now saw, might have been red from the smoke, but they were also swollen with weeping.

"Come," Doris said, and took Lila's hand.

★ ★ ★

Pa lay six feet from the crater the bomb had dug in the centre of his potato bed. He lay on

281

his back, with his hands folded on his chest, and his head comfortably pillowed on an old coat, and it was only when Lila went closer that she saw that the coat was soaked in blood, soaked darkly in it, and that the blood was coming from the back of Pa's head. Or what was left of it.

She knelt down on the earth beside him. Someone had closed his eyes, perhaps the same person who had laid his hands across his chest, across the old dark blue seaman's jersey that Lila had known as long as she had known anything. His face was very pale, and a little muddy, with a streak of blood across his forehead, but he looked composed, almost decided, and his tufty hair, unaffected by his dying, stood up above his forehead as determinedly as it had ever done.

"Was he killed at once?"

Doris nodded. Tears were pouring down her face, and down the faces of her sisters, and now down Carmela's too. Little Spiru looked as if he had seen a ghost.

"He wouldn't come. When the siren went, he wouldn't come. He said he would be safe in the garden."

Lila put her hand on Pa's cheek. It was cool, but not cold, and rough, stubbly rough, as it usually was. Doris and her relations came closer, creeping up around Lila and Pa, kneeling down beside them in the dug earth, sobbing and sniffing.

"He was the best of men," Doris said. "He was sent from God, he was a father to me, a grandfather to my children, he never said or

282

thought an evil word, he was like a lamp in our household — "

"Go away!" Lila yelled.

She spun round on her knees and glared at Doris, at Carmela, at the distraught huddle of black-clad women.

"Go away! Leave us in peace! Leave us, can't you? He was *my* father, mine, mine, mine! Get away from me!"

There was an abrupt and shocked silence for a moment, and then they all began to get to their feet, and to straggle away, disconcerted and shaken, towards the ruined house. Lila waited until they had gone, waited until the last black figure had shuffled through the gap in the wall, and then she lay down full length on the earth beside Pa, and put her face on his chest.

"Pa?"

She waited. "What ho!" he'd say in a minute. "Hail to thee! Yo ho ho." She moved so that she could see him and put a hand up to his face. Then she reared up a little and looked down at him. His face was quite empty, pale and stubbled and empty. Pa had gone somewhere else.

"Oh," Lila cried out, in sudden anguish, "oh Pa, oh Pa, I'm so sorry!" and then she put her head back down on his chest, against his folded hands, and cried and cried as if her heart would break.

★ ★ ★

It was not for some time that she realized she was not alone. She could feel, when her sobs subsided a little, and she could be conscious of anything but the first violence of grief, that there was someone else there with her, watching her. Carmela probably, or even little Spiru, both of whom would need, in their turn, every bit of the comfort she so badly needed for herself. She raised herself from Pa's chest, and blew her nose and dragged the sleeve of her shirt across her eyes. Even those simple tasks seemed difficult because she was shaking so. She had never wept like that in her life and maybe would never do so again. There would be more tears for sure, rivers more tears, but perhaps none like that first storm of loss and remorse and hitherto unacknowledged love.

"Carmela?"

"No," a man said quietly, "not Carmela."

Lila turned round stiffly, still on her knees. Behind her, and as smoke-grimed as they all seemed to be, stood Angelo Saliba, empty-handed, his arms hanging by his sides.

"I heard," he said. "I just came."

Lila got unsteadily to her feet. She took a little breath, bracing herself for Angelo to tell her, as Doris had done, how wonderful Pa had been, what a good man, what a gift from God.

She opened her mouth.

"Don't — "

But Angelo wasn't looking at Pa, he was looking at her.

"Poor girl," he said. His voice was hoarse. "What a loss for you. Poor girl."

And then he opened his arms to her, and Lila, without thinking, ran into them like a child.

# 23

"**S**ORRY," the government housing officer said, "it isn't safe."

Lila looked up, for the hundredth time, at the façade of the Villa Zonda. Or what was left of it. The two windows of the salone had certainly vanished, but Pa's bedroom window — tightly shuttered — and that of their little kitchen upstairs still looked absurdly as they had always done. Except that they were open to the sky.

"Surely we can still live in this end of it? The ground floor anyway. And the cellar — "

"Sorry," the housing officer said again. He wrote something in a notebook. He was probably as hungry and tired as the rest of them, but he had kept, for all that, a maddening air of petty officiousness.

"There's a whole family who live here," Lila said, "who've always lived here. If we none of us go upstairs, what harm can we come to?"

The housing officer squinted at the building.

"Impact of the bomb caused severe structural stress and cracking. Sorry. You're on the list and you'll have to go. We can't risk further deaths from unsound buildings. Probably," he added with some relish, "it will have to be demolished after the war."

Lila glared at him.

286

"Over my dead body. *And* my father's. We buried him here."

The housing officer crossed himself briefly.

"May he rest in peace."

"He wouldn't," Lila said, "if he knew what you were doing."

"Sorry," the housing officer said for the fourth time, "orders. It's orders. You have a week."

Lila walked deliberately away from him, and through the gap in the wall to the vegetable garden. The bomb crater was still there, already colonized by a few creeping weeds, and beyond it, against the wall where A. E. O. Perriam had grown his apricots and nectarines, the gentle mound of Pa's grave. They had buried him there two weeks ago, Lila and the family and Angelo Saliba. It had been the loneliest day of Lila's life.

Doris had wanted to mark the grave with a cross, but Lila wouldn't allow her to.

"It is what he would have wished!"

"It most certainly is not!"

Doris was furious with Lila, furious and resentful of Lila's angry shouting at her the day Pa died, and in front of her relations and her children! She was also bewildered by Lila's refusal to allow them to mourn together, to seek solace in remembering and lamenting, united like sisters in mutual affection and grief. But Lila wanted to be alone.

"She has much on her mind," Angelo Saliba said to Doris.

"Haven't we all?"

"I think," Angelo said gently, "she has the

287

past to consider. A long past. All her life with him."

Angelo had kept his distance since the day of Pa's death. He had held her there, in the vegetable garden, for perhaps ten minutes, while she wept and talked incoherently about things he only half heard, half understood, and then she had gently, politely, disengaged herself.

"Thank you."

"There is nothing to thank."

"But you came."

"I felt pain for you," Angelo said.

"Will you help me to bury him?"

Angelo looked down at Pa.

"In Malta, you know, it is always the church — "

"No," Lila said. "*No*. Not for Pa."

There was a pause. Then Angelo said, "He ought to be buried at sea."

"But we can't."

"No, we can't."

"So — here. He was happy here. It had become — well, home."

There was a tiny pause.

"I will help you," Angelo said.

It took them three nights to dig the grave. Carmela was afraid to help them — Doris had pronounced the whole enterprise to be wicked — but she lurked in the courtyard while they dug, unable to resist conveying her sympathy, her support, even if it was only by crouching in the pale spring darkness under the carob tree, where she had read Pa 'The Lady of Shalott'.

"Gloomy girl," Pa had said of the Lady,

"don't you think? Always in the dumps."

Tears prickled behind Carmela's eyelids when she thought of Pa, when she looked at little Spiru, sitting on the kitchen step nursing his wooden aeroplane, waiting for Pa to come back, when she saw Lila going yet again into the vegetable garden where Pa's mound was, under the south wall. Doris had said, and still kept saying, that Pa was like a father to her, that your world fell away when you lost your father. Carmela thought of Salvu, her own father, hardly seen now except for short visits home, when he seemed exhausted and exhilarated and angry all at once. What would she feel, she wondered guiltily, if Salvu were to die?

★ ★ ★

The bomb blast had dislodged no furniture in Pa's bedroom. It had sliced off the ceiling, and the roof above, depositing in the process a thick layer of dust and broken stones and tiles on everything, but it had left the bed exactly as it was, and the big cupboard and — hard to look at, this — an upright chair still piled with Pa's clothes, now fossilized with debris. The windows, being superfluous now that the room was open to the sky, were still tightly shuttered. Pa must have shuttered them that last night, before he died, when he came up, as he always did, to put up the blackout.

Lila stood in the dusty rubble and looked about her. She must excavate the bedding, as she must in her own equally damaged bedroom, and drag it down to be washed somehow, because all bedding was too precious to be wasted. She must grit her teeth, and find all Pa's clothes that she could, all those now painfully familiar shirts and jerseys and characterful pairs of thick white socks, the spotted handkerchiefs he had worn instead of ties, the stout canvas and corduroy trousers which he had always girdled round himself with lengths of rope rather than belts. Then she must open the cupboard and take out his hoarded paintings, his paintbox with the paints now hardened inexorably in their tubes, the brushes stiff and neglected, and try not to remember as she did so how profoundly discouraging she had been about his painting; sour and almost scornful. In fact, as the paints were going to cause one of the keenest bouts of remorse, she thought she had better take a deep breath and start there.

It was difficult to open the cupboard because of all the broken masonry piled up against it. Lila painstakingly cleared herself a passage with the shovel she had brought upstairs with her, and managed to open the door finally by jamming the edge of the shovel against the jamb of the doorframe and wrenching sideways. She peered inside, coughing in the dust.

There was almost nothing there. The cupboard, which Lila had expected to find haphazardly jammed with paintings on wood on canvas, on cardboard — Pa had never been fussy about what he painted on — was virtually empty. But eerily empty, as if there had once been something there, something important. All that was there now was Pa's one once-good jacket, a blazer in dark blue wool now peppered with moth holes, hanging from a hook screwed into the back of the cupboard, his paintbox lying on the floor with a bunch of brushes tied up with string, a lumpy bundle of something that appeared to be wrapped in an old tablecloth, and a small parcel roughly done up in whitish paper.

Lila stooped and touched the brushes. They were as stiff as if they were carved in wood. Then she opened the paintbox and looked at the bent, crushed silvery tubes and smelt, with a rush of nostalgia, that unmistakable oil-paint smell that had permeated the tall house in Aldeburgh from top to bottom. Then she picked up the little parcel. It was heavy and clinked faintly. She turned back the layers of rough paper, and found the brass dolphin knocker that Angelo Saliba had once tried to give her, in the salone. She touched it, rubbing at its greeny tarnish with one finger. It was a lovely thing, a charming thing. But why should it be in Pa's cupboard?

"Please — " Carmela said from behind her.

Lila turned. Carmela was standing in the doorway, very pale, holding the ends of her pigtails in both hands.

"Where are Pa's paintings?"

"He burned them," Carmela said.

Lila stared at her.

"*What?*"

"He burned them. He cut them up and put

them in the stove to make a fire for cooking."

"Oh no," Lila said, her face crumpling. "Oh *no*."

Carmela said, "You must come."

"Come?"

"Downstairs. Something has happened."

She tugged fiercely at her pigtails, as if to emphasize the importance of her mission.

Lila had her arm across her eyes.

"Not now, not just now, I'm — "

"*Yes*," Carmela insisted, "*now*."

Lila took her arm away.

"What is it," she said tiredly, "that's so important?"

"My father. My father has come home. He needs to see you."

Lila stood up slowly, still holding the dolphin in its crumpled wrappings.

"All right."

Carmela pointed.

"Bring that."

"This?"

"Yes. Angelo brought it. To keep it safe. And those," Carmela pointed to the bundle in the cupboard, "bring those. I'll help you. They are his mother's. They are treasures. We must look after them."

* * *

In the kitchen, by the big central table, Salvu sat. He did not get up when Lila came in, nor did the women, gathered behind him like a Greek chorus, say anything. The silence in the kitchen was however not one of tranquillity. It was one of shock.

"Look," Salvu said.

Lila looked. Salvu was sitting, she saw, but not, as she had first assumed, in a kitchen chair. He was in a wheelchair.

"Both legs," Salvu said, "Jerry got both legs. I made the hospital let me come home today to show my family I was not dead. I have my dressings changed every two hours. You mustn't touch me. You might infect the wounds."

Lila felt Carmela's hand creep into her own.

"Oh Salvu. Oh Salvu, I am so sorry."

"So am I," he said. He gestured wildly, almost upsetting himself and the chair. "What is to become of me?"

She was silent, quite overwhelmed.

"What is to become of me?" Salvu shouted. "Eh? Answer me that! What is to become of any of us now?"

Doris, standing behind him and weeping silently and unrestrainedly, put a hand out to touch him and, remembering she mustn't, snatched it back again and put it over her eyes. Salvu took a steadying breath.

"You came here," Salvu said, "you and your father."

"Yes."

"We helped you."

"You did."

"We gave you somewhere to live."

Lila opened her mouth to say that, actually, Mr and Mrs Perriam had done that, caught sight of the hospital blanket draped over Salvu's truncated thighs, and closed it again.

"You did."

"I gave your father rides on my motorbicycle. I found you a bicycle."

"Yes."

"Now," said Salvu, his voice rising a little in his agitation at his own powerlessness, "it is for you to help us."

Carmela's hand tightened in Lila's.

"We have to leave this house," Salvu said, "Doris tells me. We have to go." He leaned forward, and the women behind him leaned too, protectively, as if afraid that he might fall. "We have nowhere to go," Salvu said, "nowhere. It is for you to find us somewhere to live. We did it for you, once. Now you must do it for us."

# 24

THE dolphin knocker on the door of the Tabia Palace was as brilliantly polished as it had ever been in peacetime. What was different was that it now presided over a whole series of military notices and announcements, pinned to the great studded door with drawing pins, in neat serried ranks. Lila wondered what Count Julius thought of them. Drawing pins in his historic family door! Perhaps he would shrug, as he so often did nowadays, and merely say something deprecating about the philistine exigencies of wartime.

Count Julius had written to Lila. On thick cream writing paper embossed with the Tabia crest, he had written a stately but sincere letter of condolence on Pa's death, and on the destruction of the Villa Zonda.

"I am bold enough," he wrote, "to think of myself as your friend, indeed as an old friend by now in both senses of the word, and in that capacity, I would like to offer you any help I can. I am uncertain where to find you these days, but you know where to find me. I am a fixture here, lurking like an old toad in a cool hole in the wall. I expect to see you. I expect to see you soon."

The door of the palace wasn't opened by Teseo, but by a tidy young soldier in sharply creased khaki cotton. His bright little eyes took in Lila's faded shirt and shorts and dusty bare sandalled feet in a flash, even as he greeted her.

"Morning, miss."

"Morning," Lila said. "I'm here to see Count Julius."

"Sunday morning," the soldier said. "It's Sunday, you know. The Count has gone to church."

"Then I'll wait for him."

The soldier looked doubtful.

"My name is Lila Cunningham. I used to work for him."

"He left no orders — "

"He is expecting me any time," Lila said. She stepped smartly into the cool darkness of the hall, past the soldier. "Teseo knows me. Teseo will tell me where to wait."

"As you say, miss," the soldier said. He closed the great outer door with a slam and set off briskly up the stone staircase ahead of Lila. She sniffed. The air smelled of cigarette smoke and also, faintly, of beer. What on earth would the Baroness think of either?

They went through the tapestry room, past several officers yawningly reading outdated newspapers, down the corridor past Count Julius' library, where an orderly could be seen through the open door, incongruously making beds, and through a baize-covered swing door into a quarter of the palace Lila had never penetrated. The passages were narrower and darker, the doors meaner in proportion and there was a mingled smell of disinfectant and

296

institutional cooking. Even that made Lila's mouth water.

The soldier stopped in front of one of the narrow doors and rapped smartly. Then he opened it and stuck his head inside.

"Lady to see the Count, Mr Teezo."

He stood back, to let Lila go in. It was a tiny room, almost cell-like, with a single window set high in one wall, and on a small table in the centre, neatly covered with old copies of the *Times of Malta*, Teseo was diligently polishing Count Julius' boots.

"Miss Lila!"

She came forward, smiling.

"Teseo. How are you?"

He put down a boot and a polishing cloth and held out his hand.

"Still in the land of the living, miss, as you see."

"I'll leave you to it, then," the soldier said. The door shut, not quite with a slam, behind him.

"Count Julius wrote to me," Lila said, "about my father."

Teseo's hand sketched a cross above his chest.

"My sympathy, miss."

Lila looked down. The only time Pa and Teseo had ever encountered one another had been that undignified wrestling match when Pa, fortified by a little Dutch courage in the Gut, had tried to force his way into the lunch party in the courtyard. And she — well, better not to think about what she had done. And thought.

"Thank you."

"Count Julius is at church, miss."

"So the soldier said."

Teseo sighed.

"The soldiers, miss, are a cross we have to bear. The Count will be back at five past midday. I will show you to his room, to wait for him."

★ ★ ★

"My dear," Count Julius said.

He stood, as was his wont, just inside the door and bowed, very slightly. He wore a summer suit of cream linen with a cornflower in the buttonhole, and carried cream kid gloves and a Panama straw hat, banded in black grosgrain.

Lila stood up.

"Count Julius — "

He came forward and kissed her, very lightly, on the cheek.

"What do you think of my new abode?"

Lila looked round. The old housekeeper's room was perhaps one sixth the size of Count Julius' library. It had two windows, both looking into the kitchen courtyard, a narrow bed, two armchairs, a bookcase and an immense table, covered with a Persian rug and neatly piled with papers.

"Well — "

"I am devoted to it," Count Julius said. "I have found an absolutely unyielding mattress to sleep on and I have nothing superfluous." He motioned Lila to a chair. "I am so very sorry about your father."

"Your letter was so kind."

"Your father and I once spent a memorable night together. Drinking rum."

"Yes."

"He was not altogether the man he seemed, your father."

"No."

Count Julius laid his hat and gloves on the table. He said thoughtfully, "He saw, perhaps, more than he was ever given credit for seeing."

Lila said nothing. She could feel Count Julius watching her.

"Where have you buried him?"

"In the garden."

"I should have liked to have come," Count Julius said. "I should have liked to have known of his funeral."

Lila looked up at him.

"It wasn't really a funeral, it was just a burial. Very private, just the family, and me. My father — well, if my father thought there was a god, it wasn't any kind of god that the Maltese would recognize."

Count Julius chuckled.

"That's why I should have liked to be there. Did you — " he gave Lila a sharp glance — "did you invite my nephew, Max?"

"No," Lila said, too loudly.

Count Julius sank into the chair opposite to Lila. He shook his head.

"My dear. My dear, what a thing. What am I to say to you? You know whom he has taken up with?"

"Yes."

"What would my sister say?" He put his hands to his temples and pressed hard. "I can hardly contemplate it."

Lila said boldly, "Even worse than me."

Count Julius shot her a look.

"You don't lose an opportunity, my dear."

"No," Lila said, "I'm learning not to." She looked down at her bare knees. "She's a good girl, Max's Rosanna. One of Miss de Vere's protégées."

"A protégée from a fisherman's house in the Grand Harbour . . . "

Lila waited.

"My sister — " Count Julius said again and threw his hands in the air. "However, we will not think of my sister. We will think of you, and your loss and your situation. At least I flatter myself I can do something about that. I have never been able to do anything at all about my sister." He leaned forward and regarded Lila with his bright, humorous eyes. "Tell me the state of affairs at the Villa Zonda."

"Uninhabitable," Lila said. "At least the authorities think so. We have been given a week to evacuate it, of which two days are already gone."

"A direct hit?"

"No. It was that which got Pa. But the blast took the roof off and blew in one end, and the buildings in the courtyard caught fire." She stopped suddenly, and then said in quite a different voice, one much less brisk and matter of fact, "It's awful, pathetic, I hate seeing it like this, I can't bear the fact that we have to leave.

300

And we will have to leave Pa too — " She stopped again and put one hand to her face.

Count Julius said gently, "Where will you go?"

"The family have some cousins at Gharghur. They can perhaps take Doris and the children."

"Doris?"

"Old Spiru's daughter. Her husband has just had both his legs blown off." Lila took her hand from her face and put it, with her other one, between her knees. "I must write to the Perriams and tell them."

Count Julius leaned back in his chair. Through the window, from the kitchen courtyard below, came the sound of someone throwing the contents of a bucket down a drain.

"I would like," Count Julius said, "to offer you a home here."

There was a pause. In it Lila reflected how, once upon a time, she would have regarded such an invitation as a passport to Paradise. She looked at Count Julius.

"Thank you."

"Of course, I am unable to offer you anything very — "

"But I can't," Lila said.

"You can't? What do you mean, you can't?"

"I can't leave the family. I mean, I couldn't take responsibility for all of them, all seventeen or eighteen or however many there are, but I have to for old Spiru's family. Especially now Salvu is crippled."

Count Julius placed his fingertips together and considered them.

"I think, in that case, that they had better come here too."

"I will ask them," Lila said.

"My dear, this is most extraordinary talk. What do you mean, ask them? Is an offer like mine not beyond anything they could hope for?"

"They aren't used to a city," Lila said, "not even a little one. And there is no garden."

"Good heavens!" Count Julius cried suddenly, his voice rising almost to a shout, "there is a world war raging and you talk of peasant families needing gardens!"

Lila raised her chin and looked at him.

"Precisely," she said.

★ ★ ★

"I have found somewhere," Lila said to Doris. "In Mdina. Three ground-floor rooms in an old palace. It — it isn't wonderful, but you wouldn't go hungry there. Or at least, not as hungry as you would be with your cousins."

Doris sat at the kitchen table, tracing the scrubbed woodgrain with a forefinger. Since Salvu's alarming visit she had been very quiet, with the quietness that suggests someone is stunned rather than merely thinking.

"I will ask him."

"There isn't a garden outside. There's a courtyard but — well, it isn't like this one. It's enclosed. Smaller. But Mdina is safe. Much safer than here."

Doris said in a low voice, "What will become of Salvu?"

"I think Count Julius — "

Doris's head whipped up.

"Count Julius!"

"Yes. It's his palace. His offer."

"We could not live *there*."

"The palace is an officers' mess, for the army. Count Julius lives in the kitchen quarters. That's where these three rooms are."

Carmela had been watching from the corner of the room, by the stove. Now she came slowly across and leaned on Lila. She whispered something. Lila stooped.

"What?"

"Are you coming? Will you go to the palace?"

Lila hesitated.

"I must bring my mother," Doris said.

"Are you? Are you? Are you?" Carmela hissed.

"There's the school," Lila said. "I couldn't get to the school from Mdina."

"Nor could I," Carmela said at once. She looked at her mother. Doris was tracing the woodgrain again very slowly, up and down, round and round. "I couldn't stop going to school," Carmela said loudly to her mother, "could I?"

Slowly, Doris looked up at them both. Her once plump face was now haggard, with dark bruises under her eyes.

"There is no question about where you live," Doris said. "You are my daughter."

* * *

303

That evening, Lila went out to the vegetable garden and sat by Pa's grave, with her back against the still faintly sunwarmed wall. The atmosphere in the kitchen had been stifling, literally and metaphorically, with the family both bemused at being uprooted and resentful of Lila, as the person closest at hand to blame for their splitting up across the island. Doris, her mother and children, and Salvu when he was discharged from hospital, would go to Mdina. Two of her sisters and an aunt would go to the cousins in Gharghur. Further aunts and a cousin or two would try more distant relations in Mosta. They had all lived together for over twenty years and were devastated at the prospect of separation.

"We ask for help," Doris said, not looking at Lila, "and look what happens."

"I don't know what else to do," Lila said to Pa's grave. "I don't know how else to help them." She put her arms round her knees and bent her head onto them. "Especially as I don't know how to help myself."

There was a movement by the gap in the wall that led to the courtyard. Carmela's outline, identifiable by the pigtails and the shapeless frock, slipped through and came hurrying over to Lila. She knelt down very close to Lila and put her hands down firmly on top of Lila's own.

"*Listen*," Carmela said.

"I am."

"I *can't* go to Mdina. I can't. I won't."

"You aren't my child," Lila said. "You are Doris's. I can't tell you what to do."

"But you can *let* me."

"Let you what?"

"Come with you. I must, I must!"

"Carmela," Lila said, "I don't know where I'm going."

"You'll find somewhere," Carmela said confidently, "you'll find a place. And then I can come with you."

"What about Spiru?"

Carmela took her hands away.

"He is more precious to my mother. Because he is a boy."

"But he'll be lonely without you."

"And I'll be lonely without *you*," Carmela said.

Lila looked down the length of Pa's grave. It was alone, to be sure, but somehow it didn't look lonely, only tranquil and quiet.

"You need me," Carmela said.

Lila looked at her.

"Yes."

"Then I have to come!"

"I've upset Doris already — "

"Please try!"

"Carmela — "

Carmela suddenly launched forward and wound her skinny arms so tightly around Lila's neck that she could scarcely breathe.

"You must," Carmela said, "you must, you must. Can't you see how important it is?"

# 25

"YOU forget," Miss de Vere said.

She was sitting in an armchair draped in a scarlet Chinese shawl embroidered with herons, fanning herself with a copy of the *Times of Malta*. Opposite her, Lila sat on a kitchen chair, and Carmela, cross-legged, sat on the floor.

"What do I forget?"

Miss de Vere pointed the newspaper at Lila. "You forget how angry I am with you."

"Angry?"

"You never told me about your father's death."

"I didn't tell anyone."

"I had to hear it," Miss de Vere said inexorably, "from Angelo Saliba. I would have expected to hear from you. Direct from you."

Lila said nothing. Carmela bent her head, and wrapped her reddened wrists and hands in the skirts of her frock.

"I was fond of your father," Miss de Vere said. "I even pride myself on thinking that I may have been a little instrumental in changing your perception of him. I would like to have known. I would like to have been there, at his funeral."

Lila said steadily, "There wasn't a funeral. He wouldn't have liked a funeral. We — "

"We?" Miss de Vere demanded. "Who's we?"

306

Lila thought of Angelo and decided to throw no more fuel on the present fire. She edged a warning foot against Carmela.

"The family, and me. The family at the Villa Zonda. We buried him in the garden, where he'd grown potatoes, where he'd been happy — "

"And you never thought of telling me?"

Lila looked at her.

"No. I never thought of telling anybody. There was too much else to think about."

Miss de Vere slapped the newspaper down hard on the arm of her chair.

"You didn't think of telling me either at the time, or later, yet you have the effrontery to ask if I can offer you a home — you and this child — here, in this house?"

Lila's gaze didn't waver.

"Yes."

"How dare you?" Miss de Vere shouted.

Carmela bent her head so far that her forehead almost touched the floor. Lila knew that her eyes would be closed.

"Because we need to be in the city," Lila said, "for the school. Because I know you, and even though this house is damaged, it's a big one, and there's space. Because we could be useful to you."

Miss de Vere threw her head back.

"You are an impossible girl."

"Yes," Lila said, "but you've always thought that."

Miss de Vere brought her head back and peered at Carmela.

"Who is this?"

307

"You remember her," Lila said firmly, "Carmela. Old Spiru's granddaughter. She is very anxious to come with me. I have yet to confront her mother."

"And where do you suppose you will live in my house?"

"In the storerooms," Lila said, "down on the waterfront. You needn't know we are there."

"You can't bring a child to Kalkara," Miss de Vere exclaimed. "It's far too dangerous."

"So was the Villa Zonda, as it turned out."

Carmela raised her head very slowly until she was looking at Miss de Vere's knees. She tried to say something. Miss de Vere leaned forward.

"What, dear?"

"Please," Carmela said. "Please." She paused and then she said, "I can't — " and stopped again.

"What can't you?"

"I can't stay in the kitchen every day, I can't just — " she stopped and put her hands to her mouth.

Over her head Lila said to Miss de Vere, "It's a very domestic life, you see. And now that she reads and writes English so well — "

Miss de Vere grunted faintly. She said, apparently apropos of nothing that had been said before, "I worry about Rosanna and Max, you know. Max has been flying such dangerous missions. They grounded him for months and now he's hardly on the ground at all."

Lila fixed her eyes on a spot on the wall above Miss de Vere's head.

"It's what he wants, isn't it? To defend Malta? Now that he's discovered his — "

"You may come," Miss de Vere interrupted. "Talk to this child's mother."

Carmela burst into tears and cast herself across Miss de Vere's feet, encased in her invariable sturdy laced-up brown shoes.

"Now, now."

"She's grateful," Lila said, "and — and so am I."

Miss de Vere looked at her.

"I wonder," she said. "It doesn't trouble me much, but I wonder. I wonder, sometimes, what you really feel about anything. I do indeed."

★ ★ ★

"No," Doris said, "never."

The old kitchen table from the Villa Zonda had been put in the new kitchen at the Tabia Palace. Two men had brought it on a mule cart, tied on upside down with pillows and pots and pans and chairs and mattresses roped in an unwieldy bundle between its legs. Doris sat at it and traced the woodgrain with her finger.

The kitchen at the Tabia Palace was smaller than the old one, and darker. Doris said she didn't like it. She didn't like the kitchen courtyard outside it either, despite the useful proximity of the pump and the stone troughs where Count Julius had invited her to grow vegetables and herbs. She didn't like the fact that Salvu, now discharged from hospital, sat all day in the courtyard making a model of a sixteenth-century Maltese galley for Count Julius, concentrating so hard he scarcely spoke to her; nor did she like the cheerful English soldiers who came into the courtyard and played with Spiru, teaching him to bowl a stupid English cricket ball. She didn't like her new bedroom, nor being in a city, nor the fact that her mother complained all day, every day, about their confinement. But most of all, she didn't like Carmela wanting to leave her, and live with Lila in a house on Kalkara Creek.

"It's dangerous," she said. "It will be a godless house. There will be raids. You will be killed. Your place is with me, with your family. No," she said, over and over again, "no. Never."

"When the war is over," Lila said, "she will come back to you. She will live with you again, and go to school — "

"School!" Doris said scornfully. She almost spat. "School is the troublemaker. Ever since you came, all this talk of school. School is not a woman's life!"

Lila looked past her, through the open door to the courtyard. Salvu sat there, in the wheelchair Count Julius had obtained for him, at a table covered in a green baize cloth. His head was bent. He was working with the concentration he had always given to everything he did. Every day, Count Julius came down to see him several times, and they would discuss the galley and Count Julius would read passages of naval history to him.

"He is a clever man," Salvu would say, "for an aristocrat."

"What does Salvu think?" Lila said now, to Doris.

Doris said nothing.

"Does he think Carmela should stay here and help you in the kitchen?"

"He knows nothing," Doris said. "How can he? He's a wounded man."

"I see," Lila said.

She laid a hand lightly on Doris's shoulder and went past her into the courtyard.

"Salvu," Lila said.

"Yes," he said. He didn't look up. His fingers, amazingly nimble, were fitting tiny joints together with minute wooden pegs.

"I want to take Carmela with me. To Kalkara. She wants to come."

"I know."

"What is your opinion," Lila said. "What do you think she should do?"

"Go with you."

"Oh, Salvu — "

"You have made her," Salvu said, "not fit for us. You have changed her. Take her."

"I didn't mean — "

"She'll be the new Malta," Salvu said, "after the war. Malta without the English." He gave Lila a quick glance. "It's not a bad thing you have done, for Carmela."

Lila waited. Then she said, "But Doris — "

Salvu glanced at her again. He gave her

something close to a grin.

"Leave Doris to me." His voice almost had an edge of self-satisfaction. "There is something I can do for Doris. I am man enough still for that. Leave Doris to me."

★ ★ ★

"I have had to sell some of the furniture from the salone," Lila wrote on the thin crackling blue paper Miss de Vere had provided her with. "I'm so sorry, because I know it wasn't mine to sell, but Spiru's family had nothing to live on and I took the chance — no chance, I think — that you'd understand. I've kept the desk, and some chairs and a small table or two and several lamps and anything personal I could see like the little bronzes or pictures, but the rest has gone. It fetched almost a hundred pounds which, when I tell you that eggs are fifteen shillings a dozen, if you can get them, and a scrawny rabbit has people fighting over it for more than that, you will see won't go far. But it's something, and as they are now in a British officers' mess, I know they won't be allowed to starve."

She paused, and looked across the tiny, damp room she and Carmela now shared at night. Carmela, wearing her tattered petticoat and half covered by a patched sheet, was already asleep, her arms flung up above her head revealing the raw patches of scabies in her armpits which Lila was struggling to control. The last light of a late sunset was coming in through the little window, below which the sea gently slapped against the house wall. Lila liked the sound. She had never liked the sound of the sea at Aldeburgh, and the way it sucked so harshly at the cold pebbles, but this creek-bound sea, in wartime, seemed comforting and soothing, like a promise that normal life was still there, deep down, underneath the fear and noise and destruction.

"We have boarded up the Villa Zonda," Lila wrote, "or what's left of it. I hope you approve. It seemed the safest thing to do. In any case, if I can't live in it, I can't bear the thought of anyone else doing so, even for the war effort. I go up there when I can. To visit Pa."

She paused again. It was difficult to tell the Perriams about Pa because the Pa they had known was so different from the Pa of the Villa Zonda. And in any case, there was something deeply private about that later Pa, that gentler Pa with Spiru on his knee and a quietly watchful eye upon Lila. She closed her eyes for a moment, and as she did so, the rising wail of an air-raid siren came through the open window.

"Oh!" Carmela cried in her half sleep, "oh, stop them, stop them — "

Lila sprang up and slammed the window shut, pulling the curtain across to muffle the glass if it broke. The room was suddenly completely dark.

"Do we go to the cellar?" Carmela asked.

"No."

"Don't we? Shouldn't we?"

"We can't," Lila said. She groped her way across the room and crouched by Carmela's bed,

313

feeling for her hand, "We're on the water line. There isn't one."

Carmela's small, scaly hand gripped hers.

"I'm tired."

"I know."

"I don't want," Carmela said, her voice almost drowned out by the first screaming plane overhead, so close it sounded as if it were in the room with them, "I don't want anything else to happen!"

\* \* \*

In the morning, news came that Rosanna and Angelo's father had been killed by falling masonry on Lascaris Wharf. He had been evacuated out to Mqabba, with his wife, to his sister-in-law's house, but at every opportunity he would hitch a ride on an army lorry or a pony cart, around the airfield at Luqa, and back into the city. He had been born on the Grand Harbour; he had lived and worked on it all his life, and when he was away from it he was restless and couldn't sleep. His wife knew where he went when she found him missing; there was no point stopping him, no point trying to confine him in the tiny hot house with her sister's temper and the boredom and the hunger. It was only when he stayed missing at night that she began to worry, and on the night he was killed, she had dreamed of going to look for him in a Valetta that was at once wonderfully whole and yet disturbingly unrecognizable. She hadn't found him in her dream, and when she woke in the

314

morning and saw that he hadn't returned, she knew what had happened at once, long before they came to tell her.

After school that day, Lila took Carmela back to the house on Kalkara Creek.

"Where are you going?"

"Somewhere you can't come."

"Oh," Carmela said in exasperation, "I thought you had stopped saying that."

"You've got sums to do."

"I hate sums."

"Only because you won't learn how to do them."

"But I read beautifully!"

"You like reading. If you learned to like sums, you would do them beautifully too."

"What if there's a raid?"

"Close the windows and curtains and get under the bed. You know what to do. Anyway, Zanzu is here."

"How long will you be?"

"As long," Lila said, "as it takes."

It took a long time. On the road south she found an army truck, but it was only going as far as the airfield, and left her, after a few miles, on the edge of the dusty road with coils of barbed wire glinting in the sun all around her. She walked for a while, then was picked up by a man with a mule cart, who let her ride for a while among scratchy bundles of thorn branches he would later use for fuel, until he said she was too heavy for his tired animal, and made her get down again.

When she finally reached Mqabba, the sun

was beginning to go down, and the shadows in the ancient, narrow streets were dark and soft. It was amazing to be anywhere so little damaged. Settled there above the south-western cliffs, Mqabba had resisted Muslim invaders and pirates down the centuries and was now, almost, managing to elude the Germans. In a tiny square, Lila asked a pair of girls playing a game of primitive draughts with pebbles in the dust if they knew where Mr and Mrs Saliba were staying.

The smaller child stood up.

"He died," she said. "He was killed. In Valetta. My mother said."

"Yes," Lila said, "I know. I've come to see his widow."

The child looked at her companion.

"You wait," she said. And then to Lila, "Come."

Lila followed her down a side street, and then another, and then into an alley no wider than a passage. The houses were all shuttered, and there were no sounds, no voices or domestic clatter. The child laid her hand on the stone wall of a house indistinguishable from its neighbours.

"Here," she said.

Lila listened. There was almost complete silence.

"Are you sure?"

"Yes," the child said, "Mrs Saliba. The house of her sister, Mrs Kissaun. The son has gone to bring back his father's body. My mother said."

"Right," Lila said. "Thank you."

The child gave the house one last slap,

and went skipping off up the alley, back to her companion and her game. Lila looked at the door in front of her. It was wooden, unpainted and uncompromising, without either handle or knocker. She raised a tentative hand and knocked.

There was a pause. Lila knocked again. There was a further pause, and then slippered feet came slowly towards the door from inside and opened it. In the six inches allowed, Lila saw a small Maltese woman in a black headscarf, with a narrow, bad-tempered face.

"Mrs Saliba?"

"What do you want with her?" the woman said.

"To pay my respects," Lila said in her slow, careful Maltese, "for the loss of her husband."

"Who are you?"

"I know her daughter," Lila said, "and her son. She was very kind to me once, when I first came from England."

The door opened a little wider.

"Are you official?" the woman said.

"No. Just a friend."

"But you are English."

"That," Lila said, trying to stop her voice rising, "doesn't prevent my being a friend."

The woman looked Lila up and down, consideringly; the faded cotton skirt and blouse, the inevitably dusty sandalled feet.

"Wait," she said, and vanished.

Lila waited. From the inside of the house came murmurings, and then a raised voice, speaking sharply, and then there was someone else in the doorway, another woman, also in black, with dark shadows smudged under her eyes. She looked at Lila.

"I am Mrs Saliba," she said.

Lila put out a hand.

"Maybe you won't remember me — "

"I do," Mrs Saliba said, "I do. You fainted on the waterfront the day you landed. My son brought you to our house. We couldn't speak to one another because you knew no Maltese." She glanced down at Lila's outstretched hand and touched it briefly. "Our house was bombed."

"I know," Lila said.

"And now my husband — "

Mrs Saliba looked steadily at her. It was plain that she had been weeping, but she was dry-eyed now.

"He was a good man."

"I know. I'm so sorry. I came to say how sorry — " she paused. "My father was killed by a bomb three weeks ago, so perhaps I know a little, just a little — "

Mrs Saliba came out of the doorway a little further until she was very close to Lila.

"Who have you to comfort you?"

Lila hesitated. Then she said, "Oh, I'm all right, really, I can manage."

Mrs Saliba laid her hand on Lila's arm.

"I have my son, you see. And my daughter. They are all the world to me, especially my son. No-one will ever be good enough for my son."

Lila said nothing. She thought of Mrs Saliba's

treasures, carefully stored even now at the house on Kalkara Creek, wrapped in their checked tablecloth.

"It was kind of you to come," Mrs Saliba said. "It was a Christian act. I would ask you in, but my sister does not like visitors. And I am waiting for my son. My son has gone to bring me his father's body — "

Her face crumpled suddenly, and she drew a fold of her black scarf across it, to hide the tears.

"I'll go," Lila said.

Mrs Saliba nodded. She stepped back into the house.

"Thank you," Lila said, "thank you for seeing me."

Mrs Saliba gave her one last glance before she closed the door.

"I will pray," she said. "I will pray for you."

\* \* \*

On the way back into the city, three officers in a jeep stopped and offered Lila a lift as far as Cospicua. They were going down to Senglea themselves, they said, to put a bit of heart into the antiaircraft gunners down there. One of them had a bottle of whisky he'd paid four pounds for.

"Daylight robbery," he said, grinning. He brandished a paper at Lila. "Seen the new civilian ration list?"

"No."

"Pretty grim," he said. "No rice or sugar, one tin of corned beef between two a week, three ounces of cheese if you're lucky. No edible oil, and kerosene for one week only." He offered Lila a cigarette. "Poor buggers, if you'll pardon my French."

Lila shook her head at the cigarette. "We've forgotten what a good meal is like."

The officer at the wheel glanced at Lila in the driving mirror.

"We'll get you one," he said. "Nobody's going to let Jerry get away with this."

They let her out two miles from home.

"We could easily run you a bit further — "

"No," Lila said. "No, thank you. I know the way."

It was dark now, but a waning moon still shed a soft glow across the ruined streets, turning them eerily into places of romance, not destruction. Lila was very tired, tired with an exhaustion of spirit which had oppressed her for months, and certainly since Pa's death. She made her way steadily onward, one foot in front of the other, yard after yard, reaching Miss de Vere's door just as Zanzu was about to bolt it for the night.

"Where have you been?"

"I had an errand."

"She's waiting for you," Zanzu said. "She's waiting up. She's in the kitchen."

Miss de Vere sat sideways on the wicker chaise longue, in her peony printed wrapper, reading the *Times of Malta*. She tapped it smartly at Lila's entrance.

"This paper is a masterpiece. A masterpiece of disinformation. Anybody would think there wasn't a hungry Maltese or a German aeroplane not shot down on sight. I must congratulate Mabel." She looked up at Lila. "Where've you been? The child has only just gone to sleep. She's spent all evening asking for you."

Lila leaned against the table.

"To Mqabba."

"Mqabba?"

"To see Rosanna and Angelo's mother."

Miss de Vere put the newspaper down.

"Ah," she said softly.

"It took a long time."

"It would," Miss de Vere said. She looked at Lila thoughtfully in silence for a while and then she said, "I've something for you."

"Oh?"

"Two things, in fact. The first is a tin of sardines. Don't ask where they came from or what I paid for them. Just eat them. The second is that." She pointed.

"What?"

"That. On the table. That letter. Posted in England, brought to Malta by submarine and delivered, for some reason, to the newspaper offices. Who sent it on here."

"England!" Lila said. "The Perriams!"

"Maybe," Miss de Vere said. "Postmarked London."

Lila bent over the letter. It was in an airmail envelope of thin blue paper, and it was addressed to Miss Lila Cunningham, The Villa Zonda, Venera, Malta, in a bold black hand. But it wasn't the handwriting of either Mr or Mrs Perriam; it was handwriting Lila hadn't seen for over two years and had begun to teach herself she would never see again. It was the handwriting of Anton Ferroferrata.

# 26

CARMELA lay on her bed and looked at the eight sums Lila had drawn on the whitewashed wall above her, in charcoal. Four division and four multiplication. Miss de Vere had said they could draw on the wall as long as the drawings were educational. Lila had told Carmela that as far as her present stage of education was concerned, sums were more educational than reading, and then she had given Carmela her tin of sardines. A whole tin. Seven whole sardines and a bit of an eighth, which had got squashed. And then Zanzu had found her a piece of bread to soak up the oil in the tin so that nothing should be wasted. As she had eaten the sardines alone, with no-one to watch her, Carmela had also licked the tin out, very thoroughly. And then, promising herself she really would do the eight sums, she had lain down on her bed, and put her hands flat on her flatter belly and realized that with a little bit of imagination she could tell herself that she almost — *almost* — felt full.

Lila had gone up to the hospital to help with an emergency evening shift. Carmela had, of course, wanted to come, but Lila had said she had done enough for one day, and must rest. Carmela had heard her telling Miss de Vere how worried she was that Carmela was half-starved. It was exciting, in a melodramatic sort of way, to be considered half-starved, but the penalty was being made to rest by Lila, instead of accompanying her everywhere, all the time. Doris had never made Carmela rest. On the contrary, she had always found extra things for Carmela to do, things Carmela didn't want to do because she'd done them the day before and the day before that and that and that.

Carmela rolled on her side and squinted up at the sums. It wasn't just sardines that Lila had given her; she'd made her a frock out of some stuff Miss de Vere had found, white cotton printed with cherries.

"I can't sew," Lila said, "so Heaven knows what it'll look like."

It looked fine, Carmela thought. The neck was a funny shape and there were bunchy bits where the skirt was gathered on, but the cotton was new and the cherries were bright red, with green leaves. If, Carmela told herself, someone gives you a cherry frock and a tin of sardines and keeps putting ointment on you which makes the scabies better, then you ought really to do some sums for them. Oughtn't you? Except it would be so much easier, and more fun, to do the sums when Lila was here to talk her through them.

"Come on," Lila would say, "use your head. With multiplication you build things up, and with division you take them down again. But it's the same *numbers*."

Carmela sighed deeply and sat up, scratching absently at the infested places inside her elbows. The scabies was still there under her arms and inside her thighs and behind her knees. But at least she hadn't got it on her bottom. Some of the children at the dockyard school had it so badly on their bottoms they couldn't sit down.

She swung her legs over the edge of the bed and contemplated Lila's bed opposite. It was still tidily made up from the morning, with patched sheets Miss de Vere had lent them, and the old brown blankets that had been on Pa's bed at the Villa Zonda. Carmela had helped Lila wash them, in the courtyard, and they had both cried and cried all the time they were squeezing the brown wool lumps in the increasingly filthy water. Carmela thought she would turn Lila's bed down for her, to look welcoming, as she had seen Teseo do for Count Julius, and when she had done that, she would do the sums on the wall. Really she would.

She untucked the top fold of sheet and pulled it back, in a triangle. Then she pulled back the blankets — it was far too hot for blankets — and rolled them into a neat sausage at the foot of the bed. Then she thought she would plump the pillow. She picked it up and gave it a good shake, pulling it in and out like a concertina, as Doris did, to get air in among the feathers. Something caught her eye. She looked down. There was a blue envelope lying on the sheet where the pillow had been.

Carmela put down the pillow and picked the letter up.

'Miss Lila Cunningham' it said, in black ink. It was Lila's letter. It was wrong to read other people's letters, of course, and she must put it down again, at once. She did put it down. Then she picked it up again and slid the letter out of the envelope.

When Carmela had been taught how to set out a letter at school, she had been instructed to put her address at the top right-hand corner. The person who had written this letter had clearly not been taught as well as Carmela. This letter had no address at all, only a date. 'May 1st', it said and nothing else. Just that. 'May 1st'. Three months ago. More than three months.

Carmela smoothed the thin paper of the letter out on the white sheet and knelt to read it.

My dear Lila —

It has been so long that I am afraid you will have forgotten me. In fact, that fear is what has kept me from writing. That and, of course, this war. I cannot write much now, but I feel compelled to write and tell you how much I think of you, how often you are in my mind. I write this after a long night with little sleep — but of course I am used to that. I think of you and Malta, and those driving lessons along the cliffs at Dingli and the lunches in the palace when you wouldn't look at me. It is all so different here. I'm homesick. I never thought I would say that, but I am. I envy Max.

I once asked you to wait. I can't ask you that any more, but I can't help thinking of it either, alone here in the dawn, and so far from Malta. Maybe this letter will never reach you. Maybe it's better that it doesn't. But I have to write it, and tell you that this May morning, I am thinking of you. And thinking, Lila, with hope.

Anton.

Carmela folded up the letter. It was a puzzling letter. She knew all the words but she still couldn't quite tell what it was saying, except that the other baron prince had sent it, the one who sent the ring and the rose. The ring and the rose had been very romantic, as romantic as the poems of Lord Tennyson, but this letter didn't seem romantic. In any case, Carmela didn't want it to be romantic. At this moment in her life, she didn't want romance coming in and diverting Lila's attention from her own need for cherry dresses and tins of sardines. She put the letter back in the envelope and slammed the pillow down on it with emphasis. Then she stood up and faced the wall with the sums on it.

"Five nine five," Carmela said loudly. "Five nine five divided by — "

The door opened.

"Hello," Lila said. "Why aren't you in bed?"

"You look awful," Carmela said. She stood on one foot, holding the other up behind her. "I was doing my sums."

"Good," Lila said tiredly.

She came into the room and closed the door and leaned against it.

"Carmela — "

"Yes?" Carmela said. It would be so wonderful if the answer to five nine five divided by fifteen would just come to her, magically, and she could

327

sing it out, in triumph, to Lila.

"Carmela, Max Ferroferrata is missing."

Carmela let go of her foot and put it quietly on the floor beside her other one.

"He went up at eight-twenty-five in the morning, yesterday, when the raid began, and he didn't come back with the others. They can't find his plane." Lila put her head back against the door and closed her eyes. "They think he's dead."

★ ★ ★

It was the same soldier who opened the door of the Tabia Palace. If anything, he seemed even more crisply starched than before and Lila, by contrast, more crumpled.

"Count Julius isn't in, miss. Saw him go out myself. It's one of his reading mornings."

"Then — "

"He'll be in the Gonzi Palace, miss. Until midday. I'll get Mr Teezo."

"No," Lila said. "Thank you, but don't bother. I know the way."

"Just as you like, miss." Lila turned away in the brilliant morning light, hard, white August sunlight that gave one the feeling of being grilled by a searchlight. The Gonzi Palace was where Max had taken her, the charming, ancient, crumbling palace in the very walls of Mdina where she had made such a fool of herself. She would, she reflected now, crossing the tiny street in search of a narrow strip of shade on the far side, have given a great deal to be allowed

328

only to make a fool of herself a second time in the Gonzi Palace. What she actually had to do there was so very much more painful.

The little square in which the palace sat was empty of everything but sunlight and a worn string mop someone had left propped against a wall to dry. The door of the palace was firmly closed, and the windows either side blankly shuttered. "Look," Lila remembered saying to Max. "Look, no dolphin. Poor palace." Tears pricked sharply behind her eyelids. She shook her head vigorously, as if to shake the tears back. No weeping. No weeping in front of Count Julius. There'd been far too much of that in the night, as it was.

Inside, it was just as she remembered it: the marble hall and staircase, looking so cool and conventionally eighteenth-century, and then the way, at the top the stairs, that the whole building seemed to twist sideways so that it could look out of the bastion walls, and away across the island to the north east. She went quietly up the stairs, fitting her feet into the footprints already plain in the dust, and crossed the marble corridor at the top to reach the doorway of the salone, where Max had taken her.

The door was open, to allow such air as there was to circulate. Through it, Lila could see Count Julius, seated by the table upon which Max had spread their little picnic. There was a bookstand on the table, and an open book was propped on it which Count Julius, pince-nez on his nose, back ramrod straight, was reading.

329

He had opened the same lattice that Lila had opened, and a great pale slab of sunlight lay on the floor, almost reaching his feet.

"Count Julius," Lila said, softly.

He gave a little start, whipping his spectacles off his nose.

"My dear — "

"I'm so sorry to come unannounced like this."

Count Julius stood up. He gave his usual tiny, slightly sardonic bow.

"Any visit from you is a pleasure."

She came forward into the room. It seemed to her that Count Julius, who had always been something of a formidable figure to her, appeared suddenly smaller, smaller and more fragile, standing there in his perfect pre-war clothes, with his polished boots and his pince-nez on its black ribbon.

"Not this one, I'm afraid," Lila said.

He watched her.

"Won't you sit down again?"

"Why?"

"Please sit," Lila said. "Please sit down."

"My dear — "

Lila put her hands on Count Julius' shoulders.

"No," he said. He was gazing at her intently. He squared his shoulders. "No. I need not sit. Whatever it is, I can hear it standing."

Lila took her hands away. She said, as gently as she could, "It's Max."

"Max!"

"Yes. Max went up in the raid forty-eight hours ago. He didn't come back with the others.

He was reported missing. Then this morning, they found his plane and — "

"Yes?"

"Two wardens found his body. On the top of a house in Cospicua."

Count Julius drew a long, shuddering breath. The colour seemed to drain from his skin leaving it as pale and flat as the linen of his suit. Lila longed to step forward and put her arms round him, but something in his dignified, upright, self-contained attitude held her back.

"I am so sorry, so — "

With a hand that was not quite steady, Count Julius slipped the pince-nez into his breast pocket.

"Who has identified him?"

"His commanding officer. But they would be grateful — " she paused.

"If I would come?"

"Yes. A brother officer was going to come and ask you, but I offered instead."

Count Julius gave her a fleeting glance. His eyes were as dark and blank as black pebbles.

"Thank you." He put out a hand and closed the book on the bookstand. "Have we transport?"

"Yes. There's a car waiting, at the Mdina Gate."

Count Julius bent his head. Lila watched him helplessly. No Doris-like wailing for Count Julius, no sobbing and lamentation and rage and despair; only the iron grip of a tradition of centuries, where agonies were borne without flinching, with hardly a sign except pallor and

331

reticence. He looked up again.

"What about — the young woman?"

"Rosanna," Lila said.

"Yes. Does she know, is she — ?"

"She is with Miss de Vere. She has known longer than anyone, from the moment he didn't return. And she lost her father only four days ago."

Count Julius picked up his book.

"It is hardly to be borne. But it has to be." He glanced at Lila. "I shall go and see her. After, that is, seeing my nephew." He made a little gesture. "Will you take me, my dear, to the car?"

★ ★ ★

It was very quiet in Miss de Vere's kitchen. Miss de Vere herself was out, taking Rosanna to her mother in Mqabba, and Zanzu was out too, taking Carmela to school.

"I won't! I won't go! I won't go without Lila!"

"You have to," Miss de Vere said. "For today, you have to. Lila needs a day alone today."

Lila had looked at her gratefully. Carmela had glared.

"Just for today."

Miss de Vere had been wonderful. She had put Carmela's protesting hand into Zanzu's and pushed them out of the door. Then she had instructed Lila to stay at home. All day.

"I insist. I shall be occupied entirely with Rosanna."

332

Rosanna. Lila had only seen her once since Max died, still in the hospital, still working, her face a mask. She had refused sedation and, from Lila at least, she had refused comfort. Her grief was private, but it was also very plain that it was possessive. "Max was mine," her whole demeanour seemed to say. "Mine alone. In life or death. Mine."

Lila sat at the kitchen table. At one end, Zanzu had neatly stacked the bowls and plates they used every day, even though the rations they were allowed would scarcely have covered a single saucer. He had also put a sprig broken from a scarlet geranium in a wineglass of water, and Lila could smell its odd, sweetish, faintly peppery scent. In front of her lay her unfinished letter to the Perriams, started more than two weeks ago now, just after she and Carmela had come to live in the house on Kalkara Creek. It would be, she had promised herself, the one task she would accomplish that day. By the time Carmela got back from school, the letter would be finished, with all its painful burden of news. In a minute, she would start it. In a minute, she would pick up her pen and begin writing. But before that, she would give herself the luxury of a few minutes with her head on her arms on the table, eyes closed, tired mind beating its battered wings against the bars of its cage . . .

The door of the kitchen opened quietly. She said drowsily, without stirring, "Zanzu?"

"No," Angelo Saliba said, "not Zanzu. Me. I should have knocked."

Lila sat upright, pushing her hair off her face.

"Oh — "

"Did I frighten you?"

"No," she said. Then, pulling herself together, "I'm so sorry about your father."

Angelo put his hand on a chairback.

"May I sit down?"

"Oh, of course."

"You were so kind, so — so sweet, to go and see my mother."

Lila looked down at her letter.

"It was an impulse."

"That doesn't make it any less kind," Angelo said. "Maybe I am here on an impulse too."

Lila spread her hands flat on the letter, and stared at them intently.

"I was so touched that you went to see my mother, that you thought of doing so. And something made me anxious too. I thought, you see," Angelo said, "that you might have been forgotten."

She stared at him. His eyes, she noticed for the first time, weren't dark like so many Maltese, but almost green, hazel.

"Forgotten?"

"When Max died." He leaned across the table. She thought for one moment that he might be about to put his hand on hers. "I wondered if in all the concern for my sister and the concern for his uncle, anybody had remembered to have concern for you."

Lila took her hands off the table and put them over her face.

"Oh heavens — "

"Perhaps I presume," Angelo said. "Perhaps I presume to know something that never was."

There was a silence. Then Lila took her hands away from her face and said slowly, "No. It never was. But it was a hope. And hope — " She stopped.

"I know," he said. He put his hands together under his chin and regarded her. "We live on it. We could not bear one more day of this war without it." He smiled at her, a little shyly. "I have hopes for after the war, you know."

"Do you?"

"I won't go back to being a schoolmaster, after the war. I'm going to go into politics. Educational politics. I want to change things, for Malta. For the Maltese."

"You sound like Salvu."

"There are many who sound like us."

"The new Malta."

"Yes. The new Malta."

She said uncertainly, "You are such a kind man."

"That's easy," he said. "It's always been easy, with you."

"But I've been so horrible."

"Yes," he said. He was smiling. "Is that a good mixture, do you think, if I am kind and you are horrible?"

She looked at him, full in the face. She took in his brown skin and dark hair and white teeth. She also took in his sturdy Maltese build and his present thinness and his scarred workworn hands and his shapeless, unironed, coarse clothes.

335

"Oh Angelo — "

"You have never called me that before. You have never called me by my name."

She glanced at him. His face was glowing. She shook her head slightly. "I can't," she said simply.

"What can't you?"

"I can't do what you want. I can't — stop being horrible. However kind you are, however brave — "

He waited.

"Soon after I came here," Lila said, hesitating over her own words, "I — I found a dream. It's difficult to explain why it was so right for me, but it was. It was everything I had ever hoped for, full of all that bright promise my childhood never had. And then I thought I'd lost it. The war came and everything changed and — and people went away. And I thought the dream had gone. I suppose until Max came back, I was sure it had — no, I was just so afraid that it had. Then he came back, and he was like a herald of hope again and, well, I mistook him for hope — hope itself. As you know. And now, something else has happened. Something has come." She glanced down at her letter to the Perriams and laid her hand on it, as if for emphasis, "And I think there is a chance my dream is there still. While there's a chance, you see — I have to take it." She stopped. Suddenly, she couldn't look at him any more. She was afraid she might say sorry, and insult him, so she returned her gaze to her letter and fixed it there.

336

For half a minute or so, there was no sound. Then Angelo scraped his chair back on the kitchen tiles and stood up. Lila dared not look at him. She heard his footsteps go towards the door, and then the sound of the handle turning.

"I hope you find it," Angelo said. His voice was dry and hard. "I hope you do." And then the door closed behind him, with a bang, and he was gone.

# Part Three

*After the War: 1945*

# 27

THE door of the convent was as heavily studded as if it had been defending a fortress. There was no nameplate by it, but only, for identification, a little polychrome plaster statue in a niche over the doorway, the Virgin in a blue robe standing on bluer waves: Mary, Mother of God, Stella Maris, the Star of the Sea.

Lila peered in through the small iron grille let into the door. She could see nothing except a restricted space of very tidy courtyard, and two parlour palms in pots. She was, she hoped, dressed suitably for a convent, in a dark coat and skirt over a white blouse, with her hair pinned up neatly and no jewellery. She carried three white lilies, their stems wrapped in paper. Last time, she had brought a pot of honey, which had been rejected. It was difficult to know what to bring a nun, yet to bring nothing seemed awkward too, as if one were coming only for one's own sake, to ask for succour and prayers.

Beside the door, a long iron bellpull was threaded through brackets, ending in a knob burnished by centuries of pulling hands. Lila gave it a swift tug. There was a pause, and then the sound of sandalled feet in the courtyard coming steadily, but without hurry towards the door.

"Yes?" a voice said.

341

Lila stooped to the grille again. The nun inside was small and bespectacled, and in a full black habit, her hands invisibly folded beneath her scapular.

"It's Lila Cunningham, sister. You remember me? I visit Sister Rosanna."

"Ah," the nun said. She moved her head a little and her spectacles glinted in the sun. "You have an appointment?"

"I do indeed."

There was a pause, and the sound of bolts being drawn, and a key turned. Then the door swung open and revealed the whole of the courtyard, as tidy as its first partial impression, and bare of any living things except the parlour palms.

"This way, if you please," the nun said.

She secured the door again, and slipped past Lila towards an archway on the left. This led, Lila knew, to a second, inner courtyard, and that in turn led to the main convent building and the visitors' room. Lila had never penetrated further than the visitors' room, a dark, cool chamber smelling strongly of polish, with a line of chairs down the centre opposite the grilles behind which the nuns sat, for the allotted twenty minutes, shadowy and indistinct. Only on the day when Rosanna ceased to be a novice, and took her final vows and her final convent name, might Lila see the chapel where Rosanna — where all the sisters — spent so much of their time. Lila was impatient to see the chapel. For some reason, she had a feeling that the chapel might hold the key to Rosanna, that central element of her character which might explain what was so difficult, otherwise, to see.

The nun left Lila on the chair she always occupied, the last chair in the line, furthest from the door. It was an upright chair, with a hard leather seat. Lila sat down on it, balancing her lilies across her knees. She took a breath. The smell of polish was very strong. Perhaps Friday mornings were polishing mornings.

A figure moved behind the grille opposite to her, and sat down in a faint rustle of thick black fabric.

"Rosanna?"

"Good morning," Rosanna said. Her head was bent, as it usually was, so that her eyes were hidden. Perhaps it was not permissible, or considered seemly, to look into the eyes of a nun.

"I've brought you some lilies," Lila said. "I don't expect you're allowed them yourself, but I thought perhaps you could put them in the chapel."

"Thank you," Rosanna said. Her hand moved in a little pious gesture. "The flower of Our Lady."

Lila put the lilies down on the chair next to her.

"Did you hear? Did you hear that the war in Europe is over?"

"We did," Rosanna said composedly. "We heard, of course, from the bishop. There has been much thankfulness here, naturally."

"I came to Malta when I was twenty-one,"

343

Lila said. She smoothed her skirt over her knees. Rosanna was no easier to talk to as a nun than she'd been as a lay person, but the grille and the dimness of the room gave conversation an illusion of confidentiality, "and now I'm nearly twenty-eight. And almost all the time in between has been war."

"I am twenty-five," Rosanna said primly. "There has been war for a quarter of my life."

Lila leaned forward.

"Are you well?"

"Extremely," Rosanna said.

"And your mother?"

"My brother is moving her into a new house. She will live with him now. It is only a temporary house until the rebuilding of Valetta can begin. My brother" — she paused, and then she said with emphasis, "my brother is to be a member of the National Congress. With responsibility for education."

"Yes," Lila said, "I had heard." She had seen, too, in Merchants Street, quite by chance, Angelo Saliba in a formal shirt and tie getting out of an official car. He had looked solider, somehow, with more presence. Of course, they were all solider, everyone thankfully had put on weight since the supply convoys had been able to get through during the last two years, but Angelo's improved physique was not just a matter of extra flesh. It had to do with something inner, something confident.

"He was recommended by the Governor," Rosanna said. "By Lord Gort." Her hands moved again, and then Lila saw her tuck them behind her scapular. "And you?" Rosanna said. "How are you?"

"Do you want the truth?"

"Of course."

"I'm well," Lila said. "Physically, of course I am. We even had a pot of jam this week and it was all we could do not to eat it straight out of the jar. But — well, as to everything else, I feel I'm back where I started. No money, dependent on everyone else's kindness — "

"But you work."

"Oh yes, I work."

There was a pause, and then Rosanna said quietly, "Perhaps, with Miss de Vere, it is difficult to have independence."

Lila was startled by her openness.

"Did you feel that?"

There was a tiny movement of Rosanna's head. Lila leaned forward.

"Do you have independence now? Is that why you became a nun?"

Rosanna whispered something.

"What?"

"Partly."

Lila said, still leaning forward, "Max?"

Rosanna suddenly became very still. She said nothing.

"Sorry," Lila said, "I shouldn't have mentioned him." She straightened up. "Carmela has just turned thirteen, you know. I'm very proud of her. I sometimes think I — well, that she is my one real achievement here. Everything else seems somehow to have vanished." She

345

stopped abruptly, and then said, "I'm so sorry, whining on."

"You need someone to support you," Rosanna said in her cool, non-committal way, "someone to take your side."

There was a silence. It occurred to Lila to say that she seemed better at losing and alienating people than at keeping them, but to utter such thoughts also appeared horribly self-pitying. So instead, she got slowly to her feet.

"I should go."

"You can always come back," Rosanna said, "you know that. I am always here."

"Yes."

"I will pray for you," Rosanna said, standing too. "I will pray for you to find support and strength."

Then she was gone. Lila stood for a moment, gazing at the grille where she had been. She clenched her fists, feeling her nails digging into her palms. Ridiculous, she told herself fiercely, ridiculous, absurd — wasn't it? — to feel envy, for a *nun*?

★ ★ ★

There were many things now in Carmela's life which gave her great satisfaction. She was an enrolled pupil in the dockyard school, she was top of her class in reading and writing English, she had her own bedroom in Miss de Vere's house with a photograph of Humphrey Bogart on the wall and two pairs of shoes in the cupboard, and Doris had stopped asking her to come home to live.

Carmela liked to go home for visits. She liked to eat Doris's timpana, or fish with chillies, and she liked to teach some words of English to Spiru, now a stout child of almost six, and to play with the baby, little Paul, named for the saint who had been shipwrecked on the north coast of the island, and in defiance of Salvu's wishes. Salvu had wanted the baby to have a secular Maltese name, not a Catholic Christian one. Salvu now declared himself to be an agnostic and Doris pretended she hadn't heard him. She had become, by degrees, Count Julius' housekeeper, in a new black frock and a white apron, changed daily, and her elevation to that position had made her more pious than ever. The family had progressed to the possession of four rooms in the kitchen courtyard at the Tabia Palace, and in every one a lighted wick in a dish of oil burned before a holy image. Salvu took no notice of them. By day he worked for Count Julius, mending furniture damaged by the army's occupation, oiling leather book bindings, adding to the collection of model ships, and at night, accompanied by like-minded friends, he took a pony trap down the hill from Mdina to Rabat to argue politics vociferously over cups of coffee and glasses of rough brandy. He was faster now in his wheelchair, they said, than he'd ever been on his legs.

Sometimes, on these visits home, Carmela was allowed into Count Julius' library. He still slept in the old housekeeper's room, saying he much preferred it to his old far grander bedroom, but the library had been reclaimed. He allowed Carmela to play on the typewriter that Lila used to use, long ago, when she first came to Malta and, if she was very careful, to stand on a chair and gently polish Grand Master La Valette with a soft cloth. While she did these things, Count Julius would talk to her. He talked a lot of history, which Carmela disapproved of because there seemed to be so few women in Maltese history, and quite a bit about his family. When he spoke of them, Carmela pricked her ears up. She would dust most assiduously, never asking questions, in case Count Julius sensed her curiosity and became more reticent.

The Baroness, she learned, would soon be returning from America, with a sum of money she had raised there for rebuilding Maltese schools and Maltese hospitals. She would bring her son with her probably, the young Baron Anton, who had been convalescing with her, after an illness. Count Julius implied that the illness had been caused by the strain of the war, so Carmela imagined that the young baron — so very beautiful in her memory — had been ravaged by scabies as she had been, for over a year. That might make him, of course, rather less beautiful. One should never, Carmela knew, wish an affliction on any fellow creature, but it was difficult not to hope that if Baron Anton's beauty was diminished, so might his power be over Lila. There had been a number of blue letters over the last three years which Carmela had been dismayed to see. She had also been unable to find their hiding place. To be sure, their arrival had not had a marked effect on Lila, but they were only letters after all. The physical presence might be the thing, might turn Lila back to the glowing creature she had been before Baron Anton went away or, for a little while, after Baron Max came back. Whatever it did, Carmela was very certain of one thing: she didn't want it. She couldn't stop it, of course, but she needn't help it along, either. She needn't tell Lila what Count Julius had told her. She needn't tell Lila that Anton was coming back.

* * *

The vegetable garden at the Villa Zonda was thick with weeds, the starved-looking straggling weeds that are so quick to colonize waste ground. Here and there, the odd potato plant had pushed its way through from a stray potato left unharvested from three years ago, but otherwise those careful lines of carrots and cauliflowers and onions that old Spiru, and then his sons-in-law, and then Pa, had laboured over, had been entirely obliterated. Only one corner was clear, a rough oblong of ground under the south wall where Pa's grave was. Lila had kept it clear, faithfully, using the head of an old garden fork she had found among the burned out ruins of the sheds. She had planted montbretia there, dug up from the verges of lanes out in the country, and a white oleander and a rosemary bush.

"There's rosemary, that's for remembrance,"

349

Lila remembered Ophelia saying in those long ago Shakespeare lessons at school in Saxmundham. "Pray, love, remember: and there is pansies, that's for thoughts."

Remembrance and thoughts. Both came strongly upon Lila on those visits to Pa's grave. She came every week, sometimes twice, hurrying past the villa's sad, lopsided, barricaded façade, and through the gap in the wall from the courtyard. There was always a curious relief in getting there, and a real reluctance to go, as if something Pa had once said to her about his being in a sense her starting point in life — a remark which had exasperated her at the time — had in fact turned out to be true.

"Hello, Pa," she'd say, as she reached the grave, and then wait, as if hearing a faint "What ho!" in reply.

One of the best things about going to visit Pa was that she went alone. Carmela didn't like the Villa Zonda in its ruined state, so it was the one place she didn't follow Lila like a dog, and Lila could allow herself, after the busyness of the school and the renewed postwar activity of Miss de Vere's house, a little peace. It was a precious peace because she could rely upon being undisturbed. No-one knew she was there; no-one else was interested in a decayed vegetable garden with a bomb crater in the centre.

"Ah," Miss de Vere said.

Lila turned round abruptly, taken by surprise. Miss de Vere stood in the gap in the wall, in her white linen summer suit and a bamboo pith helmet.

350

"I thought I might find you here," Miss de Vere said with a small edge of triumph.

Lila put the garden fork head down and got to her knees.

"I never heard the car."

"I left it in the drive. In the shade." Miss de Vere advanced towards her. She nodded approvingly at Pa's grave. "Very nice. Very English and natural. Catholics make their graves look so urban, somehow. Your father would have liked that."

Lila said slowly, "I miss him."

Miss de Vere put a hand on her arm.

"Come into the shade, dear. We'll go under the carob tree. I came to find you because it's so hard to find a quiet corner just now. Or a corner without little Carmela." She paused and looked round the vegetable garden. "You could grow almond trees here, you know. Or oranges."

"Maybe," Lila said. "One day."

Miss de Vere grasped her arm and led her into the shade.

"One day is what I want to talk to you about."

She seated herself on the bench where Pa had spent wartime afternoons patching clothes, and patted the space beside her.

"Sit down."

Lila sat, obediently.

"I've been watching you," Miss de Vere said. "I know you think I don't notice, but I do. We've spent the last six years hoping and praying that the war would be over, and now it is, we

351

don't know what to do with ourselves. Am I right?"

Lila looked at her.

"Am I?"

Slowly, Lila nodded.

"You need a choice," Miss de Vere said, "that's your trouble; that you feel you are stuck, that you haven't got one. Well, I'm going to give you one. I'm going to give you a choice, a look at something else." She took off the pith helmet and fanned herself vigorously with it. Then she looked directly at Lila. "I'm going to send you home for a while," she said. "I'm going to send you back to England."

# 28

"I AM very contented here," Mrs Saliba said.

She looked round with satisfaction at the little room in which she and Lila sat. It was very ugly. It had a tiled floor, patterned in green and brown and white, and several enormous pieces of overbearing furniture, and a cactus in a pot. In the centre of the room was a table covered in a brown and white checked cloth, and on the table stood the box that Lila had brought.

"My son isn't content," Mrs Saliba said, "he doesn't like this house. But to me, it is modern and excellent."

Lila sat upright on the chair she had been offered, and clasped her hands in her lap.

"I believe your son is doing very well."

Mrs Saliba nodded. Her face, old long before its time, wore a look of deep complacency.

"It was his work on the guns and his ceaseless care for his school. He was bound to be noticed."

Lila glanced about the room. On a vast dresser at one side stood two photographs in ornamental frames. One was of Rosanna, taken on her day of entry into the convent, gazing calmly into the camera. The other was of Angelo. He was in a suit and he was standing against a pair of huge double doors, his hands folded in front of him.

"It was taken in the palace, in Valetta," Mrs Saliba said, "two days before his thirtieth birthday. If only his father, God rest his soul, had lived to see it."

"You must be very proud," Lila said.

Mrs Saliba nodded again. Lila tried to see in her the woman she had first glimpsed hazily after fainting on the harbour front, a lively looking woman with good teeth and bright dark eyes and an air of energy about her. Six years of war and hunger and strain and the loss of her husband had taken away all that former vitality. Mrs Saliba, stoutly encased in black, with black woollen stockings and no ornament except a gold cross around her neck, and a stolid expression on her now heavy face, had become a typical Maltese matron.

Lila stood up and put a hand on the box on the table.

"These are yours," she said.

Mrs Saliba looked at the box.

"Mine?"

"Yes. They are pictures and ornaments that your son brought to my father after you were evacuated from your house, for safekeeping. When our house was hit, they were luckily in a strong old cupboard, so they weren't damaged. I took them with me to Kalkara."

Mrs Saliba rose slowly from her own chair and approached the table. Lila opened the flaps of the box and pushed it across to her.

"Your candlesticks, your mirror, your crucifix — "

"Ah," Mrs Saliba said. She leaned forward,

her face lit up with pleasure. "I thought they were lost."

"No. I had them safe in Kalkara. Under my bed, in fact."

Mrs Saliba lifted out an object still wrapped in clean rags and tenderly extracted a brightly coloured picture of the Virgin Mary holding the Christ Child, framed in fancy metalwork.

"Ah," Mrs Saliba said again. She kissed the picture. There were tears in her eyes.

"I'd have brought them anyway," Lila said, "now the war is over. But I wanted to do it before I go back to England."

Mrs Saliba had set the Virgin down and was unrolling a Spanish fan from its wrappings.

"England?" she said. Her voice was amazed, as if Lila had said 'the moon'.

"Yes," Lila said, "I'm going home. To England. Will you — will you tell your son?"

Mrs Saliba gave her a long look.

"Yes," she said. "Yes. I will tell him." She looked down again, at her box of treasures. "Thank you. Thank you for these. You are a good girl."

★ ★ ★

"I have to come with you!" Carmela screamed. Her fists were clenched. "I have to! I have to!"

Lila, close to tears herself, went on steadily marking the pile of exercise books on her table.

"You can't."

"Why can't I? Why can't I? Why, why, why?"

"Because I have to go alone. Because I have to decide things by myself. Because I have to have time and quiet to *think*."

Carmela flopped onto her knees. She wore her hair in a single pigtail now, and when she was agitated, would pull it over one shoulder and tug fiercely at it, as if it were a bellpull.

"I won't *speak* to you," Carmela said, tugging violently, "I promise. I won't say one *word*. I'll come to England and I'll be like those nuns who never speak. I'll just nod or shake my head when you speak to me. I will be *silent*."

Lila put down her red marking pencil.

"Look," she said. She pulled a handkerchief out of her skirt pocket and blew her nose hard. "Look, I feel awful, leaving you. *Awful*. But it would be far more unkind to take you. England is so different from here. You'd be cold, and everything would be strange. The food would be peculiar, there wouldn't be any family, there wouldn't be anyone you know there, except me. You'd be unhappy. Really unhappy."

"I am really unhappy now," Carmela said, and lay face down on the floor.

"I'm leaving you with people here who know you and love you. And with your family. And with school."

"I don't want them. I don't want family *or* school. I want to come to England. With *you*."

Lila picked up her pencil again.

"You can't come."

"You are horrible!" Carmela shouted from the floor.

356

"So are you," Lila said, "horrible and ungrateful. You don't know how lucky you are."

"Lucky? Lucky?"

"You've got a family," Lila said steadily. "You've got a father and a mother and two brothers and a grandmother and enough aunts and cousins to fill a church."

There was silence from the floor.

"And I," Lila said, "haven't got anyone. No relations at all. None."

Very slowly, Carmela sat up. She regarded Lila for some moments, and then she said, "Is that why you're going to England?"

Lila wrote 'Better. But use your dictionary to check spellings' in an exercise book. Then she closed it and pulled the next one from the pile towards her.

"In a way," she said. She opened the book. She didn't look at Carmela. "I want to see — if I belong there."

★ ★ ★

Out on the apron of tarmac at Luqa airfield, a small plane sat. Two mechanics in oil-smeared overalls were casually moving its propellers to and fro, as if to see if they would actually spin. The plane looked very small to Lila, almost as small as Max's plane, which was the only other one she had ever seen at close quarters. Small or not, however, it was to take her to Sicily, another plane was to take her to Rome, and then yet a third to Paris. In Paris, she was to

357

board a train to Calais, and take the ferry across the Channel to Dover. Miss de Vere said that she must now learn to take aeroplanes in her stride, and also that if she were to return to England in a proper frame of mind to decide her future, she must definitely do it via the white cliffs of Dover.

There were only four other passengers, all men, in ill-fitting suits with, like her, a single permitted piece of luggage. They had all been herded into a small, dingy room with shrapnel scars in the walls, furnished with a few wooden chairs and a battered card table bearing an ashtray. All the men smoked incessantly, and two of them talked together, in low voices, in Maltese. Lila suspected that it was a first-time flight for all five of them.

It had been hard, saying goodbye. Zanzu had taken Carmela off to school before Lila left, and Lila's last sight of her had been her still skinny little figure, with the bobbing pigtail, her hand firmly in Zanzu's grasp, but her head turning constantly to give Lila another glimpse of her pink, swollen, sobbing face. After she had gone, Lila had cried too, out of Miss de Vere's sight, in case it should seem ungrateful to cry after being the recipient of such generosity. The day before, she had borrowed Miss de Vere's car and driven out to Mdina to see Count Julius. He had not been there. He was, Doris explained with her new air of importance and authority, in Gozo for a few days.

"He has left me in charge," Doris said. She had a bunch of keys at her waist and her hair was pinned back with great severity. "Quite in charge."

"I should have let him know," Lila said. "Before, I mean. But it was all decided so quickly."

Doris surveyed Lila. Salvu said they owed Lila a good deal for Carmela's education and increasing independence of spirit, and for their situation in the Tabia Palace, but Doris couldn't forgive her for Carmela's emancipation. She looked at Lila's short skirt, and the hair she wore on her shoulders still loose, like a girl, held back with red combs. *Red*.

"I will tell the Count," Doris said, in a tone that implied she doubted the news would be of any interest to him.

"Thank you," Lila said. She looked at Doris. "Any news — of the family?"

Doris stared back. Her expression was quite blank.

"None," she said.

Perhaps, Lila thought now, staring through the dirty window of the little airfield waiting room, this is all meant. Perhaps this is the end of a chapter; perhaps all the links I've made — except for Carmela and Miss de Vere — are severed now. Naturally. If links with people that have been that strong can ever be naturally broken. Perhaps I have to recognize that a whole period of my life is over now, that I have to turn a page and look at a blank sheet, and start again. I just wish, I just wish that I really believed that, instead of feeling I have to grit my teeth and accept it. I just wish I felt it was an opportunity, and not the great empty space left by loss . . .

The door of the waiting room opened. Lila turned from the window, expecting to see one of the plane's crew, announcing that the flight was now ready for boarding. But it was not a crew member. It was Angelo Saliba, in a grey suit, holding a felt trilby hat in his hand.

"Miss Cunningham — "

The four men in the room fell silent.

"Oh!" Lila said, astounded. She clutched her handbag in her arms like a baby, as if for comfort.

Angelo Saliba glanced round the grubby little smoke-filled room. He said to Lila clearly, in English, "The plane isn't leaving for fifteen minutes. I've just asked the pilot. Will you spare me just a little time, out in the open air?" He indicated her suitcase. "Your luggage is quite safe here. I have told them about it."

He stood back and held the door open. Lila went past him and as she did so, he took her elbow and steered her lightly down a short corridor and out into the windy sunshine.

"This way," Angelo said, "away from the noise of the plane."

He led her round the battered little building to a sheltered corner overlooking the wartime landing strips, still fenced with coils of wire. He grimaced.

"Hideous. How I long to clear all this up. The British are granting us thirty million pounds for rebuilding."

"Good," Lila said faintly.

Angelo turned her gently so that the sun was no longer in her eyes.

"I'm sorry to surprise you like this. I'm afraid it is a bit melodramatic. But I couldn't let you go back to England without saying goodbye."

"No."

"And my mother only told me this morning. She forgot. She forgets everything now that doesn't touch her own life." He paused and then he said, "I hope the smallness of your luggage means that you are not going back for ever?"

Lila looked at him, almost shyly.

"I don't know."

"Please," he said, and then stopped, turning his hat in his hands as he once used to turn his shabby cotton cap.

"I've nothing left to stay for now really," Lila said. "Maybe the war kept me longer than I might have stayed without it. But I have to see — " She paused.

"What do you have to see?"

"If England — "

"Yes?"

"*Is* home."

There was a silence. Lila prayed that he would not mention the dolphin knocker, now in Carmela's keeping and locked in her cupboard with her precious shoes. He didn't. He turned his hat for a while and then he said, "The war has changed my mind about that. Now I wonder — is home a place at all? Or is it people?"

He looked at her.

"Will you write to me?"

She shook her head.

He gave her a reluctant grin. "It would not have been in character if you had agreed."

She said, "At least I've always been honest with you."

"Is that a compliment?"

"I suppose so. Of sorts, in any case."

"Lila — "

"Yes."

"I hope you will be happy."

"You sound like an American film."

He grinned again. "I *feel* like an American film." Then his grin vanished. "I do not want, you see, to say goodbye to you. I do not want you to go."

He took one hand away from his hat and laid it on both hers, still clasping her handbag.

"Seven years — "

"Yes."

"Tell me one thing."

"All right."

"Are they over? Those seven years? Is this the end of this chapter?"

She looked down at his hand, square and brown on her paler ones. Then she looked at his face. It was impossible to tell him everything, to explain just how much seemed to have ended, come to nothing. She said slowly, "I think so."

"I see," he said. He gave a tiny sigh, and then took his hand from hers and leaned forward and kissed her fingers, so lightly she could hardly feel the touch of his mouth.

"Goodbye," he said. "Godspeed."

# 29

THE tall house in Aldeburgh had been painted yellow, a pale yellow, like primroses, and the sea and the wind had already buffeted it until the corners were grey and the pebbles of the stucco showed through in patches like darns on an old jersey. Lila sat on the seawall in a stiff June breeze and looked up at it. The paint on the frames of the three windows, stacked one on top of each other like boxes, was dark green and already blistering. Perhaps the people who now lived there didn't know how destructive the sea was as a neighbour, or maybe they had painted the house before the war, and then the war had come and scattered them, as it had scattered so many people, and they'd never been able to come back and do the repainting. Pa had said you had to repaint every three years, if your house was by the sea. Of course he'd never actually done it, but he talked as if he did.

Lila looked up. There were no curtains at the topmost window, her old bedroom, only a painted toy parrot in a wooden hoop suspended from the curtain rail against the glass. Perhaps it had been a child's room, the room of a child who hated the dark and wouldn't have curtains drawn, who wouldn't even have curtains. Lila had been afraid of the moon as a child, she remembered. She thought it was looking at her.

Pa used to give her one of his old neckerchiefs to tie round her eyes at night, like a blindfold, so she couldn't see the moon trying to look at her. She had one of those neckerchiefs on now, a faded red spotted one, tying back her hair in the sea wind. She put her hand up to touch it, for reassurance. It was disconcerting to be here, looking up at the old house on this unchanged seafront, without Pa.

Straight ahead, in the downstairs sitting room, she could see a table and some armchairs and one of those revolving bookcases with bars at the sides to stop the books falling out when you spun it. It didn't look a much used room. They hadn't used it much either, Pa and her. Pa had hung his paintings to dry in it and the dismal procession of housekeepers had tried to make a cosy sitting room out of it with crocheted mats and rag rugs and knitted cushions, but the smell of oil paint had invariably driven them out in the end. Above it — blue curtains now, Lila saw — was the room which had been Pa's, the room where he'd pored over those maps of Malta the night he'd accepted they'd have to go there, the island set in a blue sea with harbours full of ships, all waiting to be painted. "Gulls," she'd said to him, "and sun. Blue sea and hot sun."

Lila stood up. There was sun today, in Aldeburgh, but it was a light sun, straining against the wind, and the sky it shone out of was as clear a blue as if it had been recently rinsed and hung up to dry. The houses, even the neglected houses, looked pretty too, characterful in all their variety, hung with little white balconies and flagpoles. To an eye wearied by the relentless yellow stone of Malta, Lila thought, it was a prospect of sheer charm, lighthearted, delightful. She looked back at the sea. She had never liked that sea, all those years she'd lived by it. She'd come to see it as a cold, grey, noisy menace. But today it was blue, deep strong northern blue, flecked with foam and bobbing gulls riding the waves. It had never looked more appealing.

She moved away from the seawall and went down the dark little alley that ran beside the house and connected the seafront to the little street behind. The greengrocer who had stored his crates of cabbages there was still in business — how had he managed in the war? — and Lila's old kitchen window was curtained in red gingham. Lila paused, and looked at the red gingham. The window was so close to the street she could have peered inside with ease. But she found she didn't want to. Aldeburgh might be at its most charming today, but that kitchen, with its dankness and beetles and gloom, and memories of haddock and beetroot, could dispel all other charms at a single glance. Better not even, Lila decided, to risk that single glance. If she did, she might catch a glimpse of the ghost of her thirteen-year-old self — the age Carmela was now — dumping a bag of schoolbooks and a bag of groceries on the table with a sigh. It wasn't a ghost, she told herself firmly, that it would do her any good to see.

She looked at her watch. It was ten to four. At

four o'clock, it had been arranged, Tuttle would motor in from Culver House, pick up Lila's bag from the pub where she had left it, and meet her outside the post office in the High Street. She had protested against this, on the telephone from the dingy little hotel in London where she had spent her first few nights back in England.

"I can get a bus. Or a taxi. I won't hear of it, being so much trouble — "

"It is no trouble," Mr Perriam had said. "The motor needs a run, and in any case, we couldn't think of you struggling onto a bus."

In the High Street, Lila paused by a shop window and looked at her reflection. She had no gloves and no hat. Tuttle would expect her to be wearing a hat. Her hair, despite Pa's neckerchief, was windblown, and her clothes, which had looked perfectly respectable in Malta, appeared home-made and dowdy in England, even in provincial England. Well, there was nothing to be done about any of it. She was here, in a cotton dress and jacket made by Miss de Vere's dressmaker in an attic in Senglea, without a hat, and everyone, including Tuttle, was going to have to accept her as she was.

★ ★ ★

"Well," Mrs Tuttle said, "*you* haven't put on any weight, and that's for sure."

Lila looked round the kitchen with pleasure. It was wonderfully the same: the big scrubbed table, the dresser hung with cups and jugs, the hook behind the door to the hall where she used

366

to hang her coat, the small square figure of Mrs Tuttle, one hand on the hissing kettle.

"It was the war, Mrs Tuttle. The Germans besieged Malta so we didn't have enough food. Now there's more food, of course, but you can't get out of the habit of feeling you must make it last."

Mrs Tuttle grunted. "Wasn't no picnic here."

"No. I know."

Mrs Tuttle took the kettle off the range and poured boiling water into the familiar elegant straight-spouted silver teapot the Perriams had used at teatime for almost half a century.

"Sorry to hear about your father." She paused and then she said, matter-of-factly, "We lost our second boy. North Africa."

"I'm so very sorry."

"Reckon we all lost someone. Reckon we're all in the same boat." She put the kettle down on the range again, and jerked her head in the vague direction of the library. "They did, too. That nephew. The one that was going to inherit all this. Italy it was, for him."

Lila looked down at the tea tray waiting laid on the table. White bread sandwiches, brown bread sandwiches, scones, a ginger cake studded with walnuts. She hadn't seen so much food in years. How had Mrs Tuttle done it, with rationing?

"I like to feed them," Mrs Tuttle said. "It's a small comfort but it's a solid one. I have my ways and means."

Lila put out a finger and touched one of the teacups, the achingly familiar teacups patterned

367

with azaleas and peacocks.

"Poor them. Poor Perriams."

"They'll be waiting for you. In the library. I'll let this brew, then I'll bring it in. You shouldn't keep them waiting. In you go."

★ ★ ★

The Perriams sat, as if transfixed by time, either side of the library fireplace. Being summer, there was a fan of pleated white paper in the fireplace, and the windows were open and a few fronds of a pink climbing rose had nodded in over the sills. Mrs Perriam wore her oriental shawl over a cream linen summer dress, and her hair was still in its tight small grey bun. Their little gold spectacles glinted above the pages of their books as if they hadn't raised their heads from reading since Lila said goodbye to them, seven years ago.

She said softly, in the doorway, "It's like Sleeping Beauty."

"My dear!"

"My dear Lila!"

They put down their books, carefully, as they always had, marking the place with their folded spectacles, and rose slowly to their feet. They were stiffer, Lila noticed, and slower, and Mrs Perriam seemed even smaller and more fragile, like a little moth. She held her arms out to Lila.

"Oh my dear. My dear child — "

Lila bent to kiss her.

"I can't believe it. I can't believe I'm back, that I'm here."

"Nor can we," Mr Perriam said, holding out his hand. He had tears in his eyes.

Mrs Perriam took a tiny handkerchief out of the sleeve of her dress.

"You have had such terrible times, such calamities and privations to endure. If we'd only known, if we'd only even guessed, we should never have sent you there. Night after night, we've blamed ourselves — "

"You shouldn't," Lila said gently. "Of course you shouldn't. How could you possibly be to blame?"

Mrs Perriam looked up at her. Her eyes had faded to palest forget-me-not blue.

"Your poor father — "

"That was a freak accident. Nothing anyone could predict or prevent."

Mr Perriam put a hand on her arm.

"We should sit down. We should all sit down." He smiled at Lila. "We began to think we should never see this day."

Lila seated herself on the stool she had so often sat on in the past.

"I thought about here so much. All through the war, I thought about you and this room and the Chinese rugs and the Japanese prints. When I first got to Malta and found it so hot and so yellow, I used to dream about the birch trees and the cold sea. It was a kind of balm."

Mrs Perriam leaned down and touched Lila's hands, clasped about her knees.

"We thought of you, every day, too. I think most days we spoke of you, too. Especially after John died. Our nephew, John, you know.

Landing at Salerno — "

Mr Perriam said softly, "He was to have had all of this, you see. A scholarly boy."

"I'm so very sorry."

"But we have you!" Mrs Perriam said. She had put her spectacles back on, and behind the polished lenses her eyes looked magnified, and full of affection. "You have come back to us, you see! Haven't you?"

★ ★ ★

Later, Lila changed for dinner in a room overlooking the drive and the birch trees. She had never slept at Culver House before, and it was extraordinary to be in a bedroom of such solid comforts — a broad mahogany bed made up with linen sheets, mounds of pillows, rugs laid over carpets, dressing tables and writing tables and looking glasses and hatstands, an armchair and a footstool and lamps on every surface with pleated pale silk shades. Next door there was a bathroom of the kind Lila had almost forgotten existed, with a huge old-fashioned tub, and a chintz-covered chair, and a rail of snowy towels, enough for three people, terrycloth and linen, the linen ones embroidered with Mrs Perriam's initials.

Lila had brought her only formal dress. It was black, and not very well cut, copied by the dressmaker in Senglea from a photograph in an American magazine called *Ladies' Home Journal*, which had come Lila's way. With it, she could wear the string of graduated branch coral Miss de Vere had given her.

"Coral is for girls, my dear. You take it. I'm far too old and stout to wear coral."

It was Lila's only jewellery, apart from her battered wristwatch and Anton's ring, which had lain unworn in the envelope in which it had arrived for almost three years now. Picking the corals up gave Lila a sudden pang, a sudden flash of missing Miss de Vere, of feeling . . . She shook herself sternly. In this comfortable house, with this warm and affectionate welcome, how dare she feel anything but gratitude and pleasure to be here?

They ate dinner in the dining room, under a lamp let down on a pulley until it cast a soft golden glow on just the circle of their three faces and hands. There was poached fish, with potatoes and peas from the garden, and raspberry tart — "No cream," Mrs Perriam said regretfully. "Even Mrs Tuttle can't conjure up cream" — served on a blue and white oriental dinner service so thin it was almost translucent, accompanied by a pre-war hock, in glasses as fragile as bubbles. There were roses on the table in silver bowls, and linen napkins, and the night air coming through the open window brought with it the faint, clean, salt breath of the sea.

They talked of the war, inevitably, and of Pa and the clever lost nephew and of the ruin of the Villa Zonda and the fate of Spiru's family.

"You have done well," Mr Perriam said. "You have been their guardian angel."

"They were mine," Lila said, "when I came. The poor house looks so sad." She looked at

Mr Perriam. "What will you do with it?"

He touched his napkin to his mouth.

"Time enough to think of that. Time enough, when we have settled the future."

"The future?"

He smiled at her.

"Yes, my dear. The future. Now that you have come back." He glanced at his wife. "Shall we tell her now?"

Mrs Perriam crumpled her napkin softly beside her plate, certain, as she had been quietly certain all her life, that the next meal would produce a fresh one, starched and ironed, as pure as a lily. She beamed at Lila over the silver bowl of roses.

"By all means."

Lila waited. For some reason, her hands were clenched in her lap. Into her mind, unbidden, came the picture of her twenty-year-old self, crouched on the stool in the library, and the great atlas, with its map of Malta, being lowered in front of her bewildered eyes.

"What you may not like," Mr Perriam had said then, leaning forward out of his grey damask chair, "is the kind of help we have in mind."

Lila shut her eyes.

"My dear," Mr Perriam said. His voice had the smallest hint of reproof in it.

She opened them again. They were both looking at her, loving, courteous and confident.

"Since John died," Mr Perriam said, "we have cast about as to what we should do with this house, with our collection, with our — " he cleared his throat delicately — "our *property*, after our deaths. He was our only close relation, my sister Hilda's only son. There is no-one else in the more extended branches of our family to whom we feel sufficiently close to make them our heirs. We could, of course, leave everything to an institution, to a university, perhaps, even to a teacher training college with a sufficiently enlightened approach to educating the young. But that idea has not appealed to us, we find. It seems cold. This has, after all, been our home." He looked at his wife and smiled at her. "Our home, all our long and happy married life."

Lila reached out for her water glass, and took a sip. Through its cut glass sides, the light from the lamp fell refracted, broken into a hundred little random glittering pieces. Her mind felt the same, scattered and unable to take in what every fibre of her being told her was coming.

"What we would like," Mr Perriam said his voice warming with the prospect of the pleasure he was about to give, "is to feel that Culver House will go on being a home. Even better, a home to a family who can grow up here; the children, perhaps, that we never had but whose imaginations have been our life's work. What we would like to offer you is a home here, a home for ever, a home when you marry, to bring your husband to, and to share with him, and your future children, after our deaths."

He paused. There was an extraordinary silence in the room, a kind of high, singing silence as if the tension itself was making a sound of its own. Mrs Perriam leaned forward across the table to

Lila, her little pale hands clasped earnestly in front of her.

"You shall live with us as our assistant, our — our *daughter* assistant, until you marry. It will be just like it used to be, except that we will give you your own rooms, and a little motor, of course, for your independence. We have talked of it so much! Perhaps you will bring your friends here. Perhaps you will help us to entertain some of our academic colleagues." She unclasped her hands and held one out to Lila above the roses. "My dear child, my dear Lila, is this not, for all of us, a most admirable plan?"

# 30

IN the morning, it was raining. Soft light English summer rain blew through the birch trees in front of Culver House in grey veils of damp. Lila pulled back the thick chintz curtains lined in rose-pink sateen, and looked at the gentle wetness, and the fresh pale green of the birch leaves, and the curious silvery gleam of the tree trunks. The drive was glistening. The yellow roses round her window were spangled with drops and the air was clean and kind.

She leaned out of the window and let the drizzle scatter itself across her face. It was reviving, especially as she had hardly slept, lying wakeful hour after hour in her cushioning bed, staring into the darkness.

"You overwhelm me," she had said last night, her hands still in her lap, screwing her napkin into a damp rope. "I don't know what to say. You completely overwhelm me."

They had seemed gratified. They had risen from the table and come to pat her shoulders and tell her that she was exhausted, of course she was, that she was to say nothing then, nothing, overcome as she must be by all the sensations of being back in Aldeburgh, back in Culver House, yet without her father and after all those terrible hardships. She nodded violently, grateful to have to say nothing further. Mrs Perriam had stooped to kiss her goodnight, leaving a breath of jasmine-scented cologne behind her.

"In the morning, we will talk," she said. "In the morning."

It was a phrase from childhood, from growing up. In the morning you'll feel better; in the morning your pain will be gone; in the morning, you'll see things our way. Lila had gone upstairs to find the lamps in her room glowing and the bed turned down by Mrs Tuttle's practised hand. There was a carafe of water by the bed and the latest copy of the *Illustrated London News*, and a cream and blue silk kimono had been laid across the plump quilt. Everything was comfortable, everything was thoughtful, everything was serene and timeless and secure. It *was* like Sleeping Beauty, it *was*, this calm and lovely and civilized house dreaming on inside its impenetrable hedge of thorns. The trouble was, Lila thought, settling herself almost guiltily on the mound of soft pillows, that she had spent the last seven years on the other side of that hedge.

Now, Lila looked at her watch. Twenty-five past eight. Breakfast at Culver House — the porridge kept warm by a spirit lamp, kippers for Mr Perriam under a silver dome — was at half past. At nine, they laid aside their letters and newspapers and, weather permitting, went arm-in-arm into the garden. At nine-thirty, they went into the library, closed the door, and a deep, soft quiet descended on the house like a muffling cloud. The telephone, that necessary but uncouth fact of modern life, was switched through to the kitchen where

376

Mrs Tuttle answered it with a bark. "Culver House," she'd say. "Culver House."

Lila drew her face in from the rain reluctantly. She longed to be out there, walking through the trees, running through the shallow dunes towards the sea. She turned resolutely towards the looking glass on her dressing table, and smoothed her hair back behind its combs, and tugged at her dress. She hoped she didn't look as if she had hardly slept.

In the dining room, a white cloth had been laid for breakfast. There was a smell of toast and coffee, and the roses of last night had been removed — too lavish for the morning. Mr and Mrs Perriam were already seated, paper-knives poised above their letters, spectacles in place. Lila went round the table and kissed them, conscious of a kind of hypocrisy in seeming already to play the role of a dutiful daughter.

They made gentle small talk, enquiring if Lila had slept well, displaying a new pamphlet published on the symbolism of the crocodile in the tradition of Punch and Judy, remarking on the number of butterflies to be seen on a sunny morning — "Tortoiseshells, my dear, so pretty" — on the buddleia outside the dining-room window. Lila poured coffee, removed used plates, helped herself to a tiny crustless triangle of white toast.

"My dear. Is that all you want?"

"Yes, I — "

"Mrs Tuttle will be dismayed. Can you not manage just a little porridge?"

"I'm — I'm afraid I didn't sleep very well."

"Oh!" Mrs Perriam said, her face full of real concern. "Were you not comfortable? Was the room not warm enough?"

Lila turned to her.

"I was never more comfortable in my life. It wasn't that. It was my mind. My mind just went over and over what you — you offered me last night."

Mr Perriam laid down his knife on his toast plate, very quietly. Mrs Perriam took off her spectacles and folded them up on the crocodile pamphlet. She saw their faces turn to her, full of confidence and affectionate pleasure. Her heart sank within her.

"Nobody has ever had such friends as I have had in you. You saved me and my father, quite literally, in the past. You saved us and you saved us without strings, asking nothing in return. I wouldn't like you ever to think that I didn't appreciate your generosity to the full, that I don't know how lucky I have been."

She paused. She couldn't look at them any more, but even without looking she knew their expressions had become puzzled, even dismayed. How was she to phrase to them that they were offering her everything a virtually homeless penniless girl without family could want, and that she was going to turn it down? How could she say that life at Culver House for her now, despite all its charm and culture and quiet comfort, would simply suffocate her? How could she explain to them that she had learned about freedom the hard way during those gruelling years in Malta, and that no amount of motor

378

cars and separate rooms could give it to her here? She took a deep breath.

"I cannot accept your offer."

Mrs Perriam gave a little cry and put her napkin to her mouth.

"You are so good to make it. Too good. Certainly too good for me. It is wonderful of you, generous and imaginative. I can see how I must appear to you turning it down. I can see how incomprehensible my behaviour seems, how heartless even. But — but," she forced herself to turn and look directly into Mr Perriam's astonished and pained eyes, "I have grown to need to go forward now. It's taken me so long. I wondered, in the night, if it actually took a war to make me even begin to stand on my own two feet. But I have begun. I see that now. I have begun and I must go on."

Mrs Perriam put down her napkin and felt in her sleeve for another tiny handkerchief.

"I don't want to distress you!" Lila cried. "I don't want to hurt you, you of all people. Believe me, I don't."

Mr Perriam said quietly, "I think it is too late for such a wish." He put a hand out to his wife. "My dear — "

Mrs Perriam looked at Lila. Her faded blue gaze was blurred with tears.

"Where will you go? What will you do?"

"It is our fault," Mr Perriam said. "We acted too quickly. You had only been in England a few days, a few days after the strain of all those years away. How could you decide anything?"

Lila held the table.

"You are so kind, to think that way. But it isn't too soon. If anything, it's too late, years too late." She stopped a moment and then she said, "I didn't really want to leave Malta. I felt I should; I felt that if I left it, I should be able to make up my mind — " She stopped again.

Mr Perriam stood up, and moved round the table to take his wife's elbow.

"Then it seems you have succeeded, my dear."

Lila rose too.

"I'm so sorry, so very, very sorry."

They regarded her from across the table, across the mild confusion of the breakfast things.

"Then at least," Mr Perriam said, "we have that in common."

★ ★ ★

"I wonder," Lila said, "if Tuttle could run me to the bus?"

Mrs Tuttle was shelling broad beans. She didn't look up.

"And where might you be going?"

"To London," Lila said. "Well, to Croydon actually. To the airfield."

Mrs Tuttle put four beans in the pot in front of her and laid their empty pod on the pile beside it. She looked at Lila. Lila was wearing the cotton dress and jacket she had arrived in, and her suitcase was in her hand. Mrs Tuttle indicated the suitcase.

"You better put that down. Looks heavy."

380

Lila obeyed.

"One night," Mrs Tuttle said. "One night only. Hardly worth making up the bed."

Lila said quietly, "I didn't know what would happen."

"True," Mrs Tuttle said.

"They're the last people I'd want to hurt," Lila said. "The last. They've been better to me than I'll ever deserve."

Mrs Tuttle surveyed her.

"You going back then?"

"Yes."

"Less than a week, and you're going back?"

"Yes."

"I'll say this for you," Mrs Tuttle said, "I don't know anything about this Malta place, but it's taught you to make up your mind."

She went over to the sink and washed her hands vigorously.

"I'll put you up a sandwich."

"No, really, I — "

"You didn't eat nothing at breakfast. Toast untouched on your plate. If you're travelling, you can't do it on an empty stomach. Egg and cress?"

"Thank you," Lila said. She sat down suddenly in a kitchen chair and leant her elbows on the table, her face in her hands. "Will they be all right, Mrs Tuttle? Will they?"

Mrs Tuttle spun the roller towel on its wooden pin.

"I'll see that they are."

"I can't bear to cause them pain, I just never dreamt — "

"No more of that," Mrs Tuttle said. Her voice was quite sharp. "What's done is done. No use crying over spilled milk." She looked at Lila's bent head and then she said, relenting, "They wouldn't have done it if they weren't proud of you. Where would that pride be, I wonder, if you'd said yes?"

Lila looked up. There were tears on her cheeks.

"Do you mean that?"

"When," Mrs Tuttle demanded, "did you ever hear me say a thing I didn't mean?" She pushed the beans aside and banged a bread board down on the table. "Now I'll make you that sandwich," she said, "and then I'll call Tuttle."

★ ★ ★

The plane ride south was bumpy. Lila, along with most of the other passengers, was sick, and grew thankful that the last refuelling stop, in Sicily, meant overnight on the ground, even if the accommodation was a row of army cots in a disused German aircraft hangar. It was very hot. The supply of bottled water ran out quite quickly, the first mosquitoes of the Mediterranean summer were busy, and the mattresses not only appeared to be stuffed with golf balls, but also to have a disconcerting interior life of their own. But at least they were on the ground. Lila lay listening to the snores and grunts of the other passengers, and to the sinister tickings and twitchings beneath her until

382

she could bear it no longer, and crept out of the heavy black darkness of the hangar and into the moonlight outside.

It was very bright. The moon, a huge silver disc, seemed to hang unnaturally close in the deep blue southern sky, almost at treetop level. Lila found a stone slab and sat down on it, her back against the rough concrete wall of the hangar, and gazed upward. She should have felt exhausted, worn out by the strain of her few days in England and the discomfort of the journey, but she didn't. She felt, in an odd way, at peace, as if, for all the pain she had caused the Perriams, she had not only done the right thing in turning down their offer, but the only thing possible.

She pulled her knees up against her, and put her arms around them. She hadn't seen the Perriams to say goodbye. Mrs Tuttle had said they were in the garden.

"Best leave them there. Best not to say anything further."

"Should I leave them a note?"

"What'll you say?"

"I don't know. I just thought — "

"Least said," Mrs Tuttle said, "soonest mended."

Tuttle had driven her all the way to Ipswich.

"No," she had protested. "No, you mustn't. I'll get the bus from Aldeburgh."

"Orders," Tuttle said briefly. "Mr Perriam's orders. Ipswich station."

He hadn't spoken to her all the way there except to say that if it was going to rain, he wished it would make up its mind and do it properly. When they reached Ipswich station, he had carried her bag onto the train, and presented her with a rail ticket, and a letter.

"But — "

"Orders," Tuttle said again. He held his hand out. "Goodbye, miss."

The letter was addressed to her in Mr Perriam's hand. She couldn't open it all the way to London nor on the second train down to Croydon. It was only there, waiting to see if there would be a seat for her on the flight south, that she finally persuaded herself that if she was brave enough to turn down an offer like the Perriams', then surely she was brave enough to open a mere letter. It was very short.

'My dear Lila,' it said.

You will forgive us not saying goodbye. You will forgive me, too, for the brevity of this letter.

Time, I hope, will enable us to see matters in the light in which you so plainly see them already. In the meantime, I should be obliged if you would call on Mr Arturo Boffa, at your convenience. He is a lawyer, and his offices are in Kingsway, Valetta, close to the junction with Britannia Street. I have reason to believe he has not been forced to vacate them during the war. I will apprise him of your coming.

With every good wish for your future happiness,
Edward Perriam.

384

The letter had made her cry. She read it twice, and then she put it into her bag because people were beginning to stare at her, no doubt thinking it was a love letter. Well, it was a love letter, of a kind; a letter of forgiveness. Lila closed her eyes now, and let the white moonlight bathe her face as she had let the East Anglian rain bathe it, less than twenty-four hours ago.

"What's done is done," Mrs Tuttle had said. "No use in crying over spilled milk . . . Least said, soonest mended."

Lila opened her eyes again. The same moon, no doubt muffled in cloud, hung over Mrs Tuttle now, and Tuttle himself, and Mr and Mrs Perriam, in their cool sweet northern night. She hoped they were sleeping, she hoped they were sleeping as they deserved to. And to the south — well, to the south, under that moon lay Malta. She had not chosen Malta seven years ago, but yesterday, in the Perriams' dining room, she most definitely had.

★ ★ ★

It was grey when they landed, overcast and hot with a fierce dry wind blowing up from Africa, whirling dust and rubbish stingingly against walls and legs and vehicles. There were two taxis waiting, old bull-nosed Morrises, and one agreed to take Lila to Kalkara as long as he could drop two other passengers off first.

She was, by now, with the length of the journey and the strain on her emotions, very tired. She wedged herself in one corner of the back seat of the taxi and rested her head against the fawn moquette-covered side, and closed her eyes. The other passengers ignored her. So did the driver. She let their streams of chatter flow over her like water, or wind.

It was midday when she reached Kalkara. The street was empty, and Zanzu had plainly been round bolting all Miss de Vere's shutters against the wind. Lila opened the street door, pulled her suitcase inside, and let the door fall to behind her.

"Hallo! Hallo!"

Zanzu appeared in the kitchen doorway, holding a spoon. He looked amazed.

"Miss Lila!"

"I'm back," she said, unnecessarily.

"Miss Lila — " he said again. He seemed agitated.

"What is it?"

"I wanted to telegraph you," Zanzu said. "I wanted to, but she wouldn't let me — "

Lila stepped forward.

"Who wouldn't let you?"

"Miss de Vere," he said, making the name sound, as he always did, as if it were just one word. Mizdeveer.

"Miss de Vere?"

"The day you left," Zanzu said, "the very day." He gestured down one side of his body. "She fell ill. She was ill, here in this house. Oh, Miss Lila, you must go to her. You must go at once. She is in the hospital."

# 31

"IT was a stroke," the ward sister said. She wore a grey cotton uniform with a white apron and her hair was pinned back under a sweeping white cap, like a nun's. "She had one stroke, and we were most hopeful of her recovery, but now she has had a second. You will find her much changed."

She paused in her brisk walk down the polished corridor, and put her hand on a cream-painted door.

"We put her in here. For privacy. It is essential she is given complete quiet, you see, for any hope of recovery." She looked up at Lila and said gently, as if by way of preparation for the worst, "We fear that the second stroke was caused by the rupture of a larger blood vessel than the first."

She opened the door. The room beyond was dim, with a bulky shape on the bed and beyond it the outline of a window almost entirely shaded by a dark green blind.

"If you speak to her," the sister said in a whisper, "do it in as low a voice as possible. And no sudden movements. Would you like a junior nurse to stay with you?"

Lila looked at the shape on the bed.

"No, thank you," she said, "I should like to be alone with her."

"Ten minutes," the ward sister said, and closed the door.

Lila eased off her shoes and tiptoed in bare feet to the bed.

There was a chair placed nearby, as if other visitors — Zanzu, maybe Miss Strickland and other distinguished English friends — had already been to sit and hope and whisper. Miss de Vere lay on her back, her grey hair spread on the pillow in a way Lila felt she would hardly have approved of, with her right hand on her breast. The other hand lay by her side. It looked awkward, as if it somehow no longer belonged to her. The left side of her face looked strange too, slack and slipped, giving her an unfamiliar mask-like appearance. Paralysis, Zanzu had said. He had been close to tears. "She is paralysed on one side. On her left side. Where the heart is."

Lila sat down and put her hand gently on Miss de Vere's right one. At least she was not in some undignified hospital robe, but in one of her own unmistakable nightgowns, voluminous white cotton tents gathered into the neck and cuffs with brightly coloured embroidery.

"I'm here," Lila said. "It's Lila. I'm back."

Miss de Vere's nearest closed eyelid flickered a little but there was no other response. Lila bent closer.

"Can you hear me?"

A faint sound came from Miss de Vere's throat, like a groan.

"They asked me to stay," Lila said slowly, in a whisper. "The Perriams did. They asked me to stay and be like a kind of daughter, inheriting the house after them. That was so kind, don't you think?"

Miss de Vere's hand, under Lila's, gave a tiny, sudden movement. Lila slipped her fingers round it and held it firmly.

"But I said no. I found I didn't want to. I found I couldn't leave you and Carmela and Malta. I found I couldn't leave the person I had become and return to being the person I once was. So I've come back. I'm staying."

Again the curious little sound came from Miss de Vere's throat and her eyelid trembled. Lila bent her head.

"I want to cry, seeing you like this. It shouldn't have happened to you. It shouldn't. Not after all you've done, all you've been through."

"It was the war," Zanzu had said, his voice bitter, "that's what it was, the war! She exerted herself too much! It is the Italians and the Germans who are responsible for this!"

Lila leaned forward. Even as ill as this, Miss de Vere retained a pink English wholesomeness, and smelled of the eau de cologne soap she always used, that she said her father had used. That father whom she had adored, whom she had tried to compensate, for the loss of his only son.

"You've taught me so much," Lila said, "given me so much."

The door opened. A junior nurse, in a much smaller cap, put her head in. She smiled at Lila.

"Ten minutes are up."

Lila looked down at Miss de Vere.

"May I come back?"

389

"'Course," the girl said cheerfully, "tomorrow. Usual visiting hours."

"Can't I come any time?"

"Sorry," the girl said. "Rules and regs. You know."

Lila rose and then stooped to kiss Miss de Vere's cheek. It had lost its usual resilience and felt soft and fragile.

"Goodbye," Lila whispered, "God bless you."

★ ★ ★

The door of the building in Kingsway stood propped open with a wooden wedge, displaying a grim little tiled hallway inside and a stone staircase with an iron handrail leading up into darkness. Bedside the door, screwed into the wall, a brass plate announced that on the first floor could be found Dr J. Azzopardi, and on the second, the offices of Mr Arturo Boffa and Mr Mifsud Bugeja, lawyers and commissioners for oaths. Lila stepped out of the sunlight of the street into the darkness of the hallway, and began to mount the stairs.

Dr Azzopardi's door was firmly closed. 'Surgery hours strictly from 8 – 10 a.m. and from 5 – 7 p.m.' said a notice in a decided black hand, pinned to it. Beyond his door, the stairs seemed to climb ever more steeply, illumined faintly now by the light from a dirty skylight in the roof above. On the second landing, someone had made a small effort. There was a worn square of Turkey carpet, an umbrella stand, and a fly-spotted engraving of the Grand

Harbour, as it was in the eighteenth century, framed in black and gold. On the door, the two lawyers' plates were screwed, in an even-handed manner, side by side.

Inside, a young male clerk sat in a reception area the size of a broom cupboard. He rose at the sight of Lila, his hand going at once to his white collar, as if to make sure his tie was straight.

"I am Lila Cunningham," Lila said. "I believe Mr Perriam from England notified Mr Boffa that I should call."

The clerk nodded.

"Yes, madam. The letter came yesterday, madam. I have your papers in readiness, madam. If you will take a seat, I will inform Mr Boffa that you are here."

He indicated a chair tucked into a corner under a sagging shelf of ledgers.

"Is it convenient?" Lila said. "For Mr Boffa, I mean."

"Oh yes," the clerk said, "perfectly. Madam."

He sidled out from behind his desk and vanished down a narrow dark corridor. Lila perched on the allotted chair and looked around. Not only had these offices survived the war, but they appeared to have survived, completely untouched and certainly by any duster, for comfortable decades before that. No doubt when A. E. O. Perriam had first climbed these stairs to make the acquaintance of Mr Boffa's father before the First World War, the piles and stacks and towers of bundles of papers and black japanned deed boxes and brown leathercloth-covered ledgers had been exactly the same.

"Mr Boffa will see you now," the clerk said, flattening himself against the deed boxes to let Lila pass. "Second door on the left."

Mr Boffa was short and square with curly grey hair, dressed in black, complete with waistcoat, despite the heat. He stood up behind a desk as cluttered as everything else in his offices seemed to be, and held out his hand.

"Miss Cunningham."

Lila shook it.

"Mr Boffa."

"Not content, I gather," Mr Boffa said, twinkling a little, "with being starved and terrified here the last few years, you've decided to make Malta your home."

"Yes," Lila said. "I almost surprised myself."

Mr Boffa motioned her to sit down.

"Between us," he said, "my late father and I have looked after the Perriams' affairs in Malta since 1908. Not that they have been complicated, mind you, or at least not since the late Mr Perriam stopped trying to take pieces of Maltese prehistory home with him. Are you, Miss Cunningham, interested in prehistory?"

"I might be," Lila said, "when I know something about the future."

"Your own future?"

"Yes, Mr Boffa."

"Well," Mr Boffa said, drawing a buff folder towards him. "Well I think I can tell you something about that." He opened the folder and drew out a letter. "It seems, Miss Cunningham, that you are to have a house at least."

Lila clutched the arms of her chair.

"A house!"

"Well, what's left of a house would be more accurate. Mr Perriam says here that he and his wife wish ownership of the Villa Zonda to be transferred to you, along with the gardens and all lands attached."

Lila's face was glowing.

"But that's wonderful!"

"Is it?" Mr Boffa said. "Is it? To inherit a bomb-blasted ruin?"

"I don't mind that," Lila cried. "I don't mind that at all! I can mend it, I can — "

"What with?" said Mr Boffa.

She stared at him. He tapped the letter.

"There is no money, I fear, to go with the house. Merely the house and two hectares of land. Mr Perriam says — " he paused and looked at Lila. "May I read you what Mr Perriam says?"

"Of course."

Mr Boffa held up the letter.

"You will find," he read, "that Miss Cunningham is a young woman of high independence, to whom an offer of money might prove entirely unacceptable. I believe she would, in fact, prefer to be given a ruin and all the challenges it presents, than to have her path made in any way easier."

Mr Boffa looked at Lila.

"Is Mr Perriam right?"

Lila had clasped her hands together. Her eyes were shining.

"He is."

"Then I may proceed with the transfer of

393

ownership as Mr Perriam suggests?"

Lila beamed at him.

"Oh you may," she said. "You *may*."

★ ★ ★

Carmela sat at the kitchen table in front of a plate of bread and butter. She wore her cherry-printed frock — which she now almost fitted — and had tied her single pigtail up in a loop behind her head in a way that caused two boys in her class to call her Teapot. The nickname made her absolutely determined to go on wearing her hair like this until they stopped, and stop they would in time, she was sure of it; stop and start offering to carry her schoolbooks instead. In the last few months, Carmela had been increasingly aware of the power of her own personality. Hadn't it, after all, brought Lila back to her?

Zanzu had cut her the bread and butter. Lila said he was not, absolutely not, to wait on Carmela, she was to do things for herself, but Zanzu liked waiting on her, especially with no Miss de Vere to fuss over, and Carmela liked to be waited on. As she sat at the kitchen table with her bread and butter, she would pretend she was a lady in a café in Paris wearing perfume and gloves, being attended to by an obsequious waiter. Lila said she was going to teach Carmela French next, and maybe one day, if she worked hard, they would go to Paris together and eat in a café. It was as well, Carmela considered, to get in some practice.

Zanzu was washing up. Normally his washing up was very slapdash, but since Miss de Vere had gone into hospital, he had scoured every pot and pan and polished every spoon and glass. He had also swept under beds and cleaned the windows and hung rugs and blankets over the windowsills to air. It was plain he wanted Miss de Vere to come back to a gleaming house. The cleanliness was going to be an offering to her, a tribute, a celebratory gift. He even put flowers in her room every day, though she wasn't there to see them. Carmela respected that. When Lila went to England, Carmela had done the same. Well, almost the same. What she had actually done was to make a little shrine in Lila's room, with a picture of the Virgin Mary and an old rosary and an empty meat paste jar for flowers with a ribbon tied round it to disguise its utilitarian outline. In front of this, Carmela had prayed daily and fiercely.

"Make her come home! Oh please do, please! *Make* her come back!"

It had worked. Carmela had come home from school a week ago and Lila had been there, in the kitchen, making a pot of tea. Carmela had cried and cried. So had Lila. And then Zanzu did. They cried because they were all together again except for Miss de Vere who lay marooned in her high bed in the hospital, with nobody knowing what she could hear or see.

Carmela folded a piece of bread and butter into a neat sandwich and bit into it. Zanzu always left the crusts on, which made his bread and butter tougher to eat, but easier to hold.

"In geography," Carmela said, "we are doing drought. Drought and deserts and dried-up rivers."

Zanzu wasn't listening. He was thinking of the days before the war when he used to help organize all Miss de Vere's projects, when he worked with paper and typewriter instead of a mop and a wooden spoon and a pot scrubber. He'd do anything for Miss de Vere, but sometimes he looked back on those days with nostalgia because he felt he had had some kind of significance then. Perhaps, when — if — *when* she was well again, she would take up all her old work again, the special schools, the maternity clinics, the crèches, and he could leave the sink and blow the dust off his typewriter and join her.

"The definition of a desert," Carmela said, "is a barren place, where no-one can live because nothing will grow."

The front door of the house opened. Carmela put down her bread and butter.

"Hallo!" Lila called. "I'm home!"

She appeared in the kitchen doorway, holding a white box and a bunch of cornflowers. Her eyes were shining. Zanzu turned from the sink.

"Good news?"

"Not the news we want," Lila said. "Not news from the hospital. But other news, lovely news." She put the white box on the table. "I bought a cake. A shop cake. To celebrate."

Carmela pushed her plate aside.

"What is it? What is it?"

Lila laid the cornflowers beside the cakebox.

"We've got a house."

Carmela stared.

"A house?"

"Mr and Mrs Perriam have given me the Villa Zonda!"

"But it's broken!" Carmela cried.

"We'll mend it," Lila said. "We'll mend it and then we'll go and live there and grow flowers in the courtyard and have hens again and plant onions where Pa used to plant them."

Carmela held the edge of the table hard.

"You and me?"

Lila came round the table and stooped to put her arms around Carmela.

"Of course you and me. Who else would I live with?" She glanced at Zanzu, over Carmela's head. "And you too, of course, if — if ever you should need to."

"Thank you," he said.

"Is this for ever?" Carmela said, her arms tight round Lila's neck. "Is this for ever and ever now?"

"Yes," Lila said, "yes. It's as for ever as you want it to be. I'll get a job and you'll finish at school, and that's where we'll come home to, every night."

Carmela stiffened suddenly.

"I remembered something."

Lila loosened her arms.

"About living? About home? About your family?"

Carmela shook her head. Her face was pink. She wriggled sideways out of Lila's arms and stood up.

"No," she said. Her chin went up. "About a letter."

"A letter?"

Carmela took a step back against the table and took a breath.

"A letter came when you were in England."

"And you forgot to give it to me when I came back?"

"No," Carmela said, "I remembered but I didn't give it."

"Why not?"

"Because I didn't want you going away again. I didn't want you going to live somewhere I couldn't come. But now you've got the Villa Zonda, it will be safe. If you've got your own house, you won't want someone else's, will you?"

Lila rose from her crouching position by Carmela's chair, to her feet.

"Carmela," she said, "did you open this letter?"

"No," Carmela said. It had been agony restraining herself, but she'd managed it.

"Then what on earth are you talking about?"

Carmela flashed a look at Zanzu for support, but he was watching Lila.

"I just knew," Carmela said. "After the ring and the flower and the other letters — I knew the writing." She paused and felt behind her head for her teapot handle of hair. "Anyway the letter came in a car. From the Tabia Palace."

Lila fumbled for a chairback and sat down.

"Go on."

"He gave it to me," Carmela said. "He was

398

wearing clothes for playing tennis and he gave it to me. He said — "

"What did he say?"

"He said, 'If she comes back, make sure this is the first thing she sees.'"

# 32

LILA parked Miss de Vere's little car under the umbrella pines outside the Mdina Gate. It was blazingly hot, and there was nobody about except a dog and an old man asleep in the shade together, oblivious of anything. Lila got out of the car and smoothed down her skirt. It was the skirt of a black and white spotted sleeveless dress she had made the night before. She had felt ashamed of herself for making anything new for this occasion, but had been unable to stop herself, either. She had made it very quickly and roughly, not finishing the seams, but the effect was surprisingly good. Or, at least, it would look good until she saw it beside the Baroness's summer silks, when all the old feelings of sartorial inadequacy would flood back and she would be twenty-one again, twenty-one and gauche, with no money and no social position and an embarrassing father.

Pa. A lump rose suddenly in her throat. She put a hand up to her hair which, Tabia Palace or no Tabia Palace, she had tied back with one of his red handkerchiefs. For comfort, she told herself; for courage, for solidarity. Then she put the keys in her handbag, and crossed the moat into the shadows and silence of the little city.

The Tabia Palace looked exactly the same. The bleached yellow stone walls, the graceful double-arched windows of the first floor, the

400

cornices and mouldings, the great central doorway under its softly pointed arch with the dolphin knocker glittering below, all looked as if the war years had never happened, never been thought of. Nor did Teseo look much different; older perhaps, a little more gaunt in the face, but precise in his black and white, holding the door as he had done to Lila that first morning, so long ago, when she had cycled through the fields of red clover, her heart in her mouth, to ask for work.

"Are the family all here?"

Teseo glanced at her. It was a fleeting glance but, to Lila, a disturbingly knowing one.

"No, miss. The Baroness hasn't yet come from America and the Count has taken Salvu to the hospital. For a check-up."

"He's very good."

"He is indeed," Teseo said with emphasis. In his peaceable, traditional, obedient view of things, Salvu's political opinions were little better than those of a revolutionary. Why Count Julius should have so taken to the man was beyond Teseo and the cause of certain undeniable difficulties. Indeed, Teseo would have felt open jealousy and resentment towards Salvu, if his own relationship with Salvu's wife hadn't been so very good. Teseo had never married, but if he had, Doris was exactly the kind of woman he would have chosen, pious, domestic and thrifty. Teseo spent many hours in the kitchen courtyard watching Doris at her tasks and suggesting to her that she was wasted on a man like Salvu. She, sighing heavily and delighted, would shake her head and agree and declare that it was inevitable, it was the will of God. These conversations made them both very happy.

"Baron Anton is in the courtyard," Teseo said now.

Lila nodded. It was suddenly almost impossible to speak.

"You will find him much better now. Of course, he will always walk with a limp."

Lila said faintly, "A limp? I thought he had been ill — "

"A car crash, miss. He always was a fast driver. Between you and me, the Ford doesn't handle quite the same after Baron Anton has been driving it."

He paused in the doorway to the courtyard.

"Shall I announce you, miss?"

Lila looked out into the shade-dappled sunlight of the courtyard at the urns and the flowers and the fountain. Diagonally opposite, leaning back in a chair reading a newspaper, with a straw hat tipped over his eyes, was a long figure dressed entirely in white. Just as she remembered. She swallowed hard.

"No," she said. "No thank you."

Teseo moved back into the house. Lila stood and looked and looked. It was an extraordinary sensation to see Anton actually lounging there, in the flesh, the reality at last, after all those yearning, hoping, dreaming hours of the war. Her eyes filled with sudden tears. A limp ... She made a little helpless gesture with her hands and at the same time, gave a small involuntary cry.

At the sound, Anton looked up. He looked slowly, as if he too were emerging from some kind of dream, and then he let the newspaper slither to the ground, and tossed his hat away, and rose to his feet.

"Lila," he said.

She couldn't move. He stood as tall as ever, but slightly crookedly now in a way that was poignantly reminiscent of Pa.

"Oh, Lila," he said again, and held out his arms.

She began to walk forward. She wouldn't run, she *wouldn't*. Two paces from him she stopped and looked up. He was smiling. He was also tanned and healthy-looking and, although slightly softened along the jawline, still beautiful. He leaned forward a little and took her hands in his and kissed them. Then he drew her slowly into his arms and held her against him, his cheek against her hair.

"Lila," he said. His voice sounded as if he was laughing. "Lila. Relax."

She stared along the line of his shoulder, almost unable to believe that under the white linen lay Anton, his blood and flesh and bone. She whispered, "What happened to you?"

"A prang."

"Teseo said it was a car."

"Well, yes, it was a car. Two cars actually. One driven by me with great competence and one by some idiot who wasn't looking where he was going."

"Does it hurt?"

"Not much now," he said. His hand moved

403

from her back to her shoulder. "You're too thin."

Lila took her face from his neck and looked up.

"Did it happen in England?"

His eyes were very close. Clear, like his skin, full of well-being.

"England?" he said. His voice was suddenly very jaunty. "Why do you ask?"

"Because that's where you've been, isn't it?"

The expression in his eyes changed a little, became veiled. Lila gently pulled away from his close embrace, even though he still held her by the shoulders.

"All these years," Lila said, her voice suddenly shaken by the intensity of the memory of them, "all these years of the war while we were so hungry and frightened and I longed and longed for your letters, you were in England, weren't you? Doing something hush-hush. Your uncle said, Max — " She stopped, and then she said, "Oh, I am so sorry about Max."

Anton's hands dropped from her shoulders.

"Poor old Max."

"He was so brave."

"So I gather."

"He had begun to feel passionately about Malta, he wanted to fight for Malta — "

"And to marry a Maltese," Anton said. The lightness had gone out of his voice. He turned away from Lila. "It's pretty hard, you know, to come back and have everyone forgetting to welcome you because they're too busy telling you what a hero your brother was."

"I do welcome you," Lila cried passionately, "I *do*! Oh, if you only knew, you only — "

He looked at her over his shoulder.

"I do know. I missed you too. Why do you think I wrote to you? Why do you think I've come back to Malta now? I've been so homesick, Lila, so homesick. For here, for the past, for you." He turned to face her. "Lila," he said, "why do you think I sent you a ring?"

Lila hesitated. She said faintly, "Your note said 'Wait'."

He came so close to her she could see the little pulse beating at the base of his throat.

"Well?" he said, and his voice had a hint of his old imperiousness in it. "Well? And have you?"

She drew a huge breath. "I can't believe you've asked me that."

"Why not?"

"All that silence!" she cried. "Months, years of silence and now you ask me — "

She got no further. He had seized her in his arms and begun to kiss her, all over her face and neck, holding her head with one hand cupped behind it, to imprison her. She wrenched her face sideways.

"Don't."

"I've come back for you!" he shouted. "Haven't I? What more do you want?"

She put her hands flat against his chest and pushed him from her, hard. She was panting.

"Where were you?" she said.

"What do you mean?"

"Where *were* you?"

405

"In America. Recovering from the crash. You know that."

"No," she said. "Before that. When everyone said you were doing secret work. In England."

"I *was* working."

She fixed her eyes on his face.

"What work?"

"War work."

Her voice was rising. "What kind of work? Military work? Spy work? Resistance work? And where were you doing it? Where were you doing this famous work that no-one will speak about?"

There was a silence. Anton put his hands in his pockets. Then he said casually, "It was fund-raising. For Malta."

"*Fund*-raising?"

"Yes."

"But your mother was doing that! In America!"

Anton shifted his weight onto his good leg. "Yes."

"You were in America?" Lila said, her voice a horrified whisper. "You were in America, all the war, with your mother?"

Anton said nothing. Lila took a step away from him, clenching her fists at her sides.

"I thought you went to Cranwell, with Max."

"I did."

"What happened?"

He said, with a touch of bravado, "They threw me out."

"And so you went to America. You gave up the thought of any kind of help for the war effort

406

and — " she paused and then said with disgust, "you went to *America*."

"We raised over two million dollars," Anton said. "Nearly two and a half."

Lila was shaking. "No wonder you didn't write! No wonder you let me believe you were doing something secret and useful!"

"I never lied to you."

"Not in so many words!" she shouted. "Not a sin of commission but a sin of omission for sure!" She stopped and took a breath. "Did your uncle know? Did Max?"

"Yes," Anton said. His tone was sullen.

"But were sworn to secrecy, I suppose? To save your cowardly skin!"

"Lila," Anton said, "Lila, please calm down. I don't think you understand at all — "

She held her hand up commandingly, as she used to do in those unruly wartime classes in the dockyard school when she wanted silence.

"Oh but I do," Lila said. Her voice was very steady. "I understand perfectly. I don't know why you were thrown out of Cranwell, and I don't want to know, and nor do I want to know why you ran away to America. But after that, I *do* know. Or at least, I can guess so accurately that it virtually amounts to knowledge. You had a wonderful time in America, didn't you? You were young and handsome and wealthy and titled and exotically foreign and everyone made a fuss of you, especially the girls. Oh, Anton, the *girls*. So many lovely American girls that there wasn't a moment, was there, to write to a very ordinary English girl stuck in a siege in Malta and simply *living* on the hope of one day getting a letter? She was just a detail, wasn't she; a bit of innocent fun that had enlivened a dull summer at home with nothing to do? I'll tell you what happened. News of Max's bravery came, and all those nice Americans began to wonder why one brother was prepared to fight and, as it tragically happened, die for freedom, while the other was perfectly happy to play about in America while his countrymen half starved, going to the beach and driving fast cars. Didn't they? And then they thought, perfectly reasonably, that perhaps you weren't so wonderful after all, and they stopped making a fuss of you and the lovely girls went off to find *real* heroes, and you found yourself alone, even shunned. And *then* — " Lila stepped forward and thrust her face into Anton's, "*then* you thought, oh dear, nobody loves me. But wait! Somebody does! Ordinary little Lila in Malta, now *she*'s faithful, *she*'s adoring, *she* won't mind what I've done or what I haven't done! So you wrote me that letter, didn't you, all about sleepless nights and loneliness and missing me, and you got someone to post it from England, so that I shouldn't know — yet — where you were. Isn't that right?"

Anton said stiffly, "You have no business to speak to me in this way."

Lila moved away from him, her head bent. When she spoke again, it was in a much more remote voice.

"You're right," she said, "I have no business speaking to you, never mind the way I do it. I have no business being here with you, either; in

408

fact I have no business even knowing someone like you."

She glanced at him. He had half turned away from her and was leaning against the nearest urn, his hand to his face in a gesture which, in her present mood, spoke to her of nothing so much as self-pity.

"It's so sad," Lila said, "isn't it? So sad, so infinitely sad that all these years, all this love and patience and hope should end like this — in — in something so *tawdry*. But end it has, hasn't it?"

"Your choice," Anton said. He was standing upright now and staring ahead of him. "Your choice entirely. Without hearing one word in my defence."

"There's nothing to hear," Lila said. "Nothing. Or at least, nothing that would make any difference. Has anyone ever uttered the words 'too late' to you before?"

He said nothing. She took one last look at the courtyard, at the jasmines and the plumbago and the stephanotis and the stone dolphins. And then she looked at him.

"Goodbye," Lila said.

He didn't move. For a fleeting second, a second in which all the intensely romantic hopes of the last seven years seemed to be compressed, Lila had an impulse to rush over to him and fling herself into his arms. She closed her eyes. Then she opened them again, and said, "Please give my best wishes to your uncle," and turned away from him towards the doorway into the palace.

"It is not visiting time," the little nun in spectacles said through the grille.

"I know," Lila said, "I'm so sorry. But I would be so grateful to see Sister Rosanna for ten minutes."

The little nun eyed the sleeveless dress.

"You are improperly dressed."

"I know. I came on impulse. Perhaps you would lend me a shawl to cover my arms?"

The little nun seemed to consider for a moment.

"Wait, please," she said, and vanished.

Lila leaned against the warm stone wall. It had indeed been an impulse to come, a sudden impulse after twenty minutes of uncontrollable weeping in Miss de Vere's car under the umbrella pine, gravely watched by the old man and the dog who had both had, Lila reflected, the good manners and sense not to interfere. She had untied Pa's handkerchief and soaked it with tears, so that it now hung damply down her back after she had re-tied her hair with it, to be respectable for the convent.

The little nun reappeared at the grille.

"You may come."

The door was unlocked and opened just wide enough for Lila to slip through. The nun held out a black woollen shawl.

"Ten minutes only."

Rosanna was already in the visitors' room, a dim outline behind the grille. Lila went up to it, and knelt on the polished tiles.

"You should sit," Rosanna said.

"I know. But I need to be close to you. I need to feel private."

Rosanna said, "You've been crying."

"Yes."

"Miss de Vere?"

"No. She's no better, but she's still alive. It's — "

"Tell me," Rosanna said.

"It's about Max's brother."

There was a perceptible increase of tension the far side of the grille.

"Anton."

"Yes," Lila said, "he's come back."

"I'm glad for you," Rosanna said with some effort. "I am happy for you."

"No." Lila leaned forward and held the grille so that her face was almost touching it. "No, it isn't glad or happy. It's a sham. It's the end."

There was a little hiss of breath.

"A sham?"

"He didn't do *anything* in the war," Lila said, her voice full of horrified amazement at what she was saying. "He didn't even try. He was expelled from Cranwell, so he didn't try to do anything else. He — he just let Max do it."

There was a little pause and then Rosanna said softly, "I know."

"You know?"

"Max told me. I was the only person he told."

"And I," said Lila angrily, "was the only person who needed to know."

"No. You would never have believed us. You

would have thought it was spite. You had to learn for yourself."

Lila sank back on her heels.

"Well, now I have."

"And in time," Rosanna said calmly, "the knowledge will free you." She stood up. "I must go."

Lila rose too.

"I feel," she said, "as if my focus has gone, as if there's an empty space at the centre."

"You will fill it," Rosanna said, "in time. You will fill it in a way that perhaps you don't expect." She moved towards the doorway that led deep into the convent and then stopped. "Lila. One thing."

"Yes?"

"Don't think, in your pain, in your confusion, of turning to my brother. Please don't think of that."

"I wasn't — "

"No," Rosanna said, "not immediately. But later. Later, you might have thought of it. Don't." She turned her head and Lila got a pale glimpse of her face. "Don't," Rosanna said with emphasis. "You have tried him too far."

★ ★ ★

It was dusk when Lila got back to Kalkara. The last of the sun had slipped into the western sea, and swifts were darting and swooping in the hyacinth blue air. Across the harbour, in Valetta itself, lights were beginning to come on — the most heart-lifting sign, Lila sometimes thought,

412

that the war was actually over.

She locked Miss de Vere's car in its garage — a precaution Zanzu insisted on in the current acute shortage of driveable vehicles — and opened the house door. The lamp in the hall, a Venetian glass globe of red and blue to which Miss de Vere was devoted, was glowing softly, and the house was very quiet. Carmela and Zanzu would no doubt be in the kitchen, Carmela doing her homework (she always preferred to do it in public) and Zanzu filleting fish or slicing onions. There would be a companionable silence, broken only by chopping sounds or Carmela's sighs, and they would both turn to greet her with pleasure, reminding her not just of where her heart lay, but where it was both safe and valued.

She opened the kitchen door. The oil lamp was lit, standing, as it usually did, in the centre of the kitchen table. There was nothing else on the table, either side of which Carmela and Zanzu sat, staring at the wooden surface, in silence. The atmosphere in the room was not companionable, but something else, something sadder . . .

"Hallo," Lila said gently.

They both raised their heads and looked at her. Carmela's face was swollen with crying.

"Mizdeveer," Zanzu said. His voice was hoarse. "Mizdeveer is dead. She died this afternoon. Where were you?"

# 33

"SO many people," Zanzu whispered.

From her place in a front pew, Lila looked round. St Paul's Anglican Cathedral — so English somehow, with its great, light, neoclassical spaces, built by the Dowager Queen Adelaide over a hundred years before — was indeed almost full. And full of Maltese too, who, despite their ardent Catholicism, had come to an Anglican church to pay their last respects to Miss de Vere.

"So many people loved her," Zanzu said. He wore a black suit, with a tiny scarlet sprig from one of Miss de Vere's geraniums in his buttonhole.

Lila nodded. The congregation was not only large, but wonderfully various, English and Maltese of all ages, people who had known Beatrix de Vere as a benefactress, as an employer, as a friend of Malta, as a friend pure and simple. All the women's heads were covered, a gently nodding sea of black straw and black felt, black scarves and black shawls with, here and there, the graceful black silk sweep of the ancient Maltese faldetta.

Carmela, who had never been in an English church before, and certainly never in a church lit by so many windows, stood beside Lila in a new black frock with a white collar, and on her head a straw hat with a deep black band.

She had her first gloves too, made of fine black cotton, and black shoes which fastened across the instep with a strap and a shiny black button. Lila had taken Carmela shopping for all these things with money the lawyer had given them. He had given them enough money for Zanzu's suit too, and Lila's black silk frock and hat.

"I want Miss de Vere to be proud of us," Lila had said. "And nobody could be proud of us looking the way we do at the moment."

Miss de Vere's coffin lay ahead of them, between the choir stalls. It stood on a bier between four tall lit candles, and on the top of it was a sheaf of lilies and a posy of pink roses. Carmela had been allowed to put the roses there.

"They are from you," Lila said. "You and me."

Lila had been very quiet since Miss de Vere died, quiet and thoughtful. She had been to see Miss de Vere's lawyer three times, at his request, and then to see the priest at the Anglican cathedral to arrange the funeral. Zanzu had found his old typewriter and had typed lists for Lila, and letters in response to letters from some of Miss de Vere's relations in England who wanted to know, Lila said, if Miss de Vere had left them any money. She had given a tired smile when she said this.

"I'll refer them to the lawyer," Lila said. "He can deal with them. Money! Is that all they can think about?"

Carmela looked down at the hymnbook she held in her black gloved hands. It was bound in red cloth, and it said *Hymns Ancient and Modern* on the spine. It was an English book, with English hymns, and it was as well, Carmela reflected, that Doris couldn't see her holding it. Doris would probably think her daughter had become a heretic, holding a book of Anglican hymns. The organ, which had been softly playing while everyone filed into their pews, played a few final grave chords, and stopped.

Lila touched Carmela's arm. She looked up. A priest was standing at the head of Miss de Vere's coffin, a priest in a white surplice and an embroidered stole, holding a book open in his hands.

"I am the resurrection and the life, saith the Lord," he read in English. "He that believeth in me, though he were dead, yet shall he live: and whosoever liveth and believeth in me shall never die."

Slowly, Carmela looked up at Lila, to see the effect of what the priest had said on her. Lila was looking straight ahead, straight at Miss de Vere's coffin, and there were tears running down her face quite freely, and she was doing nothing to stop them.

\* \* \*

"Listen to this," Lila said.

She was kneeling on the floor of Miss de Vere's sitting room, by the bookcase, and she had a book in her hand. Zanzu, who had come in to bring her a cup of tea, waited politely.

"I've found a bit of poetry," Lila said,

416

"English poetry. Elizabeth Barrett Browning."

Zanzu shook his head. "I wouldn't know."

"Can I read it to you?"

Zanzu shifted. It had been a long, hard, sad day and they had only just persuaded Carmela to go to bed. What he wanted was the kitchen to himself for a while and a glass of beer.

"I wouldn't understand, miss."

"You would," Lila said, "I know you would. Listen." She turned to him, still on her knees.

"God answers sharp and sudden
      On some prayers,
And thrusts the thing we
      have prayed for in our face,
A gauntlet with a gift in it."

She looked up.

"Isn't that right? Isn't that lovely?"

He shook his head. "I couldn't understand it — "

"It means that there is always something we need or want hidden in something we don't want. We didn't want Miss de Vere to die, we prayed for her not to die, but the memory of her and all she gave us will always be with us, even though she's dead. And that memory, and the love we had for her will comfort us." She paused, and then she said more quietly, "Maybe, if we love someone, nothing can take that love from us. Not even death."

Zanzu smothered a small yawn in a sigh. Lila glanced up at him.

"I'm sorry," she said, "I shouldn't bombard

417

you with poetry when you're so tired."

"We're all tired."

Lila closed the book and slipped it back into the shelves.

"We'll have to clear all this," Lila said. "That'll be hard. Taking Miss de Vere's life out of this house."

Tiredness abruptly forgotten, Zanzu froze in the doorway.

"Clear this house?"

"Yes," Lila said. She rose from her knees and sat on the edge of the nearest chair. "I was going to tell you tomorrow, but I think I should tell you now. Won't you sit down?"

"No," Zanzu said. "No thank you."

"I saw the lawyer again today. After the funeral. He said he could now tell me for certain what Miss de Vere's final wishes were. He will of course tell you, formally, himself."

Zanzu put out a hand to steady himself, on the nearest chairback.

"Miss de Vere wanted this house to become a school. A special school, for deaf and dumb children. She said there was no such provision on Malta, and so she was going to make the first. It's to be the Beatrix de Vere Special School."

Zanzu said, almost in a whisper, "I thought she would give the house to you."

"No," Lila said, "no. She didn't know, you see, if I was coming back to Malta, and in any case, I think she'd had the school plan in her mind for years. She's been wonderfully generous. She's left me some money. And you. She's left you some money too. And a job for life at the school, if you want to take it."

Zanzu put his arm up across his eyes.

"I've got enough now to repair the Villa Zonda," Lila said. "So you can come with me, if you want to. Or stay here. She's thought of everything, you see. She's given us all our choices."

Zanzu took his arm from his eyes and crossed himself.

"It is wonderful," he said. His voice shook. "I don't know what to say, what to — "

"Don't," Lila said. "Don't say or decide anything. Go and see the lawyer first and then decide. It doesn't matter what you choose. There's no hurry. You must do what you really want to do."

She stood up.

"Zanzu — "

"Yes."

"There's just one other thing."

He looked full at her.

"Yes?"

"Was — " Lila said, and stopped. Then she said in a rush, "Was Angelo Saliba there, at the funeral?"

"No," Zanzu said.

"Are you sure?"

"Very sure," Zanzu said. "His mother came, but not him. I wouldn't have missed him. Don't I know him like my own brother? Would I have missed him if he'd been there?"

Lila looked away.

"Isn't it odd? That he shouldn't come? To *her* funeral, of all people's."

419

Zanzu said awkwardly, "I can't explain it."

Lila moved away across the room to the window and looked across the creek to the city. It was nearly dark, and the lights of Valetta seemed almost to dance across the water towards her.

"I can," Lila said softly, as if to herself.

"I beg your pardon?"

She turned to him, trying to smile. "Nothing."

"Then — "

"You go," Lila said. "You go to bed. You must be exhausted. In the morning, I'll telephone the lawyer and make an appointment for you."

He gave a little bow of thanks, ducking his dark head with his hands clasped before him.

"Good night."

"Good night," Lila said, "and sleep well."

When he had gone, she pulled the nearest chair up to the window. It was the chair she had sat in on that first visit to Miss de Vere in 1938, and then the chair had worn a wonderful covering of yellow brocade. Now it was down to its original shabby leather, dark red, and split here and there so that little wiry tufts of horsehair sprouted through. Where the yellow brocade had gone, Lila had no idea. Perhaps it had been ruined when the bomb hit the house, or Miss de Vere had given it away for someone to make curtains out of. She gave so much away. This airy first-floor sitting room, which Lila remembered as resembling an oriental bazaar in its colourful riot of fabrics and cushions, was now almost

420

austere, stripped to the bare necessities of chairs and a table and an old Persian rug on the floor showing the Tree of Life. Lila bent forward from her chair and laid her hand on the rug. She would take that with her, to the Villa Zonda. It would be a talisman for her, to have Miss de Vere's Tree of Life on the refurbished stone floor. She would need a talisman, she reflected, because even with the generosity of the Perriams and now Miss de Vere, she was about to embark on a journey with only Carmela for company: a journey for which, as yet, she could not convince herself that she had a map.

She straightened up and looked out of the open window. Out there, the dark waters of the creek melted into those of the Grand Harbour, spangled brilliantly here and there where the lights from the shore caught them. Into those waters, the night after Miss de Vere had died, Lila had thrown Anton's ring, and the pressed white rose — now a handful of whispering brown petals, like tissue paper — both so light they disappeared beneath the surface without a sound. Carmela, materializing as usual at Lila's side, had watched them fall, her face solemn.

"Are you sad?" she'd said.

Lila stared at the water.

"Yes."

"Because he cometh not?" Carmela persisted.

"No," Lila said, "not because of that."

"Then — "

"I'm sad," Lila said, "because I'm such a fool.

Because I've wasted such years and years being a fool. Because I was too proud to listen to anyone who pointed out however gently, what a fool I was being."

Carmela pulled her pigtail over one shoulder and tugged it.

"Why were you a fool?"

"You wouldn't understand."

"I would!" Carmela cried indignantly. "I would! I would!"

Lila turned her face from the window and looked down at her.

"Maybe you would. Maybe, if I tell you, you won't make the same mistake."

Carmela put the end of her pigtail into her mouth. Her eyes bulged with earnestness.

"I persisted," Lila said, "in loving what I wanted to see, not what was there to see. I thought I longed for something so much that nothing else would do, ever, but I never looked at that thing closely, I never saw what it really was, I just saw my imaginative picture of it. Do you know what a mirage is?"

Carmela took her pigtail out of her mouth. "Of course. We've just done deserts at school."

"Well, I've been like someone who absolutely will not believe that a mirage is only an illusion."

"It was a nice ring," Carmela said.

Lila smiled.

"Yes, it was. And it was a nice palace and a nice motor car and a nice way of life. But not, as it turned out, anything like nice enough. Not deep down."

She put her hands up to her eyes, now, and rubbed them. She had promised Carmela that if Carmela went to bed when asked, she, Lila, would not go to bed herself without coming to see her. Carmela was her responsibility now, her dependant, and if Miss de Vere had still been here, she would have told Lila she was lucky to have her. She was lucky, she knew it. However uncertain and unknown her future might look from the vantage point of this sad, tired evening after Miss de Vere's funeral, what would it have been like if she hadn't had Carmela to take into account, to work for, to share it with?

She stood up and stretched, glancing at her watch. It was ten minutes past ten. Carmela would be waiting.

\* \* \*

"I was waiting," Carmela said severely.

"I hoped you'd be asleep."

"When you are an old lady and I am looking after you, and I say I'll come and see you in bed, I *will come*."

Lila sat down on the end of Carmela's bed. Carmela was sitting upright against the pillows wearing striped, English, boy's pyjamas which had been part of a clothes hand-out at school, and holding Miss de Vere's Edwardian edition of *Alice in Wonderland*.

"I'm sorry," Lila said, "I was talking to Zanzu."

"Will he live with us?"

"He might. He'll decide when he's seen the lawyer."

"He can if he likes," Carmela said kindly. "I like him and we'll need people to fill that big house up."

"I know," Lila said.

"Until I get married, anyway."

Lila grinned at her.

"I see."

"I shall have six children. You can be their extra grandmother."

"Thank you. You're too kind."

"I'm not having the girls making lace," Carmela said. "They're going to school."

"I'm glad to hear it. I'm glad you have a plan for your life all ready like this. It's more than I have."

Carmela leaned forward and patted Lila's arm maternally.

"You'll feel better when we go back to the house. You'll see."

Lila blew her a kiss.

"Thank you. Actually, the house reminds me — "

"What?"

"Where is my knocker?" Lila said. "Where is my brass dolphin?"

Carmela didn't move. She said, casually, "In my cupboard."

"Will you get it for me?"

"Why?" Carmela said.

"Because I want to see it."

Very slowly, Carmela closed *Alice in Wonderland* and laid it on the sheets. Then she turned the covers back and climbed out of bed.

"He didn't come to the funeral," she said, without looking at Lila.

"I know," Lila said.

"He always comes."

"I know."

Carmela looked at her.

"Zanzu said I wasn't to tell you he wasn't there."

Lila said quietly, "He meant to be kind."

Carmela padded past her to the cupboard, hitching the too-big pyjama trousers up around her waist as she did so. She opened the cupboard. Her few clothes hung inside, in perfect precision, and her new straw hat sat in state on a shelf, on a cushion. She stooped down and lifted out a parcel wrapped in a white cloth with a red line down the middle. Glass Cloth, said woven letters in the red line, Irish Linen. Carmela turned and dumped the bundle in Lila's lap.

"There."

Lila folded back the glass cloth. Inside, the dolphin lay smiling, its forked tail at a jaunty angle.

"It needs polishing," Carmela said.

"Yes."

"Miss de Vere said it was good workmanship. The way the scales are done."

Lila put out a finger and touched the dolphin's head.

"It's lovely, isn't it?".

Carmela looked at it. Then she put her head

425

on one side and looked at Lila.

"Yes," she said and paused. She folded her arms in their striped sleeves. "Yes," she said again, "it's lovely. But what are you going to do with it?"

# 34

I N the courtyard of the Villa Zonda, two kittens, no doubt the descendants of the yellow cat which had so menaced baby Spiru lying in his basket in the kitchen doorway, played by the Roman wellhead. They were yellow too, and thin, with winglike ears and a feral wariness about them. When Lila came into the courtyard from the drive, they halted their game, whisked round to stare at her with wide eyes and then streaked for shelter in one of the lower rooms of the villa. Lila followed them, pulling open a shutter on creaking hinges. Inside was a room which had once been one of the family's bedrooms, Carmela's maybe, containing iron bedsteads and a heavy cupboard for storing linen. Now it was empty except for the cupboard, whose doors had been torn off, and it smelled of cats. Lila leaned in over the sill.

"I'm giving you an eviction notice," she said. "Work starts here next week and you'll have to go."

She stepped back into the sunlight and shaded her eyes to look up at the peeling yellow façade. The salone was still a ruin; the shutters of Pa's bedroom window were still pointlessly closed on a room open to the sky; the little end kitchen where she had fried fish and washed up in a chipped enamel basin was still intact.

That kitchen was going to become a bathroom, a bathroom, she assured Carmela, where hot water came out of one tap and cold out of another, with a blue and white floor of Maltese tiles. Pa's bedroom would be Carmela's, and her own she would return to, hanging up again, if she could find them, the little round looking glass in a gilded frame with the two doves on top, and the watercolour of an English garden complete with delphiniums and a beehive. She had first hung the watercolour up to remind herself of what she thought she was missing; she would now hang it up to remind herself of how she had changed.

She moved back across the courtyard and perched on the wellhead, patting it affectionately for still being there, for surviving the war as it had survived the centuries. "Roman," Mr Perriam had said of it with a touch of disappointment. "Late, I must admit, but Roman."

"I don't care how late you are," Lila said to it now, "I'm just grateful you're still here."

The stone was warm through the cotton of her skirt. She looked pleasedly about her, at the ragged dark shade of the carob tree with Pa's bench under it; at the ruined sheds and barns which would become, she rather thought, a colonnaded room for lemon trees in winter; at the windows and doors of the family's old quarters which would become *her* kitchen, *her* storerooms, as well as somewhere for Zanzu to live, if he chose to come. As for the salone, well, she would repair it but she would change

428

it. It would no longer be an English Edwardian sitting room full of stout velvet chairs and polished mahogany bureaux and cupboards, but a different kind of room, an airy room with the Tree of Life rug on its polished tiled floor, and long windows opening onto a loggia where the descendants of Miss de Vere's geraniums could rampage over the balustrade. She would paint it white, with white curtains, and look for furniture in the villages — Maltese furniture, made for those silent shuttered houses clustered round their yellow stone churches. And in the evening, she and Carmela could sit on the loggia and look down on the courtyard which would be filled with flowers; all the flowers that Count Julius said had once grown there, in A. E. O. Perriam's day, jonquils in spring, roses in early summer, with, beyond them in the old vegetable garden, a restored cypress walk and a grove of oranges and tangerines. And perhaps, she thought, remembering all Pa's endeavours, there would be a small corner for some onions and cauliflower and a row of beans, just as a reminder that besides beautiful things, life required useful things as well.

She slipped off the wellhead and walked slowly through the gap in the wall to the vegetable garden. It was a mass of tired, late summer weeds, bleached and dry, their seedpods rattling in the faint breeze. She must regard this weary space as a blank canvas, making a garden here from nothing, in memory of the garden that once had been there, in memory also of Pa.

She made her way to the cleared space by the

south wall. The rosemary bush she had planted had flowered, and now needed clipping, and the montbretia had faded and stiffened in the heat. Lila sat down, as she always did, at the head of the grave with her back against the wall.

"Hallo, Pa."

She waited, her eyes closed. The curious peace this little space of earth always brought her began to play round her, like gentle waves.

"We're coming home to you, Pa. Thanks to the Perriams and Miss de Vere, we're coming back here. We're going to mend it. The schools are going to start running buses down into Valetta, so Carmela can go to school on the bus, just as I used to do, to Saxmundham. I don't quite know what I'll do. I'm not really qualified to go on teaching now the war's over. Maybe I'll get involved in Miss de Vere's special school. Maybe I'll train for something different. Journalism, perhaps. Or perhaps I'll take paying guests, like all those seafront landladies used to do in Aldeburgh, and work out my grievances against life by putting up notices saying Don't all over the place. Except — " She paused and laid her hand on the earth beside her. "Except I don't have grievances any more. Regrets, maybe. Remorse — oh, remorse all right. But the bitterness has gone, quite gone." She patted the earth. "That'll please you, won't it? You didn't know the meaning of the word."

She opened her eyes.

"Pa?"

In front of her the weeds whispered in the hot breeze.

"Pa, I'm going at last to do something you approve of. Or, at least, I'm going to try. It's probably too late, but unless I ask, I'll never know, will I?" She leaned over the grave, in the speckled shadow cast by the spires of the rosemary bush. "Wish me luck."

★ ★ ★

"Please wait," the girl said.

She indicated a line of chairs, not unlike those in the convent's visitors' room, except that instead of facing a grille, they faced a wall with a rack of badly printed pamphlets on it, pamphlets on hygiene and primary education and a campaign for universal literacy. The rest of the room, huge and high, with an ancient coffered ceiling, was bare except for the reception desk and a sluggish electric fan, its walls painted pale grey. Lila chose a chair in the exact centre of the line and sat down. She sat bolt upright, her hands squeezed together in her lap, and tried to breathe slowly and calmly.

She sat there for almost ten minutes. There was no sound except for the uneven whirr of the fan and a big fly banging itself against one of the high windows. No-one came. The telephone on the reception desk rang twice, briefly, and was intercepted somewhere else in the great building. Lila stared ahead of her. There were three rows of pamphlets in the rack, printed smearily in black on rough whitish paper, and the rack was of varnished wood with big brass screws at the corners. If the girl did not come back

431

before fifteen minutes were up, Lila would take it as an omen. Her mission was not destined to happen. She had made a mistake — yet another mistake, she told herself ruefully — and must go away accepting it. She glanced at her watch. Nine minutes. She began to count the seconds, slowly. In sixty times six, she would get up, without hurry, and leave the room and the building.

The door of the reception area opened. Lila turned, expecting to see the girl who had asked her to wait.

"Miss Cunningham," Angelo Saliba said.

Lila sprang up, flustered, seizing her bag from the chair beside her where she had laid it.

"Oh, Mr Saliba, I never meant you to come down to me, I merely asked if I might make an appointment — "

"Of course I'd come down to you," he said. He wore a dark suit and polished shoes and his hair had been cut differently. He came forward into the room, the receptionist pattering behind him in a manner Lila saw was plainly respectful.

"I'm grateful — "

"Not at all." He halted a yard from her. "What can I do for you?"

She said impulsively, "You didn't come to Miss de Vere's funeral."

"No."

"But I thought — "

"I went to the cathedral later," he said, "alone. I didn't forget her. I'll never do that."

She looked down. He was managing, as he so

often had in the past, to make her feel slightly ashamed.

"No, I never meant that."

"Is it Miss de Vere you wanted to see me about? Her special school? Of course we are delighted at her suggestion, and very much want to make it part of our educational programme — "

"No," Lila said again. "No, it wasn't that."

He indicated the chairs.

"Can we talk here? I'm afraid my office is rather public."

"I'd rather not. It — it needn't be now, it needn't be immediately — "

"I have some time," he said. "I have half an hour." He moved a little nearer. "The Lower Baracca Gardens are very close. Would that suit you better?"

She looked at him. She tried to remember the face of the boy on the quayside in the Grand Harbour, the boy in the salone at the Villa Zonda, the young man by Pa's body, the young man across the kitchen table in the house on Kalkara Creek. The eyes were the same, but . . .

"I'd be grateful," Lila said. "Yes. The gardens would be lovely."

★ ★ ★

"Such a view," Angelo said. "Look at that. Rinella Bay, Kalkara Creek, Dockyard Creek, Senglea, French Creek, Fort St Angelo. And look at the rebuilding. It's wonderful, isn't it,

433

seeing Malta rising again like this?" He turned from his contemplation of the prospect across the Grand Harbour to where Lila sat on a bench behind him. "We are working on the re-establishment of self-government, you know. Perhaps we'll even get our status changed, from crown colony to dominion. Just think! There may be Maltese members of parliament at Westminster yet!"

Lila said smiling, "Even better than being kissed by Queen Victoria."

"What do you mean?"

"The Ferroferrata boys' grandmother was so aristocratic she was kissed almost as an equal by Queen Victoria."

Angelo said quietly, "I'm sorry about that."

Lila looked at her lap.

"Anton."

"Yes."

"You — know about it then."

"I'm afraid half Malta does."

Lila took a breath.

"You were right, after all. Weren't you?"

He sat down beside her on the bench, leaving a space between them.

"Right?"

She couldn't look at him.

"About me. About my dream. Because — it wasn't a dream. As you could see. It was a delusion."

"It doesn't," he said, "give me any satisfaction to be right about that."

"Thank you."

He leaned forward, putting his elbows on his

knees, his face turned towards the view again.

"What did you want to see me about?"

"I — I don't quite know where to start — "

"Start anywhere," he said.

"I have the Villa Zonda now," Lila said slowly, "and a legacy from Miss de Vere. And I have Carmela to look after."

She paused. He said, still staring straight ahead, "And I have my mother."

"I am Protestant — "

"My mother and I are Catholic. I fear there may come a time when my faith and my political ambitions for Malta are going to collide." He grinned. "My mother may be faced with a very late adolescent rebellion." He gave Lila a quick glance. "So, with the Villa Zonda and the child, you are staying?"

"Yes."

He said nothing, but gazed ahead again.

"You have a career," Lila said, her voice not quite steady, "and family. And I have a house and someone to care for, and I shall find a career. But — but, is that enough, do you think for either of us? Even with that, is there — is there a space at the centre?"

Very slowly, he took his gaze from the view across the harbour and looked at her.

"What are you asking me?"

"Wait," Lila said. She turned away from him and fumbled in her bag for a moment, drawing out a bundle wrapped in a white cloth with a red line down the middle. She laid it on the space of bench between them, and with fingers she

435

couldn't seem to prevent from shaking, folded back the fabric.

"I was wondering — "

"Yes?"

"Will you — would you help me to put this up?"

There was a silence. Both of them stared at the dolphin but neither of them touched it. Then he said, very gently, "No, Lila. No, I couldn't do that. You must do that for yourself."

She nodded. She said, hurrying over the words, "Oh, I understand, I understand why you say that when I've behaved to you as I have, but I have to ask you, had to, I mean — "

She stopped again.

"What?" he said.

She whispered, "I can't ask it."

He waited. He put a hand out and touched the dolphin's nose, above its smiling mouth.

"Angelo — "

"Yes?"

He glanced up. She was looking at him now, full at him, with an expression he had never seen on her face before, an expression that on anyone else's face he would have described as almost eager.

"Angelo, I will put the knocker up. I'll put it up myself. And when it's up, when it's there on the door of my home in Malta, will you come then? Will you?"

There was another pause. Then Angelo leaned forward and put his hand on Lila's for a moment, a quick, warm, firm pressure.

"Will you?"

He rose to his feet, so that she was looking up at him.

"Will you?"

"When it's up," he said slowly, "ask me again. I can't give you an answer now. But ask me again then," and then he stooped and lifted the dolphin to put it in her lap, and before she could say another word, he had gone, walking swiftly away from her among the little trees of the gardens, the sound of his feet sharp on the gravel path.

Lila looked down. The dolphin lay there, slightly on its side, its fins extended as if for forward movement. She slipped her hand round its solid little brass body and held it hard.

"Right," she said out loud. "Right. 'A gauntlet — a gauntlet with a gift in it.'" She lifted the dolphin and struck it once against its knocking plate. "Right?"

## THE END

*Other titles in the*
*Charnwood Library Series:*

## PAY ANY PRICE
### Ted Allbeury

After the Kennedy killings the heat was on — on the Mafia, the KGB, the Cubans, and the FBI . . .

## MY SWEET AUDRINA
### Virginia Andrews

She wanted to be loved as much as the first Audrina, the sister who was perfect and beautiful — and dead.

## PRIDE AND PREJUDICE
### Jane Austen

Mr. Bennet's five eligible daughters will never inherit their father's money. The family fortunes are destined to pass to a cousin. Should one of the daughters marry him?

## THE GLASS BLOWERS
### Daphne Du Maurier

A novel about the author's forebears, the Bussons, which gives an unusual glimpse of the events that led up to the French Revolution, and of the Revolution itself.